BLOOD AND THUNDER

THE MEMOIRS OF NATHAN HELLER:

Blood and Thunder
Carnal Hours
Dying in the Post-War World
Stolen Away
Neon Mirage
The Million-Dollar Wound
True Crime
True Detective

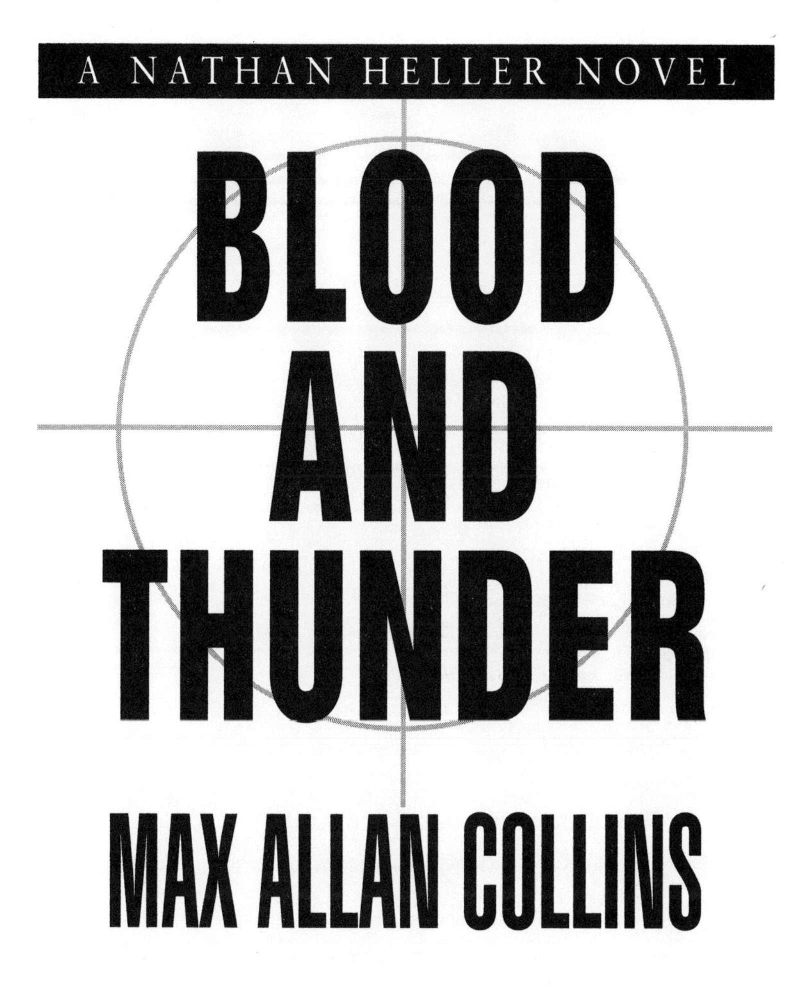

A NATHAN HELLER NOVEL

BLOOD AND THUNDER

MAX ALLAN COLLINS

A DUTTON BOOK

DUTTON
Published by the Penguin Group
Penguin Books USA Inc., 375 Hudson Street,
New York, New York 10014, U.S.A.
Penguin Books Ltd, 27 Wrights Lane,
London W8 5TZ, England
Penguin Books Australia Ltd, Ringwood,
Victoria, Australia
Penguin Books Canada Ltd, 10 Alcorn Avenue,
Toronto, Ontario, Canada M4V 3B2
Penguin Books (N.Z.) Ltd, 182–190 Wairau Road,
Auckland 10, New Zealand

Penguin Books Ltd, Registered Offices:
Harmondsworth, Middlesex, England

First published by Dutton, an imprint of Dutton Signet, a
division of Penguin Books USA Inc.
Distributed in Canada by McClelland & Stewart Inc.

First Printing, August, 1995
10 9 8 7 6 5 4 3 2

LIBRARY OF CONGRESS CATALOGING-IN-PUBLICATION DATA

Collins, Max Allan.
Blood and thunder : a Nathan Heller novel / by Max Allan Collins.
p. cm.
ISBN 0-525-93759-5
1. Long, Huey Pierce, 1893–1935—Assassination—Fiction.
I. Title.
PS3553.O4753B56 1995
813'.54—dc20 94-45895
CIP

Printed in the United States of America
Set in Sabon
Designed by Leonard Telesca

PUBLISHER'S NOTE
This is a work of fiction. Names, characters, places, and incidents either are the products of the author's imagination or are used fictitiously, and any resemblance to actual persons, living or dead, events, or locales is entirely coincidental.

This book is printed on acid-free paper. ∞

In memory of Keith Larson,
who helped me hear
the music in words

Although the historical incidents in this novel are portrayed more or less accurately (as much as the passage of time and contradictory source material will allow), fact, speculation and fiction are freely mixed here; historical personages exist side by side with composite characters and wholly fictional ones—all of whom act and speak at the author's whim.

I am not gifted with second sight, nor did I see a spot of blood on the moon last night. But I can see blood on the polished floor of this Capitol. For if you ride this thing through, you will travel with the white horse of death.

Mason Spencer,
Louisiana State Legislature, 1935

ONE
A VEST FOR THE KINGFISH

August 30—September 12, 1935

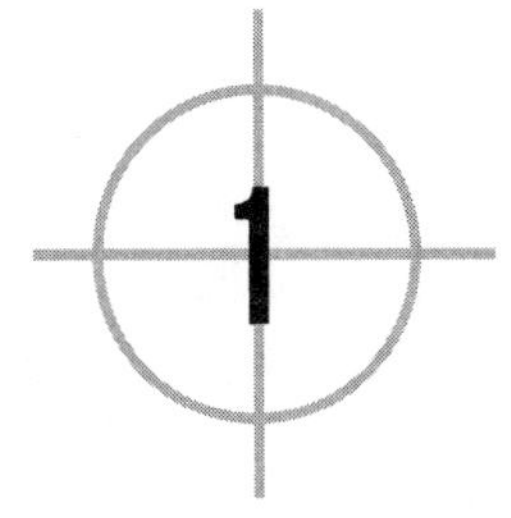

All the attractions at the Oklahoma State Fair on this sunny Labor Day afternoon paled next to this one. Kewpie dolls and lemonade had nothing on the speaker who prowled the flag-draped platform; a prize-winning hog, a local beauty queen in tiara and gown, a championship tosser of horseshoes could provide no real competition. Not the two-headed calf or the living mermaid or even the girl who turned into a gorilla.

None of these wonders could compare to the surprisingly lean, five-ten package of enthusiasm who was flailing the air with windmilling arms, raving, ranting, swearing, sputtering. The farmers—in their best straw hats, suspenders over sweat-circled white shirts—and their wives—in Sunday-go-to-meeting bonnets and frocks and heels—were wide-eyed, gaga with wonder, if not always admiration. Even the kids, nibbling their cotton candy and hot dogs, were spellbound. Man, woman and child, they all had heard about this phenomenon, in the newspapers, possibly even heard him speak on the radio, maybe seen him in the newsreels.

But in the flesh, the afternoon's guest speaker was a real sight to see. And, so, the hicks gathered 'round.

Duded up in a natty gray suit with a huge white gladiola in one enormous lapel, his necktie fire-engine red, his shoes spiffy black-and-white numbers, he would stalk the stage as if seeking a victim, dragging the microphone on its stand with him, removing his straw hat from time to time to mop his brow. Finally he just tossed the hat away, a casual gesture that further won over the crowd. After all, it was noon, and the sun was high and hot.

To a sophisticated literate like me, he seemed a figure out of "Li'l Abner": a caricature of a politician, his wavy reddish hair (coincidentally, the same color as mine) falling in a natural spit curl, his ruddy complexion freckled, his nose impudent and upturned, his bulldog jaw deeply cleft. From this distance, he seemed jowly, but I'd seen him up close. Those weren't jowls: that was just the slightly odd, deceiving shape of his face.

In fact, he was lean and hard and fit. But his oval mug, his quick grin—he was always ready to punctuate a tirade with a rustic joke and a fleeting infectious smile—gave a false impression of softness, just as the down-home inflections and his slangy speech gave a false impression of the speaker being a "common man."

"Hoover and Roosevelt," the speaker said, making hostages in the same sentence of the previous president and the current one, "put me in mind of the patent-medicine drummer that used to come 'round Winn Parish."

A parish was a county in Louisiana. I wasn't from around these parts, but I picked up quick.

"He had two bottles of medicine," the speaker said, in a rumbly baritone that managed to be both casual and grand. "He'd play a banjo, and he'd sell two bottles of medicine. One of those bottles he called High Popalorum; and the other one of those bottles he called Low Popahirum."

That quick grin told the crowd they could laugh at this, and they did.

"Fin'lly, somebody 'round there said, 'Is they any difference in these medicines?' An' the drummer said, 'Why, considerable—these is both good, but they's diff'rnt.' "

He was rocking, almost bobbing, like a child's top, and it gave a rhythm to his speech, and held the eye.

"He said, 'High Popalorum we make by takin' the bark off the tree from the top down. And Low Popahirum, we make by takin' the bark off the tree from the root up.' "

He raised his eyebrows by way of devilish punctuation, spurring a gentle wave of laughter.

His voice rose in timbre. "And these days the only diff'rence 'tween the two parties in Congress is the Republicans are skinnin' ya from the ankle *up*, and the Democrats are skinnin' ya from the ear *down*!"

The crowd roared with laughter.

Now the speaker ended the anecdote with a blast of fury; there was no humor in his thundering voice as he said, "Skin 'em up, or skin 'em down, but *skin* 'em!"

As the laughter turned to applause, several voices called out over the din: "You tell 'em, Huey!" "Give 'em hell, big boy!" "Pour it on, Kingfish!"

And this indeed was Huey P. Long, the self-anointed "Kingfish" (after the blackface radio rascal of "Amos 'n' Andy" fame), former governor of Louisiana, currently United States senator and, for all intents and purposes, dictator of the Pelican State, which he ruled through a yes-man figurehead whose name, appropriately enough, was O.K. Allen. Allen was so used to rubber-stamping Huey's edicts, it was said that when a leaf blew in the window onto O.K.'s desk, he just signed the fool thing.

This was the populist mastermind seducing the South with his "Share the Wealth" plan, promising each and every American family a yearly income of no less than five thousand dollars, old-age pensions of thirty bucks a month, a homestead, a car, a refrigerator and a radio. This would be accomplished by confiscating from the wealthy anything they possessed in excess of three million dollars. The details shifted, according to the crowd and his own mood, but the Kingfish's gospel was seductive, in these hard times, and it was spreading.

In this rural crowd, there was at least one damn Yankee: me, Nathan Heller, president (and everything else) of the A-1 Detective Agency of Chicago, Illinois. At the moment I was working as one of a team of three bodyguards traveling with the Kingfish, who was making his way back to Louisiana, by train and car, fresh from his latest Senate-floor filibuster in Washington, D.C.

This visit to the fairgrounds in Oklahoma City was just one of several unofficial campaign stops planned along the way. Just about everybody in the country, even an apolitical nincompoop like yours truly, knew that Huey was gearing up for a presidential bid in 1936. That was why so much of his energetic speechifying this afternoon was devoted to bashing FDR.

I didn't fit in here, exactly, but nobody seemed to notice, or anyway, care. I was sipping an orangeade in keeping with my wardrobe—a lightweight white suit and wide-brimmed Panama hat I'd brought back from a job in Florida a couple years ago. My complexion was a city gray compared to these Indian-dark, leathery-faced farmers, and at six foot, one hundred-eighty-five pounds, I made a less than inconspicuous presence.

But that didn't bother Huey. He liked having his bodyguards noticed. He was, after all, the sort of individual who brought the whole subject of paranoia into question. His behavior was classic paranoid, but you know what? A hell of a lot of people *were* out to get him.

While most of this crowd either loved the Kingfish or

were, at least, entertained by his showmanship, other elements clearly resented his attacks on the President of the United States on a platform decorated with the stars and stripes.

"You're a two-bit Hitler!" somebody was yelling, interrupting another anecdote.

Huey paid the heckler no mind, and continued with an attack on his fellow congressmen.

"Let me tell ya, folks, about this moss-back, pie-eatin', trough-feedin' brigadc . . . back in Loozyana, at revival meetin's . . . we called 'em camp meetin's, back then . . . the preachin' lasted all day. And it was hot, of course, hotter than even today. To keep the preacher from bein' disturbed, it was customary for the mothers to mix up a little dry biscuit, butter and sugar. Well, they put that in a rag and tied it with a string, and called it a sugar tit."

This impudent turn of phrase created a ripple of titters (well, it did) but the moment was spoiled a tad when that heckler—whose red face suggested both rage and alcohol—called out again: "Go back to the swamp, Crawfish!"

The guy was on the perimeter of the crowd, off to my left. Through the crowd, something—someone—was moving, causing a wave in the sea of straw hats and Sears & Roebuck chapeaus, with the single-mindedness of a shark.

This, I knew, was trouble. I started moving through the crowd myself, even as Huey continued.

"Ladies an' ge'men, I'm here to tell you that Prince Franklin Roosevelt, Knight of the *Nourmahal*, enjoyin' himself on that million-dollar yacht with the Astors and royalty, lettin' the farmers starve . . . why Prince Franklin, he was *born* with the sugar tit in his mouth. Been sucklin' ever since. He's worn out a dozen of 'em . . . now he's grabbin' for more."

"Fascist!" the guy hollered.

I could see him better now, and I could see something else. Someone else.

Knocking people out of his way like bowling pins now, ignoring their cries of "Hey!," "Watch it, bub!" and the like, a squat, swarthy figure in a dark, baggy gangster's suit was zeroing in on the heckler.

I picked up speed, earning a "Watch it!" or two, myself.

But Joe Messina—thick-necked fireplug of a man that he was, with a round face as free of thought or morality as a newborn baby's—was already on the heckler, a skinny redneck in white shirt and red suspenders. The heckler was saying, "You backwoods Hit," and never got to the "ler," because that's where Messina's blackjack stopped the sentence.

The man's howl was short and loud, when Messina laid that blackjack across the side of his head, but by the time the crowd had looked in that direction, Messina was hustling the guy off, behind a nearby tent.

Over the loudspeakers, Huey was in the process of explaining the difference between a hoot owl and a scrootch owl.

I found Messina, behind one canvas tent and between it and another, out of public view, hovering over the heckler sprawled on the grass by the tent posts, bending over him as if to give him a hand.

Problem was, that hand still had the blackjack in it and Messina was waling the guy with it, hitting him all over his arms and on his side. The heckler wasn't heckling now: he was whimpering, weeping, begging in a barely audible voice for mercy.

A word, like so many other words, that wasn't in Messina's vocabulary.

Messina's coat was flapping, as he drew back his arm to put force into his blows, revealing the pearl-handled .38 on his hip. His arm was like that when I grabbed it by a massive wrist.

"That's enough," I said.

Somehow that bull neck managed to allow the medicine ball head it supported to swivel toward me. The round empty face took on a snarling expression.

"Stay out," he said; his voice was oddly high-pitched, and breathy.

He yanked his hand free and slammed the blackjack into the heckler's shoulder, and I spun him around and grabbed him by both lapels.

"I said enough!"

He pushed me away, but what I'd done gave the heckler a chance to summon what little energy he had left, and he scurried away, scrambling between the tents. Messina started after him, and I followed, but we both saw the man disappear down the midway, getting lost in the crowd. Not everybody was listening to Huey speak.

"A hoot owl," Huey's amplified voice informed us, "barges right into the roost and knocks the hen clean off her perch, and catches her while she's fallin'. . . ."

Messina turned slowly and faced me; his upper lip peeled back over his teeth and it wasn't a smile.

His hand seemed to be drifting for the pearl-handled .38 on his hip; he looked like Spanky from Our Gang playing western gunfighter. Only quite a bit more intimidating . . .

"But a scrootch owl," Huey continued, "he slips into the roost and just scrootches up to the hen and sweet-talks her. And then the hen falls in love with him, and the first thing you know . . . there ain't no hen!"

The crowd laughed, on the other side of the tent. Back here, two of Huey's own people were staring at each other coldly. I had a gun, too—a nine-millimeter Browning in a shoulder holster. This would be a first: shooting it out with somebody I was bodyguarding with.

"Now Hoover was sure enough a hoot owl," Huey's booming voice continued, "but Roosevelt—he's a scrootch owl!"

There was laughter and applause, and I said, "Don't do anything stupid, Joe."

Messina's tiny dark eyes—like the black beaded eyes sewn on a rag doll—narrowed in something approaching thought, reminding me that anything this beefy little bastard did was bound to be stupid.

Huey said something else, but I wasn't listening. I said, "Joe—you were making your boss look bad. I was just trying to help."

"Heller's right," a commanding male voice said, and we both turned to see Big George McCracken, the third member of our bodyguard squad, come lumbering up. Burly, with the puffy, lumpy features of an ex-pug, his dark baggy suit from the same thug haberdashery as Messina's, McCracken was no dope.

Especially compared to Messina.

"Those people saw you smack that sumbitch," McCracken said to Messina.

Messina's head drooped like he was a scolded school kid and McCracken the teacher.

"You want the lyin' papers to pick up somethin' like that?" McCracken asked. "Next time, jest yank 'im outa there, and don't commence to beatin' on 'im 'til you're behind the goddamn tent."

"Okay," Messina said, reluctantly.

"And be careful. You don't wanna kill some fucker. Just shut him up, teach him a little lesson, and shoo him off. Got it?"

Messina nodded.

"Now get back out there, and keep an eye on the crowd. Shee-*it* . . . there's murder plots afoot, and you're back here havin' a good time! Get out there and protect the boss."

Messina nodded again, flashed me a glare, and shuffled away, around the tent, back into the crowd.

McCracken's battered pan cracked into a smile. He put a hand the size of an outfielder's glove on my shoulder.

"Don't mind Joe," he said. "When it comes to the Kingfish, ol' Messina's loyal as a dog."

"And damn near as smart," I said. My heart was in my throat. I wondered how close I'd really come to shooting it out with that mental midget.

McCracken and I returned to the crowd; nobody seemed wise to the little melodrama that had just played itself out. McCracken moved up by the stage, and I worked my way to the back of the crowd.

"Now, Roosevelt's boy Jim Farley," Huey was saying, "why, he can take the corns off your toes without removin' your shoes—he's that slick."

I was studying the audience. In a bodyguard situation like this, when a public figure is up there making a target of himself, you study faces and reactions. With a politician as loved and hated as Huey Long, the most suspicious expression is a blank one.

A very pretty female face caught my attention, as pretty female faces are wont to do, but it sure wasn't blank. In fact, it was smiling and sparkling-eyed and animated.

She was blonde with Shirley Temple's curls and Jean Harlow's body, and wore a wispy white summery dress with red polka dots and had a big purse tucked under one pale arm.

Something about that all-American-beauty face was a little harder than it ought to be; this was what you got when you asked the madam at a bordello for a virgin. But she was good: the clothes were just sexy enough to attract attention, but not so sexy as to outrage a matron.

Right now she was moving through the crowd, stopping occasionally to look toward the platform, where Huey was managing to find still more unflattering things to say about the President of the United States. Then she would move along, weaving her way through the throng like a snake with lipstick.

I was fairly sure I knew what this was about, but I didn't make a move yet. I waited till she stopped for longer than just a moment and, finally, she did.

She paused beside a heavyset, well-dressed, patently prosperous farmer with a square, bare head and short-cropped white hair, standing with his thumbs in his suspenders, like Clarence Darrow at the monkey trial.

He was alone—his wife either home, or entering a bake-off or something, in a pavilion elsewhere on the fairgrounds.

As she pretended to watch Huey, the lipstick cutie was doing something else. Specifically, she was fanning her mark, checking for a fat wallet, and then she dropped her purse, and both her pretty head and the farmer's square one disappeared under the sea of other heads. He was picking her purse up for her, no doubt, and she was flashing her smile and her baby blues.

A flirt is the best kind of stall there is, in a two-handed pickpocket mob.

Their heads appeared again, and he was smiling and blushing at her, handing her the purse—his hands kept busy, which is the way a stall frames her mark—and she was acting all coquettish, like. The blond pale boy of maybe twenty who could have been (and maybe even was) her brother moved through the crowd, behind them, brushing by just barely; he was wearing a white seersucker suit, not unlike mine.

By this time I had angled up to Joe Messina, who glared at me like a fifth-grade bully planning to get me after school.

"Want to do something useful, for a change?" I whispered.

"Huh?"

"See that dame? With the curls and the shape?"

"Yeah. So?"

"See that guy moving through the crowd, over there?"

"Yeah. So?"

"So they're dips. Not *your* kind: pickpockets."

He lurched forward and I grabbed his arm; his bicep was like a cannonball.

"Wait 'til they clear the crowd," I said. I hung back a few seconds, then said, "Come on."

We moved slowly through, as Huey was explaining to the crowd that FDR didn't scare him ("Never touch a porcupine, less'n you expect to get some quills stuck in your hide"). We excused ourselves; we weren't moving fast: we had our quarry in our sights.

Out on the midway, where on either side of us in open tents the barkers sang their siren song, the terraced hoopla stands behind them laden with such treasures as stuffed toys, bottles of perfume and pen-and-pencil sets, we trailed behind the pretty girl and the blond boy. We wandered past a brick pavilion as the scent of popcorn mingled with that of disinfectant and manure. We wove through kids with cotton candy and balloons on strings, and circumvented guys arm-in-arm with gals, the former in search of shooting booths where an eagle-eye might attain a prize that might coax an even better reward from the latter.

And we watched as the blond boy in seersucker white sidled up to the pretty girl in the dress with red polka dots; saw him hand her the fat wallet, and her hand him a smile.

He put his hand on her rump and her smile turned dirty. Maybe they weren't brother and sister. In this part of the country, maybe just cousins.

"You take the boy," I said.

"You take the girl," Messina offered shrewdly.

"Nothin' gets past you, does it, Joe?"

We slipped up beside them, and I took the dish by her soft arm and said, "On you, that dime-store perfume smells good."

She frowned at me, tried to pull away. "Don't handle the merchandise, buster!"

Beside her, Messina had halted her fella, too, clutching him roughly by the arm.

"Just dump the goods on the sawdust, sis," I whispered, "and we'll leave the coppers out of it."

It was only half a smile, but with that mouth and that lipstick, it would have got a rise out of an archbishop.

Cotton candy had nothing on the sound of her voice. "Isn't there some *other* arrangement we can make?"

I grinned, sighed. "If it was just me . . ."

Then she shoved me, hard, and her fella shoved Messina, and they both took off, down the midway, bulldozing fair-goers aside ("Hey!"), and rounding the corner down another sawdust pathway.

I was on my ass; Messina hadn't gone down—buildings don't topple, just 'cause you shove them.

He helped me up. Apparently he wasn't holding a grudge.

"What now?" he asked thickly.

"We go after them, you lamebrain!"

And I was running. Messina, huffing and puffing like a steam-engine train, was bringing up the rear.

"I'll take the girl!" I yelled.

"I'll take the boy!"

What a fucking imbecile.

She was faster than her boyfriend, but I was faster than both of them, and I brought her down with a flying tackle that sent us tumbling onto the grass under the shadow of a Ferris wheel. It was fun, for a while. She was a sweet-smelling bundle of blonde hair and soft curves and silky-stockinged legs, but when a little hard fist went flying toward my nuts, I gave her the side of my leg to hit, and slapped her, once, hard.

The boy was still running.

Messina had stopped, and was standing there, bent over,

hands on his thighs, trying to catch his breath; muscular as he was, the beer belly had stopped him.

"Get him!" I yelled.

And then Messina did something that damn near made me dirty my drawers.

He drew that pearl-handled revolver from its holster.

I was hauling the bundle of pretty pickpocket to her feet, and getting to mine, when I called, "No . . ."

But it was too late: Messina fired.

The gunshot cracked the afternoon into a million pieces.

Screams of surprise and fright seized the midway, and Huey's amplified voice said, "Shit!" Knowing the Kingfish, who was not the bravest individual I ever met, he'd be cowering on the floor of that platform about now.

Amazingly, Messina had had the presence of (his excuse for a) mind to fire into the air.

And the blond boy stood there, on the grass, by a merry-go-round, frozen, and slowly put up his hands.

Messina lumbered over to him like a squashed version of the Frankenstein monster, the revolver thrust forward in a trembling hand; he was breathing like an asthmatic, and his frog eyes were bulging. Veins stood out in his forehead like exclamation marks.

"Joe . . . " I said.

He was headed for that blond kid, who had turned around, hands still in the air, to find himself looking down the barrel of that .38.

"Don't shoot him, Joe," I said.

"Don't shoot him, Joe!" the girl called out, hysterically, as if she knew Messina. I had the wallet in one hand, and her arm in the other, and was hauling both toward Messina, who was facing his quavering captive, looking very much resolved to remove him from the planet.

"Joe," I said, nearing him, "no . . . *no*. It would make the Kingfish look bad."

"What the hell's this about?" an authoritative male voice called.

"Drop those guns!" a second male voice chimed in.

We turned and a pair of uniformed cops, whose own guns were drawn, were closing in.

Messina lowered his revolver.

"We're bodyguards for Senator Long," I explained.

"That don't give you leave to go wavin' rods around," said the older of the cops, "shooting 'em in the air like a goddamn Wild West show." Like many a cop, he could say all this through his teeth, barely parting his lips. It's an art.

I pulled the girl over, virtually handed her to the second cop. Messina monkey-see-monkey-do'ed, pushing forward the blond kid, who looked both frightened and relieved. Couldn't blame him.

"Couple dips working the crowd," I said.

Messina and I stood to one side, while the cops searched the pair. The kid had several watches and assorted jewelry in his coat pockets, and—when dumped out on the grass—the girl's big purse was laden with wallets and watches.

"How'd you spot 'em?" the older cop asked.

"I used to be on the pickpocket detail," I explained, "back in Chicago."

He made a disgusted face. "Well, what the hell are you doin' *here*?"

Good question.

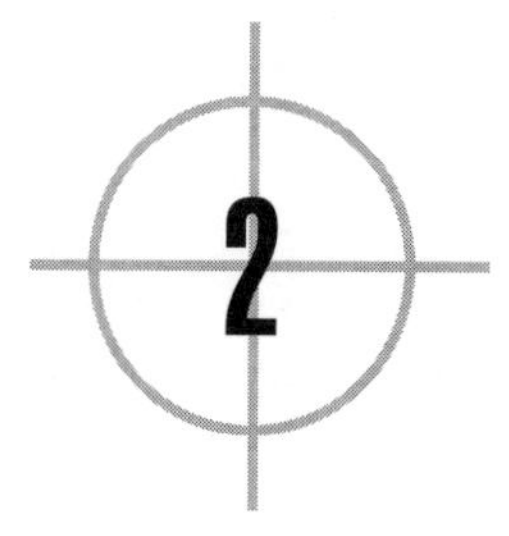

On a pleasantly warm afternoon, the Friday before, a taxi I'd caught at Newark Airport deposited me in Manhattan on Eighth Avenue between Thirty-fourth and Thirty-fifth streets, just to the rear of Penn Station, near the garment district. I paid the cabbie off, tipping him well, in return for sparing me any sight-seeing remarks on the ride in.

I alighted with valise in hand, a spongy but surprisingly heavy brown-paper package tucked under my arm. Oblivious to the bored, busy New Yorkers whisking by—shoppers, stenographers, businessmen, office clerks—I stood gaping up like any damn-fool out-of-towner at the second-tallest hotel in the city. Back in Chicago, the forty-story Morrison advertised itself as the tallest structure in the city that invented skyscrapers. But the Hotel New Yorker, with its wide, truncated, vaguely Egyptian structure and its intricate art deco setbacks, would have been impressive even if it didn't trump the Morrison by three stories.

The air-conditioned lobby was a low-ceilinged, sprawling affair that managed to be both stately and modern. I strolled past the coffee shop, newsstand, and a vast bank of elevators, over to the marble check-in counter, where I found myself expected.

"Your room is ready, Mr. Heller," bubbled a dark-haired, bright-eyed, cheerfully efficient clerk. "I'll let Mr. Weiss know you're here. . . ."

In my racket, you're seldom so graciously received, but I knew I was basking in reflected glory, and didn't take it very seriously. I took my valise, my paper-wrapped package and my travel-weary behind over to a soft chair and kept a potted fern company for a while.

Not a long while, however.

I'd been glancing around the lobby, cataloging the pretty girls mostly, when suddenly he was standing before me, like he'd just materialized. The apparition was bald, bottle-shaped and extremely well-dressed, his natty dark brown lightweight three-piece suit set off perfectly by a green-and-brown striped tie with diamond stickpin; my rumpled brown Maxwell Street number was no competition.

He was the kind of homely, slightly overweight man who tried to make up for his physical shortcomings via sartorial elegance.

But Seymour Weiss—Huey Long's second-in-command—had a lot of homeliness to overcome: wisps of brown hair atop an egg-shaped head like dying desert grass, bulbous nose, bump of a chin, dark dead eyes.

"Good to see you again, Mr. Heller," he said, and his small line of a mouth made itself into a tiny smile.

"Pleasure, Mr. Weiss," I said. "Elliott Wisbrod asked me to deliver this package to you, personally."

"Splendid!"

I handed him the brown-paper package and he held it in both hands, like an award he was gratefully accepting.

"I understand this is the Wisbrod Company's latest model," he said.

"That's what Mr. Wisbrod said."

Seymour beamed at me, pointed a stubby finger at my chest. "I'd like you to deliver it personally to Senator Long."

Was that why I'd been asked to play messenger, for a package the mails or R.E.A. could have easily handled?

I thought I knew the answer, but I asked anyway. "Why is that, Mr. Weiss?"

"Huey likes you," Seymour said quietly. "Maybe coming from you, he won't be so quick to dismiss this effort. . . ."

"If you say so," I said, shrugging a little.

After all, I'd flown out on his ticket, and I wasn't due to fly back till tomorrow, anyway. And an encounter with the Kingfish was always a memorable affair.

"Good," he said, and smiled his tiny smile, and thrust the package back into my arms, where it crinkled like Christmas paper.

As for the Kingfish liking me, that seemed an overstatement to me. I did know him, or at least we'd met. Friendly acquaintances was as far as I'd push it. Huey Long wasn't exactly the kind of man it was easy to "know."

But back in June of '32, when I was a plainclothes dick on the Chicago P.D., I'd got duty as police liaison to Long and four bodyguards, in town to attend the National Democratic Convention, at which Huey was lobbying for the nomination of Franklin Delano Roosevelt. In fact, he and his group showed up a week early, so Huey could play politics, get some press and check out the local nightlife—at least 'til *Mrs.* Long arrived for the convention itself.

Sergeant Sapperstein, my boss on the pickpocket detail, said somebody upstairs wanted Huey and his boys baby-sat. Seemed Huey's bodyguards had been deputized as Chicago police officers to give them firearm-carrying privileges; apparently the Kingfish was nervous about assassination attempts.

Huey wasn't the only nervous one: so was whoever got the payoff for allowing a Louisiana goon squad to go around town carrying guns—otherwise, I wouldn't have been showing the governor of Louisiana where in the Windy City one might violate the Eighteenth Amendment, not to mention two or three of the Ten Commandments.

"As I recall, you and Huey got along famously," Seymour said, as we stepped into an otherwise unoccupied elevator. It was one of those modern, self-service jobs; he pushed a button on a panel with more numbers on it than a punchboard.

"Yeah, Huey was okay," I said. "Even offered me a position. Should've taken it." I shook my head. "Thought I had a police career going."

"What happened?"

"Testified against some bent cops."

"Sounds noble."

"Not really. I did it to keep Frank Nitti from having me killed."

"Oh," he said. He cleared his throat. "And how was your flight?"

"Fine."

"Flying doesn't bother you?"

"Nope. Not since I went up with Lindy."

Seymour blinked. His expression was that of an iguana studying a fly. "You flew with Lindbergh?"

"Yeah, I was the Chicago police liaison on the kidnapping. In the early days, they figured Capone was responsible."

"I remember," Seymour said, nodding.

"Anyway, Slim's a real practical joker. I'd never been on a plane before, and he went on one of his hedge-hopping stunt-pilot binges, just to initiate me. Ever since, nothing any pilot can do can faze me."

On the other hand, this elevator was making my ears stop up. The button Seymour had punched read 32.

He seemed faintly amused. "Frank Nitti. Colonel Lindbergh. You've become something of a name-dropper, Mr. Heller."

I hadn't meant to be; or maybe in the back of my head I wanted to let Huey Long's majordomo know I'd been around.

"But I do wish you'd taken that job Huey offered you," Seymour said glumly.

"Yeah?"

"He could use you on his staff about now."

"From what I read in the papers, Huey doesn't go anywhere these days without a *battalion* of bodyguards."

"Trigger-happy thugs, most of them," Seymour said. "Huey'll be lucky not to get caught in a cross fire."

"Which is why you ordered this." I hefted the brown-paper-wrapped package.

Seymour nodded. The hard dead eyes got as meditative as they were capable of. "Huey engenders strong feelings in the populace," he said. "He's worshipped by many. . . ."

"Yeah," I said, "but you've also had armed insurrection in the streets of New Orleans."

"And Baton Rouge." Seymour shook his head, his expression grave. "He most definitely needs protection."

The elevator came to a stop and the door slid open, as I stepped out, swallowing to pop my ears back into full service. I followed Seymour, and it was the damnedest thing: he took small, almost mincing steps, the steps of a guarded man, yet he moved quickly. I almost had trouble keeping up. . . .

He used a key in the door (with a gold plate labeling it 3200) at the end of a hall. I was ushered into an outer sitting room where, at a table meant for dining or perhaps a business conference, two characters out of Damon Runyon sat in a cigar-smoke haze, playing cards.

I knew them both—they'd attended the Chicago convention with Long as part of his four-man bodyguard contingent.

"Hey, it's the red-headed mick from Chicago!" Big George McCracken said, his lumpy fighter's face approximating a smile.

Actually, nobody I ever heard of named Heller is a mick, but my Irish Catholic mother had bestowed on me those physical characteristics, whereas all I got from my apostate Jewish father was a last name and bad attitude.

"How you doin', George?" I asked.

"Can't complain." McCracken was in his shirtsleeves and suspenders, but had his crumpled fedora on. A smoldering stub of a cigar was buried in his cheek as he looked up from a hand of gin. He was winning.

No surprise: his opponent was Joe Messina, who had the mental capacity of a tree stump, and about as much personality. Messina glanced back at me and grunted a greeting, as if my showing up after a three-year absence was completely unremarkable, and studied his cards with all the intensity he could muster.

"Nice to see you again, too, Joe," I said.

"Comin' to work with us?" McCracken asked. Next to him, leaned against his chair, I noticed, was a big paper sack, a grocery bag, and in it was a Thompson submachine gun.

A hole in the side of the sack gave him access to the trigger.

"Nope," I said, following Seymour, who hadn't bothered speaking to Huey's roughneck rabble; he was heading past a pair of male aides or secretaries who were seated at another table, going over some papers. They didn't speak to Seymour or he to them, as he moved toward a closed door, from behind which came the muffled, but enthusiastic, sound of a woman singing.

"Just playing delivery boy," I added to McCracken, lifting the brown-paper package, and Seymour opened the door.

". . . man a king," the female voice sang in a pleasantly chirpy, Betty Boop-ish way, "every man a king, for you can be a millionaire . . ."

I trailed Seymour into the large, lavishly appointed, wall-to-wall carpeted bedroom, where next to the window, sun filtering in through sheer drapes, was a spinet piano in front of which stood a pretty little blonde in a slinky white-dotted navy taffeta number. She was swinging a cute fist as she punctuated the lyrics.

"But there's something belonging to others," she warbled, "there's enough for all *pee*-ple to share . . ."

At the piano was another cutie; neither one of them had seen twenty-five. This one was brunette and wore taffeta, too, white with navy dots, like the photo negative of the other girl's frock.

"When it's sunny June, and December, too," the blonde sang, "or in the wintertime or spring . . ."

Jumping in enthusiastically, and off-key, from time to time, was their musical director—in green pajamas and bare feet—directing the musical ensemble as if he were guiding a plane in on a runway. With one arm windmilling in a manner that had nothing to do with the beat, the Kingfish was, as usual, in charge.

Then in a croaking baritone, the senator from Louisiana joined in with the blonde on the bouncy melody, "There'll be peace without end, every neighbor a friend, with ev . . . ry man . . . a . . . *k-i-i-i-i-ng*!"

A little man sitting across the room began to applaud enthusiastically; wire-frame glasses pinched his sharp nose, a red bow tie adding a splash of color to his drab brown suit.

"Lovely, Lila," Huey said, placing one of the blonde's small hands between his two bigger ones like he was pressing a prom rose in a book. She beamed at him. Then he let go and touched the shoulder of the brunette at the piano who had turned to smile up at him in awe; this was a celebrity, after all.

"I like that 'un best," he said, "don't you, ladies?"

The two girls nodded.

The little man in wire-frames rose from his chair, still applauding, which seemed like overkill to me, and through a strained smile he said, "Very nice, Kingfish, very nice indeed."

"Well, now, thank ya, Lou."

Lou went to the piano and tapped the sheets of music manuscript. "But I think you may want one of these *new* songs we commissioned. I mean, Kingfish, this is for your presidential campaign . . . the public might be a little tired of 'Every—' "

"Lou," Huey said with a smile as casual as it was patronizing, "as a theatrical agent, you're a humdinger. But as a judge of musical composition? Ya ain't worth the powder and shot it'd take to kill ya."

The agent frowned in frustration, lifting the handwritten sheets of music and waving them flappingly in the air. "We have compositions from some of the *top* talent on Tin Pan Alley. . . ."

"I like the song *I* wrote. Iffen it's good enough for the LSU marchin' band, it's good enough for the American public."

"But you wanted a *campaign* song. . . ."

Huey put his hand on the little man's shoulder. "Tell ya what—we'll take a vote." He winked at the blonde and she blushed, or pretended to. "I'm the chairman, I vote we use *my* song, and the motion is carried."

Seymour and I had been standing just inside the bedroom door through all this, and had as yet to be acknowledged. I stood with my fedora in my hands, wondering if there was a chance in hell the Kingfish would even recognize me.

Suddenly, as if my thoughts had summoned him, Long turned to us. His happy bumpkin face turned into a scowl.

"Where'd *you* run off to, Seymour?" he asked irritably. "I was makin' a goddamn point!"

"But you and Mr. Irwin have important business," Seymour said, gesturing to the bow-tied agent.

"We *had* our business," he said. "Lou, I'll see you at supper tonight."

"Looking forward to it, Kingfish."

Huey slipped one arm around the blonde and the other around the brunette, and walked them toward the door. "It was real sweet of you kids to help the ol' Kingfish out this afternoon," he said.

"It was an honor, Senator," the blonde said, and fluttered her false lashes.

"You thank Nick for me, now, hear?"

"You bet," the brunette said.

The Kingfish shut the door behind them and his affability evaporated as he walked over to the big double bed and flopped there on his back. There were no pillows; he apparently liked to stretch out, flat. Also, at some point in the last ten minutes, I seemed to have turned invisible.

Seymour wandered over and stood at the bedside, like a butler awaiting his wealthy master's whim. Huey ignored him, removed a cigar from a box on the bedstand, biting off the tip, spitting it who-knew-where, then lighting up the cigar with the tall flame of a silver Zippo. He puffed, got it going, then picked up a newspaper on the bed next to him, the *Washington Post.* He read and smoked and then, finally, spoke.

"Like I was sayin', Seymour, 'fore you so rudely run off . . . you *know* I don't mind a few little ol' isolated pockets of insurrection . . . after all, even fleas got their use—they keep the dog awake." He turned the page of the paper and it drooped and he shook it erect, making a whip-crack sound.

"And, anyway, I cain't make a speech worth a damn 'less I'm raisin' hell about what my enemies are up to."

Seymour shifted on his feet. "I hope that means you've come to your senses on the Judge Pavy matter. . . ."

Huey thrust the paper angrily aside, tightening his fist as he did; the crumpling was like distant thunder. His eyes and nostrils flared. He was an enraged bull in green silk pajamas.

"Come to my senses is right! Them stubborn hayseeds in St. Landry Parish need to be taught some god-*damn* respect." He smiled but it turned quickly into a sneer. "Come Sunday, we'll gerrymander Judge Pavy slap damn to hell and gone."

Seymour patted the air cautiously. "Judge Pavy is very popular around Opelousas way. . . ."

"I'll teach those peckerwoods to git off the sidewalk and bow down good and goddamn low when the Kingfish comes to town." Huey's cigar had gone out. He sat up on the bed, and reached for the Zippo on the nightstand. "Who's that? New bodyguard?"

The Kingfish had finally noticed me.

Seymour smiled. "Old friend of yours. From Chicago."

Slowly, his face began to light up, like a kid handed a candy bar.

He hopped off the bed and came over with his hand extended; it was as if he planned to stab me with it. But we only shook hands, warmly, though truth be told, the Kingfish had a strangely cold, clammy handshake.

Like shaking hands with a corpse.

"Well, well, if it ain't the smart-ass Chicaga boy hisself! Nat Heller!"

I gave him half a smile. "It's Nate. But I'm surprised you remember me at all, Senator."

Both eyebrows lifted momentarily. "Why, 'cause of them speakeasies we damn near drunk outa business?"

"Man like you meets a lot of people, Senator."

He shook his head. "Not that stands up to me. I scare the bejesus out of ninety-nine out of a hun-erd men, but I guess maybe you're that *other* one."

"I don't know. Pay me enough money and I'll be glad to grovel."

His laugh was a howl, and whether sincere or just part of the rube persona he affected, I couldn't say. He slipped an arm around my shoulder.

"You know," he said, "if you didn't have the same color hair as me, mebbe I wouldn't cut ya so goddamn much slack. . . ."

I ran a hand through my reddish-brown locks and grinned. "Maybe there was a Long in the woodpile."

This time the laughter was a roar, and he gestured for me to follow him over to a sofa, where we both sat. Seymour took a chair nearby, but sat quietly.

"Forgive the pajamies, Nate—kinda got to be a trademark with me. People half expect it."

"If it's good enough for the German consul," I said, "it's good enough for me."

"But it *wasn't* good enough for that Heinie son of a bitch," Huey said good-naturedly. "That's how these things got to *be* my trademark."

We were both referring to a notorious international incident that had made great press for Huey. In New Orleans, at Mardi Gras time a few years ago, the commander of a German cruiser and the German consul called on the Governor of the Great State of Louisiana in the latter's hotel suite. Huey greeted them in his blue robe, green pajamas and red slippers (he later admitted he'd looked like an "explosion in a paint factory"), unintentionally insulting the dignitaries. The press got hold of it and had a merry time with the story, and ever since, Huey had played up the rustic fool business, probably because it softened his American Hitler image.

"So," Huey said, using the Zippo again, "what brings the Chicaga Police Department to New York? Bigger and better graft?"

"That might do it," I said. "But me, I went private back in '32."

"Hot damn." He slapped his thighs. "Hope that means you come here to fin'ly take me up on my job offer!" He shook his head. "Them sorry-ass, shif'less, worthless Cossacks of mine . . . I can *use* somebody that don't think with his fists."

"Isn't Murphy Roden still with you? He's a good man."

His mouth twitched. " 'Ception to the rule. He's drivin' my Caddy from D.C. down to Baton Rouge for me. He'd be pleased to see you—took a real shine to you."

"Huey," Seymour interjected, "Mr. Heller is here at my invitation."

"Really? That's one good idea you had lately."

Seymour's eyes tightened. "I . . . I wanted to give you something special. For your birthday."

Huey smirked at me, rolled his eyes. "Big day. Big deal. The ol' Kingfish is gettin' on in years. So, Seymour. Is Chicaga here my gift? Why ain't you wearin' a big red ribbon, Heller?"

"The cake I was going to jump out of fell," I said.

Seymour nodded toward the brown-paper package I had laid next to me on the couch. "I asked him to bring you a present from Chicago. . . ."

I handed him the crinkly package and he took it eagerly, his smile making his cheeks fat, his eyes those of a greedy child; he tore at the wrapping, but as the contents were revealed to him, his glow turned to glower.

In the Kingfish's hands was a thick, bulky tan canvas sleeveless garment, a vest of sorts that would cover its wearer neck to waist.

Disgusted, he threw the gift at Seymour who caught it, flinching.

"I don't need no goddamn bullet-proof BVDs, Seymour! Jesus H. Kee-rist! I'd look, and *feel*, like a damn fool in the fucker. Send it back!"

Seymour's homely face was tight with concern. "Huey . . . please . . . with these death threats . . . you have to have protection."

"The kind of protection I need ain't the kind you *wear*."

"I simply thought . . ."

"That's your problem, lately. Simple thinkin'." He shook his head and the spit curl flounced. "Well, ya did one thing right, anyway—you invited my ol' pal Heller here to come to my birthday shindig."

Seymour managed a smile that was a sickly half-moon.

Huey waved dismissively in the air, as if shooing a fly. "Seymour, check on them train reservations."

"I already have. . . ."

"Double-check. Don't you understand? I want some privacy here. I want a private consultation with my Chicaga security advisor."

Seymour nodded numbly, rose, and carrying the tan bullet-proof vest in his hands like something he needed to bury, went out, shutting the door behind him.

The Kingfish slapped me on the shoulder; his grin was tight and somewhat glazed; he was, after all, at least a little crazy. "So . . . you're in private practice now, are ya, son? Ya know, I'm serious about that job offer still bein' good."

"That's flattering, Senator."

"Huey. Call me 'Huey,' or 'Kingfish.' Senator is what you call them numbskulls back in Washington."

"All right . . . Huey. But I got a nice little business goin' back home."

He jerked, as if I'd slapped him. "In this goddamn depression? Under Prince Franklin? Are you joshin'?"

Actually, I kind of felt the depression was letting up a little, and I'd voted for FDR; but I didn't share that with the Kingfish.

"Well, I have clients to consider. Retail credit, insurance investigation . . . can't just walk away from them."

And I had no desire to move to bayou country, even temporarily, though I didn't share that thought with him, either. Swamps and gators weren't my style.

"Can you give me jest a little ol' month of your time, son?" His voice had turned surprisingly gentle; the soapbox nowhere to be seen. "Even jest a measly li'l ol' two weeks?"

"Well, I might be—"

He leaned forward; his dark brown eyes fixed on me in a manner that was both seductive and discomfiting. "I need a *man* . . . a man I can trust."

"What about Seymour Weiss?"

"I trust him like a brother," he said flatly. Then he leaned back, and draped his arms along on the top of the sofa. " 'Course, on t'other hand, I don't in particular trust my brothers."

"You said yourself, Murphy Roden's a good man."

"So he is, and so, in his inimitable way, is Joe Messina—he'd die for me."

"He also needs help tying his shoes."

"That's a God-granted fact," Huey said, and grinned. "So . . . what I need is a man I can trust, who's also a man with brains. . . ." He winked at me. "An *outside* man to be my *inside* man. What's your goin' rate, Detective Heller?"

"Twenty-five a day." For those clients I figured could afford it, anyway.

He raised his eyebrows and looked down the double barrels of his shotgun nose at me. "Son, I'll pay you ten times that with a minimum retainer coverin' a week's work—cash on the barrelhead."

I perked up. Despite that cornpone drawl, he was talking my language now.

"And," he said, with a flourish of a hand gesture, "I'll toss in a ten-thousand-dollar bonus . . . iffen you come through for me."

"Come through *how*?"

He used the Zippo to light up the cigar again; from the aroma, I'd bet a C-note it was a Havana. Oddly, considering how hard-drinking he'd been back in Chicago in '32, there was no sign in the suite of a bar or liquor cart or even a bottle.

Then, as casually as if he were asking somebody to pass the salt, he said, "Sometime in the next week or so . . . give or take . . . somebody's gonna try an' kill the ol' Kingfish."

But before my new employer could elucidate, the door burst open and the cute blonde who'd been singing at the piano was back again, this time wearing a black beaded, low-cut gown that exposed lots of creamy white flesh. Additionally, she was holding a big creamy white frosted cake that looked almost as good as she did; it was elaborately decorated with birthday greetings and frosting flowers, all in a shade of green near that of the Kingfish's silk pajamas. Atop the cake, a forest of little green candles burned.

"Happy birthday to you, happy birthday to you," the stunning young woman sang, as Joe Messina, Big George McCracken, the agent Lou Irwin and others in the Long retinue, male secretaries and what-have-you, crowded around, following her into the bedroom. All were gaily joining in except a glum Seymour who trailed after them.

"Happy birthday, dear Huey," they all sang—even Seymour joined in, finally—as the Kingfish approached, his eyes damp, apparently genuinely touched.

He blew out the candles.

Huey P. Long was forty-two years old.

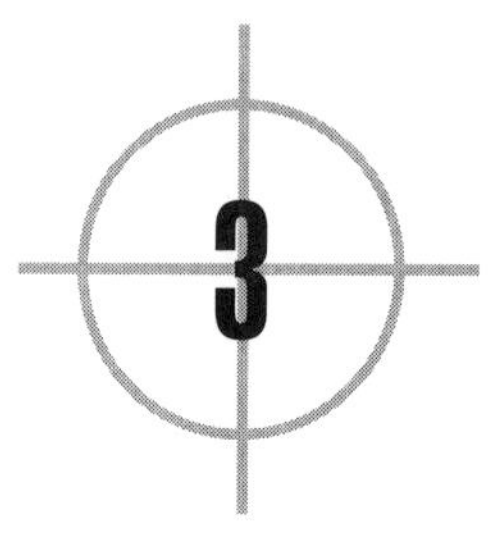

The Stork Club, that legendary habitat of café society and newspaper columnists, with its white-lettered navy blue canopy and entryway murals of top-hatted storks, seemed an unlikely venue for the birthday party of a Louisiana Kingfish. But the theatrical agent, Lou Irwin, who had booked the orchestra in the club's main room, told us owner Sherman Billingsley had just hired a new French chef who made the best onion soup in the world.

And Huey, through an enormous mouthful of frosted cake, said he liked the sound of that "jes' fine."

I still needed to check into the hotel, and several others wanted to tidy up before going out, so it was just after dark when the group—including the bodyguards, but unfortunately minus the blonde, who was a singer with Nick Lucas's band in the New Yorker supper club—piled into two taxi cabs and headed uptown. I rode with two male aides and Seymour Weiss, who looked like a headwaiter in his tuxedo.

"Huey says you've come aboard," he said, seeming in a better mood.

"For a week or two, anyway," I admitted. I tried not to let my uneasiness show: thanks to the interruption of the birthday party, getting any details from Huey about his supposedly imminent assassination would have to wait.

Like the rest of the country, I'd seen in the papers that Huey had, on the floor of the Senate, accused FDR of aiding and abetting a murder plot against him; something about conspirators meeting at some hotel somewhere. But I'd really merely read the headlines, skimmed the stories. Nobody was taking it very seriously. After all, Huey made a habit out of such accusations. He was a wolf who kept crying little boy.

The Stork Club was, obviously, for the class customer—the affluent, the prominent. Seymour was the only one in the party in a tux, however, though Huey had traded his green-silk pajamas for a light tan poplin suit, an expanse of tie that looked to have been splattered by its green-and-red colors and a lavender shirt with a checkered pattern. Explosion in a paint factory was right.

Messina and McCracken were in their usual baggy mobster suits (McCracken had left his tommy gun in a bag behind), while I probably looked a little gangsterish myself in my rumpled dark suit. There hadn't been time to have it, or my lightweight white spare, pressed at the hotel.

But we were part of Senator Long's party, and none of the stuck-up Stork Club staff dared say a word or risk a disapproving glance; the hatcheck girl, a curvy little redhead, even gave me a wink, a smile and a celluloid token in return for my fedora.

Leaving the real world behind and entering into the fantasy realm of the rich, you were stopped at nothing so common as a velvet rope: the Stork Club had an eighteen-carat gold chain. This glittering barricade was lifted from our path by a dinner-jacketed captain who ushered us to the left, past a long, oval bar where, over cocktails, men in tails looking for tail murmured at frails in gowns that were no more expensive than your average Buick. Pretty chichi company for hoi polloi like me.

Beyond a scattering of bar tables was the main room, where the Frank Shields Orchestra, on its tiered stage, was performing a rather listless "Begin the Beguine." I hoped the onion soup was better.

There were eight in our motley little party, all males, seated at a long table in the midst of the room like an island of riffraff in a sea of sophistication. All around us were men in white ties and ladies in dark gowns, both sexes smoking with that casual elegance only the rich (and, of course, movie stars who grew up in ghettos) can effortlessly affect, from barely legal debutantes to the barely living debauched, and all ages between, all dressed to the nines.

Whether they were Manhattan society or tourists from Peoria who slipped the maître d' a ten-spot, they were here to dine on the Stork Club's specialty of the house: celebrity. You might see H. L. Mencken or Eddie Cantor; Ernest Hemingway or Claudette Colbert. Tonight, the main course was Kingfish.

Not that anybody—except, perhaps, a tourist or two—gawked or gaped or any such thing. These raised-pinky types were more discreet. But out around the edges of their elegance, they were watching the Kingfish's antics, taking it all in. What were they thinking, these rich people whose money Huey wanted to reclaim for the poor (and himself)?

When a distinguished-looking older couple, on the way to the dance floor, stopped for a moment to pay their regards to the senator, he played modest. "Aw, I ain't nothin' much—only a little Kingfish from off yonder there."

When our waiter came for his order, the Kingfish said, "All I want's a bowl of this here onion soup I been hearin' so much about. And if it's not up to snuff, tell that French chef of yours, I'm gon' be back there next to 'im, with my coat off, teachin' him how the Cajuns cook."

When the head bartender brought him over a complimentary gin fizz, a drink widely reported in the press to be Huey's favorite, the senator at first declined, then relented, saying, "You know, I ain't had a drink in eighteen months, but I'll sample this, son, in order to be able to assure ya that it's gen-you-wine." He took a sip, said, "I think that's all right, I think that's all right . . . better be sure about it."

And he took another big drink, and flashed his rascal's grin of approval around at all the eavesdroppers.

But that was the last sip of anything alcoholic I saw him sip that night, or ever again, for that matter.

When the onion soup arrived, it was damn good, a flavorful broth under a crust of browned swiss cheese that passed Huey's muster. But when other people's meals began to arrive, Huey—who hadn't ordered anything but the soup—began casually plucking this and that off the plates of those around him. A boiled potato here, a carrot there, a bite or two of fish.

Nobody at the table said a word about it, or even reacted; I wasn't surprised, either—I'd noticed this behavior, back in Chicago in '32. Par for the course, at mealtime with Huey. The only difference was, back then he ordered a plate of food for himself, as well.

But now he was slimming down; preparing for the battle royal against "Prince Franklin."

In any case, I had positioned myself as far away from the Kingfish as possible. Nobody was getting a fork in this butter-smooth medium-rare New York strip steak but Nate Heller.

As Huey dined on morsels plundered from the plates of others, he expounded on his enemies: Roosevelt's postmaster and confidant Jim Farley was "the Nabob of New York," Secretary of Agriculture Henry Wallace was "that ignoramus from Iowa," Secretary of the Interior Harold Ickes was "the chinch bug of Chicago."

Mostly, though, he railed about FDR.

"He's very popular right now, Huey," Seymour Weiss said quietly, eating the few tidbits of lobster tail that Huey had left on his majordomo's plate.

"I can take him," Huey said pugnaciously. "He's a phony. I can *take* this Roosevelt. He's scared of me, Seymour." He snorted a laugh. "I can out-promise that son of a bitch *any* day of the week, and he *knows* it."

"Excuse me, Senator," someone said. The voice was male, mellow, slightly nasal.

At first I thought it was Jack Benny, and there *was* a resemblance, but then I realized this was another, if lesser, radio star: Phil Baker. I'd seen him in vaudeville in Chicago—the Benny similarity extended to his use of a musical instrument, an accordion substituting for Benny's violin. Baker was a better musician, a pleasant singer, but not, in my opinion, particularly funny.

"The *Armour Jester*!" Huey said, standing, brimming with enthusiasm. "Why, son, you're the best thing *on* the Blue Network!"

As they shook hands, the smiling Baker, hair slicked back, in a dark blue suit with dark blue bow tie, said, "I'm not gonna be on for Armour, anymore, Senator. I'm movin' to CBS, for Gulf Oil."

"So long as it ain't Standard."

They both laughed; everybody knew Huey Long and Standard Oil were bitter enemies.

"I just signed the contract today, actually," Baker said. "Real piece of luck."

"What's that, son?"

"I'm getting Will Rogers's Sunday time slot."

Will Rogers and Wiley Post had died in a plane crash in Alaska two weeks ago. Real piece of luck.

This good fortune had Baker bubbling. "Senator, I want you to meet the two most beautiful girls in New York, my wife, Peggy, and her niece, Cleanthe Carr."

Baker, who my trained detective's eye placed at around forty, had a younger, quite attractive wife with dark blonde hair, chic and shapely in a black-and-white print satin evening dress with matching gloves.

But next to her was a honey-blonde eyeful of probably eighteen, blue-eyed and sparkling of smile, her slender curves well served by a rose-color brocade taffeta gown that left her arms bare. Her shoulders were covered by puffs of sleeve tied with bows, her heart-shaped neckline modest but alluring.

"Well, howdy do, ladies," Huey said elegantly.

"A pleasure, Senator," Mrs. Baker said.

"Cleanthe is Gene Carr's daughter, Senator," Baker said, as the Kingfish approached the girl with the same look in his eyes he would give the person-next-to-him's plate of food.

"What a charmin' child," he said, taking her hands in his. " 'Cleanthe'—that's a nice Southern-soundin' name for an East Coast kiddo like you, honey."

Her smile dimples seemed about to burst her pretty face; even for someone with a radio-star uncle, meeting the Kingfish was a big deal. And getting fussed over by the famous is hard to shrug off, even if you aren't an eighteen-year-old girl.

"Gene Carr is her father," Baker told him again, as if that were important.

"Gene Carr?" Huey asked absently, his eyes bulging and full of the girl.

"The syndicated cartoonist?" Baker asked, seeking recognition. "His panel, 'Metropolitan Movies,' is very popular."

"Oh, *that* Gene Carr," Huey said. He was still holding the girl's hands. Staring at her. "Don't imagine there's a cartoon man anywhere on earth, under God's livin' sun, that's better known."

I'd never heard of Carr, although Huey may have. Of course, I didn't read the comics. But I would have said, "What about Walt Disney?" if I'd been part of the conversation, which I wasn't.

The girl, however, was beaming, hearing this praise heaped on her father.

"Pull yourselves up some chairs, and join us!" Huey said gaily, nudging Seymour to make room for the honey blonde. Lou Irwin, on Huey's other side, made room for Baker and his wife. I was next to Seymour, and scooted down accordingly.

"Ha! Ha! Oh boy," Baker said, treating us to an inane radio catch phrase of his. "Imagine finding a Kingfish inside a stork."

But Huey didn't laugh or even seem to be paying attention to Baker; he was massaging the honey blonde with his eyeballs.

"That's my orchestra, you know," Baker said, nodding toward the stage. "Frank Shields and his boys, I mean. They're on my radio show."

"You want some champagne, young lady?" Huey asked her. "Seymour, pass that bubble water down heah!"

"Cleanthe is an aspiring artist herself," Baker said, finally grasping the only subject that interested Huey at the moment. "She's going to study in France."

"Why get involved with *them* highfalutin' suckers?" Huey asked her earnestly. "Honey, we got art classes at LSU."

The orchestra was making a decent enough job of "I'm in the Mood for Love." Reading Huey's mind, perhaps.

"Just how good an artist is this little girl?" the Kingfish

asked Baker, eyeing her in a manner that seemed unlikely to assess artistic skill.

"She's every bit as good a cartoonist as her father," Baker said.

Huey grabbed one of the napkins, with its top-hatted stork emblems. He dug in an inside pocket and came back with a fountain pen. He put the napkin before her, and held out the pen like a dare.

"Then let's see ya sketch *me*, young lady!"

The young woman, who as yet had not spoken, did a quick, deft caricature of Huey with the fountain pen; in bold strokes, she caught him without flattering, or insulting, him, which was a good trick for any caricaturist. She depicted him frozen in mid-hellfire speech: arms out, hair flying. Mouth open. It seemed the most natural way to depict him.

He held the little napkin before him like a pocket mirror he was looking into, his eyes wide, his face a blank putty mask. Then he smiled, as if he relished the reflection.

"Normally," she said, in measured tones at odds with her college-girl good looks, "I work in wash, or charcoal."

"How would you like a job?" he asked her. He wasn't looking at her with backwoods wanton lust anymore; he was appraising her as the talented young woman she was.

"You mean, in the art field, Senator?"

"I don't mean in the cotton field, missy. I jest finished writin' my latest masterpiece . . . li'l ol' tome called *My First Days in the White House.* Thought I best write my memoirs of my presidential years *'fore* I got there, 'cause I'll be too busy durin', and after's way too late."

I was eating my desert, some cherry cheesecake; but sweet as it was, this latest explosion of Huey b.s. made me smile more. The guy was outrageous; you had to give him that.

"Miss Carr," he said almost formally, "I have been considerin' adding some caricature illustrations to my book. Of myself and the other public figures depicted therein. And I think you're the perfect man for the job. So to speak."

Her eyes were as wide as they were blue. She seemed flabbergasted, but had the presence of mind to say, "Why, I'd be honored, Senator."

"Is he serious about that book?" I whispered to Seymour.

Seymour, who was pouring himself some champagne, nodded, and whispered back: "He finished dictating it last week. Intends it to be a major tool in his presidential effort —that's why we're in New York."

"What is?"

"To place the book with a publisher."

Huey was saying, "Do you know what I want for my birthday, young lady? To show you how we cut a rug back in Loozyana."

He pulled her by the hand toward the dance floor, and she went willingly. As they were gliding around out there, he was making her laugh, obviously charming her, but the lack of animation in his features indicated he'd shifted gears. He was in that one-on-one mode of his, where he could exude a different sort of magnetism. Where he could harness the bull of himself and project a seductive gentleness. . . . I'd seen it this afternoon, when he'd told me how he needed a *man* . . . a man he could *trust*. . . .

"Hello, Seymour," a female voice said; it was a melodic soprano.

When I glanced up and back, I thought for a moment Claudette Colbert *had* shown up.

"Well . . . Alice Jean," Weiss said, clearly shaken by her presence. "Hello."

The bodyguards and male secretaries mumbled their hellos; I gathered her last name was "Crosley."

She was in her mid-twenties, slim yet bosomy, in a black satin dress with ruffles at the throat and cuffs, touched with winking rhinestones here and there; her hat was a black beret plumed with black ostrich feathers, at a rakish angle.

The delicate features of her heart-shaped face were highlighted by hazel eyes, framed by perfect dark curls, though her mouth was thin, making a little bow of a smile.

But the smile didn't last long. It flattened into a single hard line at the sight of Huey dancing and flirting with Miss Carr.

Seymour, noticing this, got suddenly conversational, half-turning in his chair. "What brings you to New York, Alice Jean?"

"What do you think, you phony son of a bitch?"

Alice Jean cut as straight a path as possible through the tables out to the dance floor, where the Kingfish and his new illustrator were taking the orchestra's rendition of "Cheek to Cheek" literally. She tapped Cleanthe Carr on the puffy-sleeved shoulder.

When Huey looked back to see who was cutting in, he frowned in surprised displeasure; even from this distance, his reddened face looked fearsome as he spat some harsh words at the pretty intruder.

I couldn't hear exactly what he said, but his young dancing partner looked as shocked as Alice Jean did hurt.

Alice Jean almost ran from the dance floor, moving as fast as the tight gown would allow. She was biting her lower lip with tiny perfect white teeth, her big hazel eyes liquid with tears as she rushed out of the room, wearing dozens of café society eyes.

"A dame with a shape like that," I said to Seymour, "usually gets a warmer reception."

"She's lucky Huey didn't slap her," Seymour said. "He told her to stay away."

"Why? Who is she?"

"Alice Jean Crosley."

"I gathered. Who *is* she?"

Seymour was pouring himself another glass of champagne. "She used to be his confidential secretary."

"Used to be?"

He nodded. "She wanted to go to Washington with him, but he told her she couldn't." Seymour's voice was only faintly edged with sarcasm, as he said: "After all, how would it look, an attractive girl like Alice Jean . . . and the senator, a happily married man with children . . ."

"A 'happily married man' with his eye on the White House, you mean."

Seymour nodded.

"So he gave her the brush," I said, "and she's pissed off."

Seymour laughed soundlessly. "Hardly. He left her home in Louisiana, all right . . . but he made her Secretary of State."

Before I could inquire of Seymour just how even a Huey Long could get away with appointing his mistress to a high office like that, the Kingfish was back at the table, holding the chair out for Miss Carr, his spirits high again.

"Son," he said to Baker, even though they were probably about the same age, "your niece is as light on her feet as she is proficient with a pencil."

The girl seemed a little unnerved, which didn't escape the Kingfish's notice.

"Folks, I'm sorry about that nasty little spectacle out there," he said. " 'Fraid I lost my temper with the child." He shrugged. "But when people throw stones at me, I throw brickbats back at 'em."

"Excuse me," a female voice said.

We all looked back and there she stood, Alice Jean Crosley, hands fig-leafed before her, head hanging, like a repentant little girl.

"Could I please join the party?"

She didn't address him directly, but it was Huey she was talking to.

Huey was glaring at her, but as he stared at her, something like real affection melted the stern expression. He nodded, and pointed down toward my end of the table. She pulled out the chair next to me, and sat.

She leaned her head out to look down the table toward Huey. "I just wanted to surprise you for your birthday," she said meekly.

The Kingfish nodded. "I know you meant well, darlin'. Have yourself a li'l ol' drink, and relax some."

Baker said, "Aren't you having anything, Senator?"

"Nope. But jest 'cause I'm off the likker don't mean everybody else shouldn't have a party." He found a Havana in an inside pocket of his suit coat. "I'm jest gonna smoke this heah birthday cigar . . . the last one I'll smoke 'til my presidential campaign is over. In keepin' with my new, wholesome public image."

He winked at the honey blonde.

Frowning, Alice Jean poured herself a glass of champagne. She drank it quickly, without glee.

"My name's Heller. Nate Heller." I held my hand out. "Pleased to meet you, Miss Crosley."

She smirked at me, ignoring my offered hand, poured herself another glass; she kept pouring and drinking—I lost count, how many times. She just sat drinking quickly, quietly, morosely, while Huey held court down the table, trading laughs with the unfunny radio comic.

"Ha, ha! Oh boy," Baker said, for no apparent reason. "If you really want to see what Cleanthe can do, you should come up to my penthouse."

That got double takes from just about everybody at the table, and Alice Jean spilled a little of her latest glass of bubbly.

"We've got her portfolio back there," Baker said, "and some of her watercolors and some serious things, hanging on the wall. Why don't we go there for a nightcap?"

"That's generous of you, son," Huey said.

"We could discuss the illustrations for your book," Cleanthe offered.

She was no dummy; she wanted something in writing.

"*Everybody* come," Baker said, looking down the table. "You're all welcome. . . . And if you've had your fill of spirits, Peggy'll whip up some good black coffee. . . ."

Going to a radio star's New York penthouse sounded good to everybody, with the exception of Alice Jean, who hadn't said anything for a long time, but whose expression was getting surly.

Then the caricature that was Huey's real face was looming next to me, as he bent down to whisper.

"Min' doin' the Kingfish a li'l ol' favor, son? Escort Miz Crosley back to the hotel, would you? That's a good boy. . . ."

He patted my shoulder, and he and the party were wandering off, as "Miz Crosley" sat up in her chair, glaring at them as they went, and then at me.

She was about to say something very nasty, I'll bet, when she threw up in my lap.

Ha ha.

Oh boy.

4

My arm around her waist, I guided the still very tipsy Alice Jean Crosley down the carpeted hallway of the thirty-fifth floor of the Hotel New Yorker; she was no help in the effort, and frequently stumbled, but had no trouble expressing herself.

"Lousy bastard," she said, referring to Huey, not me (I didn't seem to exist). "*I'm* bad for his public image . . . *me*! *Bad!* Lousy goddamn bastard . . ."

I had heard slurred, Southern-tinged variations on this theme all the way back from the Stork Club, where the help had been gracious about getting the two of us cleaned up. Posh as the Stork Club was, it was a saloon, and people had thrown up in there before.

Alice Jean had managed to get very little on herself, and it was mostly liquid anyway, mostly that champagne she'd been swilling. So the front of me was damp, from where I washed it off in the Stork Club men's room, but that was about it. No rank smell or anything. Why, glancing at me, you wouldn't think I'd been thrown up on, at all; merely that I was incontinent.

Getting a room for her had been no problem; apparently the management kept several rooms free, on the Kingfish's floor, for the senator's use, at his discretion—whether in anticipation of business or pleasure or both, the desk clerk didn't say.

"This way," I told her, as she tried to veer down the wrong direction.

"Tell me this," she said. "Will you tell me this one thing? Tell me this."

I walked her along.

"Tell me why *I'm* bad for his public image," she said, "and pawin' that little blonde chippy, out in fronta God and the Astors and ev'rybody, isn't. Tell me *that*!"

She leaned against me, and I continued supporting her with an arm around her waist, as I worked the key in the door. The ostrich feathers on her beret tickled my nose, and I blew at them, to get them out of my line of vision. Even leaning against me, she was weaving. Spewing that champagne from her system and onto my poor suit hadn't seemed to make her any less drunk.

The room was small but, typically for this hotel, well appointed: dark, modern furnishings, a pale green carpet muffling the elephant footsteps of our double entry.

I risked allowing her to stand on her own steam. She wobbled, but didn't fall; she was watching the floor with frowning fascination. What she perceived the floor as being up to, I couldn't hazard a guess.

"Are you going to be all right now?" I asked her. I was standing at the door, which was open.

"Shut the door," she said. She tossed her beret toward a chair, missed by a mile. "What's your name again?"

"Nate Heller."

She looked like she was going to cry. "You been awful nice. *What's* your name?"

"Good-night, Alice Jean."

But before I could go, she stumbled over to me, and fell into my arms: it was not an embrace. More a collapse.

Hugging me, to keep from falling, she said, "Goddamn bastard. Goddamn bastard. Undo me."

"What?"

She stood away from me, weaving, but more or less keeping her footing. She wiggled her fingers. "Bananas."

"What?"

"Got bananas for fingers. Can't do a thing with 'em. Undo me." With considerable effort, as if backing a big automobile into a tiny parking place, she maneuvered her body, turning her back to me, and I got the message: she needed help with her zipper.

I unzipped the black gown and a beautifully curved, wonderfully pale back revealed itself, right down to the dimples over her full little ass. She wore scanty step-ins, but no camisole, under the gown. The banana fingers managed to brush the dress off either shoulder and the garment dropped to her feet in a black beaded puddle.

Somehow she stepped out of the puddle without falling, but when she tried to take her right heel off, I had to catch her, a bundle of drunken but firm and beautifully rounded flesh in my hands. While I supported her, she got the heels off, then she stumbled a few steps, in the cream-color lace step-ins, matching garter belt and dark-seamed silk stockings.

A man of true moral fiber would have been disgusted by this drunken display; me, I had a raging hard-on.

She stumbled toward the room's single bed and fell face down; instantly, she began to snore. I studied her for a few moments; one of her bare breasts, her left one, ballooned interestingly on the bed as she pressed her slumbering weight against it. What would a man of true moral fiber do? Neither I, nor my hard-on, had a clue.

She was tiny, and lifting her in my arms was no trick,

though getting the bedspread and sheets pulled back, while cradling her like that, was. I deposited my pretty, unconscious bundle between the sheets, making sure her head was resting comfortably against a fluffy pillow, and I tucked her in.

And that—believe it or not, to quote Mr. Ripley—was all I did.

Back in my own room, on the same floor, it took me forever to get to sleep. I lay in the dark on my back and stared at the ceiling and thought about the perfect little body on that foul-mouthed, drunken little dame; thought about holding her, naked, in my arms. Thought about tucking her in and leaving. Thought about what a schmuck I was.

I didn't even realize I'd fallen asleep when the phone on the nightstand rang, startling me awake.

"Y-yes?"

"Kingfish speakin'. Over at Phil Baker's place."

My fingers fumblingly found the switch on the lamp by the bed; I could see my watch, but my eyes weren't focusing yet.

"Yes?" I said again. It was the best I could manage—my mind was as fuzzy as my mouth.

Huey, on the other hand, was peppy as a pup. "Meet me in the lobby, long 'bout fifteen minutes from now. So we can finish up what we were talkin' about, before."

Now my eyes could see the time. "Jesus, Huey, it's after three a.m.!"

"See ya in fifteen, son."

I stumbled to the sink and threw some water on my face; powdered up my toothbrush and got the sour taste out of my mouth. Did the Kingfish ever sleep, I wondered? My suit was still damp, but I'd put my lightweight white seersucker on a hanger, and the wrinkles had pretty well hung out.

The lobby was quiet, the coffee shop closed, though a skeleton crew manned the marble check-in, a lone bellboy was on duty, and the newsstand was apparently open all night. I bought a *Racing News*, just in case I had time to get out to Saratoga while I was in the area.

So I sat reading my paper, minding my own business, chaperoning a potted plant, enjoying the solitude of the nearly empty lobby, when I noticed the guy.

He looked respectable and, yet . . . he didn't. He was small, pale, brown-haired, probably in his mid-forties, very average looking . . . except. Behind his thick, almost scholarly glasses, wild eyes flashed; and—despite the air-cooled lobby—that high, intelligent forehead required an occasional mopping with a handkerchief. His mustache was well tended, but his cheeks were stubbly—he needed a shave. His dark suit looked expensive, but it also looked rumpled, and his tasteful striped silk tie was loose. He carried his hat in one hand and a briefcase in the other, and he prowled the lobby like a nervous cat.

Several years before, I had been on the scene when an assassin named Zangara shot Mayor Anton Cermak of Chicago, in Miami, Florida, where the mayor was sharing the spotlight with the supposed intended victim, Franklin Delano Roosevelt.

Perhaps that made me more suspicious than most, even propelled me toward outright paranoia, possibly; but looking at this jumpy, off-kilter character, knowing that Senator Huey P. Long, the Kingfish himself, was not only staying at this hotel but on his way to this very lobby this very instant, made me wonder if I was observing a specimen of that oh-so-special breed: the potential political assassin.

I was trying to decide whether to buttonhole the guy when through the front entry, like a train noisily entering the station, the Kingfish and his retinue rolled in. McCracken was out front, followed by Huey, Seymour and the male aides (the theatrical agent, Irwin, was gone) and that bulldog Messina bringing up the rear.

The nervous little guy with the briefcase perked up, seeing the entrance of the Kingfish, who was moving quickly, his voice echoing as he animatedly expressed some opinion or other to a patient, weary-looking Seymour.

Then Huey stopped at the newsstand, checking out the front pages of several papers' early-bird editions.

The nervous guy, making a beeline toward Huey, was about to pass by where I sat.

I raised my leg, like the gate of a toll crossing, lowered my *Racing News* and said blandly, "Something I can help you with, pal?"

"Are you with the hotel?" he asked, annoyed at being stopped this way, eyes tight behind the Coke-bottle glass.

I folded the paper, tossed it on the chair next to mine, rose.

"No," I said.

There was a flash of fright before his expression turned eager. "You wouldn't happen to be part of Senator Long's staff, would you?"

Did he have a bomb in that briefcase?

"Suppose I am," I said.

He frowned. "Well, are you or not?"

My nine-millimeter was in my valise, in my room; I was not licensed in the state of New York, and hadn't seen any reason to carry it.

"I'm on his staff," I said.

A big sigh of relief ruffled his mustache. "Thank God. Could you take me over and introduce me?"

"Depends on who you are . . . and what you have in that briefcase."

He blinked. "Oh, this? Business papers. Contracts! I represent the *Telegraph* in Harrisburg, Pennsylvania. . . ."

"You want an interview?"

"No! We want to publish Senator Long's new book."

The little guy filled me in, and then I sat him down where

I'd been parked, over by the potted plant, and went over to where Huey was waiting while Seymour paid for a stack of newspapers.

"Thanks for baby-sittin' Alice Jean, son," Huey said, by way of greeting.

"She puked in my lap. Hope you're willing to front the dry-cleaning bill."

He snorted a laugh. "I'd be a pretty sorry cuss iffen I didn't."

I pointed over to the chair where I'd deposited the publisher's rep. "See that shrimp in the glasses, with the briefcase? He's from Harrisburg."

Huey thought about that. "You know, we'll be goin' home through there, on the train. Little early for a reception committee."

"It's a little early for anything. His bosses heard about your new book, and heard, too, that you came to New York looking for a publisher. They want to make a serious offer. Tonight."

His smile plumped his cheeks; his eyes danced. "Seymour! Go tell that little feller with the caterpillar on his lip to come on up to our suite in ten minutes. Gotta talk to Heller here, first."

Seymour had overheard what I'd told Huey. He frowned and said, "We have morning appointments scheduled with several prominent New York publishers."

"Didn't you say it would take 'em six months at least to get the book on the stands?"

"Yes . . ."

"Well, a newspaper publisher'll understand the importance of timeliness. We'll talk to 'em."

"But the New York publishers . . ."

"Can go slap damn to hell. Nate! Come 'long with me, now. . . ."

Seymour and the male secretaries went over to talk to the

little man, while Huey—his arm around my shoulder—walked me over to the elevator, and Messina and McCracken trailed after.

On the way up, Huey told me how lovely the Carr girl's drawings had been; that he indeed intended to have her illustrate *My First Hundred Days in the White House.* Apparently Phil Baker had entertained, as well, playing the accordion, singing a few songs.

"Sorry you missed out on the fun, son," Huey commiserated, unaware that I'd had instead the pleasure of tucking in his nude (and stewed) mistress.

In the bedroom of his suite, the Kingfish slipped out of his coat and loosened the loud red-and-green necktie. Unbidden, Messina brought us each a warm bottle of Coca-Cola and a cold glass of ice.

"Right now's 'bout the time," Huey said, as we sat down on the sofa where we'd spoken before, "when I miss a gen-you-wine nightcap. What's your drink, Heller?"

I raised the glass of Coke. "This, with rum in it. Or if I gotta choose between 'em, just rum'll do fine."

His expression turned wistful. "Give me a sixteen-year-old bonded whiskey and ginger ale, any day." He shrugged away the nostalgia, and raised the glass of Coke in a toast. "Here's to the common man . . . and the uncommon leader."

I raised my glass of Coke and clinked it against his. "Here's to you, Kingfish."

He smiled at that, took a sip, and then said, casual as commenting on the weather, "Former law partner of mine had a tip, yesterday. Says a plot's been formed to murder me."

I sat forward. "A tip from who?"

Huey shrugged. "All my friend could tell me, bein' a lawyer bound by certain rules of ethics, was that the tip come from a 'conscience-stricken enemy.' "

"Sounds a little vague."

The protuberant brown eyes rolled. "Oh, there were some specifics, all right. This killin' is supposed to take place 'fore the special session of the Louisiana legislature adjourns."

"And when is that?"

"Session starts the seventh of September. And it won't last long . . . day or two. That's all it'll take to ram my bills through."

I frowned. "That's just a week from now."

The casualness, I finally gathered, was his version of false bravado; studying his face, the bulging eyes, the faint tremor of his hands, I could see the Kingfish was well and truly scared.

"That's right," he said. "This 'conscience-stricken enemy,' seems he's willin' to fight me, politically . . . but, much as he'd like to see me silenced, he draws the line at shutting me up permanent, through violence."

"And that's all you know, about this specific 'plot'?"

Huey nodded, sipped his Coke, raised his eyebrows. "That's the sum total."

There were several long moments of silence—an unusual occurrence in a room shared with Huey Long.

I said, "You don't have to be from Louisiana to know Huey Long's got no shortage of enemies." I shook my head, sighed heavily. "A week isn't much time to sort through 'em all."

"No it isn't."

"Who do *you* think might be behind the plot?"

He twitched a humorless, disgusted smirk. "If we were talkin' about some individual," he said, "some sorry shiftless skunk who don't cotton to my take-charge kinda gov'ment . . . the list could run in the thousands, anyway." He looked at me, hard. "But a conspiracy—somethin' organized—a *'murder'* plot? That narrows it way the hell down."

"How far down?"

He held up three fingers, began to tick them off. "It's one

of three, you can be damn sure. . . . It's either my old friends at Standard Oil, who don't take kindly to my idea of taxation . . ."

Even I could've guessed that one.

". . . or certain gamblin' interests, here in New York, who ain't been happy 'bout me changin' the terms on 'em, terms of a deal we made a while back. . . ."

And I knew Huey had some mob ties—I'd witnessed that in Chicago, in '32.

". . . or the Square Deal Association—that buncha sorry, good-for-nothin' political malcontents . . ."

But I had no idea in hell what the Square Deal Association was.

Much as I wanted to take Huey's $250 a day, not to mention a chance at that ten-grand bonus, I was beginning to sense just how far in over my head I was.

I spread my hands. "What do you expect me to do? I don't know Louisiana. I'm a goddamn outsider. . . ."

His grin was nasty. "That's what I like about ya. *You* I can trust. Easiest way somebody like me gets taken down is if somebody on the inside, somebody I trust, some dog-faced son of a wolf Judas Ice-carry-it betrays me."

"Okay. Okay. Three main possibilities, then. But how would I go about looking into it?"

"You're the detective. You tell me."

"No," I said. "You tell *me*—where to look. Who to talk to."

He pointed a manicured finger at me. "Tell you what. I'm gonna give you three names outa my private son-of-a-bitch book. Each one of these names'll represent one of them three groups I mentioned. You figure yourself a way to check up on jest these three individ'als, and in one hell of a hurry, we'll have a *damn* good idea whether there's any dang 'murder plot' or not."

The Kingfish looked at his watch, shambled to his feet. I had a feeling I was about to be dismissed.

He said, "That fella from the Harrisburg paper oughta be here, long about now. You best run along."

I stood. "Huey, if I'm going to do this job for you, I'm going to need an in-depth briefing. . . ."

He shook his head, no. "Not from me, you ain't. Far as the rest of the boys go, far as even Seymour Weiss and my aides and all are concerned, you're just another bodyguard. Got it?"

I nodded. "But I still need . . ."

He took me by the arm, leading me toward the door. "You'll ride back on the train with my party. I'm takin' Alice Jean along, takin' her back home where she can't cause me no trouble. You can talk to *her*. She'll fill ya in on any background you might need."

I couldn't believe what he was saying. His spurned mistress would be my background contact?

He answered my unasked question.

"Don't misjudge that little gal. Alice Jean may look like Clara Bow, but just 'cause she's built like a brick shithouse, that don't make her no goddamn floozy. She's got the mind of a college professor."

What, in a jar?

"But, Huey—I need to ask you about that FDR hotel conference . . . how does *that* fit in? . . ."

"Ask Alice Jean."

Then he was opening the door, and I found myself leaving even as the little bespectacled man with the briefcase was brushing eagerly past me. The publisher's rep was taking his four-in-the-morning meeting with the Kingfish, and being greeted in a typically warm, typically demented Huey Long manner.

"Howdy do, Mr. *Telegraph* Man—never mind the

money. We can talk 'bout that, second. First question is, can you boys get my book on the stands by next month? I need that sucker in print *now*, fer out on the stump. . . ."

And the door shut behind me.

On the way back to my room, all I could think of was two things: Alice Jean's pale, bare, curvaceous body . . .

. . . and that she made a likelier suspect than information source.

The phone rang me awake to a still-dark room, and again I fumbled for the receiver and the lamp switch. I ignored the second ring, plucking my wristwatch from the nightstand.

It was a few minutes past five a.m. I'd slept maybe an hour.

"Yes," I said into the phone, cutting the third ring in half.

"Get your things packed."

Seymour Weiss's voice.

My response was typically articulate: "Huh?"

"We're leaving in ten minutes. We just have time to catch the Broadway Limited to Harrisburg. The meeting's just breaking up now. . . . Huey's gonna make a deal with the *Telegraph* to publish his book."

"Doesn't that S.O.B. *ever* sleep?"

"Occasional naps. That's about the extent of it. Shake a leg, Heller . . . oh, and collect Miss Crosley, would you? She has her phone off the hook."

There was no time to bathe; I threw some cold water on my face, quickly shaved, nicking myself a couple times, threw my things in my valise, got into the white suit, snugged on my Panama. Within three minutes of Seymour's call, I was at Alice Jean's room, knocking.

I knocked quite a while.

Finally something clattered against the door, on the other side, startling me. A shoe she'd tossed, perhaps.

Raising my voice, I said, "Miss Crosley! The Kingfish is leaving—you want to come?"

I stared at the door and it stared back at me. Then I heard the squeak of bedsprings; some rustling around in there. Finally the door cracked barely open and one large, long-lashed, very bloodshot hazel eye peeked out at me.

"The Kingfish has a train to catch," I said. "Can you throw yourself together in one hell of a hurry?"

The eye studied me. Then it narrowed, uncertainly. From the slice of her I could see, she'd slung on a pink satin dressing gown.

"Did I throw up on you last night?" she asked.

Her voice carried no embarrassment, no regret—just curiosity.

"Yeah."

"Suit looks none the worse for it."

"Different suit."

"Oh."

She shut the door.

Then it opened again, a little wider, just enough for me to see both eyes and the generous curve of one breast peeking out from what I could now confirm was indeed a pink dressing gown, with pink ostrich-feather trim.

"You mind waiting for me?" she asked. "I have two bags and could use some help."

"Not at all."

"Your name was . . . ?"

"Nate Heller." I risked a little smile. "Still is, in fact."

She was too hungover to be amused; the door closed, and I waited for perhaps three minutes, and then suddenly she was next to me in the hallway, ready to go.

For a little past five in the morning, considering she hadn't even had time to sleep it off yet, Alice Jean Crosley didn't look half bad. Actually, she didn't look bad at all.

A flower-trimmed navy blue bandeau hat with an angled brim set off the short, flapperish hairdo framing her round cutie-pie face; her bosomy frame was tucked into a mannish lightweight suit—tan waistcoat with navy buttons, navy blue skirt. A navy-and-white print silk scarf was arranged at her throat.

I took her traveling bag and walked her down the hall.

"How did you manage it?" I asked her.

"What?"

I raised an appreciative eyebrow and set it down. "Would've taken most women two hours to put themselves together like this. You look like you stepped out of a band box."

The hard little mouth traced a faint smile, but only momentarily.

"I've known Huey for some time," she said. "I've had to learn to pull up camp stakes quickly. You're bleeding."

"What? Oh. Cut myself shaving."

"Should've stuck a little toilet paper on it. Here."

She stopped and so did I. She put her bag on the floor, and licked the tip of the middle finger of her right hand and touched the damp digit against the spot near my mouth, held it there hard. Released it. The hazel eyes, under naturally long lashes, looked at the place, head moving side to side. She was a pretty thing.

"There. That's better."

And she picked up her bag and moved down the hall quickly, on her high heels; I followed the impertinent sway of her rounded rear, having trouble keeping up. And I wasn't in heels, or hungover.

At Suite 3200, Huey and his entourage were emerging noisily, bags in hand; no one spoke to us as we fell in step.

Nobody bothered checking out—we just barreled through the lobby and down a wide stairway into an underground tunnel that connected the hotel with Pennsylvania Station.

In the vast, echoey main hall of the station, while Seymour Weiss was at a ticket window making arrangements, shielded by the ambience of footsteps, chatter and amplified announcements, Huey ambled over to Alice Jean and whispered in her ear a while. She looked at him blankly, nodded, and he gave her a half-moon grin, patted her on the shoulder and went back to pretending she didn't exist.

Not long after, out on the train platform, in the bustle of passengers and redcaps, under a cloak of steam and clanging bells and hoarse train whistles, Huey appeared at my side, his hand on my arm, his mouth to my ear.

"You been assigned to watch Alice Jean," he whispered. "That'll give her time to fill ya in on things, and nobody the wiser."

We boarded the sleekly modern train, with its black streamlined engine looking like something out of *Buck Rogers*, and trailed along to a car where Huey had a private compartment. He and Seymour and the little publisher's rep holed up there, to talk about Huey's book, presumably. Messina and McCracken took turns standing in the narrow hallway outside the door.

In the next car down, I took a similar position outside the door of Alice Jean's compartment. There was no room for a chair. Bone tired, I stood leaning against the wall, letting the rattle of wheels over track joints lull me. It was going to be at least a three-hour ride.

On the other hand, for $250 a day, I could learn to sleep standing up.

After about fifteen minutes, the door opened and Alice Jean seemed startled to see me.

"What are *you* doin' out here?" she asked.

"I'm assigned to guard you."

"You should have knocked. Huey says I'm suppose' to help you out on some things."

"That's right. But for appearance's sake, I'm your bodyguard."

She nodded that she understood, and squeezed out in the hallway; there really wasn't room for all four of us—me, her and her breasts. But I didn't mind.

"I was just going to get some breakfast," she said. "Would you care to join me?"

"Sure."

I followed that swaying rump to the dining car, where she had a very full breakfast—scrambled eggs, bacon, orange juice, cottage fries, toast—for a girl who'd tied one on last night. If she threw this up, it wasn't going to be pretty.

A doughnut and coffee was all I felt like.

We just sat there in the posh car, with its linen tablecloths, pristine china, and colored waiters in spotless white, and dined quietly, enjoying the air of affluence. She seemed the picture of poise, and it surprised me when she suddenly blurted out that she was sorry for the night before.

"Excuse me?" I said.

"There's really no excuse for my drunken behavior of yesterday evening." She was just enough of a Southern belle to make that sound like poetry.

"It's not a problem. Really."

She raised her coffee cup to sip; without looking at me, she said over it, "I was . . . undressed, when I woke."

I nodded, sipped my own coffee.

"Did you . . . undress me?"

"You asked for my help." I gave her half a grin. "We at the A-1 Detective Agency aim to please."

That seemed to embarrass her, just a little, and she put the coffee cup down and folded her hands; they were small, like a child's. "You didn't . . ."

"No. I didn't take advantage. I would be lying if I said it

didn't occur to me. You're a handsome woman, Miss Crosley. If it's not out of line, my saying so."

"Thank you. For not . . . taking advantage of the situation, I mean. That was kind, Mr. Heller."

"How would you feel about calling me Nate?"

Her smile was tentative, but lovely. "I'd feel fine about it . . . Nate. And, when no one else is around at least, why don't you call me Alice Jean."

"I'd like that," I said.

"I think I would, too."

No one from Huey's party was in the dining car right now, so it didn't seem an inappropriate time to begin getting some of that background material out of her. For about an hour, she filled me in about the feud between Huey and the so-called Square Dealers, and even gave me the name and address of the man I should call on—Edward Hamilton, an attorney.

"Hamilton and that hawk-faced wife of his, Mildred, have been tryin' to bring Huey down for years," Alice Jean said.

Later, when we made our way back to the car where her compartment awaited, I took my position in the hall, back to the wall, arms folded, a cigarette-store Indian in a Panama hat.

"You look beat," she said.

"Huey kept me running last night."

"So did I." She was standing with the door to her compartment open; she nodded toward the inside. "It's a double berth. Wanna take a nap, 'til Harrisburg?"

I grinned. "Are all you Southern girls this hospitable?"

Her smile may have been tiny but it was enormously winning. "My hospitality extends only to lettin' you take a nap in the upper berth. Period."

"That's plenty. Probably all I have energy for, anyway. . . ."

So we let down the upper berth, and I climbed up there and stretched out. It took me a while to go to sleep—thanks to that cup of coffee—but in a few minutes the jostle of the train and the rhythmic song it sang over the tracks had soothed me into slumber.

The train was whining to a stop when she shook me gently awake.

"Harrisburg," she said. She was small enough to have to stand on tiptoe to look at me in the upper berth.

"You're the best-looking train conductor I ever saw," I said, and swung out of there.

"Do you know what the plan is?" she said. "Nobody bothered telling me."

"Well, we change trains here," I said, "but we've got a layover of a couple hours that Huey's going to use to talk to the people at the *Telegraph*, who want to publish his book."

A smirk dimpled her cheek. "I don't suppose he'll want *me* around."

"I'll keep you company," I said.

We joined up with the entourage out on the platform of the Harrisburg station. It was dark as night on the covered platform, and Huey and Seymour, the bodyguards and aides, too, were huddled around the little publisher's rep like conspirators.

Alice Jean and I kept back, staying to ourselves, and after a bit, Seymour broke away from the little group and approached us.

He pointed off to the left. "The *Telegraph* office is just a couple blocks away. We're gonna hoof it over there, for a conference . . . you two wait in the station."

I nodded, and escorted Alice Jean inside; a newsstand separated us from the cavernous waiting room area, and baggage was off to the far right. But at left there was a diner-style coffee shop, where we parked ourselves in a booth and drank coffee.

"You snore," she said.

"Don't spread the news," I said. "People might misinterpret how you came by the information."

"You're kind of a flirt, aren't you?"

"Do you mind?"

She shrugged. "Not really. Shall we take advantage of the time?"

I nodded, and she continued with her background briefing, shifting from the Square Dealers to Standard Oil; it took about forty-five minutes, with me interrupting only occasionally as I jotted down a few pertinent facts in my pocket notebook.

"The man you should talk to, the lobbyist I was referring to," she said, "is Louis LeSage. You can call him at the refinery."

And she rattled off the phone number.

I took it down in my notebook.

A remarkable girl, Alice Jean. She may have been Huey's mistress, but she was no tramp, or at least not a stupid one. She was, as Huey himself had indicated, one sharp cookie.

"Could I ask you a question, Miss Crosley? Alice Jean?"

"Why, certainly."

"Are you really the Secretary of State of Louisiana?"

She pursed her mouth into what might have been a kiss but was really a smile. "You find that hard to buy, Mr. Heller? Nate?"

"Not really. With your brains, you could be governor. I just wondered how you managed it."

"You mean, how Huey managed it. Mind if I smoke?"

"Not at all."

She took a pack of Chesterfields from her purse and tamped one down and lighted it up with a Zippo identical to the one I'd seen in Huey's bedroom at the New Yorker.

"Actually, I'm not Secretary of State anymore . . . I haven't been since '32. Who told you that . . . Seymour?"

I nodded.

"He's a jealous S.O.B., Seymour is. Always has resented me. Fact is, I was only appointed to serve out the term of a poor gentleman whose heart expired."

"Oh. So now you're out of a job?"

"Oh no. Huey appointed me Supervisor of Public Accounts and Collector of Revenues."

That meant Huey's mistress controlled the purse strings of the state's economy.

"Shall we have a sandwich, Nate? Who knows when we'll be catching that next train."

So I took luncheon with Louisiana's Supervisor of Public Accounts—bacon-lettuce-and-tomato sandwich for her, a fried-egg sandwich for me—and pretty soon moved into the third and final phase of the trio of possible Huey murder plotters: the Syndicate, specifically, Frank Costello, with whom Huey had recently gone into the gambling business.

"You'll want to talk to Costello's man in New Orleans," Alice Jean said blandly, as if referring me to a tailor. " 'Dandy Jim' Kastel . . . he has a suite at the Roosevelt. Don't write that down: just remember it."

"All right," I said. I checked my watch. "We've been sitting here for at least two hours. You want to take a walk or anything? My butt's getting sore."

"I wouldn't mind."

"Maybe we could find a nice quiet saloon. I could use something stronger than coffee. How about you? Ready for some hair of the dog?"

She smirked and nodded. "I sure am. But what if Huey comes back . . . ?"

"I'll check at the ticket counter and see when the next train to St. Louis leaves. That's our next stop."

Funny how that hard little mouth could transform itself into such a soft, sweet smile. "You *are* a detective, aren't you?"

The next St. Louis train wasn't until six-thirty, so I asked the shoeshine "boy" (he was in his sixties) where the nearest bar was, and he pointed the way. We walked toward the river, through a lively commercial district—it was Saturday, and the five-and-tens and department stores were doing a brisk business—until we found a quiet little gin mill. The place was almost empty; we ordered at the bar, then took a back booth.

"Here we are sitting again," she said.

I sipped my rum-and-Coke. "Yeah, but my butt doesn't hurt anymore. Mind if I ask you something personal?"

"You can ask."

"How does a girl . . . how old are you? Twenty-five?"

"More or less."

"How does a girl twenty-five, more or less, wind up Secretary of State and Supervisor of Whatever?"

"You mean, besides by being the Kingfish's girlfriend?"

"Is that what you are?"

She looked sourly into her beer. "Not anymore, I guess." Then she made three words of it: *"Not any more."*

I studied her through narrowed eyes. "Alice Jean, if you don't mind my saying so . . . you're no dummy."

"How flatterin'."

"I mean, I can tell just by talking to you that you're up to any job in government that might get thrown at you. I just wondered how it happened. Are you a college girl?"

She laughed. "Not hardly. Tenth-grade dropout."

"Hard to believe."

She shrugged. "I developed secretarial skills, even so. My daddy used to run a well-known newspaper in the state. The *Shreveport Caucasian*?"

This last was posed as if I probably would have heard of it, which of course I hadn't. Might as well have been the *Natchitoches Negro*.

But I said, "Is that right? Well, that is impressive."

"Daddy helped me get a nice secretarial job, in Baton Rouge. . . . Then when I was eighteen, I went to work in the Long gubernatorial campaign. Pretty soon I was his confidential secretary. One thing sorta led to another."

One beer led to another, too. By the third one, Alice Jean's bitterness was starting to show.

"You sign your resignation yet?" she asked suddenly.

"What do you mean?"

She shrugged again, poutily, swirled her beer in its glass. "Usually when you sign on with Huey, you have to sign an undated resignation, too. He does that with all his employees."

"No kidding."

"Sure. You know what every state employee in Louisiana does, first thing every morning?"

"No. What?"

"Checks the morning paper, to see if they resigned yesterday." She grinned one-sidedly, but the grin was caustic. "Has he paid you anything yet?"

"Yeah. He gave me a retainer."

"Bet it's in cash. That's how Huey does all his business."

As Supervisor of Public Accounts, she was in a position to know.

"Is he makin' you kick back five percent? 'Cause that's what *all* state employees do. Five percent right off the top of your paycheck—a 'dee-duct.' And you know where it goes?"

"Where?"

"Right into the ol' dee-duct box."

I checked my watch. The afternoon was drifting toward evening. I figured maybe Alice Jean had had enough to drink; I didn't want to get that breakfast I saw her eat, plus that bacon-lettuce-tomato sandwich, all over my remaining suit.

So I asked the bartender if there was a city park around, where we might take a leisurely stroll, and he pointed the way to nearby Harris Park, which fronted the river. The day was warm, but not hot, and a gentle breeze riffled the leaves of the elms, maples, oaks and sycamores shading the quiet park paths. After a while, we bought some popcorn from a stand, found a bench and fed ourselves, and the pigeons.

"He told me he was going to take me along," she said.

"What?"

"To Washington. To the Senate. I was supposed to be his secretary. But then he hired a *man*. I'm bad for his 'public image.' Hell, in Louisiana, I used to stay in the damn governor's mansion, when his wife was back home! For months on end, sometimes! But *now* I'm bad for his public image. . . ."

"Alice Jean," I said, tossing a kernel of popcorn toward the birds, "seems to me he's trying to do some good things for people. His style may be a little unorthodox, but at least he's not afraid to take on the rich bastards that . . ."

"Rich bastards," she snorted. "With the exception of Standard Oil . . . and Huey's got it in for them for purely personal reasons . . . there's not a politician in the country that has cut more deals with rich men than Huey P. Long. He's no friend to labor—or to the colored, either. . . ."

Maybe I let her have one beer too many.

"And you know what? He ain't much in the sack, neither."

"Alice . . ."

"You've seen him eat! Fast and sloppy and not particular . . . not to mention stealin' off of other folks' plates. That's his *real* idea of 'share the wealth'! Same damn thing with sex . . . fast and sloppy and selfish. Nothin' truly excites that man except power, and more power, and *more* power."

"Then what in the hell do you see in him, Alice Jean?"

She seemed to be staring at the birds, but she wasn't. "I don't know. Don't rightly know. Maybe . . . maybe I see a farm boy turned patent-medicine drummer who was so smart, so dedicated, he mastered a three-year law course in seven months."

She was talking to me, but it was like she'd forgotten I was there. Her words were for her own benefit.

"Maybe I see a self-made lawyer fightin' for the little guy in court, a little guy himself who got pushed around by big business and ran for office to do somethin' about it—for himself, and for all the little guys."

She sat quietly for a while; I didn't say anything—I just watched. Suddenly her thin line of a mouth hardened.

"Or maybe I'm just a woman who likes to rub up against a powerful man."

We sat quietly for perhaps another half hour, and then I walked her back to the train station, where before long Huey's entourage returned, piling onto the St. Louis train. Added to the group were an editor from the *Telegraph* and a pair of stenographers, young and female and pretty, which irritated Alice Jean further.

In what seemed like a blink, I was standing outside another compartment in another train, keeping guard over the woman who used to be Huey Long's mistress. The afternoon seemed to have skipped dusk and gone straight to night—the windows outside poured in nothing but darkness.

Seymour Weiss found me. "Gonna be a long night."

"Yeah?"

"Yeah. Huey and that publisher decided, for the book to be out as soon as Huey wants, they gotta cut two hundred pages of what he dictated, before. We're going to be hackin' away at it, 'til dawn and then some."

"Are we getting off at St. Louis?"

"Just to catch the train to Oklahoma City. Huey speaks there, tomorrow afternoon. Labor Day at the fair. He wants to be done with the book by the time we catch that train, tomorrow morning. You gonna be okay? You need me to have Messina or McCracken relieve you at any point?"

"No. I'm fine."

Seymour nodded, then rolled his eyes, shook his head, and walked back toward the adjacent car, and Huey's compartment.

A few seconds later, the door to Alice Jean's compartment cracked open. She was wearing the feathered pink dressing gown again. The dark curls framed her round face perfectly; her lipstick was fresh and cherry red, and her hazel eyes weren't bloodshot in the least. She smelled like Chanel Number Five.

"I heard you and Seymour talking," she said.

"Really."

"You don't think you need to be relieved, huh?"

"No."

"I think you're wrong."

She took me by the wrist and tugged me into her compartment. This wasn't a sleek, modern train, like the Broadway Limited, but one of the older-fashioned—and better—Pullman Standards. Fresh cut flowers in wall vases. Wood paneling; dark furniture. No foldout berths, but a single bed, with the sheet turned down.

I heard the click of the door locking behind us, and when I turned, she took me into her arms, and I gathered her in mine, eagerly, lowering my lips to hers.

There was nothing hard about that mouth, now; it was a soft kiss, at least at first, but before long it turned yearning, then finally, as her tongue flicked its way between my teeth, demanding.

I drew away, gasping for breath, and watched as she gave me a burning look that would have done any silent-movie vamp proud, dropping the pink robe to the floor, revealing again that beautifully rounded little body, like a young teenage girl's—wasp waist, wispy pubic triangle, slender legs, but a woman's generous bosom with aureoles so pale they almost disappeared, the tips erect and pointing up at me, accusingly, scolding me for what I had in mind.

Then we were on the bed, and I was kissing every part of her while she was loosening my tie, working at my buttons, her other hand on the front of my trousers, gripping me through the cloth; my hands found the incredibly firm globes of her breasts, their tips hard as diamonds, so much of them my hands were filled to overflowing. Already the bed was rocking with its own rhythm, the train tracks be damned, and then somebody knocked at the door.

It startled us both.

She hid herself under the covers, almost demurely, and I stood and straightened myself, snugged my tie, fixed my buttons, minimized my erection, found a handkerchief to rub off the lipstick, checking the mirror over the basin to see if I'd done the job.

Then I answered the door, just cracking it open.

Huey's face—like him, larger than life—stared at me, eyes bulging.

"Heller," he said, "this is the first I could get away."

"Really. How's the work going?"

"Fine. Jest wanted to check up on you, son. I know things went a little tough last night, with Alice Jean. She can be a handful."

"Oh, I know."

"So how are you two gettin' along?"

"Better," I said.

Huey smiled, nodded. "Well, I got work to do. These sumbiches say my book's too long, and this is the only way I can get 'er out in time to do me any good. Take care, now."

And he was gone.

I shut the door, and took several deep breaths.

Then I locked the compartment, turned off the light, and took off my clothes.

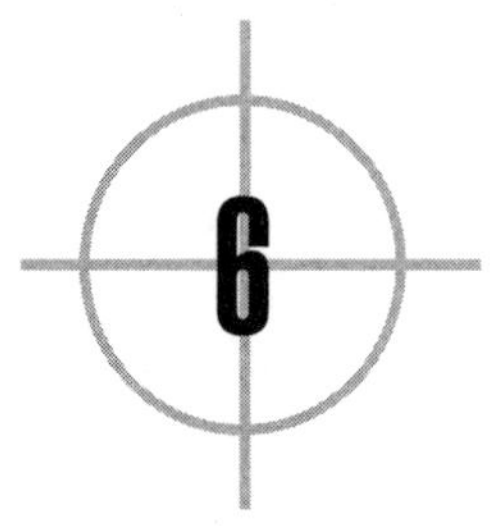

For a twentieth-century capital city in the United States of America, downtown Baton Rouge had a surprising number of ancient, wood-frame buildings; the Reymond Building, however, wasn't one of them. The gray granite office building might have been a post office or some other government facility, with its chiseled eagle decorations and sleek, modern, yet unostentatious lines.

But it certainly wasn't part of Huey Long's government: though a few pro-Kingfish supporters maintained offices in the Reymond, it was generally known as the city's foremost anti-Long enclave.

The Square Deal Association did not have an office here per se, but its founder, attorney Edward Hamilton, did, on the sixth floor.

It was Tuesday afternoon.

On Sunday morning, the Long party had arrived in St. Louis, with Huey greeting a rally-size crowd at the station, where we'd had only five minutes to make the train to Oklahoma City. Lack of sleep—and an attack of hay fever

—finally slowed the Kingfish down, and our stay at the Black Hotel in Oklahoma City, that night, was uneventful—although my bodyguarding duties remained interesting and rewarding, thanks to the remarkable female whose body I was guarding.

After the Labor Day speech at the Oklahoma State Fair, the Long group caught the only available eastbound train; Alice Jean and I continued conferring in her compartment.

By that evening I was finally in Louisiana: at Dallas, two more Huey Long bodyguards (their names were Two-Gun Thompson and Squinch McGee—enough said) had met us in black unmarked State Police cars. Our party had been escorted to Shreveport, where the Kingfish summoned me to his room in the Washington-Youree Hotel.

As usual, he'd been spread out, flat as a stiff on a morgue slab, on the double bed of the suite, in his fabled green-silk pajamas.

We were alone.

"I'm gonna be burrowed in, in Baton Rouge, with my attorneys and advisors and such," Huey said, "for the next two, mebbe three days."

"Okay," I said, because he'd left a rare hole in the conversation for me to fill.

"Me and the boys got thirty-one bills to polish up, for the special legislative session, Sund'y. You ready to start pokin' around some for me, son?"

"Sure."

"Alice Jean, she's gived all you need?"

"Oh yes."

"Well, that's fine. She's a good girl. Jest a little too ambitious. Ambition can be a mighty destructive thing."

If I hadn't been banging his girlfriend, and taking $250 a day from him for the pleasure, this is where I would have made a smart remark.

"Run along 'bout your bizness, now. On the way out, ask Seymour for your Bureau of Criminal 'vestigation badge, and the car keys."

"What car keys?"

"I sent for an unmarked B.C.I. buggy for ya to use while you're workin' for me."

So I'd driven down from Shreveport this morning, in a big black Buick that made me feel like a gangster (not an unusual outlook for a Huey Long bodyguard, really), following State Highway 20 along the Red River. I knew I was in the Pelican State because the highway signs bore an ungainly cartoon version of the bird. The road rolled by rich farmland and eerie wilderness alike, giving me glimpses of sprawling antebellum-style cotton plantations, as well as swampy expanses with willows, cottonwood and cypress trees. At Alexandria I picked up US Highway 71, swinging south, away from the Red River and into wooded bottomland, where truck farms, cotton and sugar-cane fields and uncultivated fields were alive with the colors of wild flowers.

I arrived in Baton Rouge, two hundred miles of Louisiana the wiser, with a solid sense of just how big a fish out of water I was, here.

And you know what pelicans do with fish.

The sixth floor of the Reymond Building did not look like an enemy encampment: gray-and-black speckled marble floor; dark-wood-and-pebbled-glass offices; names of attorneys, doctors and insurance agents in block-letter respectability on the frosty glass. No barbed wire or armed sentries in sight.

And on guard in Edward Hamilton's outer office was a schoolmarmish matronly secretary who interrupted her typing to note my arrival and my business card, and announced my presence by intercom.

My card, incidentally, said "Hal Davis—*Chicago Daily News*." I had taken half a dozen of these out of Hal's billfold, a few months back, when he'd drunk himself to sleep on the bar next to me at my friend Barney Ross's joint.

"Mr. Hamilton is expecting you," she said, and parceled out a smile before returning to her work.

And he *was* expecting me: I had called from the hotel this morning, before I left Shreveport. I'd had no trouble getting in: I said I'd traveled South to "get the truth" about "Dictator Long" for my paper.

While I hadn't spoken to Hamilton personally, but rather this matronly secretary, she had passed my message along to him, coming back almost immediately with an afternoon appointment.

Now he was rising from behind his desk, extending his hand, a white-haired, dark-eyebrowed and -mustached, medium-sized man in a well-tailored gray three-piece suit and blue tie that suggested both dignity and prosperity. His handsome face had a lived-in look, and the easiness of his smile was offset by deep-socketed sorrowful gray eyes that had seen way too much in half a century or so.

"I'm pleased to see you, Mr. Davis," Hamilton said, in a mellow, Southernly soothing but quietly commanding baritone that must have served him well in a courtroom.

"My pleasure, Mr. Hamilton," I said as we shook hands. "Thanks for seeing me at such short notice."

A chair opposite him was waiting, and I took it.

I had glimpsed a sizable law library off the reception area, but Hamilton's own office was modest, though that mahogany desk must have cost a small fortune. Vintage prints of riverboats, a signed photo of FDR and a few diplomas were the sole wall decorations; a couple of file cabinets were against a side wall. On his desk were a few framed photos, facing away from me; family photos, no doubt. One of them would be of his wife, Mildred—organizer of the anti-Long Women's Committee of Louisiana.

I knew, from what Alice Jean had told me, that Hamilton

had been special counsel to two state boards, patronage appointments from the previous administration, before the Kingfish had fired him, and battle lines had been drawn between them ever since.

I didn't even have to ask a question: Hamilton was ready, willing and eager to speak his anti-Long piece.

"If you in the North think Huey Long is a peculiarly Southern phenomenon, Mr. Davis, you may soon learn how sadly mistaken you are." He was sitting in a swivel chair and he rocked back easily in it as he spoke; his smile was gentle, his eyes hard. "First of all, the 'Kingfish' is no clown. . . . The Northern papers take that rustic-fool facade entirely too lightly, too lit'rally."

I shrugged. "Makes good copy."

"It makes good sense for Huey to sugarcoat his tyranny."

" 'Tyranny' is a pretty strong word, Mr. Hamilton."

His smile stayed gentle, amused; and his speech remained softly Southern in cadence. But the words themselves were harsh.

"Make no mistake, Mr. Davis," he said. "The Kingfish is an American Mussolini, a home-grown Hitler . . . a queer mixture of Fascism, baloney and old-fashioned bossism, Tammany Hall–style."

That seemed a little overstated to me, but I merely nodded, and made notes.

"Louisiana under Huey P. Long," the attorney continued, "is a banana republic with a particularly odious, megalomaniacal dictator. He owns the state government, the governor, the state university, the treasury, the state buildings and the Louisianians inside 'em. With a few isolated exceptions—my friend Judge Pavy, for one—Long owns the courts, as well. His secret police terrorize, and kidnap at will—"

I raised my pen as I interrupted. "My understanding is

that Huey won his last election, handily. And that his candidates for other offices are usually big winners, too—"

Hamilton's sorrowful eyes flared with anger. "He *runs* the elections, he counts the votes! He wields life-and-death power over private business, through his bank examiners, his homestead agents, his boards and commissions. . . ."

"Is that why a law-abiding citizen, like yourself, took up arms and rose up against him?"

I was referring to uprisings in both New Orleans and Baton Rouge.

Last year in New Orleans, Huey—at odds with local politicians—had passed legislation giving the state (i.e., himself) control over the New Orleans police and fire department; and usurped the city's authority over voter registration and election machinery, as well. Huey had Governor O.K. Allen declare martial law, and soon the New Orleans police and an "army" of local citizens were facing down the National Guard. The comic opera situation had attracted both the national press and the White House, and—eventually—civic leaders had convinced both sides of the conflict to declare an armistice.

But the Baton Rouge uprising, earlier this year, had been the work of Hamilton's Square Dealers. The group consisted largely of embittered Standard Oil employees who feared Huey's personal war on Standard would drive out the company that kept the community financially afloat.

"Armed insurrection was not our goal," Hamilton said quietly, the rocking in his swivel chair ceasing. "Only to rid the state of obnoxious dictatorial laws."

I gave him a smirk. "Come on now, Mr. Hamilton. You wore little blue uniforms, you formed 'battalions,' you marched and drilled. . . ."

His frown turned his dark eyebrows into one straight, furrowed line. "We were a paramilitary organization. So are the Boy Scouts. Neither group is inherently violent."

"Your slogan was 'Direct Action.' One of your members spoke openly about hanging Huey and his puppet governor and all the rubber-stamp legislators—"

He bit the words off: "It was not our purpose to assassinate or murder anybody. For God's sake, man, we numbered two ex-governors among our membership, and the mayor of New Orleans." He shook his head. "I must say, I'm disappointed with the tack you're takin', Mr. Davis. I'm not certain this interview should . . ."

I replaced the smirk with an easygoing smile. "Mr. Hamilton, please understand. The things that are happening down here are difficult for folks up North to grasp."

His eyes were scolding. "That's the point I've been tryin' to make. Don't feel so smug about it. Huey's already in Washin'ton, and he's knockin' at your door. He'll smile and grin and guffaw his way into America's house and steal off with the Bill of Rights and the Constitution and every man, woman and child's immortal soul."

That all seemed pretty arch to me, and perhaps my expression showed it. Hamilton sat forward, leaned his elbows on the desk and looked at me, wearily.

"You see, Mr. Davis, after our impeachment efforts failed, and when Long began pushin' through his 'special legislature sessions' in 1934—there have been *six* such sessions in the past thirteen months—well, it created a sort of . . . *wildness* in the air."

" 'Somebody oughta kill that guy' became more than just a wisecrack, you mean?"

Sitting back, Hamilton nodded gravely.

I asked, "Is 'a wildness in the air' why three hundred armed Square Dealers stormed and occupied the East Baton Rouge courthouse, last January?"

He winced at the memory. "You must try to understand, Mr. Davis. . . . Long sneaked a bill through that gave his stooge O.K. Allen leeway to appoint new members to the governing board of our parish—our last vestige of representative government had been stolen from us."

"I thought storming the courthouse had to do with one of your people being arrested."

He nodded slowly. "Yes, that did fuel the ill-advised episode."

"So Huey sent the militia in, and the Square Dealers folded."

He shook his head, quickly. "No. We received word that our arrested member had been released, and we went home. The irony is, that 'member' was an undercover agent of Huey's all along. In fact, during his 'arrest,' he was probably reportin' in, deliverin' names and phone numbers. That would certainly explain the airport debacle."

The morning after the seizing of the courthouse, a hundred armed Square Dealers had arrived at the Baton Rouge airport, where they were greeted by five hundred national guardsmen with machine guns and teargas.

The sorrowful eyes took on a haunted aspect. "Most of the Square Dealers were gassed, and one was shot. Half a dozen were hospitalized. No fatalities, thank God. Some of us made it to our cars, or into the woods, before anything serious happened . . . other than abject humiliation, that is."

"What possessed you to send a hundred of your men to the airport, anyway?"

His laugh was short, deep, humorless. "That's the most humiliatin' part. Even those of us in leadership capacities didn't know *why* we were there! We all received urgent anonymous phone calls, urgin' us to get out to the airport."

"Phone numbers provided by Huey's spy?"

He sighed. "I can only assume so. At any rate, that was the end of the Square Dealers, for all intents and purposes. A while later Huey banned the organization, officially. Martial law wasn't lifted in Baton Rouge until only just last month."

"When you say the Square Dealers are 'officially' dead, do you mean . . . ?"

A brave smile formed on that lived-in face. "That unofficially, the anti-Long movement is very much alive? Oh yes, Mr. Davis. Yes indeed."

"Alive, like at the DeSoto Hotel conference?"

The smile disappeared and he winced again; sat forward. "That's been highly exaggerated, Mr. Davis. Most of what the press has said about that conference is based upon Huey's own irresponsible hyperbole on the floor of the Senate of the United States."

"He named FDR as a conspirator in a murder plot against him," I said, raising an eyebrow. "That's either irresponsible, or goddamn disturbing. The idea of the President of the United States, conspiring to have one of his challengers killed . . ."

His frown was dismissive. "It's absurd! The DeSoto Hotel conference was aboveboard and respectable—four of the five pro-Roosevelt Louisiana congressmen were present, for God's sake, as were ex-governors Sanders and Parker, and Mayor Walmsley. . . ."

"All gathered to discuss the Huey Long problem?"

"It was a political caucus, sir, plain and simple. The business at hand was to select anti-Long candidates to run in the comin' primary election."

"What about Huey's claim of having a transcript of the conference taken from a dictaphone his men planted?"

"Ludicrous."

"Maybe so, but colorful as hell." I checked my notes from my briefing by Alice Jean. "Among the tidbits Huey reported on the Senate floor was one unidentified speaker's offer to 'draw straws in a lottery to go out and kill Long. It would only take one man, one gun and one bullet.' "

"Please, sir, don't dignify—"

"Another unidentified voice supposedly said, later, 'Does

anyone doubt that President Roosevelt would pardon anyone who killed Long?' "

He was shaking his head, slowly, his smile one of frustration. "Mr. Davis . . . how often do you suppose someone in Louisiana says 'Somebody ought to kill that Huey Long'?"

"Every thirty seconds or so?"

"Precisely. It doesn't mean they'll do it, or even that they're thinkin' serious of it. It's just a kind of . . . wish. A daydream."

He made it sound wistful.

"Mr. Hamilton," I said, "I have an admission to make."

He looked at me sharply.

"My name isn't Davis," I said, "and I'm not a reporter. Name's Nate Heller—I'm a bodyguard on Senator Long's staff."

He almost lost his balance in the swivel chair; he tried for indignation, but his fear was showing, as he said, "This is outrageous, sir! I must ask you to—"

My hands patted the air. "Whoa," I said, "settle down. I said I was a bodyguard, not a spy. . . ."

He stood. Pointed at the door. "Leave. Now."

"I really am from Chicago," I said pleasantly, crossing my legs, smiling up at him, ignoring his commands. "The Kingfish took a shine to me back at the Democratic Convention in '32, when I was his police bodyguard. I came down on an errand, and he offered me a position. . . ."

"What is your point, Mr. Heller?"

I arched an eyebrow, smiled half a smile. "My point is that I'm from Chicago, and I'm on the inside of the Kingfish's personal staff . . . and did I mention I'm willing to do just about anything for money?"

He sat, slowly, studying me carefully. "I was just beginning to gather that."

I shrugged. "So . . . if there's any information you, or any of your Square Dealer or DeSoto conference pals, might need . . . anything you might need *done*. . . . Catch my drift?"

"I'm beginning to."

The attorney swiveled in his chair and faced the window behind his desk, looking somberly out at the city the Kingfish had taken away from people like him.

"Just over a year ago," he said very quietly, "a goodly number of 'law-abiding citizens' were gathered in this very office . . . most of them armed. We seriously discussed stormin' Long's suite in the Heidelberg Hotel . . . just a few blocks away . . . bravin' the nests of machine guns and such to rid the world of a tyrant."

"What made you change your mind?"

Hamilton shrugged. "Cowardice, perhaps. Reason, possibly. At any rate, we didn't resort to assassination then, and I seriously doubt we would do it today . . . much as we might like to."

"I see."

"We are not barbarians, Mister . . . Heller, was it? We are civilized men in the grasp of a barbarian."

That would've seemed arch, too, if Hamilton's expression hadn't been so tragically grave.

"Well," I said, as I stood. "I appreciate your time."

He nodded noncommittally, numbly.

I went to the door. "And I apologize for the deception. But if you change your mind, or talk to any of your friends who might see things . . . differently . . . well, don't hesitate to contact me."

"In that unlikely event," Hamilton said, "where are you staying?"

"At the Heidelberg," I said, at the door. "Just down the hall from the machine-gun nest."

And I left him there, to ponder the possibilities.

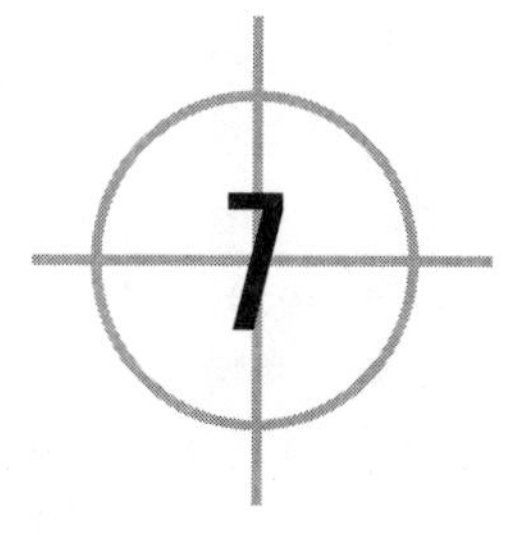

Industrial sites were nothing new to a Chicago boy like yours truly; the steel mills and factories of the South Side, and of Gary, Hammond and East Chicago, Indiana, were like a foul-smelling forest just beyond my backyard.

But approaching by car, after dark, heading north from Baton Rouge, I felt overwhelmed by the sprawling otherworldly Standard Oil refinery. Appearing at first like some modern artist's semi-abstract, geometrical vision of a metropolitan skyline, the vast facility soon filled the horizon, blotting out the world of woods and bluffs it emerged from, dwarfing even the Mississippi along whose banks its shadows fell. Security spotlights and billowing flares adding soft-focus radiance, scaffolding clinging like exoskeletons, the turrets of cat-crackers and the cannon-barrel towers of white-smoking chimneys loomed over a Paul Bunyan's playground of baseball spheres and bullet tubes and cake-pan storage tanks.

The guard in the booth at the chain-link gate looked at my business card (or that is, Hal Davis's card) and checked his clipboard. I was expected. He threw a switch and the gate slid open with a metallic whine that seemed only appropriate, and I guided the Buick into this city of steel and flame and smoke.

Louis LeSage—chief lobbyist for Standard Oil, and vice president of public relations—was waiting out in front of a three-story brick administration building. He rocked on his feet, hands clasped behind him, a tiny, balding man with a round cheerful face on a slender body. His wispy waxed mustache, like his cream-color suit and crisp red bow tie, somehow underscored his air of confidence.

When LaSage spotted me, he lighted up as if we were old friends—we had of course never met—and he walked over quickly to the side parking area where I was climbing out of the Buick. His arm was thrust out like a spear as he offered me his hand.

"Mr. Davis," he said, exuberantly, his voice high-pitched and only faintly Southern, "I'm so very pleased to meet you. We don't often get representatives of the Northern press down to have a look at our little facility."

I let him pump my hand for a while, then dug out my notebook, looked up at the towering smokestacks and columnlike cat-crackers. "Just how 'little' is this facility?"

He gestured. "Shall we stroll?"

"Why not? It's a pleasant enough evening. I'm surprised the air isn't fouled by all that smoke."

He established an easygoing pace as we walked down a cinder street; but he was holding back—he was in the energy game.

"You don't see any black fumes, messin' up the sky, do you, Mr. Davis?" he asked, but it wasn't a question. "We're a clean business, here at Standard. Oh, you may get a nasty little whiff of this or that . . . but for the most part, we pride ourselves at not foulin' our nest. As for how 'little' we are, this is the biggest refinery in the world. Even bigger'n Bayonne."

I didn't doubt it. Right now we were strolling past a row of steel sills that could have kept Kentucky in moonshine for decades.

"We process 110,000 barrels of crude oil, each and every day, day in day out . . . am I talkin' too fast for ya, Mr. Davis?"

"No. But, frankly, this isn't the kind of information I'm after. . . ."

He smiled; the ends of the mustache pointed upward, emphasizing the smile's smugness. "I know. You indicated on the phone your primary interest was in Senator Long."

"That's right." I glanced around at the monumental spires of industry rising into the night sky; the smoke really was white—as if they were a cloud-making factory. "And seeing all this, it's frankly hard to understand why Huey Long would make an enemy out of such a boon to his state."

LeSage stopped. "Have you met the Senator, Mr. Davis?"

"No."

"Well, if you're able to get an interview with him . . . and you probably will be—he likes to show off for the 'lyin' press,' 'specially likes to play monkey for the Northern papers, keepin' you folks off your guard . . . but when you get to talk to him, you'll find out that logic is not one of his stronger suits."

"I understand he's a brilliant man."

"He's a brilliant *child*, Mr. Davis. Yes, I would say Standard Oil is a boon to this state, you're correct. At this facility alone, we employ five thousand workers . . . several hundred more in management positions."

Actually, I hadn't seen more than a handful of workers, in their hard hats and jumpsuits; but that was deceiving. With a place as expansive as this one, it wouldn't take long for handfuls of workers to add up to a number like five thousand.

LeSage began to stroll again; I fell in alongside him. His

smile seemed mildly amused as he said, "Do you know why Huey Long has it in for Standard Oil?"

"For the same reason he has it in for Wall Street, I suppose. He thinks 'robber barons' should be stopped, and the wealth should be shared with the little guy."

LeSage chuckled; it made his bow tie bobble. "Huey's feud with Standard Oil has nothing at all to do with helping 'the little guy' and takin' on the evil rich."

"It doesn't?"

"No. Not in the least." He paused for effect. "It's about Huey Long not gettin' rich himself."

LeSage stopped again; he gestured gently, with a lecturing forefinger, waving it like the laziest flag in the world. "When Huey was a young lawyer in Shreveport, he used to take payment for legal services in royalty shares and acreage allotments."

"I don't understand. . . ."

"Oil had been found in the Pine Island area, nearby, and there was a boom on, y'see. Huey figured he'd be joinin' the ranks of oil millionaires by the time he was thirty."

"But he didn't?"

LeSage shook his head, kept smiling that knowing little smile under that tiny twitchy mustache. "Not when the only available pipeline belonged to the Standard Oil Company."

"And owning the pipeline made Standard the only game in town?"

"An astute observation, Mr. Davis."

"And they weren't exactly paying top dollar."

The smile kept going. "If you don't mind, since you *are* takin' notes, and presumably plan to quote me . . . I'll allow you to draw your own conclusions. But it would be fair to say, the shares and allotments Huey dreamed would make him so very wealthy were, in fact, next to worthless."

This was all new to me—Alice Jean had filled me in on none of the facts behind Huey's feud with Standard.

Despite her bitter outbursts, Alice Jean still retained some admiration for Huey's defense of the common man and his interests. Now, as I strolled with Standard's own lobbyist through the bowels of the fire-breathing dragon St. Huey so frequently battled, I finally understood what motivated the crusade.

"Revenge, Mr. Davis," LeSage was saying. "Revenge, not public concern, fueled Huey Long's Holy War against Standard Oil."

"Didn't you come close to getting him impeached, in '29?"

"You know what they say about 'close' only countin' in horseshoes, Mr. Davis." LeSage shrugged. "Huey bought himself enough votes to stave off impeachment, more or less permanently. Ever hear of the Round Robin? You cover *that* story, up North in your papers?"

"Not that I know of."

We were walking, again.

LeSage said, "He got fifteen senators to sign a document pledgin' that no matter what Huey ever did, they'd never vote to impeach him; just enough votes—actually one extra—to block impeachment, no matter what the charges. He rewarded 'em with cushy jobs and patronage spoils. Like Huey says, he plays the legislature like a deck of cards."

"You sound like you know Huey, personally."

His laugh was barely perceptible. "Of course I do. I'm a lobbyist, Mr. Davis—I spend the majority of my time over at the capitol building, swimmin' in that particular slough. I know Huey well. We get along just fine." He grinned; so did the mustache. "You know where they say Huey used to hide that Round Robin document of his, for safe-keepin'?"

"Where?"

"In his girlfriend Alice Jean's brassiere."

Well, it wasn't there now.

"What were the grounds of impeachment?" I asked.

"Huey tried to push through an exorbitant five-cents-a-barrel crude oil tax, in one of his 'special sessions' of the legislature. While obviously we didn't get his behind tossed out of office, the fuss was enough to block the tax . . . for a while. Then—just last Christmas—he finally snuck it through."

"That's what got the Square Dealers so riled up, isn't it?"

LeSage nodded; he gestured to the industrial landscape surrounding us. "Baton Rouge is a one-company town, Mr. Davis. We have thirty thousand inhabitants in our fair capital city—and some twenty-five thousand of them depend on Standard Oil's payrolls. It's not just our employees, you understand . . . it's banks, retail businesses. . . ."

"And, because of Huey's tax, your company threatened to pull out of Baton Rouge."

"Exactly."

"Which led to armed insurrection in the streets of two American cities." I shook my head. "Hard to picture, in this modern age."

Now the cheery little man revealed a streak of cynicism. "There's nothing modern about the Huey Long approach, Mr. Davis," he said. "It's a technique that dates back to Genghis Khan, or Julius Caesar. Tyrants are as old as civilization."

"Doing something about tyrants goes way back, too."

He stopped; frowned at me. "Doing something? . . ."

"For every Caesar, there's a Brutus."

His mouth twitched with irritation. "Mr. Davis, are you fishin' for some provocative comment, to titillate your readers? Because I'm afraid I have to say, as a representative of Standard Oil, I would only deplore any extralegal tactics that might—"

"The only law in Louisiana, it seems to me, is Huey Long."

Only the sounds of fluid pumping and metal wheels turning filled the silence. A whiff of sulfur drifted through; was a deal with the devil about to be struck?

"There are those," he said, "who would agree with you."

I shrugged with my eyes and mouth, and said, "And I would imagine your company would be favorably disposed toward a 'repeal' of that law."

"Mr. Davis . . ."

"My name isn't Davis."

LeSage's affability and confidence evaporated; he was standing out in the midst of this snarl of pipes and tanks and tubes, in a darkness broken only periodically by security lighting and billowing flames above, at a location in one of the most chaotic states of the union, in the presence of an individual who had misrepresented himself and was talking murder.

"I'm afraid I don't under—"

"My name is Heller. Nate Heller. I'm a bodyguard for Huey Long."

He began to back up, in more ways than one. "I never said a word against Huey! If anythin', you were puttin' words in my mouth!"

I caught him by the arm; he was trembling. For a lot of people in Louisiana, it seemed, fear was always nearby.

"Take it easy," I said. "I'm no reporter, but I *am* from Chicago."

I gave him the same spiel I'd given Hamilton, about meeting Huey in Chicago, and recently landing this job as one of Huey's inside men, and so on.

He was getting my drift; and he was settling down. His expression was sly as he said, "You say you're willin' to do just about anything for money?"

"Now you got it."

His eyes narrowed to slits of suspicion. "How do I know you're not an *undercover* agent for the Kingfish? He's been known to do this very kinda thing. . . ."

I gestured with open palms. "Hey, any meetings we have will be one-on-one—in locations like this one, that can't be bugged with a dictagraph or whatever."

He seemed to be considering that.

I shrugged one shoulder. "Try me out. You're a lobbyist—one of the things you traffic in is information, right?"

He nodded slowly.

"Well, if there's any information you need, just say the word. Or anything you need done. *Anything.*"

He said nothing.

"You'll get value for your dollar," I assured him.

He turned and, with no particular sense of urgency, headed back toward the administration building where my car awaited. I walked alongside him. Our shoes scuffed the cinders. For perhaps a minute he was silent, as if mulling over my proposition.

Then, suddenly, he stopped and faced me. "It's an interestin' offer, Mister . . . Heller was it?"

I nodded.

He nodded, too. "But I'm afraid I'll have to pass."

"Okay, but don't 'pass,' " I said. "Pass it *along.*"

He said nothing, studying me.

I continued: "If you, or your bosses, need anything done—*anything*—you can get in touch with me at the Heidelberg."

"Really? Now that is convenient."

"You mean, because that's where the Kingfish stays, when he's in town?"

The smile under the tiny mustache turned enigmatic. "No. Because that's where *I* live, too. . . . Good evening, Mr. Davis, uh, Heller."

He disappeared into the brick building and I returned to the Buick, wondering who had thrown who the curve.

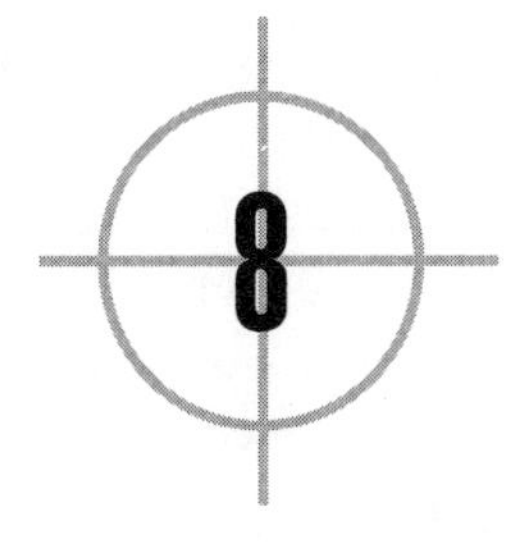

The eighty-six paved miles of Air-Line Highway, from Baton Rouge to New Orleans, would have been an arrow-straight ribbon of roadway but for a single curve that represented Huey punishing a stubborn, greedy landowner who wouldn't accept the Kingfish's generous price. The monotony was broken up, for this Northerner at least, by the variety of countryside—ghostly still bayous and luxuriantly overgrown swampland, predating civilization, were interspersed with old-fashioned sugar plantations and industrial sites that spoke of two very different eras of man's intrusion, here.

Huey's roads were concrete evidence of his good works for the Pelican State. According to Alice Jean, the Kingfish was responsible for two thousand miles of it, and that didn't count another four thousand or so of asphalt and gravel. For all the talk of dictatorship I'd been hearing, there were plenty of dissenters delighted to live in the realm of the Kingfish, eager to brag about it to a wandering Yankee like me.

Like the gas-pump jockey who filled the Buick even as he extolled Huey's roads and bridges and schools and hospitals. Or the busty redhead behind the counter of the roadside sandwich joint who wondered if they had free schoolbooks up North like they did in Loozyana, and in the Catholic schools, too!

Probably the biggest exponent of the Kingfish's jovial dictatorship I encountered in the most unlikely place.

Actually, the place itself—the marble-colonnaded lobby of the sixteen-story Roosevelt Hotel, at Canal and Baronne in downtown New Orleans—wasn't so unlikely. After all, Huey himself maintained a twelfth-floor suite here. But so did gangster "Dandy Phil" Kastel, the third of my trio of names culled from Huey's "son-of-a-bitch book."

And I hardly expected, calling upon Kastel, to encounter such a big pro-Long cheerleader.

I'm not talking about Kastel himself, but rather his second-in-command, one "Diamond Jim" Moran.

Short, paunchy, beetle-browed, mustached, with the slightly battered puss of an ex-pug, Moran rolled across the lobby toward me like a tank, his wardrobe making the Kingfish seem, by comparison, a man of the finest sartorial taste: sky blue double-breasted suit; pink silk shirt; wide red tie; white flourish of handkerchief pluming from a breast pocket. A jaunty homburg matched the light blue color of the suit, as did the round tinted lenses of his gold-frame glasses.

I'd never met the man, but I knew him at once. Why? First, I am a trained detective. Second, the words "Jim Moran" were spelled out in glittering stones—presumably diamonds—on a pin on his tie.

He confirmed the pin with an introduction, and I gave him my name—my real one—as we shook hands. Then he said, "Didn't mean to keep you waitin', Nate—phone started ringin'. Okay I call ya Nate? You call me Jim. *Mister* Moran? That's my old man, rest his soul."

He spoke a peculiar mixture of Italian immigrant (Moran was apparently an alias) and Southern gentleman.

Ten minutes ago I had called up to Kastel's business suite

in the Roosevelt, and Moran had asked me to wait here in the lobby. Maybe his phone really had started ringing, but I figured it was more likely he was calling around, checking up on my story.

He was moving; he waved for me to fall in step. "Dandy Phil's at our warehouse, over on the French side. He's expectin' us."

He walked me out onto Canal Street, and we crossed the wide thoroughfare with the light, skirting a trolley car as we went.

"Ever been to the Vieux Carré?" Moran asked.

"First time."

"I prac'ly grew up there. First job I ever had was a barber shop over on Chartres."

"Boxed some, didn't you?"

His already jovial countenance brightened even more. "Why, you see me fight?"

"No. I see your nose."

His laugh was immediate and infectious. He was a pleasant enough lunatic to be around.

"So you're pals with Frank Nitti, huh?" he asked, as we strolled down Dauphine into the French Quarter. We had crossed a street into another country: tall brick buildings with wrought-iron balconies hugged the sidewalks of the narrow street, ranging from shabby dilapidated affairs with sagging doors and rusted ironwork, often standing empty and in ruins, to structures painstakingly restored as private residences. Others, taken over by shopkeepers, were somewhere in between.

"I do the occasional job for Frank," I admitted.

"But you're workin' for the Kingfish now?"

"That's right."

Going into the den of gangsters required leaving my newspaperman masquerade behind: I needed to stick as close to the truth as possible. I had told Moran, on the phone, that

I was a Chicago private op who had just gone to work as a bodyguard for the Kingfish; and that Frank Nitti had asked me to pay my respects to Phil Kastel.

The latter wasn't true, of course, and the Outfit connections I'd implied were an exaggeration; but I did have a friendly relationship with Capone's successor, Frank Nitti. In fact, he considered himself in my debt, to some degree.

So if Moran had checked up on me with his Chicago sources, my story would seem confirmed.

"I used to work for him myself," Moran said.

"You worked for Nitti?"

"No! Somebody hit you in the head real hard, boy? The Kingfish! I was one of his first bodyguards, sure 'nuff."

We strolled along past an unconventional conglomeration of shops and residences: a tea room next to a flophouse, an art studio next to a corner grocery, a nightclub beside a curio shop. Like Greenwich Village in New York, and Tower Town in Chicago, the French Quarter catered to local eccentrics and slumming tourists.

And I was ambling along with a one-man tourist attraction, in the form of Diamond Jim Moran with his light blue suit and matching tinted spectacles. The locals, whether bohemian types (poets, artists, models) or street denizens (gamblers, winos, beggars), or even ordinary working folk (icemen, shopkeepers, hookers)—paid this walking advertisement for Technicolor little heed. But the out-of-towners, from debutantes to bank presidents, from sailors to nuns, took in Diamond Jim, in wide-eyed wonder.

I was stunned by him, too—but it wasn't his wardrobe.

It was the notion that one of the mobsters I was investigating as a possible Huey Long murder plotter was one of the Kingfish's former bodyguards.

And, apparently, a loyal one.

"Yeah, I love the Kingfish, and the Kingfish, he loves me," Moran was boasting good-naturedly.

"When was this?" I asked.

"When was what?"

"You working for the Kingfish."

"Six, seven years back. . . . I worked weekends, mostly—'cause of my other business in'tr'sts." He touched a bejeweled finger to his pink-shirted chest. "*I'm* the one intr'duced the Kingfish to Bourbon Street! Singin', dancin', drinkin' fools we was, back in them days."

"He's on the wagon now."

"Yeah, and I hear he slimmed down, some. Gotta be in fightin' trim to take on the president." He let out a single loud laugh. "The boss is sure 'nuff lucky *I* ain't around!"

"Oh?"

His smile pretended to be modest. "I used to cook for him. He's a fiend for my spaghetti and meatballs."

Told you he was Italian.

"Why'd you stop working for him, Jim?"

"Well, Uncle Sam sorta stopped me. They nailed me on a bootleggin' rap, in '30 . . . did a year inside. . . ."

In case you were wondering what his other "business in'tr'sts" were. . . .

"So now you work for Kastel."

His beetle brow furrowed; it was almost a frown. "I don't work *for* him, Nate . . . I work *with* him."

"I see."

We passed a restaurant oozing the scent of tomato sauce; the neighborhood was Italian, too—French Quarter or not.

"Phil's a right guy. Been around. Smart sumbitch. One of Arnold Rothstein's fair-haired boys, way back when."

"Impressive company."

"You're tellin' me! High-class operator. Phil was only inside once, and that was on a securities scam."

High class.

"But working with Kastel," I said, "it's not like working for the Kingfish, I guess."

"Not hardly." He gestured to the world around him. "I'm tellin' ya, that Kingfish is the best damn thing that ever happened to this state."

Never mind that we had turned down a shabby side street where unkempt children scurried in and out of gloomy alleyways, and overflowing trash cans decorated the sidewalk, attracting flies and vermin. The lovely wrought-iron balconies on slender iron pillars, adorning buildings that were shabby shadows of their former splendor, looked down on the scruffy ragamuffins in mocking reminder of the wealth Huey Long promised he would one day share with them.

"Take this bizness we're in, now," Moran was saying.

"Which business is that?"

"The slot-machine bizness! You know why the Kingfish cut that deal with the Politician, to bring the machines down from New York?"

The Politician was Frank Costello, also known as the "Prime Minister"—the biggest big shot of the New York mob.

"Because Fiorello LaGuardia threw Costello's slots in the East River?"

He smirked disgustedly. "I'm not talkin' 'bout why the *Politician* made the deal; I'm talkin' about why *Huey* made it."

"Oh. Well. For the money?"

He shook his head, as if disappointed in me. We had paused at a modest-looking church called St. Mary's; a raggedy man with one leg sat on the stone steps trading pencils for contributions. Moran put a dollar in the man's hat and took a pencil.

The beggar's grin was yellow-green. "Thank you, Jim!"

"Thanks for the pencil," he said affably, tucking it in an inside pocket, as we moved on past decidedly nontouristy businesses—a small grocery, a dry cleaner's, the courtyard to a private but rundown home with a hand-lettered sign tacked over the stone archway saying HEMSTITCHING.

"You poor feeble-minded Yankee," he said. "You really think ol' Huey's in it for the money, do ya?"

Money and power, I thought, but didn't say it; just shrugged.

"Hell, no!" he said, answering his own question. "The Kingfish is goin' to pass an ord'nance for the poor and the blind—stir up some relief money for these unfortunates, outa his percentage off the slot-machine take." He shook his head in admiration. "That Huey . . . always thinkin' of the little guy. . . . Well, here we are."

We were at a small warehouse; over a single garage door was a wooden sign with block letters: BAYOU NOVELTY COMPANY. We went in a door beside the garage entry, but it didn't lead into an office, just the warehouse itself, a brick, two-story-high area with a small glass-and-wood office partitioned off in one corner.

Most of the room was taken up by an unmarked semi truck, whose back doors were open, a ramp up to the back accommodating a pair of truckers in caps and work clothes, carrying out bulky wooden crates each about the size of a midget's coffin. It took both men to carry one crate.

A dark-haired pair of workers, not in work clothes but in dark suits and ties, used crowbars to open crates that had already been unloaded; then they would lift out the contents. Standing like silver totems against the wall were the previously uncrated slot machines with the distinctive emblem of a bronze Indian chief's head over the dial.

The semi truck had Cook County plates, and that was no surprise: these slot machines, known as Chiefs, were a product of Jennings and Company, a firm on the west side of Chicago.

Outfit territory.

Supervising all this was a handsome, dapper man of perhaps forty-five in a gray silk suit, leaning forward with both hands on a gold-tipped walking stick; he achieved effortlessly a suave, stylish air epitomizing the elegance and class Diamond Jim tried so hard, and so ineptly, to attain.

Moran introduced us, and Kastel took his weight off the walking stick and shook my hand, bestowing me a friendly, if cautious smile.

"It's nice of you to stop by, Mr. Heller," he told me. "I consider Frank Nitti a true gentleman. One of the smartest, shrewdest businessmen in our field."

"He speaks highly of you, as well." Of course, I'd never heard Frank Nitti so much as utter a word about Dandy Phil Kastel; but a guy with a gold-tipped walking stick obviously had a certain sense of self-importance, so I played into it.

"What brings you here, Mr. Heller? Other than to 'pay your respects.' "

"Well, uh . . . that's basically it. Courtesy call." I gave him a hard look that tried to send a signal: I didn't feel comfortable talking in front of Moran. His eyes tightened ever so slightly—it was barely perceptible—but he'd gotten the drift.

Kastel gave Moran a bland glance that apparently sent its own signal.

Moran cleared his throat. "Yeah, well . . . if you don't need me here, Phil, I'm gonna head back to the office, and mind the phones."

Kastel nodded his approval of that notion, and the chatty, overdressed mobster left me there with his boss. Or, that is, the man he "worked with."

I gestured toward the slot machines, lined up St. Valentine's Day Massacre-like, against one wall; others were being added to the lineup as the wooden crates were crowbarred off. "I see you have friends in Chicago."

His smile was slight and sly. "Frank Costello has friends everywhere, Mr. Heller."

"Call me Nate," I said.

But he didn't ask me to call him Phil.

"What's the story on Moran?" I asked. "Is he Huey's boy?"

"Only in spirit."

"He says he doesn't work for you."

"Diamond Jim represents local interests. He's something of a . . . liaison."

"What, with Sam Carolla's camp?"

Carolla was the New Orleans equivalent of Frank Nitti.

His glance seemed benign, but he was assessing me. "If you know anything about Frank Costello," Kastel said, "you'll know that his style is to cooperate, to collaborate, with local business."

By local business, of course, he meant the local mob.

"Now, Mr. Heller . . . Nate. Why are you here? *Really* here, I mean."

I shrugged a little. "Back in Chicago, I heard rumors that you guys are having some problems with the Kingfish."

He laughed silently. "Interesting, how word travels. How is it you happen to be working for Long as a bodyguard?"

I explained about hitting it off with Huey at the Chicago convention in '32, and how Huey had offered me a job when I delivered a package to him recently.

"I just thought if there was any package *you* wanted delivered," I said, "you should be aware you have a friend in the enemy's camp."

He twitched a smile; his eyes were hooded, near sleepy in a face almost movie-star handsome. "I see. That's white of you."

"I just wanted you to know where my loyalty lies. That if you need any help, in any way, you have but to ask."

"That is generous. But I hope it won't be necessary."

"But it *might* be?"

He seemed to be tasting the little smile; he shrugged his shoulders, Cagney-like, and leaned on the walking stick. "I admit there have been . . . problems with the former governor. When he invited us down here, I expected the hospitality to be longer lasting."

"And it hasn't been?"

He shook his head, no. "Problems have arisen, due to Senator Long's lack of control over the local municipal administration. We discovered, too late, that Sam Carolla had much more influence, in that regard, than the Senator."

"Huey promised something he couldn't deliver, you mean."

"That's a minor irritation. With Diamond Jim's help, we were able to iron things out. Senator Long agreed to provide political protection, statewide, to Mr. Carolla's various . . . business activities. Prior to this, New Orleans had been Sam's sole bailiwick."

"Well, then, what's the problem?"

He lifted his eyebrows. "The problem is that the redoubtable Kingfish, who had agreed to a very reasonable piece of the action . . . ten percent . . . recently upped the ante."

"To what? Fifteen? Twenty?"

His lips pursed in amusement. "He wants a flat fee, Mr. Heller . . . Nate. He wants three million a year."

"That's a lot of dough. . . ."

He gestured around the room, where the truck was nearly unloaded now. "This is not a huge operation, Nate. By the end of the year, we'll have six hundred machines around town—in drug stores, saloons, cigar stores."

"Lucrative . . . but not lucrative enough for a three-mil yearly payoff."

"Correct. Just a moment. Carlos!"

One of the well-dressed workers who'd been uncrating

the slot machines turned and looked our way. A dark-haired, hook-nosed bucket-headed tough, short but burly with a face that seemed set in a permanent scowl, young Carlos lumbered over sullenly, though his voice was respectful.

"Yes, Mis' Kastel?"

"I appreciate you and your brother helping out, with this physical labor."

"T'ink nuttin' of it, Mis' Kastel."

"Would you pay off these truckers, and see about getting our little Indians into the designated locations?"

"Dey be in dere by midnight, Mis' Kastel."

If I'd thought Moran's Italian-Louisianian accent was something, this kid was something else.

Carlos wandered back and, reaching for a wad of dough in one pants pocket, began peeling off bills and handing them to the grinning truckers, who'd finished unloading.

"Well, you've obviously got work to do," I said, heading to the door. But I made the point one more time: "If you need anything done—from gathering inside information to, well, *whatever* . . . I'm up for the job."

"If Frank Nitti trusts you," he said quietly, "that's all the reference necessary."

He shook my hand again. "Where are you staying?"

"Tonight, the Roosevelt, here in town. After that, back to the Heidelberg in Baton Rouge."

He walked me to the door; he used the walking stick, but didn't seem to have any sort of limp. "Well . . . we'll be in touch if anything comes up."

"Nice meeting you, Mr. Kastel."

"Call me Phil."

I was back on the street; he filled the doorway. His smile was as charming as it was meaningless.

"And, uh, Nate—you didn't mention any of this to Diamond Jim, by any chance? Your willingness to . . . help with the Kingfish problem, I mean."

"Why, no."

"Good."

"Why is that?"

"Oh, because he'd very likely kill you. A very loyal boyo, our Mr. Moran."

And he shut the door.

Normally, I don't like playing any kind of game with mobsters; too many characters who underestimated the likes of Diamond Jim and Dandy Phil wound up dead in a ditch.

Nonetheless, I figured I'd put my scam across, and didn't feel terribly intimidated. Or maybe the dangling carrot of the Kingfish's ten-grand bonus was just clouding my normally conservative (where my skin is concerned) judgment.

Whistling "Anything Goes," I strolled into the Roosevelt's lavish, story-and-a-half lobby feeling pretty good about how I'd handled myself. That was when I spotted a familiar Chicago face. Seated between a potted palm and a marble column was Frank Wilson—dark-haired, jug-eared, round-jawed, the dour Wilson, with his black horn-rimmed glasses and baggy suit, might have been a schoolteacher.

But he wasn't. He was a fed—specifically, one of the IRS team that, in tandem with Eliot Ness and his Capone Squad, had put Big Al away.

Feeling a little cocky, I sauntered up and said, "Hiya, Frank—what brings *you* to New Orleans? Investigating Huey Long's taxes?"

His long face got longer and the eyes between the round lenses flared.

Whoops. . . .

Wilson was on his feet in a fraction of an instant and his hand clamped on my forearm and he whispered, harshly, in my ear: "Keep your mouth shut, Heller. . . . We're goin' for a ride."

This was a new one: getting taken for a ride by a G-man.

But I was in no position to argue. I let him walk me quickly along to the corner doors and out onto the street, where in a few paces we were at a parked-at-the-curb black Ford that he indicated was his by shoving me toward the rider's door. He got in. Me, too.

Wilson, glancing behind him like a getaway driver pulling away from a just-robbed bank, swung the Ford out onto Canal.

"To answer your question," Wilson said tightly, "yes: I am here investigating Huey Long's taxes."

"Hey, Frank . . . it was just a smart-ass remark. . . ."

"Whatever, you hit the bull's-eye." He stopped at the light, glanced over at me. "Sorry about the bum's rush. But I'm undercover."

This guy couldn't have looked more like a fed if he tried.

"Ingenious disguise," I said.

His smirk was fleeting and disgusted. "I'm posing as a radio station executive."

"A radio station executive? What for?"

He turned right, onto St. Charles. "There's a radio station at the Roosevelt that Long's right-hand man Seymour Weiss is involved in; gives me a natural inroad with the Longsters."

I'd never heard that one before: Longsters. But it was apt enough.

Wilson was saying, "You see, I'm having difficulty getting my FCC permit. . . ."

"Oh. So you're cozying up to Seymour, to get the Kingfish's help cutting federal red tape."

He flashed a little smile. "Bingo. I'm spreading some dough around. I've even played poker with the Kingfish—who's a lousy damn loser, by the way."

"Sounds like you made the inner circle."

He smirked again. "As long as nobody heard you call me 'Frank' in the lobby."

"That was stupid of me. Sorry. . . ."

"I think we're all right. But I had to get you out of there. And you better talk to the boss."

"Is *Irey* here?"

He nodded. We were cruising past the grand old many-columned St. Charles Hotel. Elmer Irey had been chief of the IRS tax unit that put Capone away.

"Irey doing fieldwork?" I shook my head. "I thought he was strictly Washington, D.C., these days. . . ."

"This is a big effort, Nate. Louisiana is crawling with grafters, and the President sent the boss down, personal. Long and his gang are stealing everything that isn't nailed down, and they're using the claw end of the hammer to pry up the rest."

"Heaven forbid they're not paying taxes on their ill-gotten gains."

That made him smile, a little. "What are you doing in this part of the world?"

We were passing the Whitney Bank; I set my watch by its two gigantic square bronze clocks and said, "Working for Huey Long."

He damn near ran the car up over the curb. "What?"

"Yeah, I'm one of his bodyguards. We met in Chicago at the '32 convention—I was police liaison with him and his goons."

"Why the hell didn't you tell me!"

"Why? You think it's pertinent?"

He glowered, and pulled the car over into a space in front of the United Fruit Company Building, an elaborately decorated granite structure with bas-relief baskets of fruit over the windows.

"You guys gone undercover as banana craters?" I asked pleasantly.

"Come on," he growled, leading me down the street to the eighteen-story stone edifice that was the Masonic Temple. We went through the middle of a trio of high vaulted entryways and used the elevator to one of the numerous floors of offices above the meeting hall.

A pair of armed uniformed private security guards were waiting as we got off the elevator. Wilson nodded to them.

"You guys got *armed guards* posted?" I asked him, incredulous.

"Twenty-four hours a day," Wilson said, as we wandered into the big open room filled with agents sitting at desks, typewriters and adding machines making mechanical music. Whirring fans overhead mingled with street noise leaching in through open windows; phones rang, occasionally. No partitions separated the bustling agents, who were frequently moving from their desk to a brother's to share a piece of information, although at the right was a wall of small, glassed-in offices. Only one of these was in use, and in it sat Elmer Irey.

Irey was another dark-haired, jug-eared, round-jawed professor in black horn-rimmed glasses. He and Wilson were the Gold Dust Twins of the Internal Revenue Unit. The only difference was, Irey's hairline was making its escape more slowly.

He glanced up from a desk filled with papers, reports and adding-machine scrolls, and glimpsed me through the glass. His expression was at first confused, then irritated. He stood as we came into the cubbyhole, Wilson shutting the door behind us, muffling the din of the busy office.

Rather reluctantly, I thought, Irey extended his hand across the desk and I shook it as he said, "What the hell are you doing in New Orleans, Heller?"

"Nice to see you, too, Elmer. I'm on Huey Long's bodyguard staff. Why would that be of interest to a bunch of IRS agents?"

Irritation dissolved into disgust as I helped myself to a chair. Wilson, Irey's bald reflection, stood beside me and recounted, in the nasal whine of the grade-school tattletale, my approaching him in the Roosevelt lobby.

I shrugged. "It was a thoughtless slip. I already apologized a dozen times, and hell—there was nobody around to pick up on it."

Irey looked sharply at Wilson. "Is that right?"

Wilson sighed, nodded, said, "I don't think anybody heard him."

Irey sat, motioning Wilson to do the same. The IRS chief was lining me up in gun-sight eyes. Not much missed this sharp son of a bitch: he'd put men away for a misplaced decimal point.

"How's your friend Ness?" he asked.

"Still keeping the world safe from illegal hooch."

"Where is he? Ohio? Kentucky?"

"Yeah. Glorified revenooer."

Irey's mouth twitched. "He deserves better. Hoover's no prize."

Though a certain amount of tension existed between Irey and Eliot Ness—both of whom had been dubbed by various members of the press as "the man who got Capone" (as had Wilson)—Irey knew Eliot's backwoods banishment had to do with FBI chief J. Edgar Hoover's jealousy of anyone who grabbed more headlines than him. Just ask Melvin Purvis.

"Nate . . ."

Not "Heller"—Nate. Chummy, now.

"Nate, I can't buy you uprooting and giving up your agency . . . I hear you're fairly successful now. . . ."

I shrugged. "Not doin' bad. Still a single-man operation but prospering, considering the times."

"Good. That's just fine." He leaned back in his chair; made a tent of his fingers. His smile was a line curved at both ends, like a deft scalpel slash. "So why would you give that up to play bodyguard for a monster like Huey Long?"

"Is this meeting confidential?"

He nodded. The smile released a glimpse of teeth. "Don't you trust Uncle Sam, Nate?"

"The question is, do I trust Uncle Elmer . . . not to mention Cousin Frank."

Wilson said, "I'm the one who's undercover, Heller."

"Yes," I said, and I looked at Irey while jerking a thumb toward Wilson and added, "And as I was saying to Frank, earlier, you guys are putting together some remarkable disguises these days. Why, Sherlock Holmes couldn't top this one."

"Go to hell," Wilson said.

Irey patted the air with one hand. "Let's keep it civil. Nate . . . what in God's name are you up to?"

So I copped to it. I told them about my investigation of the latest Huey Long murder plot, and that I'd been undercover recently myself, seeing if anybody with assassination on their minds or in their hearts would recruit me for help, or possibly even the job.

Irey was slowly nodding through all this. "This sounds more like you. I couldn't see you joining the ranks of Huey's Cossacks, no matter what the paycheck was."

"The high opinion's appreciated," I said, "but I reserve the right to sell out if the price is right."

"I wish you luck on this," Irey said. "As a general rule,

I'm against assassination . . . even when the target is a corrupt, money-grubbing bastard like Huey Long."

"Lot of people in this state love him."

"At least as many hate him—he can't even trust his own people. That's why he hired you. Now, I'm prepared to shake you loose, if you promise not to expose Frank, here."

"Expose him? You have my word—at no time will my hands drift anywhere near the fly of his trousers."

"Fuck you, Heller," Wilson said.

I frowned in thought. "Isn't there a government directive about the use of profanity by agents?"

"Nate," Irey said, ignoring the floor show, "our investigation into Long and his Longsters has reached a point where an indictment is imminent."

"Really?"

"Really," Irey said. "Although, frankly, we're focusing as much on Seymour Weiss as the Kingfish himself."

"Seymour? I take him for a glorified gofer."

"Only around Huey Long," Wilson said.

"To everyone else in Louisiana," Irey said, "Weiss is a mover and shaker. That hotel you're staying in? The Roosevelt? He owns it."

That was some hunk of real estate.

"This is news to me," I said, and it was: Alice Jean had told me next to nothing about Seymour.

"He used to manage the Roosevelt barbershop," Wilson said, "before he hooked up with the Kingfish. Few years later, he buys the place."

"Owns the New Orleans Pelicans baseball team, too," Irey said, "and a soda pop company, and . . . well. Let's just say he's a very well-heeled gent."

"But does he pay his taxes?"

Irey grinned like a skull; I knew the way to make an IRS agent smile, didn't I?

"Louisiana is honeycombed with graft," Irey said, savoring his own words. "It's the shakedown capital of America—puts Chicago to shame. One contracting firm alone paid the Long machine graft in excess of half a million."

"But can you track the money to Huey?" I asked. "Huey's like Capone—he's got one hell of a lot of buffers. . . ."

"He *is* like Capone," Irey said ominously. "And where is Capone now?"

He had a point.

"Trust me," Irey said, "Weiss and all the others will take a very big fall . . . including the Kingfish. We've put a lot of man hours in. . . ."

"Going back to 1930," Wilson said wearily. "That was when the letter campaign started."

"Letter campaign?" I asked.

Irey nodded. "Thousands upon thousands of letters from respectable citizens in this state, wanting us to do something about Long's brazen thievery."

"Organized, you think?"

"Perhaps. But what's the difference? They were real letters, from real citizens, with real concerns."

"If you've been at this since '30," I said, "and if Long's such a 'brazen' crook, why haven't you nailed him yet?"

Irey's expression darkened, and Wilson sighed heavily.

"The investigation was shut down for a time," Irey said quietly.

I grinned. "I get it! You started lookin' into Huey's finances when the Republicans were in office, then when FDR came in, you shut it down! After all, Huey helped get Roosevelt the nomination—it was payoff time."

Irey's shrug was barely perceptible; Wilson was looking at the floor.

"But now that Huey's making noises about running for the presidency himself," I said, "and hangin' FDR in effigy in every public speech he makes, you guys are back in business!"

Neither of them spoke; but they didn't deny it, either.

I stood, and the chair scraped the floor. "Hey—you guys want to nail Huey, Capone–style, that's your business. But he strikes me as a tough prospect."

"Oh?" Irey said.

"Like he said to me, he prefers doing business 'cash on the barrelhead.' "

"That's certainly true," Irey admitted. "Huey and his boys have collected millions in graft . . . but finding a receipt or a canceled check in this case is about as easy as finding an honest man in the Long administration."

"Hey, I'm in the Long administration."

"And you're probably the most honest man in it . . . and isn't that saying something?"

Another good point.

"So, I take it, you've found something?" I asked, wandering to the door.

"Let's put it this way," Irey said, with a tiny enigmatic smile. "Big crooks shouldn't commit little crimes."

"Then you are ready to indict?"

"We are," Irey said, "but you'll understand, I'm sure, my reluctance to share the details with one of Huey Long's personal bodyguards."

"Fair enough," I said. "But like I told you—I'm working a specific investigation. I don't see that what you're doing has anything to do with what Huey hired me to do. I'm prepared to keep it to myself."

"Good," Wilson said.

Irey lifted a warning forefinger; the professor's expression and tone were scolding. "Foul us up," he said, "and I'll personally guarantee you and the A-1 Detective Agency an annual audit."

"Mum's the word," I said, half-out the cubbyhole door. "How about a ride back to the Roosevelt, Frank?"

"Hoof it," he said. "It's not that far, and I don't want to be seen with you."

Irey called out to me: "Oh, and Heller?"

Not "Nate"—Heller.

"If Huey's paying you in cash," Irey said, waggling a parental finger, "don't forget to declare it. . . ."

I spent several uneventful days back in Baton Rouge, in my room at the Heidelberg, waiting for the phone to ring. None of the bait I'd tossed out to the Square Dealers, Standard Oil or the Syndicate had as yet produced a nibble. So I shifted my undercover efforts to Alice Jean's bed; her suite was just a few doors down from mine. Tough way to earn $250 a day.

By Friday afternoon, Alice Jean having stayed behind in Baton Rouge, I was again at the Roosevelt Hotel in New Orleans, this time in the Kingfish's twelfth-floor suite, where the man himself—in his uniform of green-silk pajamas—was entertaining a steady stream of advisers, ward-heeler types and influential citizens. The joint was also crawling with bodyguards, and the scene was even more chaotic than what I'd witnessed on Huey's birthday at the New Yorker.

At one point, Seymour Weiss tried to corner Huey with a fat handful of papers, saying, "Huey, we've only got seven days to get these income taxes filed."

Huey, who was pacing at the time, frowned as if a pesky

gnat was buzzing his ear. "You got all the necessary papers—bills and canceled checks and such like?"

"Yes. Of course."

"Well, then you deal with it. Fill everythin' out and I'll sign it when I get back here from Baton Rouge on Monday or Tuesday." His expression softened; he put a hand on Seymour's shoulder. "Then you know what we'll do? We'll go on a vacation together, just you and me—no bodyguards or anythin'. Be like old times."

"That would be nice."

"We'll just climb in the car and go wherever we want to, and not make one single, solitary, slivery plan in advance."

This moment indicated a depth of friendship between the two men that I hadn't picked up on before. I found it oddly touching, although I wasn't touched enough to tell these two friends, in the midst of their income-tax discussion, about Elmer Irey's "vacation" plans for them. I'd rather have a root canal than an IRS audit.

In the midst of all this, Huey was going over his notes for a speech he was going to give, via that Weiss-controlled radio station in the Roosevelt that Frank Wilson had mentioned.

So I'd had no opportunity to get Huey alone long enough to fill him in, properly, about what I'd been up to.

The green-pajamaed Southern-fried potentate was flat on the bed, stomach down, going over his notes in pencil when he suddenly called me over. I went.

"You like golf?" he asked.

"I don't know if I like it, exactly. I've learned to put up with it—I do a lot of work for bankers and insurance people, you know."

"Well, you won't have to play, son. Jest caddy."

"Caddy?"

"I always use my bodyguards as caddies," the Kingfish

said, glancing up from his notes with a sly smile. "I don't want nobody makin' a hole-in-one in *me*."

Speaking of Caddies, a few minutes later I was sent down to wait for Murphy Roden, the Long bodyguard who'd been dispatched to trade in the Kingfish's last-year's-model Cadillac for a new number. I stood outside, near the Roosevelt entry that straddled the corner of Canal and Baronne. A New Orleans P.D. sawhorse reserved a parking place, and when the shiny-new, midnight blue buggy rolled in, I cleared the way.

The long, rakish Caddy purred like a thousand kittens; behind the wheel, Roden's blond, brown-eyed, roughly handsome countenance lighted up with a grin, upon seeing me.

We had hit it off, back in Chicago in '32, which is something I couldn't really say about any of Huey's other Cossacks. Murphy was a small-town boy who'd wanted to be a flyer, but washed out and joined the Louisiana State Police, where he set countless sharpshooting records—I heard one of the other bodyguards say that Murphy could empty a .38 into a four-inch target at fifty feet.

He got assigned to the Kingfish as a driver for one upstate visit, and Huey took such a shine to him, Murphy became his personal chauffeur, and easily his most trusted bodyguard.

"Nate Heller!" he said, climbing out of the Caddy, dropping its silvery keys into a pocket of his tan suit. "I *heard* you joined the circus!"

Murphy was probably thirty, and he was brawny but not big: maybe five seven, five eight.

"Just short-term," I said, as we shook hands. "Your boss has had some death threats and wanted to put on some extra security."

"He always did like you, Nate." He cocked his head,

raised an eyebrow. "Death threats are pretty much old news around here, but the boss is takin' this one serious. He's reassigned every available highway patrolman and B.C.I. agent to the capitol. So—what do you think of my spandy-new wheels?"

"Yours?"

"Well, the boss never drives 'em. Maybe we can take a spin, a little later. I need to show you the French Quarter."

"I saw it."

"Daytime or nighttime?"

"Daytime."

"Then you ain't seen it, nohow."

I walked down the sidewalk, along the endless length of the new Caddy; sun glinted off in cross fires of glare. "I see what Huey means by 'sharing the wealth.' Doesn't this rub his dirt-poor constituents the wrong way?"

"Hell, no! He leaves the slouchy duds and horse-and-buggies for the also-ran candidates. He wants people to think he's somebody special—and they do."

"How does this thing handle?"

Murphy put his hands on his hips and appraised the vehicle. "Well, I've only driven it a mile or so, over from the dealership. But these babies handle fine . . . leastways, now that Huey paved the roads. Back when I was navigating *gravel* roads, at eighty miles an hour, we used to go through windshields twice a month. And hell, I must've blown out more tires than Carter's got pills."

I winced. "On gravel roads?"

He nodded, and his sunny smile was seductive. "I tell ya, when I had a blowout on a downgrade, and was strugglin' to keep control of the wheel, them folks in the backseat, they really come alive. If I'm lyin', I'm dyin'."

"I believe you."

We strolled into the Roosevelt's block-long, chandeliered

lobby, and Murphy asked me how I was getting along with Messina.

I shrugged. "No real problems, since Oklahoma City."

"You know, he loves the boss. Sleeps near his feet; plays valet for 'im. He'd do anything for the boss."

"You mean, he handles the murders."

Murphy shook his head and laughed, a little. "You ain't changed much, Nate."

That evening, around seven, as I sat on the rider's side in the front seat of the big blue Caddy, Murphy Roden switched on the radio. A lively live rendition of "Every Man a King" was emanating from the speakers, straight from the Roosevelt Hotel's Fountain Lounge.

"The boss told Seymour to reserve a three-hour time slot," Murphy said, grinning over at me. His arm was elbowed out the window, his blond hair ruffling in the breeze the buggy was stirring up out of this hot humid night.

"This is Senator Huey P. Long talkin'," the Kingfish began, "and since the lyin' newspapers won't tell you these things, I'll have the boys play a little music so you can call up your friends and neighbors and tell 'em I'm on the air. . . ."

Murphy switched off the radio, shook his head, grinned over at me again. "The boss is a cutter, ain't he? You ready to learn why they call N'Owluns the city that care forgot?"

"I'm sure."

"You're sure you're sure?"

"If I'm lyin', I'm dyin'," I said.

The next morning—on the plushly green links of the Audubon Park Club's golf course—two bleary-eyed caddies, both of whom were entirely too hungover to be carrying handguns in holsters under the jackets of their white linen suits (though they were), followed a pair of golfers up a slope. The golfers were Huey Long—in a short-sleeve white shirt with a loud red-and-green tie, tan slacks and white golfer's shoes—and Seymour Weiss, atypically jaunty in green cap, white sport shirt and brown knickers with matching socks.

A third member of the party, with his own armed (but apparently not hungover) bodyguard, was off to the left somewhere, chasing a ball in the rough.

The strap of the bag of clubs slung over my shoulder created a band of pain that almost equaled the ache in my legs as we scaled the hill.

"Have a little too much fun last night, kiddo?" Murphy Roden asked; he was grinning, but he couldn't have felt much better than me. His eyes were filigreed with red.

"I don't remember anything after the tequila."

"La Lune! Now *there's* a club. . . . Don't tell me you could ever forgot the *Dog* House."

I winced as I tried to think. "Was that a colored show?"

"Ycs sir, but so was Popeye's. And Mama's Place."

For whatever reason, these words summoned images of flickering lights and floor shows with barely clothed high-yellow gals stomping in abandon to red-hot jazz. I trudged up the hill, following the Kingfish's tan-trousered behind.

"Murph . . . did we pick up a couple of girls?"

"Sure 'nuff did. College gals from Philadelphia."

"Legal age?"

"I don't believe we asked."

Huey had reached his ball, where it rested at the hill's summit like the cherry on a sundae. He walloped it a good one, and it sailed down the fairway two hundred fifty yards, easy.

He whooped with delight.

"Nice," Seymour said.

"Top *that*, sucker!" Huey cackled.

Actually, Seymour was winning. Huey had power, but no

finesse. It didn't seem to bother him, though, when he flubbed a shot; the glee when he really connected with one made up for it.

We began to trudge down the hill, to where Seymour's ball waited.

"These college girls," I said to Murphy. My head was playing the Anvil Chorus. "Do I remember us goin' to their hotel room?"

He shrugged. "I don't know. Do you?"

"Was mine a redhead?"

"I believe so."

"I'm not *married* or anything. . . ."

"I couldn't rightly say."

Seymour hit the ball straight and hard and it bounced onto the green, a healthy but possible putt from the pin.

The Kingfish chipped it on, but he three-putted and then Seymour made his shot with grace and seeming ease. I was keeping score for the Kingfish, and when he reported the number of his strokes—off of which he had shaved two—I jotted it down dutifully. The shakiness of my pencil line, however, might have been the work of a recent stroke patient.

As we walked to the next tee, Seymour said, "Shouldn't we wait for Dr. Smith?"

"Hell, no," Huey blurted. "Let that slowpoke sumbitch catch up on his own time, at his own speed. I don't wait for nobody."

"Actually," Seymour said conspiratorially, "I'm glad he's not around."

"Oh?"

"Couple things I wanted to mention that I'd just as soon the good doctor not be privy to."

"Well, then, hell's bells—shoot."

Seymour tasted the sentence before spitting it out; it was bitter. "I've been able to confirm that Elmer Irey's in town."

That remark penetrated the swollen lump of pain that was my head, as I dragged my sorry ass and the ton of clubs behind them.

Huey seemed unconcerned. "That right?"

"No question there's a major investigation under way."

"They won't git anything on me. You got yourself covered, Seymour?"

"I believe so."

"Sometimes I don't know about you boys," the Kingfish said, shaking his head, teeing up. "Without me 'round to hold ya down, I'm 'fraid you'd all land in the penitentiary."

He swung, missed, said, "Shit!" then grinned back like a silly kid at Seymour and said, "Practice swing."

Then he slammed it down the fairway.

Seymour teed up. "This bad blood between you and the White House, it could ruin us, Huey. Never mind this tax threat—look at the way they're usin' patronage against us! Shuttin' us off, and givin' all the WPA jobs to our political enemies to dole out! It's goddamn blackmail."

Huey's grin was nasty as he rocked on his heels, holding his golf club in two hands before him like a riding crop. "Ever hear of the tenth article of the Bill of Rights, Seymour?"

Pausing at the tee, Seymour frowned. "Certainly. It's not exactly on the tip of my tongue. . . ."

It was on Huey's. "Anythin' not specifically permitted to the federal government or forbidden to the states is straight-out reserved to the people." He bounced over to me, handed me the club to put away in the bag.

Then he turned to Seymour, and thumped himself on the chest.

"And of course," he said, "as we all know, I *am* the people."

Seymour had been about to address the ball, but this stopped him. He frowned in concern.

"What do you have in mind, Huey?"

Huey's sneering smile made me think of a mean little kid laying out the details of a particularly nasty prank for his cohorts.

"One of the laws I'm gonna push through in this special session," he said, "forbids any federal official or employee from disbursin' any public funds appropriated or made available by the Congress . . . if, in the Louisiana state government's opinion, that spendin' would encroach upon states' rights."

"This is a *law* you're talkin' about?"

"Sure as hell ain't a request. Violators'll be sentenced to a year in jail! We'll fill the hoosegow so full of them Roosevelt henchmen, there won't no room left for the honest crooks."

Seymour seemed to have forgotten his teed-up ball; he went over to the tee bench and sat, numbly, and Huey joined him.

Quietly, reasonably, Seymour said, "Kingfish . . . you have one of the best legal minds in the country . . ."

"Why, thank you, Seymour. The Supreme Court of the United States, 'fore whom I've argued many a case for the great state of Loozyana, agrees with you."

". . . and you know, at least as well as I, that such a law would be found unconstitutional. . . ."

"I don't give a diddly damn. Either way, it'll tie up them federal funds till after the election, come January."

Seymour sighed; his expression was dark. "You're playing into FDR's hands with this one, Kingfish—with this probe he and the House of Representatives are about to launch . . ."

Huey stood, stamped his feet like a child in a tantrum. "They can *probe* my *hind*quarters till the cows come home! Claimin' Louisiana ain't a 'representative form of government' no more? Hell—*that* duck won't hunt. Everybody knows that crippled fucker is afraid of me!"

"Then you haven't . . . reconsidered?"

Huey spoke through clenched teeth; whatever subject Seymour had just broached, it was a sore one. "Reconsidered what, Seymour?"

Seymour said nothing.

Huey put his hands on his hips and leaned forward mockingly, inches from Seymour's dour face, pronouncing every word distinctly.

"Yes, I'm runnin' for president," Huey said, "and no, I don't necessarily expect to win . . . not in '36. But by God, I'll sure as hell set the stage for 1940!"

Huey backed off, folded his arms, raised his chin.

Seymour said, "Kingfish . . . we don't even have the damn South sewed up. Does the word 'Mississippi' conjure up anything? Bilbo's man just beat your candidate's ass, there!"

Senator Bilbo, another rabble-rousing populist, had backed Hugh White for governor of Mississippi; Huey's man Paul Johnson had been narrowly defeated. The papers were still full of the ongoing recount.

"That's a goddamn fluke," Huey said dismissively. "And it wasn't *me* that got beat—it's that shif'less sucker Johnson . . . he shoulda took *more* of my help! Look what my stumpin' done for Hattie Carraway! Jesus Christ couldn'ta got that prune-faced old gal elected. But *I* did!"

Seymour was shaking his head. "I've told you how expensive a campaign of that magnitude would—"

"Fuck it! We got a war chest so fulla loot we cain't close the goddamn fuckin' thing!"

"It'll clean us out, Kingfish."

He nodded, and kept nodding. "And we'll have another four years, 'fore '40, to fill the ol' dee-ducts box back up ag'in, won't we? Now, git off your ass, and hit your goddamn ball, Seymour. I ain't got all day."

A weary Seymour got up, his demeanor at odds with his sporty golf apparel, addressed the ball, hit it hard and clean, but not as forcefully as Huey, who was heading down the slope while Seymour's ball was still in the air.

"House of Representatives my ass," he was muttering. "Four hundred and thirty-five fuckin' dumbbells . . ."

As I trailed along, my pounding head barely functioning, I gathered that Huey and Seymour had moved on to discussing possible candidates for the next figurehead governor, now that O.K. Allen's "reign" was coming to an end. Huey kept saying that he'd promised this one and that one the job.

"Jesus, Huey—who *haven't* you promised this job to?"

"Hey, it keeps 'em all on my side, and when the time comes, I'll find an excuse and a fat job for each of 'em, to keep 'em there. You worry too much, Seymour."

"Fore!" someone shouted, and a ball went sailing over our heads.

"Jesus H. Christ!" a startled Huey shouted.

He stood fuming, like a bull preparing to charge, as up and over the hill came the party responsible. Trailed by his armed caddy, the blond heavyset man, with an eagle's beak nose in an incongruously blue-eyed, boyish face, trotted down the hill, smiling benignly. He wore a straw hat, a short-sleeve white shirt with no tie, an argyle sweater vest, and—like Seymour—the childish knickers so many golfers insisted upon humiliating themselves in.

"Didn't expect to get such a good piece of that, Kingfish!" he called, in a booming, pulpit-schooled baritone.

"You dumb sumbitch!" Huey shouted. "You tryin' to kill me?"

"What," Murphy whispered to me, "and end his meal ticket?"

This "dumb sumbitch" was Dr. Gerald L. K. Smith, the rabble-rousing revivalist preacher who headed up the Kingfish's nationwide Share the Wealth Clubs.

Smith knocked his ball up over the next hill and he and his caddy moved on ahead of us, for a change.

"Why do you tolerate that two-bit bible-thumper?" Seymour muttered to Huey, as they walked along. "He's only out to feather his own damn nest."

Huey snorted a laugh. "Tell me somethin' I *don't* know."

Seymour frowned, and didn't even bother lowering his voice. "The bastard's a Jew-hating Fascist, and his ravings and rantings draw us the wrong kind of attention."

"There's no such thing as the 'wrong kind' of votes, Seymour." The Kingfish laid a hand on his adviser's shoulder. "Besides—next to me, the Rev is the best damn rabble-rouser in the You Ass of A."

I whispered to Murphy, "Is Seymour right about Smith?"

"Guess you folks up North don't get the priv'lige of Reverend Smith's insights," he said dryly. "We hear 'im on the radio, a lot, down these parts."

"Really?"

Murphy nodded. "The Rev got bounced out of his home church 'cause he was spendin' too much time workin' with a North Carolina black-shirt outfit."

"North Carolina *Nazis*?"

"If I'm jokin', I'm chokin'. They advocate overthrow of the gov'mint by armed insurrection—the whole shootin' match."

We had the same thing in Chicago, of course—the Bund was always rattling imaginary swords—but I couldn't dispel from my hungover brain the absurd image of a bunch of hillbillies wearing bib overalls over paramilitary black.

Then Seymour hit a long ball that sent him out ahead of the pack, and it was Reverend Smith's turn to do the bad-mouthing.

"That Hebrew 'friend' of yours is untrustworthy, you know," Smith said, in a hypnotically mellow voice. Like so many preachers, the resonance of his voice lent Smith's words undeserved weight.

"If I can trust anybody," Huey said offhandedly, "it's Seymour."

"So Christ thought of Judas," Smith insisted. "Weiss is one of that tribe that uses both capitalism and communism to dominate the world and eradicate the godly."

Huey said nothing, as they trudged down a steep hill; his ball mocked him from a sand trap up ahead.

"And this *is* a *worldwide* problem, Kingfish," Smith continued. "Brave men all around this globe are uniting to fight these godless forces. . . ."

This guy obviously wanted to play Goebbels to Huey's Hitler, but then he made the mistake of being too direct about it.

"America needs its own Führer," Smith began.

And Huey turned on him.

"Don't you compare me to that son of a bitch!" he roared, his nose an inch from the blinking Smith's, his forehead buckling the brim of the Reverend's straw fedora. "And knock off the goddamn Jew-baitin' bullshit!"

When Huey backed away, the Reverend hung his head and said, "Please accept my apologies. I forgot myself. I bow to your more Christian instincts."

"And don't you fuckin' forget it," Huey muttered, moving on.

Two holes later, Smith and Huey were alone again. After Huey swung—and his mood was brightened by another two-hundred-yard-plus drive—the ass-kissing Reverend politely asked if he could discuss business for a moment.

"What kind of bizness, Rev?"

"Share the Wealth Club. I merely wanted to suggest that we charge our members a nominal ten cents in dues. . . ."

"No."

From his expression, you'd think Smith had been struck a blow. "But with eight million members at ten cents a month each, think what that would bring us!"

Huey looked like he was going to spit out a seed. But all he spit out were words: "We're lookin' for support, not money, Rev. The money'll come. It'll come. Now . . . what's this about you bein' against tellin' our members about my thirty-dollar-a-month old-age pension plan?"

The Reverend lowered his voice to the timbre of a very special prayer. "Dr. Townsend is promising his followers two hundred dollars a month . . . so I suggest we just put in the word 'adequate' and let every man name his own figure. . . ."

Huey roared with laughter. He slapped his spiritual adviser on the back.

"The Lord broke the mold when he made you, Rev," Huey said. I couldn't tell if that was spoken in admiration or contempt, or maybe half-and-half.

Finally, Huey and I found ourselves alone, with both Smith and Weiss off chasing their balls, so to speak. I filled the Kingfish in on my visits to the three names he provided me from his "son-of-bitch" book. I did it quickly, but in detail, and he took it all in with eyes that were hard and focused.

"I've made myself available," I said, "and easy to find. I was at the Heidelberg most of the time, as you know, but the night I called on Dandy Phil, I stayed in New Orleans. And nobody's contacted me, or approached me, about anything."

"You think you gave 'em enough time?"

I shrugged. "I think if anything was afoot, from these quarters, we'd know. Remember, I talked to Hamilton and LeSage on Tuesday, and Dandy Phil on Wednesday. Your old pal Diamond Jim sends his regards, by the way."

Huey shook his head. "God, I miss his spaghetti and

meatballs." We had reached his ball and he began to address it, then turned to me with a frown of thought and said, "You know, that tip I got said I wouldn't live through the special session."

"How long did you say the session would take, again?"

"By Monday, we'll have them thirty-one bills rammed through. Would ya mind stickin' aroun' till then? I can use another good man at my side."

I stepped back while he took a swing and raised a healthy divot.

"Practice swing," I said.

"Goes without sayin'," the Kingfish said, and waled at the thing. It went flying over the hill, just like my ten-grand advance had flown.

But another few days at $250 per wasn't a bad consolation prize.

"I'll stay," I said.

"I thought you might," he said jovially. "Considerin' how you and Alice Jean done hit it off. . . ."

He went on up and over the hill while I stood there with my mouth open.

"What's wrong?" Murph asked, as he came down over the slope behind me.

I swallowed thickly. "I think the Kingfish knows I'm bangin' his sweetie."

"Hell, Nate," Murphy said, moving on past me with a soft chuckle, "everybody in this damn circus knows that."

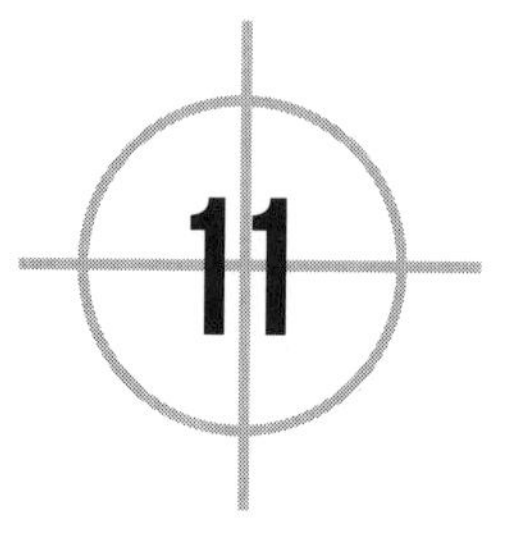

11

The midnight blue Caddy shot down the Air-Line Highway like a well-aimed bullet—no blowouts or broken windshields, this trip. Not on a hard stretch of Kingfish concrete that might have been designed for breaking speed limits; and what Louisiana traffic cop was fool enough to stop the car that bore license plate Number 1?

Murphy Roden was a no-nonsense driver: his foot was heavy, sure 'nuff, but his eye was steady and ever on the road. Affable as he was, Murph indulged in little small talk on the drive. I was in the front seat with him, and the Kingfish was by himself in back. Seymour Weiss had remained in New Orleans. It was a hot, sunny day, and the only wind was the one we stirred up; the windows in front were down.

It was the closest I ever came to seeing the Kingfish at repose, and the only time I had evidence that he ever slept. He napped briefly, and read various newspapers and sheafs of correspondence, occasionally scribbled some notes or something, for the rest of the ninety-minute trip. The gregarious, motormouth bear was in near-hibernation.

Suddenly, a gray-granite rocketship, poised to launch into

the heavens, rose above the mud flats, before my astounded eyes: Huey's skyscraper statehouse. The tapering spire of the thirty-four-story capitol was like a mirage of the future, an apparition of civilization in a world of swamps and bayous.

"Some buildin', huh?"

It gave me a start: the Kingfish hadn't spoken the whole trip, and now, when I glanced over, his shining moon face was next to me, as he sat forward, leaning on my seat, staring ahead at his art deco monument to himself.

"Some building," I agreed.

"Brother Earl calls it my 'silo.' Jealous, as usual. Only cost five millions, and I had the sucker finished within a year of the day we laid the cornerstone." Then, with no irony and not a twinge of conscience, he added, "Woulda cost fifty millions in New York or Washin'ton, what with their crooked brand of politics."

If an Empire State Building ascending from marshlands had seemed jarring, the capitol grounds dispelled that sense. As the Caddy glided through a formal, landscaped park—flower beds bursting with color, magnolias and poplars mingling with ghostlike, ancient, moss-hung oaks—the towering stone structure achieved an eerie dignity, like a single massive gravestone in a vast perfect cemetery.

Murphy turned down Capitol Drive, where parking places awaited Huey and the bodyguard car that trailed us (bearing McCracken, Messina and two other Cossacks). These were among the few reserved spaces that weren't taken: the special session began today, and Louisiana's pro-Long legislators knew the Kingfish expected their presence, and the anti-Longs weren't about to give him the satisfaction of no opposition.

The Kingfish was forgoing his private parking place in back, where he could enter the statehouse unobtrusively—but right now, with the session looming, Huey wanted to be seen. It was a time for grand entrances.

To reach the entrance of the 450-foot inverted T that was Huey's capitol—the Senate and the House of Representatives were in first-floor wings at left and right, respectively—you climbed forty-nine steps, each but the last inscribed with the name of a state. The granite stairway was flanked by somber, imposing statues of explorers, pioneers, settlers and Indians. The majesty of all this, and that of the looming monolithic capitol itself with its historical and patriotic friezes, was undermined by the all-pervasive presence of Huey's state police.

In their helmets and khakis and boots, strapped with gun- and bullet-belts, they were not a police guard, but a military encampment, standing watch along the perimeter, perched on the edges of the somber statuary, stationed on the landings of the stairway. Their presence only made Huey smile, and he said, "Hello, boys," half a dozen times along the way; their disciplined lack of response tickled him all the more, as he strutted up the granite stairway followed by Murphy and me, as well as Messina, McCracken (with his deadly grocery sack), and other assorted hooligans.

We followed the Kingfish through the glass doors into a claustrophobic bronze-and-marble entryway, and on into the grandiose main lobby known as Memorial Hall. Our footsteps echoed across the polished lava floors and up to the ornate four-story ceiling; Huey's voice echoed the same way, as he jauntily greeted legislators and tourists and tour guides.

Yesterday Huey had asked me to stick around, because he needed "another good man." But inside the capitol was crawling with even more military-style state police, as well as thuglike plainclothes dicks with conspicuous bulges under arms or on hips. The dignified bronze fixtures and patriotic murals decorating Memorial Hall—obviously the capitol's hub—were at odds with this police-state atmosphere.

It was a straight shot to the trio of elevators, whose elaborate bronze doors depicted bas-relief portraits of what were apparently (judging by the muttonchops) public figures of bygone days; but Huey was among them, up at the top right.

Murph saw me squinting at the little boxes with faces in them and he whispered, "It's a gallery of the state's governors, endin' with Huey."

I somehow felt sure that the omission of O.K. Allen was okay with the current governor.

We took the middle elevator, which bore a small placard saying PRIVATE—STATE EMPLOYEES ONLY. Huey chatted with the elevator operator, a skinny, friendly man in his sixties, inquiring about his wife and children by name.

"Boss has a photographic mem'ry," Murphy whispered.

I figured as much; nothing I'd observed would have led me to believe Huey cared about individuals like this fellow. Huey worried about only two things: himself and the masses. In that order.

We got off on the twenty-fourth floor, on the other side of the elevator, which opened onto a small, mundane vestibule. Tourists were getting off one elevator and onto another, and gasped at the sight of the Kingfish, who waved and smiled and said, "Howdy." This was the floor where the common folk could catch two things: glimpses of Huey and the elevator to the observation tower.

The door to Huey's suite—which took up the rest of the floor—was around to the right. The suite itself was furnished in a sleek, modern style—curves of wood and chrome—but otherwise reminded me of various hotel suites of recent days. The only major difference was we settled ourselves in a living room area and the Kingfish didn't get into his fabled green-silk pajamas.

For much of the afternoon the Kingfish and a small, dark, apparently Italian gent worked on a new song Huey was cooking up. It was a victory song for the LSU football team, and Huey had some hand-scribbled lyrics he'd done in the car on the ride over from New Orleans.

Murphy, McCracken, Squinch McGee and I were playing

poker—using wooden matchsticks for chips—at a card table over in one corner. I was the only one who didn't smoke, but I might as well have: the blue haze from the cigarettes hung like ground fog.

"Jacks or better," I said, dealing the cards. "Who's the ginney?"

"Actually," Murphy said, "he's from Costa Rica. Castro Carazo. Writes all the music for the boss's songs."

"He used to be the orchestra leader at the Roosevelt Hotel," McCracken said. "The boss likes him, 'cause Castro used to let him direct the band at the Blue Room, sometimes."

"What's he do now?" I asked. "Besides write songs with Huey."

"He's director of music at LSU," Murphy said. "I can open."

After Huey and his music man had roughed out their composition, the Distinguished Senator from the Great Pelican State came over and pulled us away bodily from the middle of a round of Black Mariah (sometimes called Chicago). This did not make me happy, as I had the ace of spades down, which would have entitled me to half the pot.

But you didn't argue with the boss.

I have only the faintest memory of the rah-rah number, other than its melody being suspiciously similar to "Every Man a King."

Nonetheless, I joined in with the effusive praise and applause of the other bodyguards. Messina, who had been seated nearby the musical geniuses while they composed, was smiling like a madman; his eyes were glittering with emotion.

We were allowed to return to our game—which was declared a goddamn misdeal—and were summoned back for three more performances, over the course of the next hour and a half, to hear "improved" versions, every one of which sounded identical to me.

Even for $250 a day, this was not the life for me. Murphy was pleasant company, but the rest of the bodyguard crew were untrained, on-edge thugs that Frank Nitti would have fired in a heartbeat.

With the exception of Murphy, who'd done a few years as a state cop before joining Huey, they had jack shit security experience. Messina was a damn ex-barber from the Roosevelt Hotel.

Also, I was winning at poker. Consistently winning. That didn't necessarily surprise me (I'm as self-deluded as the next average player), but these guys—even Murphy—were playing sloppy, and if there was one thing I would have confidence that guys like this could do, it's play cards.

They were nervous. On edge.

"Fuckin' death threats," Squinch McGee whispered. He had squinty little eyes behind thick wire-frame glasses—just the kind of guy you'd want handling firearms, right? "I don't take 'em serious. You take 'em serious?"

"The boss does," McCracken said, and shook his head. "I ain't seen this many cops in one place since that all-night diner shut down."

Messina was in the game now. "Why would anybody wanna kill the boss?"

"It sure ain't no picnic guardin' him," McCracken said, and shook his head again. "Cain't hardly keep up with him."

"Walks faster'n most men run," Murphy said. "Stops and starts, and stops and starts—it's like chasin' after a goddamn trolley car."

"It's like a goddamn game of musical chairs!" Squinch McGee said, holding his cards in two trembling hands.

A few hours later—after supper had been catered up to us from the cafeteria in the capitol's basement—I saw the truth of their words. Keeping up with the Kingfish, as he shuttled back and forth between the House on one side of the building, and the Senate way over on the other, was work for Jesse Owens.

Watching this banty rooster expending boundless energy was a thing of wonder: pressing the flesh, keeping an eye on what were apparently routine matters, he obviously wasn't taking any chances about getting his bills pushed through.

On one of the rare occasions I was able to keep up with him, falling alongside, I said, "Mind if I ask you something, Kingfish?"

"Only way to learn, son."

"Why do you fight so hard, when you got the battle won from the starting pistol?"

"Son," he laughed, "I ain't even begun to shoot from the taw, yet." He stopped on a dime, put a hand on my shoulder and his bulging brown eyes bore into me like needles. "Why do I run my fanny off like this? I'll tell ya why, and you'll wanna remember this: never write what you kin phone, never phone what you kin talk head-to-head, never talk what you kin nod, never nod what you kin wink."

And he winked at me, and took off like a race car.

He was halfway down the hall from us when a man in white stepped out from where he'd been standing beside a pillar and planted himself in front of Huey, blocking his way.

"Now, I don't want trouble with you, Tom," Huey was saying, as we moved quickly up.

"This time ya've gone *too* far, Huey," the man, who was elderly and frail-looking, said in a tone that managed to be both strong and quavering. Hatless, his snow white hair neatly combed, he wore wire-frame glasses and his face was handsome, dignified, but the sunken cheeks revealed the fragile skull under the creped skin.

"Now, you step aside, Tom."

"It's unconstitutional, this bill of yours. . . . We have a great president, and it shames every citizen of this fine state when you—"

By now, we had formed a half-circle around the pair. The Kingfish had made no indication he wanted us to intercede.

Huey thumped his chest. "*Ah* do the speeches aroun' here, you feeble-minded ol' fool! Git outa my way, and go slap damn to hell, while you're at it!"

The old man stepped forward, his right hand raised. "Don't curse me, you power-drunk bastard. . . ."

Huey took several steps back; his face was white. The thought of this old man hitting him had paralyzed the great dictator with fear!

There was a sharp *crack!* as Big George lurched forward and slapped the old man, knocking his legs out from under him like kindling.

Huey, brave again, stood with windmilling arms, raging over the fallen senior citizen. "You're the one who's *drunk*! Git 'im outa here! Git 'im charged with drunk and disorderly, disturbin' the goddamn peace or somethin'! And usin' obscenity in a goddamn fuckin' public place!"

"I'll take him," Messina snarled, and threw himself at the old man like a ball, grabbing the gent's collar and yanking him to his feet. The old boy looked dazed, his glasses askew.

I pulled Messina away by one thick arm; the look he flashed back at me might have been a rabid animal's. Nonetheless, I pushed myself between him and the old man. My right hand was on the butt of the nine-millimeter holstered under my left arm.

"Let *me* take him," I said to Huey, looking at him hard. "I'm done for the night, anyway."

Something akin to shame flickered in Huey's eyes when he saw my expression. Had the Kingfish been a human being, once upon a time?

Then the Kingfish gave me his prize-winning shit-eating grin. "You *have* put in a long day, Nate. Know where the Baton Rouge police department is?"

"I'm a detective," I said. "I'll find it."

A hand was on my arm; it felt like a giant's hand, but it was only mental-midget Messina's.

His eyes were glittering with emotion again, but a different one.

"Don't ever put your hand on me," he whispered, his face in mine.

"Sen Sen's only a nickel," I said. "Make an investment."

I hauled the old boy out of there, being just a little rough with him to keep the other bodyguards from looking at me too askance. We went out onto the landing of the capitol, with the forty-nine granite steps stretching down before us; the military guard remained, but at about half the force of before. The gardenlike grounds yawned before us in the pale light of a quarter moon, like a hazy paradise, but the weather made of the night a sultry, sweltering hell.

"Thank you, young man," the old gentleman said. "I've . . . I've never seen *you* before."

"I'm just passing through."

"You're from Chicago."

"How did you know?"

He straightened his glasses, smiled; his poise had returned. "I have a good ear for accents. You have a distinctly flat, nasal twang."

"I know. I'm taking something for it."

He frowned in thought. "You're no Cossack. Are you *really* a detective?"

"Yes."

"Investigating these murder threats?"

I frowned in thought. "Are you a reporter?"

"Used to be. Work for the administration, now."

"What administration?"

"Why, FDR's, of course. Publicity director for the Federal Education Program. Huey wants to pass a law so he can put people like me in jail."

"You do strike me as a dangerous type."

His smile might have been a pixie's. "If you like . . . I can direct you to the police department. . . ."

"Why, do you *want* to go to jail?"

"If you don't take me there, he'll fire you."

Fuck the two-fifty a day. The list of things I will do for money is damn near endless; but it doesn't include aiding and abetting the assault of elderly gentlemen.

"Doesn't matter," I said. "I'm quitting tomorrow. You got an automobile here?"

"Yes, indeed."

"Can you drop me somewhere?"

"Yes, indeed!"

The ten-floor Heidelberg Hotel was on Lafayette Street. The Mississippi was damn near in its backyard; and next door was a Victorian residence with a clothesline, and cows and horses grazing in the yard. Baton Rouge was the goddamndest capital city I ever saw.

The hotel's top-floor restaurant, the Hunt Room, was decorated with fox-and-hounds prints and mounted examples of the taxidermist's art. Alice Jean and I chose to sit under the canopy in the open-air section of the restaurant. We could see the Mississippi and the quarter moon's ivory reflection on its black surface; we could see cows belonging to the family in the Victorian home munching in a small pasture separated from the river by some trees. A paddlewheeler's mournful whistle echoed down the river.

I had just told Alice Jean—who looked lovely in a white organdy dress with red polka dots and a matching red beret—about the old ex-reporter getting slapped.

"If I hadn't stepped in," I said, "Messina would have beat him to a pulp, and Huey would have sent him to jail on trumped-up 'disturbing the peace' charges."

She was sipping a Ramos Gin Fizz, a specialty of the house that Huey had imported from the Roosevelt Hotel in

New Orleans. " 'Tom' you said? That was probably Tom Harris . . . they're old enemies, Huey and Tom."

I set down my glass of rum. "It doesn't bother you? Doesn't it surprise you that—"

"Nothing Huey does, at this point, would surprise me." She was smiling but her eyes were infinitely sad.

"Nothing?" I hadn't told her yet. "What if I told you Huey knows we're sleeping together?"

She almost choked on her latest sip of cocktail. I waited for her to regain her composure; she never quite did. Finally she said, "Can we discuss this in private?"

We sat in her room—the rooms at the Heidelberg were modest, at best, small, colorless studies in cheap wood veneer and cut-rate carpeting. The hotel was the tallest in the city but, remember—it had cows next door.

I was in a straight-back chair; she sat on the edge of the double bed, wrinkling the cream-color spread.

"Huey knows?"

I nodded. "In fact, I think he set us up."

Her frown was bewildered; her eyes flying. "Set us up?"

"Huey and me hung around together in Chicago, remember. Back in '32. He knows my style."

She made a disgusted kiss of her cupie mouth. "Your . . . style?"

"Yeah . . . yeah, that I'm a randy son of a bitch, okay? We've been together less than a week, and I've already cheated on you."

That was twice I surprised her.

Boy, those eyes could get big. "*Cheated* on me? Why, you son of a bitch!"

"Randy son of a bitch. I don't remember anything about her, if that's any consolation. She might've been a redhead. Murphy Roden and I apparently picked up some college girls in the French Quarter a few nights ago."

"Apparently?"

I shrugged. "Too much tequila. Jesus Christ, Alice Jean, I'm no angel, and neither are you. Don't you get it? The Kingfish was counting on that. He put us together so we'd maybe become an item, in which case I'd keep you outa his hair for a while. You're bad for his image, remember? And it worked."

"Why, that bastard . . ." But for some reason, she was smiling a little.

I smiled, too. "You gotta admire that kind of manipulation."

She was nodding. "And I gotta admit, you and me are a good match, Heller."

"Thanks."

"And all the while, he was payin' you, how much?"

"Two-fifty a day."

She shook her head. "Only Huey. Only Huey." She narrowed her eyes appraisingly. "Why'd you tell me this? When did you find out?"

"Just yesterday." I stood. "Look. You're a great gal, and more fun than a barrel of chorus girls, and I'm gonna miss the hell out of you . . . but, baby—I want *out* of this southern-fried insane asylum."

Now both her eyes and her smile were sad. "Goin' home, Heller?"

I nodded.

"Don't like the way the Kingfish does business, huh?"

I came over and sat on the bed next to her. My voice was quiet, almost tender as I said, "I can handle the idea of a little honest graft. Hell, if it wasn't for patronage, I'd never've made it onto the Chicago P.D. But this Gestapo stuff . . . shit. It's for the fuckin' birds."

She was nodding. "So, then—I would imagine you'll be donating all the money."

"What money?"

She put on an innocent air. "Why, the money Huey paid you. You'll be donating it all to charity, of course."

I grinned wickedly at her. "You wanna know what I'm gonna do?"

"Sure. I wanna know what you're gonna do."

I put my hand on one of those round, high, firm breasts and exerted just enough pressure to make her lean back and she smiled slyly as I climbed on top of her.

"I'm gonna do the same thing to you," I said, undoing my belt, "that Huey P. Long's doing to Louisiana. . . ."

The next morning—Sunday—just after nine o'clock, the House Ways and Means Committee assembled in an upstairs public hearing room at the capitol. Seated on a riser on a table that stretched horizontally along the wall, the fourteen committee members faced a small table where citizens could testify or speak their minds, and, behind that, a gallery of benches where citizens could observe the sacred lawmaking process.

Murphy Roden, Joe Messina, Squinch McGee, Big George McCracken and myself were stretched along the rear wall like a hoodlum honor guard.

The Kingfish—resplendent in tan linen, red-and-green tie, black-and-white shoes—was seated at the witness table, and his presence was no doubt responsible for the packed house. Abuzz with excitement at being in the same room as the great man, the God-fearing folk filling the gallery had either skipped church or gone to early services, men in straw fedoras and white shirts and black suspenders, women in Sunday bonnets and floral-print frocks. Farmers and other working-class salt of the earth, here to worship their rustic savior. A few representatives of the "lyin' press" were scattered throughout the gallery, as well.

The morning outside the open windows was a little cloudy but windless and dry and hot; there was no sign that God had noticed August was over and September had supposedly arrived. Ceiling fans whirred and the gallery spectators used cardboard fans, some of which said "I'm a Long Fan"; flies droned and swooped and, when swatted, died.

First thing this morning, I had asked Huey to have somebody book me a plane or a train back to Chicago, for tomorrow; this would be my last day. He'd thanked me for my services. We were still pals.

I had one last day of Loozyana craziness to endure, at the not inconsiderable $250 daily rate. And while I was almost certain to be appalled on occasion, I was equally sure of being entertained.

Right now, for example, Huey was chairing the Ways and Means Committee meeting from the witness table.

"Of course you know," Huey was saying, pouring himself a glass of ice water from a sweating glass pitcher, "I'm not here in any official capacity—I'm merely here to discuss these measures, a priv'lige accorded every Loozyana citizen. Now, shall we begin our discussion?"

All but one of the committee members nodded; a young, dark-haired fellow was glowering at the senator.

"That's Jack Williamson," Murphy whispered. "Lake Charles. He's the only anti-Long man on the committee."

"This first bill, Senator," Williamson was saying, "rearranging the thirteenth and fifteenth districts . . . you of course realize it, in effect, gerrymanders Judge Pavy out of office."

"Nonsense," Huey said. "The Judge retains his office until January 1, 1937. . . . When it comes election time, he simply has to run in a new district, is all."

Williamson arched a skeptical eyebrow. "Did the people of these districts request this change be made?"

Huey stared at the young representative for a long time; but Williamson did not wither. In fact, he repeated his question.

And Huey finally said, with a smile about as convincing as mail-order false teeth, "Yes, the people of Evangeline Parish are ever' bit behind it, and the St. Landry Parish members of the House are all for it. Now, call the question."

The bill passed committee, 13 to 1.

But at least Williamson got on the record his objections to the various bills Huey roller-coastered through, most of which were gerrymanders or assaults on Huey's enemies in New Orleans; but the anti-FDR bill sparked the biggest discussion, one that woke up the press reps in the gallery.

"What exactly is the purpose of this bill, Senator?" Williamson asked.

Huey answered grandly: "Why, to enable us to carry out the great principles of the Constitution of the Yew-nited States."

"I see. Then it's not designed to prevent the expenditure of federal funds in Louisiana?"

For once Huey was thrown; his answer was a vague muttering: "It intends to prevent the violation of the Constitution of the United States."

"What do you have in mind, Senator? What's the purpose of this bill?"

Huey flared; his voice was a roar. "That certain sacred rights are reserved to the states and the people! That whoever violates the Constitution of the United States in the great state of Louisiana is subject to a misdemeanor punishable by a fine and a jail sentence!"

"You're willing to make law of this vindictive, patently unconstitutional claptrap," Williamson said, ruffling the pages of the bill in the air disgustedly, "even though its chief effect would be to keep vast sums of federal money *out* of your own state?"

Huey slammed a fist on the witness table; his water glass and pitcher sloshed and spilled, some.

"Young man," the Kingfish said indignantly, "I will preserve the Constitution of the Yew-nited States at *any* cost! We're still Jeffersonian Democrats in Loozyana!"

Applause and cheers from the gallery rocked the room. Shouts of support echoed: "Hot dog!" "Give 'em hell, Huey!" and such like. It was the Oklahoma fairgrounds all over again.

This was a crowd that apparently relished the idea of being deprived of federal funds.

I shook my head.

"What's wrong?" Murphy whispered.

"I gotta get back to Chicago," I said, "where people understand the value of a dollar."

By early afternoon, Huey had pushed thirty-one bills through the committee.

He bragged about it, over the lunch he had sent up from the basement cafeteria to that twenty-fourth-floor suite. "That'll put a crimp in that crip's plans! Sumbitch thinks he can run *my* state!"

He sat at a white-topped table in the kitchenette area of the suite, eating with the boys. I'll spare you the brutal details, but watching Messina put away meat loaf and mashed potatoes was an appetite killer; suffice to say even *Huey* didn't eat off Messina's plate.

We bodyguards played cards again, all afternoon, while Huey entertained a stream of legislators and lobbyists and the like, on errands of patronage and politics; the only one of these I recognized from previous sessions was Reverend Smith, who dropped by with some Share the Wealth Club literature for Huey.

But the paramount topic seemed to be lining up January's primary ticket, and in Louisiana, the Democratic primary was the only election that counted. One visitor in particular seemed even more concerned about this topic than Huey.

You had to look hard and close to see that they were brothers. The cleft chin was the only near giveaway. Earl Long's eyes were dark and hard and sharp, but everything else about his face was soft, and his smile was a nervous, unsure, sideways thing, while his voice was the gravel road his words were forced to travel.

"I know we done had our ups and downs," Earl said. In a cream-color pinstripe suit, his red-and-black tie loose, the younger, slimmer Long stood before his brother, who was seated on a sofa in his shirtsleeves with an ankle resting on a knee, a foot wobbling a slipper.

"You mean, like when you swore an oath I took a ten-grand bribe," Huey said pleasantly.

"I mended that fence," Earl snapped. "I stumped this goddamn state from pea patch to picket fence for your good fren' Fournet."

Huey was nodding. "Yes, you did. Much 'ppreciated."

"Anyway, I know you're considerin' candidates for governor . . . and I remember what you tol' me back in '32, when I asked you to gimme the lootenant guv'nr slot."

"That's right," Huey said. "I said I couldn't use ya, 'cause I didn't want people talkin' 'Long dynasty.' We got enough stupid damn dictator talk goin' as it is."

"So, then, I'm not bein' considered."

"Not at this time, no, Earl."

Earl was lighting up a Camel. "Who is, then?"

"I'm leanin' toward Dick Leche."

"Leche? A goddamn state's appeals judge?"

"He used to be O.K. Allen's secretary. He knows how to take orders."

"And I don't."

"No. You're my brother, ain't ya? Or is it true Mama found ya on the porch in a picnic basket?"

Earl shook his head sullenly, and paced and smoked; he held his cigarette tight between thumb and forefinger.

"You got somethin' else on your mind, Earl?"

Earl stopped pacing and came over and sat by his brother. "I don't think you oughta be gerrymandering Judge Pavy outa his district, 'long about now."

"You don't, huh?"

"No." Earl shook his head. "Huey, things are just a little bit too hot and little bit too tense right now. I think it's a bad idea to even have a special session at all, at this here time."

Huey shrugged. "Horse is out of the barn, Earl. Too late to stop 'er now, even if I wanted to."

Earl smiled; was there sarcasm in it? Or maybe envy? "You can do anything, Huey. You're the Kingfish."

Huey smiled back at his brother; patted him on the leg. "You go on up to Winnfield, if you cain't stand it, and listen, here—nothin's gonna happen. Things ain't that hot or that tense."

Earl studied Huey for what seemed like forever; then he sighed, nodded, crushed out his cigarette in a glass ashtray, stood, waved his brother farewell, and went out.

The next subject to gain admittance to the Kingfish's court looked more like Huey's brother than Earl. He had the same oval face, similar earnest features, even a cleft chin (if not as prominent as Huey's); as with Huey, the visitor's imposing figure gave an impression of bulk that disguised strength.

The Kingfish remained seated on the sofa casually, as the visitor—immaculate in a lightweight tan suit with a brown tie, holding his straw hat in hand, a supplicant with head bowed—paid his respects.

"What brings *you* by this afternoon, Dr. Vidrine?"

"I just wanted to thank you for seeing that Charity Hospital got its full appropriation, Senator."

Huey beamed. "Well, you're welcome. You been doin' a fine job there, and, more importantly, I couldn't be more tickled with the way things are workin' out, out at LSU."

Vidrine's smile was shy. "There were a lot of skeptics who didn't think either one of us knew what we were doing."

"Them aristocratic snobs on the board at Tulane, what the hell do they know? They were overcrowded, and Louisiana needed goddamn doctors! Maybe Rome wasn't built in a day, but it just took me sayin' so, and, whiz, bang—we had a new medical school. And now what? Just four years later? What's the enrollment this fall?"

Huey gestured with a hand for Vidrine to sit next to him, and he did.

"Nine hundred," Vidrine said, humbly proud.

"Increased the enrollment times nine in only four years. Damn! Now, that's an accomplishment." He patted the doctor on the shoulder like a child who'd performed well. "When I appointed you super'ntendent of Noo Awlins Char'ty Hospital, I wanted to show the worl' that a back-country doctor like you was ever' bit as good as any big-city sawbones. Thanks for not makin' a liar outa me, son."

Vidrine nodded and smiled sheepishly; he was behaving like a new priest in the presence of the Pope.

"Got your pretty little wife along?" Huey said, and suddenly rose, and so did Vidrine, who sensed he was being dismissed.

"Yes, I do. . . ."

Huey walked him toward the door. "You put tonight's dinner at the Hunt Room at the Heidelberg on the ol' Kingfish's tab, y'hear?"

"That's not necessary. . . ."

"Don't insult me, now, by rejectin' my generosity."

"Yes, sir," Vidrine said, smiled, nodded and went out.

I was shuffling the cards. Quietly, I asked Murphy, "What's *his* background? Seems like a kinda unassuming type to be holding such fancy administrative jobs."

"Dr. Arthur Vidrine—former general practitioner from Ville Platte," Murphy said, as if that answered my question.

"What's Ville Platte?"

"Bump in the road, over Opelousas way."

I began dealing, Black Mariah again. "How does that qualify him for anything?"

"Gimme a damn spade, would you? He captained the Long campaign in those parts."

No further explanation was necessary for this Chicago boy.

A little later another unassuming character entered for an audience with the Kingfish. Heavyset, crowding six feet, he made himself seem smaller by hunching his shoulders and holding his straw fedora in front of him with two hands; under eyebrows that seemed perpetually raised, two squinty slits appeared, and a nervous smile curved beneath a nondescript beak. The overall impression he gave was of bemused embarrassment.

"You wanted to see me, Kingfish?"

"Yeah, come in and sit down!" The Kingfish was on the couch again.

"Who's *this* guy?" I whispered to Murphy.

"Jim Smith—president of LSU," he whispered back.

"Now what the goddamn hell is this about a *ridin'* academy out at the college?"

Smith shrugged, hat still in his hand; the little smile remained embarrassed. "Thelma likes to ride. I bought her a thoroughbred, and she likes wearing those cute outfits. She thought the coeds might enjoy . . ."

Huey was shaking his head. "When I hired you, on the advice of a stationery salesman I might add, the idea was to get rid of them goddamn highfalutin suckers over at the university, and put in some down-to-earth folks. Now your wife is havin' fancy parties and puttin' on airs and at her biddin' you're usin' my funds to start a fuckin' *ridin'* academy?"

"Well . . . as I was saying, it's a nice activity . . ."

"For the coeds. Right. Well, I see in the paper where two girls fell off them horses on their fannies, last week."

The smile got more nervous. "Do I have to tell you about the lying press, Senator?"

"No, you don't. I have three words for you: sell them plugs."

"Senator?"

"Sell them plugs! Get rid of them horses! No more ridin' academy. Besides which, my people tell me you may wanna talk to the missus about this handsome, strappin' former Army man she hired to be her groomsman. Word to the wise."

The smile disappeared; he hung his head. "Yes, Senator."

"Now. This comin' fall . . . those journalism students I expelled last year, they'll be back on the *Reveille*, I suppose."

"Yes sir. Except for those that graduated."

"Well, tell those prima donnas that if they print any more unflatterin' letters or editorials about me and my administration, *they* won't *be* graduatin'."

"I'll make that clear, Senator. I've already told them I would fire the entire faculty and expel the complete student body before I'd offend you, sir."

The Kingfish's grin just about burst his face. "You're my kinda educator, Jimmy. Now . . . you handpick the new editor, and tell him LSU is Huey Long's university, and no bastard is gonna criticize Huey Long on Huey Long's own goddamn money! Is that clear?"

"Crystal, Senator."

"I enjoy our little talks, Jimmy. Go, now."

He stood. "Yes, Senator."

And he was up and out.

The Kingfish sat shaking his head. He said to nobody in particular, "Now that's my brand of university president. Not a straight bone in his body, but he does what I tell 'im to."

That evening, the Kingfish was in top form, bounding across Memorial Hall, down this corridor, down that one, outdistancing his half-dozen thuglike guards, with whom I blended in disturbingly well. Brushing by lobbyists, tourists, legislators, stopping to chat sometimes for a couple minutes, sometimes a couple seconds, he finally strutted into the House of Representatives like a rich uncle arriving late at the family reunion.

The human dynamo bounded up and down the aisles, showing off that shit-eating grin, pressing the flesh, laughing loud, an important man making his minions feel important, too. Now he was crouched beside this member's seat, whispering, now he was jumping up like a jack-in-the-box at a question directed to him by another member, now he was leaning in at *that* member's seat, bellowing with shared laughter, only to suddenly propel himself up to the dais, to consult the Speaker, before strutting back down an aisle, grimacing, shouting. And then the process began again.

The balcony was packed with spectators, whose eyes followed the bouncing ball of the Kingfish, who was after all the whole show here. The legislature rubber-stamping process was devoid of drama.

Finally Huey ambled back up to the dais and helped himself to the swivel armchair by the Speaker of the House. No one objected; certainly no one was surprised.

The down-home crudity of Huey's style was at odds with this magnificent tan-and-brown marble chamber; a frieze of the state's plants and animals hugged the ceiling, and various fixtures were also decorated with stylish flora and fauna. But the massive walnut voting panel, behind the Speaker's chair, invoked an altar, and the place resembled nothing so much as a Protestant church with a very wealthy congregation.

Our hoodlum honor guard was again assembled at the rear, seated behind a rail, with the exception of Big George; maybe he and his brown-bagged tommy gun weren't welcome in the House. Huey had told us that if any pro-Long legislator got confused and pushed the "no" button on any of his bills, one of us was to guide that lawmaker's hand to "yes."

I was no judge, but the going-through-the-motions session seemed to be moving right along. Absentmindedly, I checked my watch—it was nine on the nose. When I glanced up, Huey—still seated up on the dais—was waving at somebody in the back of the room. Trying to get their attention.

It took me a while, but I finally got it.

Me? I mouthed to him.

And his head bobbed up and down, yes.

I wandered up to the dais, thinking that the floor of the Louisiana House of Representatives was one place I never expected to be, and looked up at Huey behind the dais like he was the teacher and I was about seven years old.

"See that feller over there?" the Kingfish asked.

I glanced over where he was pointing, and between the railing and the wall, a handful of people were talking. Possibly legislators, although there were reporters and various political hangers-on lurking about, as well. The only one I recognized was my old friend, lobbyist Louis LeSage.

"You mean LeSage?" I asked.

"No! The one smokin' that big old ceegar."

A dark-haired guy about forty was indeed enjoying a "big old ceegar." I recognized him as one of the many political appointees who'd stopped by the suite on the twenty-fourth floor to chat with the Kingfish this afternoon.

"I'm about to give ya your last official assignment on my staff," the Kingfish said.

"What is it?"

He raised his eyebrows and grinned like the greedy kid he was. "I want you to get me half a dozen of them Corona Belvedere cigars."

"I thought you quit smoking."

He frowned. "It would be my luck to hire the only man in Chicaga with a goddamn conscience. I'm in the mood to celebrate, son! Get me them cigars!"

I shrugged. "Sure. Where?"

"Downstairs in the cafeteria. They got a box of 'em down there, at the tobacca stand. Now go on, git outa here—make yourself useful! *Earn* that two-fifty a day. . . ."

So I went down the stairs to the cafeteria. The white-tile-and-gleaming-chrome restaurant was deserted except for the help, two girls behind the food line and a few colored guys back in the kitchen. I got myself a cup of coffee, decided against the apple pie with cheese, and took my time buying Huey his cigars, so I could flirt with the pretty blonde behind the tobacco counter. She had eyes that were a robin's egg blue and a Southern accent you could have ladled onto pancakes. She was also chewing gum: nobody's perfect.

"I get off at ten, han'some," she said. "Why? You got somethin' in mind?"

Us randy sumbitches always do, but before I could mount a reply that would combine just enough sincerity with the vague promise of sin, a sound, from above, interrupted.

Muffled thunder.

"What the hell was that?" the blonde asked.

"Not thunder," I said, and ran, pushing open one of the heavy glass doors like it was spun sugar, rushing up into the stairwell, where the rumbling sound continued and goddamn it, I knew what it was, *not thunder,* but the sound of blood being spilled: gunfire, roaring gunfire.

Not one gun, but many, an artillery barrage of handguns and maybe a machine gun. . . .

Pulling my nine-millimeter out from under my left shoulder, I went up the stairs two at a time, the echo of continuous gunfire rumbling down the stairwell like an earthquake.

I practically collided with him, as he came staggering around the corner, onto a landing of the stairway: the Kingfish!

His mouth was bloody, but his suit was pristine; his eyes lighted up at the sight of me, and he held out his arms as if he wanted to hug me.

I slipped my arm around his shoulder, as he leaned on the railing. I managed, "What the hell? . . ."

"I'm shot," the Kingfish sputtered, and in the process spit blood all over my suit coat.

We were both shouting: the echoing thunder of gunfire upstairs roared on, unabated. We were in a terrible fever dream and neither of us could wake up. He was stumbling down the stairs, weaving, and I supported him as he tried to walk, and guided him out of the stairwell, down a hallway and to a bank of glass doors at a side entrance, pushed one open with my shoulder and drunk-walked him outside.

When the glass door shut, the thunder of guns finally stopped—or did it just seem to?

I had no idea what had happened up there, except that it had been some form of hell on earth. I knew, for certain, only two things: I had failed this man leaning limply against me; and that I mustn't fail him now.

I leaned the Kingfish against the glass doors, like I was balancing a bass fiddle against a wall, and ran out under the portico into the driveway and stood in front of two approaching headlights with my arms outstretched.

The beat-up black four-door Ford screeched to a halt, more from age than speed; the legislative session—with its promise of Kingfish theatrics—had attracted a packed house of spectators, starting to leisurely clear out now that the show was over, wandering into the sultry night, getting their cars from the parking lots on either side of the building. Most of these good citizens weren't aware a second, bigger show had eclipsed the main attraction. . . .

I was still standing like a scarecrow in front of his car when the driver leaned his head out and, more startled than angry, yelled, "What the hell's the idea, bub?"

I spoke as I came around to him. "Where's the nearest hospital?"

"Are you crazy?" He was a little man in his thirties, straw hat, wire-frame spectacles, suspenders over a white T-shirt; a farmer, most likely, and a poor one. Your typical Huey supporter.

"The Senator's been shot, you dumb rube! Where's the nearest hospital?"

He opened his eyes wide and pointed. Through the portals

of the portico, the statehouse lights danced on the small, man-made Capitol Lake, and on just the other side of it, not a quarter of a mile away, the lights of a low-slung building winked on the black surface of the water, as well.

"Our Lady of the Lake," he said.

"What are you talking about?"

"It's a hospital, ya dumb city slicker!"

I yanked his door open. "Help me with the Senator. . . ."

The driver got out, leaving his motor running, and now he saw Huey leaning against the glass doors like a statue that lost its pedestal. "Jesus Christ . . . it's Huey Long."

"Help me with him!"

We drunk-walked him to the car, eased him into the backseat; Huey didn't cry out or even moan—he was barely conscious. I sat back there with him as the car drove through the portico, made a U-turn and pulled around to head north on a street that hugged the wooded lakeside. The farmer had the old sedan floored, but top speed seemed to be about forty. The skyscraper Huey had built in this wilderness receded behind us; the motor thrummed in tune with the nocturnal drone of crickets. Between statehouse and hospital was a little bitty stretch of untamed Louisiana. . . .

With both hands, Huey held on to the right side of his upper belly; he lay draped across the backseat, his head resting on my shoulder. I kept an arm around him, as if he were a big child I were comforting.

"We're almost there," I said. "Very close."

"I wonder . . ."

His eyes were wild.

"What, Kingfish?"

". . . I wonder why he hit me?"

He closed his eyes. I patted his shoulder gently as the lights of the sprawling three-story brick building that was Our Lady of the Lake Sanitarium grew larger before us.

The beat-up sedan pulled under the brick canopy of the

emergency entrance and jolted to a stop. I got out on my side and came around and opened Huey's door. The driver was still behind the wheel.

"Give me some help, goddamnit!" I said.

"I helped you," he said. "I brung you here."

I half-dragged Huey out of the backseat—he was just awake enough to be cooperative—and was standing there with the Kingfish leaning his full weight against me when the driver said, "I didn't even vote for the son of a bitch," and peeled off in a cloud of gravel dust.

Shit! And here I thought Huey had the farm vote sewed up. . . .

I lifted Huey gently up, on his back, onto a rolling metal stretcher-table that waited by the emergency room doors; he groaned, moaned, but did not cry out. He seemed semidelirious, muttering, "Why?" and "Why'd he shoot me?" and "I don't understan' " and variations and combinations. All I could see on the suit coat was a quarter-size black powder burn surrounding a small bullet hole, and some flecks of blood. But his mouth bubbled bloody foam. . . .

There was a bell to summon aid, and I rang it, rang it hard, and kept ringing, but nothing happened, so I kept ringing while I pounded my fist on the nearest of the double doors so hard the goddamn hinges started coming loose. Finally a ghostlike figure of a nun in her flowing white habit came rushing into view, and pushed open the doors.

"It's the Senator, Sister," I said.

Her pale pretty face was a cameo of concern as she went to the Kingfish, stretched out on the rolling table. "Oh, dear—what's this?"

"He's been shot."

"Help me wheel him to the elevator."

We pushed him through the doors and onto an elevator, which the Sister operated.

"What happened?" she asked. "Who shot Senator Long?"

"I don't know. I wasn't there."

I told her how he'd come stumbling down the stairs, and I'd commandeered a car to bring him here.

She was shaking her head. Then she said something that surprised me, something I'll never forget: "This was bound to happen."

We got off on the third floor; most of the lights were out in the hospital, it was after hours, but things were coming alive, nuns floating down the hallway like pelicans, and other medical personnel, nurses, interns, were starting to gather, as well. It all seemed unreal; the world whirled as we rolled the silent Kingfish down dark narrow hallways and finally toward, and through, the double doors labeled EMERGENCY OPERATING ROOM.

Suddenly the world was blinding white, as more ghosts gathered 'round the Kingfish and eased him from the metal stretcher onto a sheet-covered operating table. A white-garbed intern, with no surgical mask, a blond boy who looked impossibly young, approached with a scalpel; but all he did was start razoring off the Kingfish's clothes.

Huey was conscious, but he wasn't saying anything; he was staring at the ceiling with wide empty eyes. If his chest hadn't been heaving, I'd have taken him for dead.

Another intern, a dark-haired boy, was swabbing out Huey's mouth. "Little abrasion." He turned to glance at me; I was keeping back, out of the way. "Did he hit himself against something?"

"I don't know," I said. "Maybe he stumbled against a wall, coming down the stairwell. . . ."

The blond intern was still cutting Huey's coat open when a big dark curly-haired man with a cleft jaw burst in, sweating, breathing hard. I recognized him at once, and was relieved to see him.

"Dr. Vidrine!" the blond intern said. "We're glad to see you, sir . . . the Senator's been shot."

"Ran all the way over here, from the capitol." He was removing his coat, and a nurse was taking it. "My wife and I were attending the legislative session. . . . There was a bad shooting over there." He walked to the prone Kingfish, still speaking to the intern. "Word was it involved Senator Long, and I thought maybe somebody might have had the presence of mind to bring him over here. . . ."

"That gentleman did," the dark-haired intern said, pointing.

I nodded. "Dr. Vidrine."

He frowned at me. "Have we met?"

"I've been working as one of Huey's bodyguards. I was in the Kingfish's suite when you dropped by this afternoon."

He was leaning over the Kingfish, but speaking to me. "I see. Did you witness this?"

"No," I said, and told him briefly what little I knew.

"Your quick action probably saved this man's life," Vidrine said. He was looking at the Kingfish's wound, a small bluish hole under the right nipple. "Huey?" the doctor asked gently. "Do you recognize me? It's Arthur Vidrine."

Huey nodded.

"Senator, we're going to need to clean this wound."

"Go . . . go ahead."

"What happened here on your lip, Huey?"

"That's where he hit me! Why'd he hit me, anyway?"

This seemed to upset Huey, and Vidrine let go of the topic. He turned to the nun who'd helped me bring Huey in. "Sister Michael, can you make some phone calls, at once?"

"Certainly."

"Begin with Dr. Maes, in New Orleans. He's the best surgeon in the state. Then call Dr. Lorio, here in Baton Rouge . . . he's the Senator's personal physician. . . ."

Huey raised his head. "Am I going to live, doc?"

His voice was as casual as if he were ordering a ham sandwich; but his eyes were wild.

"Huey, I feel certain everything will come out jus' fine. Now, Sister. . . ."

"Sister!"

It was Huey, crying out. Not in pain. Fear.

"Yes, Senator?"

"You won't lie to me, Sister. How bad is it?"

"Gunshot cases are always serious," she said softly. "It's best to be prepared."

"Would you pray for me, Sister?"

She took his hand. "We'll pray together, Senator."

"Sister . . . I'm a Baptist. . . ."

The kindness of her smile was heartbreaking. "Just repeat after me, Senator. . . . Oh my God, I am heartily sorry . . ."

"Oh my God I am heartily sorry," Huey muttered.

Vidrine stepped away from the surgical table as the Sister and Huey prayed. Another nurse, a pleasant-looking brunette who was not a nun, approached Vidrine and said that she would contact the doctors for him.

"Once you've located Maes and Lorio," Vidrine said, "call Seymour Weiss in New Orleans, at the Roosevelt Hotel. Then contact the Long family. . . . Weiss will have their private number."

The nurse nodded and hurried out. Vidrine motioned for the blond intern to come over. They huddled for a conference, close by.

"I want his blood pressure taken," Vidrine said, "and blood tests for a transfusion. . . . God, I hope that isn't necessary."

"A transfusion?"

Vidrine shook his head, no. "That prayer."

"I firmly resolve, with the help of thy Grace," Sister Michael was saying.

"I firmly resolve, with the help of thy Grace," Huey weakly repeated.

"That's the Act of Contrition," Vidrine whispered.

". . . to confess my sins," the nun said.

". . . confess my sins," Huey repeated.

Even a nonpracticing Jew like yours truly knew what that was: the prayer of a dying Catholic.

Shortly after that, Vidrine asked me to leave the operating room, and I was happy to comply. I leaned against the wall, in the hallway, as hospital staff rushed in and out; I was having a look at my suit, to see just how much blood Huey had spit on it. It wasn't too bad. Luckily it wasn't the white linen.

A lanky, lantern-jawed guy in a brown suit and boater-style straw hat came down the hallway, moving like a man trying to catch a bus; his breath was heaving—he'd been running. When he saw me, his eyes narrowed.

He stood before me. "You're one of Huey's bodyguards!"

He had a husky voice and an affable manner; both rubbed me the wrong way.

"Yeah. So?"

"You're the *new* one. From Chicago."

"And who the hell are you?"

"Chick Frampton," he said, and extended his hand. I just looked at it. "I'm with the *Item-Tribune*."

That was a New Orleans paper.

He withdrew the hand, raised an eyebrow. "I'm also on the payroll, if that helps any. Statistician in the Attorney General's office."

I smiled a little. "Not part of 'the lyin' press,' then?"

"No. More, the Long organization's unofficial press agent." He gestured toward the double doors of the operating room. "Kingfish in there?"

I nodded.

He grinned. "I figured as much! I spoke to Huey just minutes . . . hell, *seconds*, before the shit hit the fan."

"What happened?"

He shrugged in frustration, rolled his eyes. "I didn't see it! Biggest story of the century, and I'm a closed door away!"

"How so?"

He leaned in, chummily, gesturing with a loose-fingered hand. "I was in the governor's office, in the anteroom, see, usin' the phone callin' an item in. I was just about to leave, my hand on the damn doorknob, when what do I hear but a shot! I crack open the door and see Senator Long stumblin' by, movin' down the hall, claspin' his side with his hands."

"Christ, man, what else did you see?"

His eyes widened, trying to recall it all; even for a trained reporter, a chaotically unfolding event can be overwhelming.

"Murphy Roden was strugglin' with a guy in a white suit; Murph had his back to me, kind of stooped over the guy, little Caspar Milquetoast feller. Then Murphy fires, and backs away, and fires some more, and the guy kinda shook, like a kid gettin' shook by the shoulders, only he was free-standin'—then, shit, all of them bodyguards of Huey's started firin' into the guy. Messina, some state troopers, too, a mess of 'em, blazin' away like a Wild West show. The guy kinda pitched forward, fell down with his head near this marble pillar, by the wall. Face to the floor. Shot to shit."

I'd missed all the fun. Thank God.

"Hell," I said. "Who was he?"

"The shooter? Nobody knows."

I thought about the old gentleman who'd had the altercation with Huey and his bodyguards last night. "Not Tom Harris?"

"Hell, no! I know Tom. I don't know this poor bastard. I don't know if anybody'll know 'im, now. Skinny little bastard must weigh a thousand pounds."

"A thousand pounds?"

His mouth twitched. "With all that lead in 'im."

He dug out a pack of Lucky Strikes and lighted one up.

I said, "You're the first one here, besides me and Huey. How'd you manage it, Frampton?"

He waved out his match. "Mrs. Frampton's little boy is a reporter. I went in the direction Huey went, and followed the breadcrumb trail of blood drops on the marble floor, and on down the steps . . ."

"I met him coming down. Brought him here."

He grinned again, snapped his fingers. "I figured somethin' like that happened! I talked to some bystanders 'round the rear entrance who said they saw somebody pile Huey into a car and took off toward here." His breathing had slowed; the cigarette had helped calm him. "Ran the hell over here. How's Huey doin'?"

"Well, that depends."

"On what?"

"On whether you consider getting read the Last Rites is a good sign."

He thought about that. Then he pulled a notebook out of an inside suit coat pocket. "I better start callin' people," he said, and rushed off.

Where any of this left me, who the hell knew? Now that Frampton would get the word out, this joint would soon be swarming with cops, bodyguards, politicians, reporters, sightseers, what-have-you. Best plan I could come up with was to get out before that started happening.

And I couldn't see where I was of any use here, anyway. So I wandered downstairs, looking for a way out, and on a first-floor hallway, just off the main reception area, I almost bumped into Murphy Roden, being guided along by a young highway patrolman as if under arrest.

Murphy's face, around his eyes, was scorched.

"Jesus, Murphy!" I said.

He couldn't see me; his eyes were tearing, but he was not crying. "Heller?"

He was blind; whether temporarily or not, I didn't know. But right now, this was a blind guy. . . .

I took his other arm. "I know how to get to the emergency area," I told the highway patrolman, and took the lead.

"What the hell happened, Murphy?" I asked.

"Muzzle flash," he mumbled, and passed out.

We dragged him onto the elevator, and I played operator, taking us up to three.

"What the hell happened over there?" I asked the patrolman.

"Damned if I know," he said. "Somebody took a shot at the Kingfish, and then all hell broke loose."

The back of Murphy's suit coat was scorched, and his neck was powder-burned, too; he'd obviously been caught in the middle of one hell of a gun battle.

Murphy came around just enough to walk a little as the patrolman and I guided him toward the emergency operating room, where the Kingfish was still being tended to. The blond intern stepped into the hall and had a look at Murphy.

"We better get those eyes swabbed," he said to his patient, and he and the highway patrolman helped Murphy toward another examining room.

I didn't go with them. I went back downstairs and out the front entry, where I could see the parking lot of the hospital—almost empty now, but not for long—and the lake with the reflection of Huey's statehouse shimmering on it.

The statehouse itself was ablaze with lights. Sirens howled in the night; horns honked. A line of cars was heading this way on the street that edged the lake.

I walked toward the tower. My suit was sticking to me; the heat was as unbearable as the tension. I walked beside the lake, on the grass, by the trees, as cars whizzed by me, on their way to help turn a tragedy into full-scale pandemonium.

The capitol had already been cordoned off. A human ring of highway patrolmen encircled the building, with a few extra at every exit. Many had riot guns or tommy guns slung over their arms. Flashing my Louisiana Bureau of Criminal Investigation badge, I got past the troops, going in the back way, through the portico entrance where I had taken Huey out. I kept the badge in my palm, showing it to the various patrolmen I encountered as I retraced my steps.

The blood drops that Frampton had trailed us by were still there; were still wet. It hadn't even been an hour yet. God, how could time crawl so? And how could it race so frantically by?

There were no gawking spectators; the building had been cleared of them. Even the legislators and lobbyists and other politicos had been banished. Only Huey's inner circle, and of course his storm troopers, both uniformed and hoodlum–style, were allowed.

And when I saw the man in the linen suit, oddly, no one was around. He'd been abandoned there, probably for just a moment, but it seemed so strange. There he was, the slender young man sprawled lifelessly face down across the base of a pillar in a vast puddle of blood pooled on the cold marble floor. Black round glasses on his face askew, frames broken, glass shattered. His back was like a punchboard, with all the punches out. It was hard to imagine how many bullets must have been pumped into him. Huey's boys must have stood there emptying their rage and their guns into an already dead man's back. Such noble warriors. Even now, almost an hour later, the smell of cordite was so thick in this hallway, you had to work at it not to cough. Bullet holes had been gouged in the orangeish marble walls. But the marble didn't bleed.

I was standing with my back to the twin doors of the

governor's office, where the narrow corridor widened just a little. This was a hell of a cramped area for a gunfight—no wonder Murphy had got powder-burned. And no wonder the echo of it had carried all the way down the nearby stairwell.

An oversize hand clutched my arm, startling me.

I turned and was facing the glittering dark eyes in the round terrible face of Joe Messina.

"We got the bastard! He shot the boss, but we got him! We got him! We got him!"

He was either smiling or grimacing; you tell me.

I said, "No shit."

Messina was beaming at me adoringly; it was the goddamndest thing. "You saved him. Everybody says so. Word's around. You saved him!"

He hugged me.

Now I knew how a toothpaste tube felt, on its last day.

"Thanks, Joe," I said, easing out of his sweaty grasp.

He grabbed my arm and tugged, like a kid trying to get his pop to take him on an amusement-park ride. His eyes were bright and crazed and wet.

"We gotta go over and see the Kingfish!" Messina said.

"No thanks, Joe. I've been over there, already."

"Okay. Okay. You done good, Heller! You done good. . . ."

I began to walk away. When I glanced back, Messina was scowling at the bullet-riddled corpse. He was pointing an accusing finger, shaking his finger at the body, as if he were putting even more slugs into it.

I shivered and found my way out.

As I walked the several blocks to the Heidelberg, the whole city seemed to be coming my way, in cars and on foot, civilians and police, mothers, fathers, children, converging first on the statehouse, then the hospital across the lake.

When I walked by the door to Alice Jean's room, I

stopped. Paused. Thought about knocking. Had anyone told her? Somebody had to. . . .

Somehow I didn't think I was the one who should bear her these bad tidings.

I moved on down the hall, to my own room. If she wanted to turn to me for comfort, she knew where to find me.

The sky was in mourning, the dome of God's capitol a rumbling, rolling black that threatened celestial tears any moment. And I hadn't packed a goddamn raincoat.

A hot hoarse wind rippled the surface of Capitol Lake as I walked along its wooded shore, between the war zone of the statehouse and Our Lady of the Lake. It was a little before ten o'clock. Like most people going to visit somebody at a hospital, I didn't really want to be here.

Not so the throng of people standing on the ground between the lake and the hospital parking lot, rural folks mostly, moms and dads and kids and grandfolks, their beat-up trucks and autos parked right up on the grass. They stood keeping vigil, staring at the nondescript three-story light-brown-brick sprawl of the hospital as if it were a holy shrine; perhaps to them it was.

This respectful mob was kept at bay by the bayonet-wielding national guardsmen who formed a human cordon around the edge of the parking lot. More soldiers were posted at each of the handful of steps rising to the front landing, where a dozen plainclothes cops, heavily armed, some with shotguns, some with submachine guns, stood shoulder-to-shoulder, blocking the front double doors. The soldiers and cops seemed to be expecting revolution, even though the crowd they were facing was adoring.

My B.C.I. badge got me inside the hospital, and past one last sentry in the surprisingly small reception area, which was teeming with cops and guardsmen and guys in rumpled suits. The hallways were a little better, but not much, and even the nuns looked ready to swear a blue streak. The place was thick with dozens of heavily armed cops, in and out of uniform, often clustering around stairwells. A large press room was up and running, with half a dozen tables cluttered with phones; it was bustling, and blue with swearing and smoke. A big fleshy state patrolman with a bloodshot nose was talking to a couple reporters just outside the press room.

The trooper was smiling, waggling a finger, saying, "Remember, now—we got orders to shoot any of you boys who try an' go upstairs an' see the Kingfish."

The newshounds took this advice without objection; this was Louisiana—this wasn't the place to make a stand over freedom of the press.

I showed the big patrolman my badge and asked, "Where's the Senator's room?"

He frowned; my accent must have made him suspicious, but my badge was legit, so he pointed upward with a thumb. "Three-fourteen. Do I know you?"

"You must," I said pleasantly. "Otherwise, why would you've given me the Kingfish's room number?"

On the third floor, politicos and bodyguards were everywhere, slumped in chairs and on couches, many of them snoring. Messina was in a corner, by a potted plant, curled up like a fetus, sleeping on his coat.

Murphy Roden was sitting by a window, looking out at the dark roiling clouds; he was smoking a cigarette. On a magazine table nearby was a little metal ashtray with dozens of spent butts.

"So," I said, "I don't have to finance a white cane and seeing-eye dog?"

Murphy turned and looked up at me and managed a smile; the skin around his eyes was reddish, and his left wrist was bandaged, and so was the back of his neck. Otherwise he looked okay.

"No dog or cane this time," he said. "All they had to do was just wash out my eyes. I'll be diggin' marble shrapnel outa my back from here till doomsday, though."

I tested the edge of the magazine table; felt like it could take the weight, so I sat on it. "I heard Chick Frampton's version," I said. "But he came in after the movie started. You up to filling me in?"

He sucked on the smoke; then blew out a gray cloud. "I'll try, Nate. But it's kind of a muddle."

"I've been in situations where guns were going off. The object is to come out alive, not with detailed notes."

He found me another smile, though not much of one, sighed, and started in: "Huey came out of the House like a runaway train, hurtlin' down the corridor. We couldn't nearly keep up. Then he ducked into the governor's office—"

"The governor's office?"

"Yeah . . . yeah, Huey wanted O.K. Allen's help roundin' up some more votes for the special session. But he just sort of stuck his head in, hollered, then was back out in the hall again. He didn't get far before Judge Fournet came up and said hello."

"Who's Fournet?"

Murphy shrugged. "Political appointee of the Kingfish, just a friend. . . . That was when this skinny young guy in black-rimmed glasses and a white linen suit come up from the other side of the Kingfish . . . on the left. Guy'd been standin' by the wall, by a pillar. He had a straw hat in front of him, both hands hidden behind it . . . then I saw the little gun in his right hand and I *dove* for him."

His eyes were wide and staring at nothing but the memory.

"I grabbed his hand as the gun went off . . ." Now his eyes looked at me; he had a point to make. "The Kingfish woulda got it right through the pump if I hadn't done that!"

"And he'd have been dead on the spot," I said, since he seemed to want the reassurance. "Go ahead, Murph. . . ."

"Anyway, I tried to wrest the gun away from the guy, but I couldn't do it, so I put my arm around his neck, kinda wrestled him, and then my heels went out from under me, on that slick goddamn marble floor, and we both went down, *wham*! And that's when I got my pistol out from under my shoulder holster and fired one into the bastard's throat, up into his head."

I'd seen Murphy's gun—a revolver, a Colt—.38 on a .45 frame. Big damn gun.

"I use strictly hollow-point ammo, y'know," he said, almost proudly. "So the son of a bitch, the assassin was dead, then and there."

Dead before the fusillade of the other bodyguards' guns turned him into that punched-out punchboard. Murphy had done him that much of a favor, anyway.

"I was barely to my feet, away from him, when all hell broke loose, Messina and the others blastin' away like the Fourth of fuckin' July. That's . . . that's when the muzzle blasts blinded me."

"A cramped area like that, it's no surprise," I said. "I heard somebody at the hotel say it's a guy named Weiss . . . no relation to Seymour, I assume."

"Not hardly," Murphy said wryly. "Dr. Carl Austin Weiss."

"A doctor? Not a *medical* doctor?"

"Yeah, a medical doctor."

"You're kidding . . ."

"If I'm lyin', I'm dyin'."

I thought about the bloody rag of a man I'd seen sprawled on the marble floor last night. "He looked so young . . . what was left of him."

Murphy nodded. "Just twenty-nine, they say. Top ear, nose and throat man in the state."

"That's goddamn odd, if you ask me."

"What is?"

"A doctor, trying to commit murder."

Murphy's smile was condescending; he shook his head. "Not murder—*assassination.* It's politics, Nate. Dr. Carl Weiss was just another of thousands of respectable citizens who hate the Kingfish. His office was in the Reymond Building . . . that's a hotbed of anti-Long cranks, you know. Something wrong, Nate? You turned white."

"Nothing," I said. "Nothing's wrong."

But I was lying *and* dying; hearing the name "Reymond Building" gave me a sick feeling, and I didn't think a doctor could cure it.

I asked, "How's the Kingfish doing?"

"Holdin' his own," Murphy said. "Guy's bullet went through him—but last night was chaos . . . that operatin' room was a goddamn vaudeville show. More doctors in there than a country club dance . . . politicians . . . bodyguards. . . ."

He waved his hands in the air, in distaste.

I rose, patted him on the shoulder. "Glad you're okay. What's a copper without his peepers?"

"You gonna leave soon?"

"Most likely."

He stood, extended his hand. "You take care, Nate. You're a good man, for a Yankee."

"We're both good men. But some son of a bitch still shot the Kingfish."

We traded disgusted smirks, and waved, and I moved down the hall toward 314. Along the way I passed the Rev. Gerald L. K. Smith. He wore a somber black suit and dark blue tie, but his mood was boisterous. He was slapping reporter Chick Frampton on the back.

"This is *great*!" Smith was saying. "The Kingfish'll get well, and what a fine piece of propaganda *that'll* make!"

Frampton's smile was skeptical. "You really think so, Rev?"

Smith gestured expansively; the hallway was his pulpit. "How many years have we been saying that the corporations have been tryin' to kill Huey? *Now* we can say—'I *told* you so.' "

I didn't stop to be part of that. But I did stop when I spotted, sitting alone in an alcove with three empty chairs in this standing-room-only house, Alice Jean Crosley.

She wore black—a black bonnet and prim-and-proper black dress. Her hands were folded in her lap like a corsage and she was doing her best not to cry. But her eyes were laced with red.

"Want some company?" I asked her.

She found a little smile for me, somewhere, and patted the chair beside her.

"I feel like a heel," I said.

That statement astounded her. "Why?"

"I didn't have the guts to knock on your door last night, and tell you. I didn't want to be the bearer of bad tidings."

She lowered her head, but the little smile was back. "I think I understand."

"We . . . we've had a great time, Alice Jean, you and I, but we're bound together by that man, and whether he's a saint or the biggest sinner the South has ever seen, he's important to us. You hate him, and you love him. Me, I don't know him all that well, frankly. How do you get to know a force of nature? I don't know if I could ever understand a man who's that motivated by power. Greed, I understand. Sex, I got a feel for that, too. But power I don't begin to get."

"What are you trying to say, Nate?"

"Just that I don't want him to die, either, Alice Jean. If for no other reason than it might cast a pall on our friendship."

She reached out for my hand and squeezed. "Will you do me a favor . . . friend?"

"Name it."

"Nobody will talk to me. The only reason I got in was my statehouse pass—and now they're afraid to cross me for fear I'll blab to those reporters downstairs."

"So what can I do for you?"

"Find out how he *really* is. See him, if you can."

"You bet."

And I squeezed her hand.

The red-laced eyes were glimmering with tears, but at least I'd made her smile.

Down the hall, just outside Room 314, I saw Seymour Weiss. He was standing with a heavy-set white-haired gent who was obviously Governor O.K. Allen; shrewd detective that I am, I figured this out when I overheard Weiss refer to him as "Governor."

Seymour noticed me, where I was standing patiently a ways down the hall—not wanting to interrupt him and the governor, after all—and came quickly over.

"Heller!" he said, with a somber smile. He extended his hand and I shook it. Why the hell was he glad to see me?

He said, "There are some people I want you to meet," and slipped his arm around my shoulder and walked me into the room just opposite 314. All of a sudden I was the guest of honor. . . .

"Rose," Seymour said, gesturing to me, "I'd like you to meet the young man who brought your husband to the hospital last night."

Chairs had been arranged and the hospital bed removed; this was a sitting room now, a lounge for family members. Mrs. Long was standing talking to a young man of perhaps twenty, in white shirt and dark tie, who was a startling replica of what Huey must have looked like at that age.

She turned to me and her smile was both dignified and brave. Rose Long was a pretty, pale-blue-eyed Irish lass who had grown pleasantly plump in middle age; she wore a dark brown dress with her namesake flower pinned to the breast.

"We're very grateful to you, Mr. Heller," she said. "This is my son Russell. . . ."

I shook hands with the boy. It was as if he'd been stamped in his father's image. But his handshake was firmer.

She introduced me to her father-in-law—a long-faced, haggard, no-nonsense-looking farmer who was seated by Huey's brother Earl—and her other two children, a pretty teenager also named Rose, and another Huey-in-the-making, eleven-year-old Palmer. They all seemed more confused than worried. It's difficult to summon concern, let alone grieve, in the midst of bedlam. Outside the window, the crowd had begun to sing, "Every Man a King." Its jaunty air seemed out of place.

Still, Mrs. Long said, "Huey would appreciate that."

"Only if they let him direct, Mother," Russell said, and they exchanged smiles. But their eyes were damp.

This group did not seem to share Rev. Smith's optimism or glee about the wounded Kingfish.

Mrs. Long clasped my hand. "My husband spoke of you just recently, Mr. Heller. He regards you highly."

I gave her half a smile. "I'm afraid my efforts didn't prove of much use, Mrs. Long."

"If you hadn't rushed him here," she said, "he'd have died last night. He asked me to thank you."

"I was hoping to see him myself. . . ."

Seymour took me by the arm and whispered, "That's not going to be possible. A word with you?"

I nodded to Mrs. Long and her family and allowed Seymour to buttonhole me in the hallway.

Seymour raised a lecturing finger. "The Kingfish wants you to keep mum about what you've been up to."

"He's conscious?"

"He's driftin' in and out . . . sometimes he's rational, sometimes not. But he told me day before yesterday, when we were golfin', what you've been doin' for him. . . ."

I smirked and shook my head. "Did a hell of a job, didn't I?"

Seymour put a hand on my shoulder. "No one's blamin' you. One man, in a few days, tryin' to sort out a lifetime of enemies. . . . And this doctor was apparently a wild card, a crank outa left field."

"How is the Kingfish, really?"

"Not good."

As if on cue, the door to 314 opened as a nun exited, giving me a view of the Kingfish in his hospital bed—under an oxygen tent.

Seymour's head was lowered as he spoke. "Dr. Maes—the top surgeon in the state—got delayed by an accident on his way from New Orleans. Last night, it got to where we couldn't wait—and Dr. Vidrine went ahead and performed the operation."

I shrugged. "I saw Vidrine in action. He seemed more than competent."

Seymour raised both eyebrows. "Mebbe so—but when Dr. Maes arrived, about an hour after the operation, he examined Huey—and then he read Vidrine the riot act."

"Why, in God's name?"

"I'll tell you as best I can, one layman to another. Dr. Maes's diagnosis was that Huey had been shot through the kidney . . . but Vidrine didn't probe the bullet beyond the intestines. Another operation was indicated, but Maes refused to do it."

"Why?"

Seymour gazed at me without blinking. "He said . . . he doesn't operate on dead men."

It looked like I was going to bear Alice Jean the bad tidings, after all.

Seymour slipped his arm back around my shoulder and walked me slowly down the hall.

"If Huey dies," I said, "there'll be an inquest. . . ."

"You needn't worry about that," Seymour said. "You didn't witness the shooting, did you? You're free to go back to Chicago."

Seymour stopped for a moment, dug inside his suit coat and came back with a fat wallet; from it, he peeled out two hundred dollars in twenties.

"Your train ticket's waitin' at the Heidelberg desk. You leave this afternoon. Acceptable?"

"Fine with me," I said, pocketing the cash. "I don't particularly need this kind of publicity. The detective hired to prevent a killing that's headline news all over the world? Not great for business."

"Here's another hundred," Seymour said, taking out another handful of twenties.

I took them, tucked them away. "I hope Huey beats the odds. Tell him that for me, Seymour. So long. . . ."

I'd taken a few steps when Seymour called out to me.

"Oh, and Heller?"

"Yeah?"

He walked quickly up to me and pressed still more twenties into my palm.

"What's this for?"

"It's what we call in Louisiana a lann-yapp."

"A what?"

He repeated it, and spelled it: l-a-g-n-i-a-p-p-e.

"Means somethin' extra, for no special reason. Somethin' for nothin'." He patted me on the shoulder, smiled, then as an apparent afterthought added, "Oh, and would you, on your way, get Alice Jean out of here? Her presence upsets Mrs. Long."

It didn't begin raining until Monday night. I was well on my way home, dry as a bone, in a private compartment, thanks to Seymour Weiss's largess. But a day later, when I spoke to Alice Jean, long distance from Chicago, she said the rain had started Monday evening and was still coming down. Not a storm, but a steady, rhythmic rain. A deluge couldn't have dampened the vigil of his followers, and when Huey died before sunup Tuesday morning, just as it was beginning to build, they were waiting, ready to add their tears to the downpour.

They had sunny weather for the funeral, except for a brief sprinkle that quickly turned to steam. It was so hot, in fact, many of the mourners used umbrellas to shield themselves and their children from the rays. Even in Chicago, you couldn't avoid the details of the spectacle. Every radio carried it live; every newspaper gave it the front page; and a week later, the newsreels were full of it.

As it turned out, his skyscraper statehouse was the only gravestone large enough to suit Huey: it had been his wish to be buried on the capitol grounds, and he was, in the sunken garden facing his art moderne memorial. But first, twenty-two thousand mourners passed by the bier as he lay, strangely enough, in a citified tuxedo, a peasant under glass in an open coffin in grandiose Memorial Hall. So many flowers were sent, they would have overflowed the hall, had they all been displayed there; instead, they were set up on the grounds and extended out over several acres.

By daybreak Thursday—the day of the funeral—mourners were streaming into Baton Rouge from all over the state, by train and bus, by limo and pickup, black and white, rich and poor, man/woman/child, hillbillies and rednecks and Creoles and Cajuns, in tailored suits, in dusty coveralls, by some estimates as many as 150,000, congregating everywhere from oak trees to rooftops, perched on statues, peeking out capitol office windows, but most of all swarming the capitol grounds.

While the LSU Marching Band played a minor-key dirge variation of "Every Man a King," Huey Long's bronze casket was carried by Seymour Weiss, Judge Fournet, Governor Allen and other key figures in the Long machine, down the forty-nine steps through the crowd's weeping gauntlet, to the resting place in the sunken garden.

At the graveside, Dr. Gerald L. K. Smith delivered the eulogy, making a bid for Huey's followers. (The next day, in a press conference at the Roosevelt, in a flurry of anti-Semitism, the Rev announced himself officially the heir to the Kingfish's throne.)

When the last mourner had drifted away, one final precaution was taken to guard Huey Long: he was buried beneath seven feet of steel and cement. Alice Jean said it was Seymour Weiss's idea. Dillinger's dad had done much the same for him. Keeps the tourists out.

A smaller funeral had been held, in the pouring rain, three days before: that of Dr. Carl Weiss. The monsignor at St. Joseph's didn't feel it had been clearly proven Dr. Weiss shot

Huey, and granted a church burial. The funeral was attended by Baton Rouge's business, civic and social leaders, as well as every doctor in town, not to mention several congressmen and one former governor.

And the Kiwanis and Young Men's Business Club sent wreaths.

Sometimes at night, in the months that followed, I would think about being in the Reymond Building, trying to ferret out the Huey Long murder plot, wondering how many offices away from the real thing I'd been.

Other times I would think about Alice Jean, who occasionally dropped me a note, sometimes even called, urging me to return for a visit; but fond of her as I was, I wasn't about to.

If I wanted to go to a banana republic, I'd hop a tramp steamer to South America.

TWO
A LAGNIAPPE FOR ELMER

October 26—November 10, 1936

The Mediterranean-style, creamy-stucco, tile-roofed two-story, in the Garden District of New Orleans near Tulane University, wasn't a mansion, exactly. Not that it wasn't impressive, with its railings and ornamentation and many windows, not to mention the manicured lawn and exotic shrubbery. Small cedars hugged the first floor and moss-hung oaks protected the perimeter, and here and there were other, more tropical trees, including several broad-leafed banana trees.

I shook my head, as I pulled my black rental Ford into the cement-block driveway: here I was, back in the banana republic of Louisiana, after all. And only one thing could have coaxed my return. Alice Jean Crosley, you're thinking? The love of a woman? How romantic.

Hardly. I was here on a thousand-dollar retainer from the Chicago office of the Mutual Life Insurance Company. The woman—a widow, who lived in this near-mansion at 14 Audubon Boulevard—had put in an accidental death claim on her husband. I had been chosen as a neutral third party, acceptable both to the insurance company and the widow (and her attorney), to determine whether her husband's death was accidental or not.

Actually, I wasn't sorry to be back in Louisiana at all. We'd had a cold snap, and Chicago had done that disappearing act it occasionally likes to perform: skipping fall and cutting straight to winter. It felt good to be in a lightweight white linen suit, walking around in seventy-degree weather, even if it was slightly humid.

The lady of the house must've had a perfectionist, raking fool for a gardener; though the oaks and cedars were losing their leaves, the lawn was free of them, and was still green and as perfect as the nearby Audubon Park Club Golf Course. I shook my head again. That's where I'd been, a little over a year ago (or was it a century?), caddying with my nine millimeter strapped under my arm.

I went up the steps to the elaborate entryway; two white plaster artichokes framed the massive wood front door. I rang the door bell, expecting a butler or maid to answer.

But she answered herself.

She hadn't changed: the tragedy was nowhere in her attractive oval face; her pale blue eyes and her smile were shy, but not insecure. Pleasantly plump, she wore a simple chocolate-color dress with touches of lace and a silver brooch at the neck.

"Hello, Mrs. Long," I said. "Nathan Heller, from Chicago . . ."

Her smile widened as she offered me her slender hand to shake, which I did. "I remember you, Mr. Heller. That's why you're here."

"Pardon?"

"I requested you."

Confused, I took off my Panama, as she led me inside, shutting the massive door with a thud. We passed through a small entryway into a larger vestibule where dark wood stairs rose to an upstairs landing; a formal living room was through a double archway at right, an immaculate dining room through a double archway at left. The woodwork was dark, the walls creamy pastel plaster, the furnishings Mediterranean and expensive. Lovely, but it didn't quite look like anybody lived here.

She paused and said, "Would you like something to drink, Mr. Heller? A mint julep, perhaps? I've just made a pitcher of iced tea, if you prefer something softer?"

"Tea would be fine, Mrs. Long . . . excuse me. Would you prefer 'Senator Long'?"

She had been appointed to serve out the remainder of her husband's senate term.

Now her smile turned embarrassed. "Actually, I prefer 'Mrs.' I'm afraid I'm playing hooky at the moment. I'm really not in Washington as often as I should be . . . public affairs and politics just aren't very interesting to me."

"Then, if you don't mind my asking, why'd you accept the job?"

"It provides a nice change of scenery . . . but mostly, it's the ten thousand dollars a year. Shall we have that iced tea? I assume you prefer it unsweetened, like most Northerners. . . ."

Soon she was escorting me through a hallway to an expansive solarium with dark-stained wicker furnishings, creamy walls and a red-tile floor. We moved past a card table to a sofa and chair, and she gestured to the chair as she settled herself on the sofa, sitting with hands folded in her lap, her iced tea on a coaster on the wicker-and-glass end table beside her. Prim, proper, but in no way pretentious.

"I like this room," she said, glancing out the slatted wooden blinds at her tropical backyard garden. A balmy breeze drifted in through the screens. "We had a room like this at the governor's mansion."

"At the risk of seeming rude," I said, sipping my tea, "why would a woman of your means have to take on a job that pays ten thousand a year?"

"Then my attorney didn't fill you in, at all?"

"No. And Mr. Gallagher, the chief of Mutual's investigative bureau, merely said that you'd worked out an arrangement where an outside investigator—sort of an arbitrator—would be brought in."

"You weren't aware that I requested you, specifically."

"No. In fact, that surprises me. All Mr. Gallagher said was, 'I understand you did some work in Louisiana for Huey Long.' I said yes, and he seemed to think that meant I knew my way around down here . . . for a Northerner, anyway."

She looked around the room; her eyes landed on a framed family portrait on a table—Huey, Rose herself and their three children, probably taken a year, maybe two, before the Kingfish died. "On the last night we spent together, in this house, my husband spoke of you."

Now that really surprised me. "Is that right?"

"Yes. The next morning he met with you on the golf course, I understand."

I nodded.

She was looking off, into the past. "He spoke of how nice it was to have someone from the outside, someone he could trust. With all the squabbling over the spoils, among his 'supporters,' from Seymour Weiss to Dr. Smith and a raft of others, I can well understand that he felt surrounded by . . . vultures. They ran on an assassination ticket, you know—and painted their podiums blood red. Most distasteful."

I was starting to feel awkward about this. "Mrs. Long, it's only fair that I tell you I failed in my mission, for your husband. He'd been warned someone was going to try to assassinate him, during the special session, and he came to me to . . ."

"I know," she said quietly. Her smile was a madonna's.

"He confided in me. On that last night. The next morning, I pleaded with him not to go to Baton Rouge, with this murder threat hanging over him. But he just laughed, Huey did, and said, 'I may not come back, dear, but I'll die fighting!' "

She dug a handkerchief out of a pocket and wept into it for a moment. I sat quietly, listening to the wind rustle the fronds of the banana trees.

Soon she had hold of herself, but she was still in the mood to reminisce. "Huey and I . . . there was a time when we were very close. He was taking so many classes, working so many jobs, and I was finding every which way to stretch a penny. I'm very much a housewife, Mr. Heller—Huey met me when he was judging a cake-baking contest . . . he was selling vegetable shortening, at the time."

I smiled. "And you were the winner."

She returned it. "I was the winner . . . for a while. But success came quickly, and wooed him away from me. He didn't spend much time with us, here in this house. I think he knew his time was short. And now . . . now I'm a United States Senator myself! Can you imagine?"

"I'm sure you're doing a fine job."

"Not really. If I didn't have Russell beside me, I'd be lost—lost without my twenty-year-old to guide me along. The funny thing is this, even when we first met, Huey was always writing letters to United States senators, at any ol' excuse. It didn't make any sense to me, and I'd ask him why he was doing it. He'd say, 'I want them to know I'm here.' And again, I'd ask, why? And he'd say, 'I'm going to be there someday myself.' Can you imagine? He was only a teenager, then."

"He already had a sense of what he wanted to do."

She nodded, rolled the pale blue eyes. "We were barely married when he first told me his 'master' plan. . . . He had it all mapped out. First he'd run for some minor office, then for governor, then United States Senate and finally, the presidency of the United States. He had it all measured out. Gave me cold chills to hear it, and to see that look in his eyes."

I sat forward. "Mrs. Long. With all due respect, you still haven't told me why a woman of your standing would take her husband's Senate seat for what must be to you a paltry sum."

Now the smile was teasing. "Do you consider ten thousand dollars to be a 'paltry sum,' Mr. Heller?"

"Of course not . . ."

Now it was gone. "And do you know the purpose of the investigation you're to pursue?"

I shrugged. "Well . . . as I understand it, I'm to determine whether Mutual's double-indemnity clause kicks in, on your husband's life insurance policy."

"That's right," she said, with one nod. "If my husband was murdered by Dr. Carl Weiss, the policy pays ten thousand dollars. But . . . if he was shot accidentally . . . for example, by the stray bullet of one of his bodyguards . . . it pays *twenty* thousand."

Money again. Another ten grand . . .

"The fact is, Mr. Heller," she said, and from her expression I could tell she found this subject disagreeable, "my husband's estate was just a little over one hundred thousand dollars. That includes the value of this home."

I felt like I'd been coldcocked. While a hundred grand sounded like all the money in the world to a small-timer like me, for a politician like the Kingfish—by all accounts, an incredibly corrupt politician, at that—to leave so little behind was absurd.

I told her so—skipping the corrupt politician part.

"Louisiana is a state of abundant absurdity, Mr. Heller. Surely you remember that from your previous visit."

I was shaking my head. "I know for a fact your husband had money tucked away. Money that the IRS didn't know about. Money that might not have been part of his estate, but that, one way or another, should have gone to you."

"If so, none of it did."

"Mrs. Long, the day I was on the golf course with your husband, I overheard him and Mr. Weiss mention the so-called dee-duct box."

She blinked. "You know about that?"

"I know about that. And from what they both had to say, it was obvious there was at least a cool million stashed away, as your husband's 'war chest' for his presidential campaign."

"Then the vultures got it," she said crisply, raising her chin. "Not me. Can you help me get that extra ten thousand dollars?"

Now *I* blinked.

"Well, Mrs. Long," I said with my practiced shy grin, "I've been hired to be impartial. I've done considerable work for Mutual, over the years, and wouldn't want to risk . . ."

"There would be a thousand-dollar cash under-the-table bonus in it, for you."

I shifted in my chair. "Well, uh . . . I'll see what I can do."

"Understand, I'm not asking you to falsify any documents or evidence. But you will be sorely tried, and tempted, along the way, I fear. . . ."

"By the 'vultures,' you mean?"

"That is correct. The inquests into the deaths of my husband and Dr. Carl Weiss were perfunctory affairs. Neither my husband's enemies, nor his supporters, were terribly anxious to question this doctor's supposed role as a lone assassin."

"Sure," I said. "Much tidier to just pin it on the mad doctor. If the bodyguards killed the Senator, it would be a scandal. And if a full-scale inquiry turned up a conspiracy, half of the Baton Rouge Chamber of Commerce might find themselves indicted."

She liked the sound of my reasoning. "Correct. And this is why you're the perfect man for this job."

"What is?"

She raised a forefinger. "Only you can accomplish this—an outsider who has already gone into the dens of both camps . . . the enemies who wanted Huey dead, and the 'friends' around him. . . ."

I lifted an eyebrow. "The 'vultures,' you mean."

"Precisely."

I scratched my neck. "I have to say, Mrs. Long, I felt there was genuine affection between Seymour Weiss and your husband. And some of those bodyguards, like Joe Messina and Murphy Roden, damn near worshipped him."

"I don't want to color your inquiry," she said enigmatically.

I kind of figured she already colored it when she bribed me with the grand.

"You do realize," I said, "I wasn't a witness. . . ."

"I know. I'm fully aware of your role in rushing my husband to Our Lady of the Lake. But you did view the aftermath, isn't that correct? The . . . what is the term?"

"Crime scene," I said. "Yes. I saw the young doctor's body."

"The poor man was shot many times, I understand."

Interesting that Mrs. Long could refer to her husband's presumed assassin in such a sympathetic way, unless she had already convinced herself of the man's innocence.

"Frankly, ma'am, I never saw anything quite so brutal. And it was a very enclosed space for so much shooting."

She was nodding again; like her husband, she could appreciate a good yes-man. "Then you feel it *is* possible that my husband may have been killed not by Dr. Weiss, but by a wild bullet from one of the bodyguards' guns."

"I do. Bullets had to have been ricocheting off that marble, every which way. But it doesn't necessarily mean anyone was lying, either, about their stories."

She frowned. "How is that possible?"

"That kind of violence, in so cramped a space, in so short a time, almost none of the eyewitness testimony can be trusted. I heard two versions—one from Chick Frampton—"

"The reporter."

"Yes. The other from Murphy Roden. They were similar stories, but there were differences."

Her eyes narrowed. "Such as?"

I shrugged. "Typical eyewitness inconsistencies. Murphy said he wrestled the assailant to the floor. Frampton merely said Murphy was 'stooped over' the doctor. Minor, but differences. I'm sure dozens, perhaps hundreds more, will turn up."

She was frowning in thought. "I already know another."

"What's that?"

"Judge Fournet claims he and Mr. Roden *both* struggled with Dr. Weiss, at the same time."

"Well, frankly, that just may be the judge trying to add some glory to his role in it. When I read in the papers about your husband being rushed to the hospital, I saw the names of half a dozen people, including several bodyguards, claiming to have ridden in that beat-up Ford I commandeered."

"They had a lot of practice," she said, "basking in my husband's reflected glory. His death was no different."

I patted the air gently. "I have to tell you, ma'am, my understanding is Dr. Weiss *did* have a motive."

It had turned out the young ear, nose and throat specialist was the son-in-law of Judge Pavy; one of Huey's special session bills had been designed to gerrymander the judge out of his district. Both Seymour Weiss and Earl Long had tried to talk Huey out of that bill.

"Do you think that's a murder motive, Mr. Heller?"

"People have been killed over a lot less . . . but, frankly, I think it's more likely the doctor approached your husband in the hall, and argued with him, maybe got physical . . . and the bodyguards overreacted. And your husband caught a stray bullet."

She was nodding again. "That's exactly how I see it. But how did you arrive at that conclusion?"

"Well . . . I noticed the papers didn't talk about it much, but your husband's mouth was bleeding. In fact, when I met him on the steps, when he came weaving down, he spit blood on my suit coat. . . . Is this distressing you, ma'am?"

"No," she said. Her eyes were hard, alert, as she leaned forward, hands clasped.

"One of the first things the intern in the operating room did," I said, "was swab out an abrasion inside your husband's mouth. This fits in with something Huey said . . . he didn't say much, he was pretty much delirious . . . but he asked, 'Why did he hit me?' "

"You think Dr. Weiss hit my husband? Not in the sense of . . . shooting him, but . . . striking him a blow?"

"It makes sense. A sudden movement, and those hair-trigger moronic bodyguards just exploded. I'm sorry to put it that way, but it's definitely a possibility."

"So," she said. "Where do you start?"

"I think the logical place," I said, "is with the dead man."

"My husband?"

"No," I said, and stood. "The other dead man."

17

The bungalow on Lakeland Drive was not a near-mansion; it was a white-frame duplex, what the locals called a "shotgun double," with separate entryways beneath an overhang, sharing a common, untrimmed-shrubbery-crowded walk up a shallow yard. A dog—from the sound of it, a big one—was barking in the backyard. The spire of Huey's statehouse loomed, a mere two blocks away.

Like most neighborhoods in Baton Rouge, this one was beautifully shaded; moss-hung oaks, losing their leaves, mingled with evergreens and poplars. But the ivy climbing the posts of the porch looked more parasitic than decorative, and the homes on this block were close together, almost claustrophobic. Perhaps it all would have struck me as cozy if I hadn't known that tragedy had visited this overgrown cottage.

I'd spent Monday afternoon with Mrs. Long, in New Orleans; it was Tuesday morning now. My interview subject had been at home when I telephoned last evening, and when I told her what my purpose was, she had seemed willing, even eager, to see me. *Knock on the door at right,* she'd said, in a gently musical voice. *Our renters are on the left.*

At first she was just a shadow behind the screen door. "Yes?"

I told her my name. "We spoke on the phone?"

"Do you have any identification?"

What happened to her eagerness? "Only my Illinois private investigator's license," I said.

"You said you worked for Mutual Insurance."

I was getting out my billfold; I found an A-1 Agency business card for her, too. "Right now I am. But I'm a private operator."

She cracked open the screen to have a look, a slender, dark-haired woman in her late twenties; with her flawless complexion, she seemed even younger, but lines of pain were etched at the corners of the large, lovely eyes. Even in a housedress (not that this navy floral-print was in any way frumpy), Mrs. Carl Weiss—the former Yvonne Pavy—was a strikingly beautiful woman.

She stepped out on the porch. Her arms were crossed, as if she were protecting herself from a chill in the air, only there wasn't one. "I'm sorry, Mr. Heller. After you called, I . . . had second thoughts. I thought you might be . . ."

"Another reporter?"

She nodded. "Or some other . . . grasping individual. I've tried to stay out of the public eye as much as possible."

"I can understand."

"I'll invite you in, but first, I must ask you to keep your voice down . . . Carl Jr. is napping."

"I see. How old is your son?"

"A year and a half. He's an active boy, and he needs his rest."

I risked a smile. "And you need yours."

I got a tiny one back, as she nodded, and I followed her inside. She led me into a pastel-wallpapered living room dominated by a brownish red overstuffed, mohair-and-walnut sofa and a matching pair of easy chairs, all with rounded arms and backs and colorful floral cushions.

"Handsome suite," I said.

"My husband and I picked it out at Kornmeyer's, just a few days before his death. In fact, I had to postpone delivery because of the funeral. Could I get you something? Iced tea perhaps?"

That seemed to be the local drink of choice. I said yes, thank you, and sat in one of the easy chairs, because that was where she'd led me.

I could see through to the dining room, where a table and chairs and china cabinet were carefully arranged. The furniture seemed a little nicer than the house, but the place was also underfurnished. As if this were a work in progress, perhaps one that had gotten stalled.

The place was showroom tidy, with the exception of a scattering of the child's toys on the living-room floor: a red rubber ball, some ABC blocks, a rubber Big Bad Wolf toy, and an Amos 'n' Andy windup car, a replica of radio's celebrated Fresh Air Taxi, with Amos and Andy riding—but the Kingfish conspicuous in his absence.

"I'm afraid I spoil him," she said, handing me the tall narrow glass of iced tea, garnished with a mint leaf.

I hadn't even heard her come back in; I'd been studying the toys.

"What else is a kid for?" I asked. I sipped the tea—it was sickly sweet. I'd forgotten to remind her I was a Northerner.

"You mind?" I asked, taking out my pocket notebook and pen.

"Not at all," she said, and sat on the couch; our configuration echoed that of me and Mrs. Long, the afternoon before.

"Do I understand," she said, almost reading my mind, "that I have an unlikely ally in Mrs. Long?"

"You could put it that way."

"Or I *could* put it that it's to her financial advantage that my husband's innocence be proved."

"You could put it that way, too. Does her motivation matter?"

"Motivation is *all* that matters, Mr. Heller." She sipped her tea. "This is my husband. . . ."

She plucked a framed picture from an end table; the picture had been facing away from me, but now it was thrust before me: Dr. Carl Weiss, in a studio portrait, his earnest eyes searching mine from beyond the grave.

And if that sounds melodramatic to you, too bad: the widow of Huey Long's purported assassin was holding her dead husband's picture under my nose and I was spooked.

Spooked by both his surface unassumingness, and an underlying intensity. The eyes behind the wire-framed glasses smoldered; the soft features, the long, straight nose, the full lips, the almost weak chin, were those of a bookworm. The kind of kid who got teased for being so smart. The kind of kid who, under the right conditions, could explode.

She withdrew the picture and her jaw was firmly set; but she was trembling as she said, "Is that the face of a murderer?"

"No," I said. But I was lying: if I've learned one thing, in this life of crime, it's how many faces murder wears.

"The newspapers have called Carl 'brooding,' and a 'loner,' " she said. She laughed—softly, bitterly. "I never heard anything so ridiculous. He was the most well-rounded, brilliant man. . . . He finished high school at fifteen, you know."

"That is remarkable."

"Graduated college by nineteen, a doctor of medicine by twenty-one . . ."

"Mrs. Weiss, sometimes brilliant students, prodigies, *are*

loners. If you've skipped grades, and are thrown in with the older kids, it can—"

"That wasn't the case with Carl. He loved to read, but he was no egghead. Yes, he was quiet, even shy . . . but he had a keen sense of humor, and he *loved* music . . ." She glanced at a spinet piano by the wall. ". . . But he was also a wonderful carpenter, and an amateur inventor . . . went to plays and prize fights, alike. . . ."

A Renaissance man who died a political assassin.

I searched for the words. "There was nothing . . . morbid in his outlook?"

The dark eyes flared. "What you mean is, were there any signs of suicidal tendencies . . . no there were not. Carl loved his work—he loved working with his father, the two of them were the best ear, nose and throat men in the state. And he was the most *doting* father . . . took dozens of snapshots of little Carl Jr., gave the baby his two a.m. feeding, wheeled his carriage. I hardly changed a diaper."

I narrowed my eyes and asked the question she wanted me to ask: "Does a man so devoted to his three-month-old son walk into a suicidal situation?"

"Of course not! Surely, already you can see how ridiculous . . ."

When she trailed off, I jumped in. "But the gun they found—it *was* your husband's weapon."

"Yes." She tilted her head; her posture, it seemed to me, had become suddenly defensive. "A lot of doctors carry a firearm, in their bags. There are drug addicts lurking on every corner."

Of Baton Rouge?

"Well, certainly," I said, smiling affably, "and it's not like guns were one of your husband's many interests."

I was just trying to fill the space with something innocuous, but I'd struck a nerve. She blinked and suddenly she nervously fingered the antimacassar on the arm of the sofa.

"Actually," she said, "guns *were* an interest of Carl's. There's nothing wrong with that, nothing unusual."

"Of course not. Was he a hunter?"

"Not really. It wasn't in his character to kill anything; he was a *doctor*, after all. But he and another physician friend liked target shooting. They had rifles, shotguns, pistols. They'd bring clay pigeons with them. Sometimes they'd just shoot at the water. Just . . . boys will be boys, you know."

I wasn't quite sure she bought that, herself.

"Where did they do this target shooting?" I asked.

She frowned. "What does this have to do with proving Carl's innocence?"

"Mrs. Weiss . . . my job is to ascertain what really happened that awful night at the capitol. I will tell you, frankly, that I am inclined toward your husband's innocence."

The lovely eyes widened. "You are?"

"I told you that on the phone. And it wasn't a lie, or a ruse, just to get some time with you."

"What makes you believe in Carl's innocence?"

I told her about Huey's bleeding mouth and his question about who hit him.

She shook a righteous fist. "I *heard* that! I *knew* they'd suppressed that evidence! That rumor was flying around Our Lady of the Lake."

Now I was frowning. "Did your husband have friends on the staff?"

"At the hospital? Of course. He did many operations there. There are only two hospitals in Baton Rouge, Mr. Heller."

I sipped my sweet, sweet tea. Smiled. "Now," I said, "where did Carl go target shooting?"

"At Carl's father's cabin. On the Amite River, over in Livingston Parish. It's a popular recreation spot."

A harmless enough response, considering how hard she'd ducked the question.

I asked, "You didn't happen to go there, that Sunday afternoon, did you?"

She tugged at the collar of the navy-print frock. "Yes, we did. We frequently spent quiet Sunday afternoons at the cabin."

Quiet afternoons, shooting.

"Did your husband do any target shooting that particular Sunday afternoon?"

"No! Certainly not!"

Bingo.

Well, this seemed to be the first time she'd lied to me, and it was an understandable falsehood at that: even if he'd spent every Sunday for the previous three years target shooting, doing so on that Sunday would seem to attain a terrible significance.

So I moved on, and said, "There were no signs, on that Sunday, that anything was disturbing him? The morning papers surely must've covered the bills Huey was pushing through. Didn't your father being gerrymandered out of his judgeship kind of spoil your Sunday?"

She sighed. "First of all, you have to understand that Carl wasn't very political at all. He wasn't involved in local politics, and it wasn't a subject he discussed much, even though his father did, all the time."

"His father had an interest in politics?"

"Particularly Huey Long. He despised him."

"What about Carl?"

Her shrug only seemed casual. "He was certainly no admirer of the man. Like a lot of people around here, he felt things were being . . . badly managed. There was some bitterness in our family, toward that administration . . . my sister Marie lost her third-grade teaching job, and my uncle Paul lost his job as principal of Opelousas High."

"Why did they lose their jobs?"

"Because they were Pavys. My papa was one of the few anti-Long judges still on the bench, you know."

I sat forward. "Which brings us back to the gerrymander. . . . Your family had just heard about it, that Sunday morning, isn't that right?"

Reluctantly, she nodded. "But it was no surprise to us. In fact, my mother was delighted by the prospect."

"Delighted?"

"Papa didn't make as much money as a judge as he could in private practice. Mama was elated he'd be stepping down. Papa himself didn't feel there was any great injustice being done to him, personally. It was just politics. Dirty politics, but politics."

"So the gerrymander, as a motive for Carl . . . ?"

"Ridiculous. We all knew Papa was ready to step down off the bench, anyway."

I hadn't taken many notes, yet. But I needed Carl Weiss's timetable. "Tell me about that day. That Sunday."

"All right." She shrugged. "It was a typical Sunday. We went to Mass, and we came home and changed our clothes, and went to Carl's parents' house—we always had Sunday dinner at one o'clock with them—fried chicken, rice, gravy, salad, all the trimmings. Carl's parents have a wonderful colored cook."

"And this is when you discussed the gerrymander bill?"

"I . . . I suppose. I remember someone said it was a kind of backhanded compliment to the judge, from Huey."

"How so?"

Her smile was small and smug. "Papa must've been a pretty good judge, if they couldn't vote him out of office."

"Did Carl seem at all . . . preoccupied?"

"No. He was skinny, you know, and we teased him about it, and I remember he ate really well, and went out of his way to compliment Martha . . . that's the cook . . . about the meal. Tom Ed excused himself . . ."

"Who?"

"Tom Ed. That's Carl's brother . . . you'll want to talk to him, too, by the way. . . . Anyway, Tom Ed went off with some of his college chums to hire a band for their rush-week dance. We went into a bedroom where Carl Jr. had woken from his nap, and I nursed him, and Carl just lay on the bed and we talked. Just talked, like husbands and wives do . . . quiet things. Unimportant things. So unimportant, I don't even remember. . . ."

And she began to weep.

I found a handkerchief for her and she took it, apologizing.

"Please don't apologize," I said. "I'm the one who should apologize for asking you to talk about all this."

"I'll be fine. Really."

Before long, she was.

"After a while, we all went to the cabin together . . . it's just a rustic, three-room affair, you can't cook there, but it was by the river and nice for picnics and swims and just, you know, relaxing. We went swimming, Carl and I, and we, well the only word for it is, we frolicked. Like children. Isn't that silly?"

"No," I said.

"Later, we all sat on the porch, staring at the river moving by. It was almost . . . hypnotic. Carl and his father talked about medicine, and Mama and I played with the baby, and the clouds threw pretty shadows on the river and on the riverbank."

"When did you get back to town?"

"About 7:30. I fixed Carl a couple of sandwiches and he ate 'em up, and had two glasses of milk, too. I kidded him about finally putting some meat on his bones. Carl Jr. was sleeping in his baby buggy, next to the table. Our dog—Peter, he's a big ol' police dog—came over and licked the baby's face, licked him awake."

She smiled at the memory.

"Carl told me I better wash the baby, and I did, and he put Peter outside, and fed him. Then he helped me wash and dry the dishes."

This domestic little scene had occurred, what? An hour and a half before the shooting?

"A little after eight," she continued, "Carl called Dr. McGehee, an anesthetist, in regard to a tonsillectomy Monday morning. Then I stretched out on our bed and read the Sunday comics while Carl showered and the baby slept. It was a perfect Sunday, really."

Almost.

"When Carl stepped into the bedroom, he wasn't in his casual clothes from camping, but a white linen suit and Panama hat . . . like yours, Mr. Heller. Only his shoes were black, not brown. His hair was messy and I made him comb it. I was still reading the comics when he kissed me goodbye. He said something about making arrangements for an operation tomorrow. I thought he was going to Our Lady of the Lake. I didn't ask him, or make an issue of it. He made hospital night calls all the time."

"And then he left?"

"No. . . . See, we'd been rocking the baby to sleep every night, after his ten o'clock bottle, and I said, just as Carl was going, 'I believe I'll let Carl Jr. cry himself to sleep tonight, and not rock him.' And Carl said, 'Well, I'll hurry back as quick as I can, and we'll try that out together.' Then he left. That was the last time I saw him. Alive."

She began to weep again. Who could blame her? She still had my handkerchief.

When the time seemed right, I said, "Mrs. Weiss, your

husband's behavior is definitely not that of an assassin on his way to perform a suicide mission."

"I know that. The whole family knows that."

"My problem is—I have to prove it. I can't promise you that that's possible."

Her half-smile was lovelier than most whole ones. "You don't owe me anything, Mr. Heller."

"I think I do. For your kindness. And patience."

"Is there anything I can do to help?"

"I'd like to talk to your father, and to Carl's father, as well. And you said I should speak to Tom Ed?"

"Definitely. He *knows* things."

I liked the sound of that.

"Can you help me make some calls? Pave the way for me a little bit?"

In the other room, the wail of the waking child cut through like a police siren.

"I'll be glad to, if you'll give me a minute." She rose, and was going quickly to her boy, when she stopped cold and said, "You know, I can sympathize with Mrs. Long."

"Really?"

"Carl's policy had a double-indemnity accidental death clause, too. But it didn't pay on death by homicide, either."

And she went out.

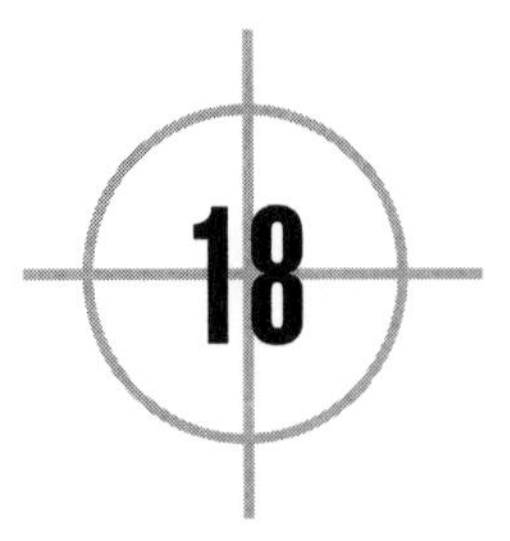

The frosted glass read DR. C. A. WEISS, M.D.—EYE, EAR, NOSE AND THROAT SPECIALIST; another doctor's name was beneath. But the bottom third of the window space was left awkwardly open—no doubt the other, younger Doctor Weiss's name had been lettered here, before thunderous gunfire in the capitol's marble halls, last year, had gotten it scraped off.

The suite of offices was on the seventh floor of the Reymond Building—I'd once visited the sixth floor—and the chairs in the spacious waiting room were filled with patients thumbing through the out-of-date magazines. Maybe they weren't here for their eyes.

Despite the crowd, the lanky brunette nurse came out from around her reception desk and showed me right in. The doctor had an impressive spread: I was led down a hallway off of which were two treatment cubicles with eye charts, and doors marked RECOVERY LAB and X-RAY ROOM. The office at the end of the hallway was small and spartan, however, just the usual diplomas, a few file cabinets and a big, open rolltop desk. I sat in an uncushioned wooden chair near the cushioned swivel one at the rolltop, and waited. Not long.

Meticulous in a dark vested suit, a silver stickpin in his blue tie, Dr. Weiss was of medium height and probably around sixty, though he looked older; he had a stern face, but the gray eyes behind the rimless glasses were gentle and, not surprisingly, sad. He was bald as an egg.

I stood and offered my hand and he shook it.

"My daughter-in-law tells me you're trying to help clear Carl's name," he said.

"I don't want to misrepresent myself, doctor. I'm working as an impartial investigator, merely trying to ferret out the truth of this unhappy situation."

He gestured for me to sit, and he settled into the swivel chair, resting an elbow on the neatly ordered desk. "That's more than can be said for any prior investigation."

"My understanding was that the D.A. who held the inquest into your son's death was no fan of Huey Long's."

He nodded slowly. "That's true. In fact, the district attorney attended the notorious DeSoto Hotel conference . . . and once that fact was thrust in his face, and in that of the press, our illustrious D.A. backed off. And the Long machine's Bureau of Criminal Investigation . . . which is investigation *by* criminals, as I see it . . . put their rubber stamp on the whole sorry affair."

"You were no fan of Huey Long's, either."

His smile was thin and bitter. "No. There were those in my family who, upon hearing the news that Long had been shot, prayed *I* hadn't done it. But thousands upon thousands of families in Baton Rouge had the same reaction about someone in their own families."

"And no one would have suspected your son of this?"

He shook his head, no, gravely. "If anything, Carl tried to calm *me* down, when I'd rant and rave about that tin-pot Napoleon. Oh, he was no admirer of Long's, and from time to time expressed a general dismay over Long's puppet government. But, like so many people who stand apart from politics, Carl accepted it as if it were inevitable."

"And you didn't?"

The gentle eyes flared, but he remained calm as he said, "To me, Huey Long stood for everything that was wrong, dishonest and conniving in mankind. He was without integrity, and felt every man had his price. He would have run roughshod over this entire country, given the chance."

"Some of the poor people in this state," I said, trying to plumb the depths of his rage, "think Huey's heart was in the right place."

He lifted his chin and peered down his nose at me. "Perhaps that *was* once the case, and he initially did pursue noble goals with an ends-justify-the-means approach. But, remember, Mr. Heller—at a certain point, to such men, the means become an end in themselves."

"I wonder if you'd mind my taking a few notes? And could you go over that last Sunday you spent with your son, as you remember it?"

He had no objection, and he told in detail a story that paralleled the young widow's: Mass, a meal with the family, an afternoon at the cabin, home by 7:30.

"Did you speak with Carl again, after that?" I asked.

"No," he said. He shook his head, adjusted the rimless glasses. "You know, when I heard the radio report that Long had been shot and a Dr. Weiss killed . . . I couldn't imagine it was Carl. But there was no answer when I tried to phone. My son—other son, Tom Ed—came home and he'd heard a rumor about Long and 'Dr. Weiss,' but didn't know any more than I did. I sent him over to Carl's to check up on the situation. I didn't wake my wife, so after a while I just . . . walked the two blocks to their house, to see if this nightmarish thing could be true. . . . There were people all over the front lawn, neighbors, reporters, police—and Yvonne was on the porch. Screaming."

He was staring into nothing.

I said, "Dr. Weiss, did your son carry a pistol when he went out at night?"

"Occasionally, he did."

"Why?"

He winced. "Well . . . we'd had prowlers in the neighborhood. And a doctor carries narcotics in his bag, after all."

I nodded. "Is it possible that your son felt as deeply about Long as you, but kept it to himself? By all reports, he was quiet, retiring. . . ."

"Not around the family and his close friends," he said. "He had a lovely sense of humor—his college friends called him 'Weissguy'! Mr. Heller, I don't equivocate in any way on this subject: I am convinced beyond any doubt that my Carl did *not* go into the capitol intending to kill Long."

I tapped my pencil on the pad. "You know, doctor, from everything I've learned, I'd tend to agree with you. But there's one snag: he *did* go into the capitol—and did, in some fashion, confront Long."

His eyes tightened; it was a riddle he'd been unable to solve, in all these months. How many sleepless nights had he spent trying to?

"All I know, Mr. Heller, is that my son was too happy to even *think* of doing what he is accused of having done. Too brilliant, too . . . *good.* Too happy with his wife, his child, too much in love with them to want to end his life after such a murder."

"Maybe he thought he could get away with it. Hit-and-run . . ."

"You embarrass yourself with the question. You can barely get it out, can you, Mr. Heller? Carl would have known that it was suicide, that he was walking into cold, deliberate self-destruction under the guns of those vicious 'bodyguards.' "

"You're right," I admitted. "But it had to be said." I closed the little notebook. "Thank you for your time. I may be back in touch."

"Feel free to contact me, any time, here or at home."

He gave me a business card with his home address and number written on it; I thanked him, shook hands with him again, and was half in the hall when he said, "He came to see me once, you know."

"Pardon? Who?"

The old doctor wore the faintest, damnedest smile. "Huey Long. The fabled Kingfish. Had a speck in his eye. Stormed into the waiting room, demanding immediate attention, cursing like a sailor."

"Did you help him?"

"He didn't want an anesthetic, but I gave him one anyway, put cocaine in his eye, removed the foreign body. But there was nothing I could do for his other problem."

"Pardon?"

His lip curled in disgust. "That foul mouth."

The same schoolmarmish secretary was at her desk, typing, when I entered the reception area of the attorney's office on the sixth floor. I asked her if Mr. Hamilton was in, and she frowned at me and asked if I had an appointment.

"I don't need one," I said, and left her huffing behind me as I moved right by her, opened the door and went on into the small office with its riverboat prints and signed FDR photo and scattering of diplomas. The white-haired attorney—dignity personified in his three-piece gray suit and gray-and-white tie—looked up from a desk spread with legal papers. His dark eyebrows furrowed at the interruption, his mustache twitched with irritation.

"What's the idea . . ." But then the eyebrows shot up, as he recognized me.

The schoolmarm was angling past me, indignation on wheels. "Mr. Hamilton, I'm so very sorry, but this *gen*tleman—"

"That's all right, Lucille," Hamilton said, batting the air, his eyes racing, "I'll make time for him."

She was breathing heavily as she went out, and shut the door, hard. I pulled up a chair and sat casually across from the worried counselor.

"What is it you want, Mr. Heller?" he asked.

"I'm flattered you remember my name."

"Actually, you gave me two names—but only the second one stuck."

I clasped my hands behind my neck and winged my elbows out. "Perhaps that's 'cause you wrote it down, and repeated it to a friend or two?"

He began drumming his fingers. "Why would I have done that?"

"Because I offered to help kill Huey Long. Don't you remember?"

He twitched a smile. "If blackmail is your intention, you've come to the wrong—"

"This isn't about blackmail. It's about the truth."

"The truth?"

An unfamiliar concept to many a lawyer.

"The truth," I said. "For example, the truth is, a few days after I came here with my offer of 'help,' somebody on the next floor . . ." I pointed up. ". . . shot and killed Huey Long."

He stood. I thought he was going to gesture at the door and demand I leave; instead, he put his hands in his pockets and looked out the slats of his blinds at Baton Rouge.

"In the first place," he said quietly, as if to himself, "there are severe doubts that Dr. Carl Weiss killed Huey Long. In the second place, the work of *other* doctors, like that political hack Vidrine, is who and what killed Huey Long."

"You know who I was *really* working for, Mr. Hamilton, when I approached you last year?"

He looked over his shoulder at me curiously.

I said, "The Kingfish."

His face whitened. He turned toward me. Leaned his hands on the back of his chair. "And who do you work for, now? Seymour Weiss? Governor Leche?"

"Actually, Mutual Insurance."

"What?"

"I'm trying to determine who *did* shoot Huey Long."

He looked like I'd hit him with a mackerel. "For an insurance company?"

"That's right. How well did you know Carl Weiss?"

He shook his head dismissively. "Hardly at all. Just to speak to."

"But he was part of your organization, the Square Dealers, right?"

"Wrong. He was not a member."

I sat forward. "What about the DeSoto Hotel conference? The Long people's 'Assassination Ticket,' last election, was predicated on evidence that Weiss attended."

"Ridiculous. I was there. Carl Austin Weiss wasn't."

"You're telling me that in this hotbed of anti-Long feeling, Carl Weiss wasn't one of the chiefs?"

He raised an eyebrow and smirked. "Mr. Heller—he wasn't even an Indian."

It took one ferry across the Mississippi to Port Allen, and another across the Atchafalya, to get to Opelousas. Highway 90 was dotted with roadside parks and tourist camps, a scenic drive that, in two and a half hours, put me in this hamlet of six thousand or so souls. Signs and commemorative markers trumpeted Opelousas as the birthplace of Jim Bowie, of hunting knife and Alamo fame—otherwise, beyond enduring a couple centuries of existence, the town seemed undistinctive. Past the typical town square, dominated by a Victorian monstrosity of a courthouse, I tooled my rental Ford through residential sections of tree-lined streets with unremarkable frame homes perched on generous lawns.

The Pavy place was an exception. It had the generous lawn, all right—a luxurious expanse with a long walkway I strode down, past two ancient, Spanish-moss-hung oaks—but was a remarkably well-preserved example of an antebellum residence. The afternoon was dwindling. Judge Benjamin Pavy sat in a rocking chair on the unenclosed porch, looking beyond the white pillars of his plantation–style home at the lengthening shadows.

He stood as I approached. A towering, heavyset, broad-shouldered old gentleman with gray mustache and full head of silver hair, he would have seemed the picture of health had his complexion not been so pallid. His round jaw was offset by a high forehead; his nose was well sculpted, almost prominent; his eyes dark and kind under curves of salt-and-pepper eyebrows.

If his home could have served as a museum exhibit, he could have passed as the tour guide, decked out in blue alpaca coat, white shirt and striped blue-and-white tie, and white linen trousers, Southern colonel–style.

"Thank you for seeing me," I said, as I accepted his firm handshake.

"A pleasure, sir," he said, and there was a French lilt under the melodic drawl. He gestured to a second rocker he had waiting for me, beside him.

I sat. Rocked.

"If you'll excuse my lack of hospitality," he said, "I prefer we speak out of doors. Talk of this tragedy only serves to upset Mrs. Pavy."

"I understand. Your daughter explained what I'm up to?"

"Yes. Yes, indeed. I will be glad to answer any questions, but I'm afraid you'll find little of use, here."

The sun going down was turning the Spanish moss into spun gold.

"He was a very fine young man, Carl was," the judge said. "Vonnie . . . my daughter . . . brought him to meet me one Sunday afternoon. They wanted my approval, but I gave it even before they could ask. They were married here in Opelousas, you know, at St. Landry Parish church."

"Judge—why did Huey Long go to so much trouble to get rid of you? With all the judges he controlled, why bother?"

The thin line beneath the mustache formed a faint, proud smile. "Because I made him look bad. You see, I stood up to him. I wasn't afraid to throw his election officials in jail for their chicanery. His pawn O.K. Allen would pardon them, mere hours later, but just the same, I was pleased to be a burr under Long's saddle."

I said, "The general thinking is that Carl Weiss snapped because Long was about to gerrymander you off the bench."

He rocked for a while before answering; his expression was as blank as a stone. "I'm afraid I've tortured myself over that possibility," he admitted, "ever since that terrible night. The thought that I, however innocently, might have prompted, or even indirectly contributed to Carl's death, gnaws at the inside of me. I keep wondering . . . if I hadn't been so deeply involved in politics, would Carl have gone to the capitol that night?"

"Do *you* think he shot Long?"

His tone was weary but not impatient. "You have to understand, young man, that Carl and I never discussed politics. . . ."

"He never mentioned Huey Long in your presence?"

He took his time before answering. "Only once, that I can think of."

"Yes?"

"Carl was a student in Vienna . . . he was a gifted boy, you know. But he had seen dictatorship in full sway, in Europe. Once, I remember he compared Long to Mussolini, Hitler and Dollfuss."

"Dollfuss," I said. "Wasn't he that Austrian dictator?"

"Yes. That's correct. . . ."

"And wasn't he assassinated?"

The old judge said nothing; merely looked out at the shadows, which were lengthening and blending and turning into darkness.

Arms folded, Tom Ed Weiss, looking very collegiate in his white shirt, lime green sweater-vest and darker green gabardine pleated slacks, leaned against my Ford, parked in front of the Sigma Pi fraternity, just off the LSU campus. The street, like so many in Baton Rouge, was lavishly shaded; a nearly full moon filtered through leaves and painted the world a perfect ivory. It was after nine, and fairly quiet, though most of the lights were on in the two-story frame frat house behind us, and an occasional couple walked by, arm-in-arm, the girl giggling and snuggling, the boy carrying a double pile of schoolbooks under his other arm; the library probably just closed. Now and then a clunker car with college kids would rumble by. This was the never-never land of academia; the controlled climate of studies and homecoming dances and bonfires and coeds and frat rats.

But Tom Ed, a handsome enough kid, his looks echoing his late brother's but minus the specs, was scowling.

"The bastards framed him," Tom Ed said.

"You really think so?" I said. I was leaning against the

car. Just a couple of pals talking, though we'd known each other about two minutes.

"Those B.C.I. sons of bitches didn't even want to hear my story," he said. "Do you know the cops never came around? Some of 'em milled around out front, on the lawn, but my family, all of us, heard about it this way and that . . . some from the radio, some word of mouth—my *mom* had a damn *reporter* come to the door and tell her!"

"*I* want to hear your story," I said.

He turned his head, sideways, to give me an appraising stare. Yvonne Weiss had told me that Tom Ed idolized his brother, though the gulf of that decade or so between them had kept them from being close; the boy was taking pre-med, not to follow in his father's footsteps, but his brother's.

"Vonnie says you're trying to help," he said.

"I'm an impartial investigator," I said.

"Compared to what's gone on before, that qualifies as a help." He looked out at the street, gazing at the pavement as if he could view the past there. "Anyway, it was Rush Week. Some frat brothers and me, we were riding around with some high-school seniors we were rushing."

"Night of the shooting, you mean?"

"Yes. We were circlin' around the statehouse, lookin' for a parking place. We thought it'd be a riot, goin' in and watchin' the Kingfish and his big show. We all thought he was kind of a royal joke, y'know. I mean, everybody laughed at him behind his back, leadin' the marching band, ridin' in parades next to cheerleaders, struttin' along the sidelines bossin' the football coach aroun'. Sometimes it wasn't so funny, like when he expelled the newspaper staff for printing one negative letter about him."

I recalled the meeting between Huey and LSU President Smith, who had catered to the Kingfish's every whim and had exhibited no particular interest in the students.

"But we couldn't find an empty spot that night," he went on; he put his hands in the pockets of his loose trousers and jingled his change nervously. "The lot was jam-packed—every farmer, every shopkeeper, every mother's son, not to mention every mother, was piled inside that capitol watching that clown perform."

"So you didn't stop?"

"We would've had to park a couple blocks away, and we said, forget it." He shook his head. "Shit. If only I'd stopped in there, maybe I'd've run into Carl and stopped it. Whatever the hell happened."

"I wouldn't waste time thinking about that. Your sister-in-law said you 'know things.' What things, Tom Ed?"

A girl's happy laughter rippled through the night; a horn honked a few blocks away.

"I was still drivin' around with my pals, along Third Street, when we noticed a crowd swarmin' around the *State-Times* newspaper office. I pulled over and got out, and somebody in the crowd said Long had been shot. Somebody else said that a Dr. Weiss did it. That gave me a chill."

"Did you think of Carl?"

"Carl? Hell, no! I thought of my dad! With his hotheaded political ideas, it'd be just like him to get in some stupid scrape with Long. Anyway, I asked the guys to take me back home, drop me off. The front porch lights were on, and Dad was standing on the front steps. He looked kind of . . . dazed. He said, 'Something's wrong. Your mother's sleeping, she doesn't know.' And I said, 'Doesn't know what?' And he said, 'I'm not sure, but I'm afraid something's happened to Carl.' "

He swallowed and touched his hand to his face; squeezed his nose. Swallowed again. I patted him lightly on the shoulder.

"Then what, Tom Ed?"

"Then I guess I told Dad what I heard at the newspaper

office. And he told me he'd heard something over the radio, and sent me over to Carl's, to see what was going on. There were all sorts of people, in the street and on the lawn; I pushed through, and rang the doorbell. Vonnie stepped out on the porch. She was very panicky. She said, 'Carl's gun isn't in the house!' "

"Why do you think she checked for his gun?"

"She'd heard the vague radio report, too. I don't know—maybe she thought Dad had taken it. Maybe she didn't know Carl had been carrying it with him a lot, lately. Anyway . . . I told her I thought Carl had been killed, and she looked out at all those faces in front of her house, and she . . . she started to scream."

I didn't know what to say. The only sounds were the jingle of his change and a distant car. Lights were starting to wink off along fraternity row.

"Dad showed up about that time," he said, "and took Vonnie inside. I was so . . . so damn frustrated! We'd had no official word! It was only two blocks to the capitol, so I decided to walk over there, and see for myself. My cousin Jim lived just down the street, and he went over with me."

"When was this?"

"Oh . . . it must have been about eleven, eleven-thirty. The capitol doors were locked; the state troopers were keeping people away. But we found Carl's car."

"Where?"

"Right in front. Just to the left of that fancy front stairway with the states on the steps. Huey Long himself didn't have a better parking space."

How had Carl Weiss managed that?

"The car was locked," he continued, "but through the window, we could see Carl's bag on the seat. I figured we ought to move the car, so we ran back home to get the spare keys. But when we came back, the car was gone."

"Gone? Did you find it?"

The boy nodded. "Somebody had moved it around on the east side of the building. When I unlocked it, I found his medical bag on the floor, on the passenger's side, and the bag was open."

"Open?"

"Somebody'd ransacked it, instruments were sticking out every which way, the whole contents in disarray. The glove box was open—they rifled *it*, too—and there was a white flannel sock on the floor. That made my mouth go dry."

"Why?"

"That was what Carl carried his gun in. 'Cause the gun had a little grease on it, and he didn't want to get anything messy."

"Did he carry the gun in his bag?"

"Sometimes. But mostly in the glove box. He caught a drunk sleepin' it off in his car one time, and had to scuffle with him, some." The boy shrugged. "He'd had the gun a long time, you know. It was a little .32 Browning he brought back from France."

"He liked guns."

He gave me a hard look. "That doesn't make him a killer. He liked music, too, but it didn't make him an opera singer."

"What do you think Carl was doing at the capitol?"

"Well, he sure as hell wasn't there to shoot Huey Long. My brother was too moral, had too much respect for life, and love for his family, not to mention a complete disinterest in petty local politics. . . ."

The same Weiss-Pavy family song.

I sang the Heller song: "But he *did* go in there. He *did* confront Long. Why?"

Tom Ed shrugged. Jingled his change.

"There's something you're not telling me, Tom Ed. Something no one in your family has told me, yet."

He looked at me sharply. "What have you heard?"

"Nothing! I'm trying to find out what the hell your

brother was doing there! No one in your family believes the gerrymander issue could have triggered this tragedy. What *did*?"

"Well . . ."

"Well, what, Tom Ed?"

He looked away from me. His voice was barely audible. "If aspersions had been cast on the Pavy family, I could . . . I could see Carl doing something about it." Now he looked at me, and his voice was not soft: "*Not* murder, *never* murder . . . but confronting Long? Arguing with him, maybe even punching the son of a bitch in the mouth? I could see that."

"What sort of aspersions, Tom Ed?"

He shrugged again. "That's all you're gettin' out of me. I gave you plenty."

I patted him on the shoulder. "Yes, you did."

A tiny half-smile formed. "Didn't mean to get smart."

"It's okay. Family honor's a big deal down here, isn't it?"

"Counts for a lot," he said. "Funny thing, though."

"What's that?"

"You'd be surprised how many people in Louisiana consider Carl a hero. A martyr. We get letters damn near ever'-day from people wantin' to fund a statue."

"Do you think your brother was a martyr?"

He bristled. "Hell no! He was a *murder* victim. You'll have to excuse me, Mr. Heller. I still have studies to tend to. . . ."

He shook my hand and headed up the walk of the fraternity house. But even this sheltered world wouldn't be shelter enough for the brother of the man who shot the Kingfish.

Beauregard Town was a residential section near downtown Baton Rouge, a stone's throw from Huey's White House-like governor's mansion. It was after ten o'clock, and the moon mingled with soft-focus streetlamps to lend the quaint, late-nineteenth-century subdivision, which ran to gingerbread cottages with small well-tended yards, a quiet charm.

I pulled the Ford up in front of one of the slightly larger, newer bungalows, a one-and-a-half-story wood-frame with a broad open porch and tapered piers; centered in the roof was a dormer with triple windows. The lights were on in the downstairs front windows.

I went up the walk, onto the gallery-style porch, knocked on the door.

It didn't take her long to answer. She was wearing a blue satin dressing gown, sashed tight around her waist, and darker blue open-toed high-heeled slippers; she seemed dressed for bed, but she hadn't yet removed the makeup from her pretty, heart-shaped face. Her cupie-bow mouth really was way the hell out of date. Fetching nonetheless, like her equally dated cap of flapper curls.

Alice Jean Crosley was a sight for sore eyes.

"Your message said you'd be up till eleven," I told her. "I took you at your word."

The mouth pursed into her kiss of a smile. "You look tired," she said, through the screen.

"I had a long day. I'm one of those working men you hear so much about."

She opened the screen door and made a mock-elegant gesture for me to enter. I did.

The small entryway opened right onto the living room, which was furnished in the modern style, no chrome, but lots of sleek walnut furnishings and a rust-color striped mohair sofa and matching easy chair with ottoman. For a single woman's living room, it seemed surprisingly male.

But there were feminine touches—floral-print draperies, a dreamy Maxfield Parrish print over the sofa, a bisque baby on a rounded radio console, creamy silk-shaded lamps with pottery bases and antimacassars on the sofa and chair arms.

"Come here, you big lug," she said.

I just love it when dames say that.

She wrapped her arms around me and gave me a long, hard kiss. It wasn't passionate, exactly; but it was a hell of a hello.

Then she led me by the hand to the sofa, where we both sat, and she crossed her legs, sharing a well-turned calf and promise of creamy thigh.

"How did you know I was in town?" I asked.

"I still have my spies in Huey's machine."

"How did *they* know I was in town?"

"Are you serious? You're staying at the Heidelberg, aren't you?"

I shrugged. "It's the only decent hotel in Baton Rouge."

She smirked. "Well, Roy Heidelberg is one of Seymour's best pals. Everybody knows you're in town. They just don't know why."

She reached for an already opened pack of Chesterfields on the round coffee table before us; a few magazines were spread out there—*Vogue*, *Cosmopolitan*, *True Romance*, *Photoplay*, *Breezy*. Apparently, Alice Jean had a lot of spare time, these days.

"Is that why you left the message for me, at the hotel?" I asked. " 'Cause you want to know why I'm here?"

She fanned out her match, sucked on her cigarette. "I wanna know how you can have the nerve to come to Baton Rouge and not look me up."

"I've only been here a day," I grinned. "And here I am."

She pretended to pout. "And I had to go begging. All those letters I wrote . . . all those phone calls . . ."

"I have great affection for you, Alice Jean. But it took money to get me to come back to this state."

"You *are* on a job."

"That's right."

"Tell me about it."

I waggled a scolding finger. "There's such a thing as client confidentiality."

"Warm in here. I oughta buy myself a nice big electric fan." She unsashed her satin robe, opened it up some; gave the globes of her bosom a chance to cool off. She was right: all of sudden it was warm in here.

"I'm working for Mutual Insurance," I said.

She inhaled. "Tell me more."

"I don't think so. Even if you take it all the way off."

That made her smile. "You know what I like about you? You're shifty, but you have standards."

"You could take it off and call my bluff, you know. Might be worth a try."

"Nate," she said, and her hand found the back of my neck and she scratched and tickled and played with my hair. "I'm not in the enemy camp. I'm just curious."

"Since when is Alice Jean Crosley not a part of the Huey Long machine?"

"Since that peckerwood Governor Leche fired me."

I blinked. "What? *You* were fired? But, Alice—you know which bayous the bodies are buried in."

She shrugged. "Didn't matter, apparently. I was friendly with Jimmy Noe, and that was all it took."

"Who's Jimmy Noe?"

"He was governor, briefly, after O.K. Allen died. Just one of the many of Huey's minions, squabblin' over the spoils. But I like Jimmy better than that fat crook Leche. And Jimmy's been lining up support around the state, and we were friendly, and so I got fired. All my relatives, too."

"Hell of a thing." I glanced around at her bungalow full of new furniture. "Looks like the Collector of Revenue may have collected a little revenue herself, over the years."

"Moral indignation, from the Chicago delegation?"

"Just an idle observation. You know, I would've thought Seymour and the gang would've been up the river by now.

When I was here last year, the tax boys were closing in."

She laughed harshly. "Are you kidding? Nothin' touches Seymour Weiss. Elmer Irey and his boys packed up their bags, not long after Huey was killed."

"What?"

"Sure! All indictments pending against Seymour and the other 'Longsters' were dropped."

"Sounds like the fix was in."

She blew a perfect smoke ring. "Of course—clear from Washington, D.C. If Huey's heirs will just cooperate with FDR's administration, all sins are forgiven. That was the rumor around the statehouse."

"Only it wasn't just a rumor. . . ."

She raised an eyebrow and gestured grandly with her Chesterfield. "Let's put it this way—last June, Seymour Weiss was Louisiana's national committeeman at the Democratic National Convention."

And I thought Chicago was something.

"So, Nate," she said, and she slipped the robe down to her waist and folded her arms across her treasure chest like a genie, "what brings you to Louisiana?"

"You really think a cheap, vulgar move like that would work on me?"

She put her hands on her hips.

I told her everything.

When I was finished, she got back in the robe, tied it tightly and got up. She began to pace and smoke.

"That isn't fair," I said.

"Fair, hell," she said, shaking her head. "You're crazy. Completely bughouse."

"Why?"

She stood facing me; her face was white. "This is one case that you *cannot* go messin' in. Understand? These people will kill you."

"I don't think so."

"You don't, huh? Do you know that when they lifted Carl Weiss's body off the marble floor, it sounded like a hailstorm, with all those bullets fallin' outa him? *You* know what kinda men you're dealin' with—Messina, McCracken, even your chum Roden. Homicidal thugs! They've been rewarded with fancy jobs, you know. They're not gonna want that threatened."

I waved at the air, dismissively. "If they kill me, it's an admission of guilt. And another investigator will follow, and another, and eventually even in this swamp of a state, it'll all catch up with 'em."

"Meanwhile, Heller, you're dead."

She had a point.

She came around and sat next to me, very close; put her hand on my leg. "Why bother with this? You're on a fool's errand. Everybody in the state knows it's possible, maybe even probable, that Huey got hit by a stray bullet in the close-quarter chaos of that hallway. But everybody also knows that Dr. Carl Weiss at the very least *tried* to kill Huey."

"I think he may have just smacked Huey in the mouth, and got shot for the trouble. Talking to Tom Ed Weiss makes me think somebody got the doctor's handgun out of his car *after* the fact. Switched it with a throw-down gun, no doubt."

She shook her head, no. "I don't think so."

She seemed certain.

"Why, Alice Jean?"

"The Weiss family knows; so do the Pavys. But I bet they didn't tell you. And if you ask them, they'll deny it."

"Deny *what*?"

Her smile was not one of amusement. "Huey had a nasty habit of smearing his enemies . . . sometimes it was with charges of mental illness in the family. Usually it was racial."

"Racial?"

"Oh, I know you people up North are much too high-minded and advanced to have any racial prejudices or racial difficulties of any kind. But we backward Southern folk haven't quite worked it out, yet."

"Alice Jean—what the hell are you talking about?"

"I'm talking about Huey needing to fight the opposition to his gerrymander bill. Oh, he could push the bill through, but there'd have been an outcry. Judge Pavy was popular, you know, respected even by his enemies. Except Huey . . . Huey didn't really respect anybody, did he?"

"You knew him better than I."

"Yes . . . and neither of us knew him at all. How could I love him, Nate? How could I love somebody capable of smearing a fine man like Judge Pavy with public accusations of the most ruinous sort? Huey . . . Huey was preparing to spread the word that the Pavy family had 'nigger blood.' "

I frowned. "Huey had done that sort of thing before?"

"Oh yes."

"And down here, it's . . . it's something you kill over?"

"You definitely kill over. If you were a father, with an infant son you loved very much, and your family was faced with such a scurrilous slur . . . you might even willin'ly die for it."

So this was the "aspersion" Huey was casting that Tom Ed had referred to.

"I'm glad to have you back, Nate," she said, slipping her arms around me; her Chanel Number Five tickled my nostrils. "But don't look into this morass of unpleasantness anymore. I don't want another man I love to die in a storm of gunfire."

She stood and slipped off the robe and turned her perfect dimpled behind to me and walked slowly out of the room.

What she'd had to say was troubling, and my mind was spinning, but you know what?

I followed her.

The Reverend Gerald L. K. Smith, his hawklike nose unable to defeat his blond boyishness, was pink and hairless and plump, like a big baby, as he lounged in the large bathtub, overflowing with frothy white bubbles.

"We're both men," the enormous child said, with a smile that had charmed many a dollar from a wallet, "so I trust you don't mind meeting with me in this fashion. . . . After all, some might consider it undignified."

I was sitting on the toilet. Lid down. The gleaming white-tiled restroom—in one of the finest suites at the St. Charles Hotel in New Orleans—was larger than some hotel rooms I'd stayed in.

"I'm grateful to get any audience," I said, "at such short notice."

He was soaping one fleshy arm with a pink bar—no washcloth for such delicate skin. "Miss Crosley said you're undertaking an investigation that may prove embarrassing to the curs who displaced from power both that fine young lady and myself."

It was nice to know that this man of God held so high

an opinion of the late Kingfish's mistress. Who, incidentally, had reluctantly agreed to help me line up a few key interviews, like this one.

"Yes sir, I am undertaking just such an investigation," I said with ludicrous formality; but sometimes the only way to deal with pompous people is to shove pomposity back at 'em. "I understand I'm lucky to catch you in Louisiana at all, these days."

He squinted one eye; a fleck of stray bubbles gave him an extra, if foamy, eyebrow. "I've presently moved my headquarters to California. I've thrown my lot in with Dr. Townsend."

Dr. Francis E. Townsend of California—a mild-mannered, far more benign version of Huey—was well known for his utopian ideals and notions of higher taxes and generous old-age pensions. His gentle approach seemed at odds with Reverend Smith's rabble-rousing style, but I could well understand that Townsend would relish inheriting the millions of Huey's Share the Wealth Club members.

The man of God's eyes narrowed suspiciously. "Mr. Heller, before we speak further, I must ask you an . . . embarrassing, but necessary, question. I already asked Miss Crosley, and she gave me certain assurances. But I must ask you, sir."

"Well, go ahead, Reverend. By all means."

"Are you Hebrew? Your last name demands the question."

"Yes, and it's a fair one," I said. "Most 'Hellers' are Jewish. My family on my father's side is German and Catholic. My mother's people were Irish Catholic."

This was, of course, a lie, except for the part about my mother.

"Frankly, I would prefer Protestant," he sighed. "But Catholicism is the far lesser of the two evils. I have a general policy of mistrusting Jews. Some consider this attitude anti-Semitic."

"No, really?"

He nodded; he had a billy-goat soap-bubble beard. "It is, frankly, a political stand. A *practical* stand. Look at the Long organization—riddled with Jews! And like jackals smelling carrion, they have torn the flesh from the true supporters of that great man."

"It's very sad, sir."

"And, of course, it's no surprise that the assassin himself, this Carl Weiss, was a Jew."

"Actually, he wasn't."

He sat up in the tub, sloshing; a few bubbles plopped onto the tile floor. "What are you saying, man?"

I shrugged. " 'Weiss,' like Heller, is a German name. There are Weisses who are Gentiles, and Dr. Weiss and his family happen to be Catholics."

This news disturbed him no end. "I find this difficult to believe."

"Nonetheless, it's true. Of course, he may not have been an assassin at all."

Patches of bubbles decorating his pink chest, the Reverend frowned in confusion; for all his abilities—speaking before the public, scheming behind the scenes—Dr. Gerald L. K. Smith was just not very smart.

"What are you saying, man? The Kingfish is our martyred leader!"

"I didn't say he wasn't."

But he was off and running. Gesturing, splashing, turning his bubble bath into a stormy sea, Dr. Smith delivered a brief sermon: "They called him a dictator, but it was the dictatorship of the surgical theater. Huey Long was a political surgeon, working for the welfare of the patient!"

"Right . . ."

"There are those who claim he was corrupt! I say he

merely yielded on lesser principles to serve a greater one. Share the wealth! Every man a king, and no man wears a crown!"

Maybe so, but I was sitting on the throne.

"The point is, Reverend," I said, hoping we could get back to it, "I believe those around Huey Long were responsible for his death."

Fire flared in the pale blue eyes. "Yes . . . I can see it. A conspiracy. Surrounded by those vile Hebrews. . . . You're saying the Jews killed Huey, just as they killed our Lord!"

"Well . . . no. I think it was probably an accident."

"It was no accident that Jesus was slain by the Jews!"

"I was talking about the other slaying. What it's starting to look like is Dr. Carl Weiss confronted Huey, about a racial slur against the Pavy family. I think Huey probably shrugged it off, and got belted by the doctor in return. Then those bodyguards started firing, and . . ."

A gleeful grin had formed. "But don't you see? Seymour and the others, they must have been in league with Roosevelt!" He swung a fist out of his soapy sea. "Yes! FDR and the Jews!"

"Well . . ."

"Don't you grasp it, man? Seymour and the Long machine, they've been campaigning for Roosevelt all year! He'll be reelected next month, in a landslide! Would such be the case if Huey were alive, and running for president himself? Would *Huey Long* have put his machine behind the reelection of that vile, crippled deceiver?"

"Of course not."

"These evil fiends. Capable of anything. Do you know what they did to me?"

"What?"

The rack? The iron maiden? Crucifixion?

"They denied me my mailing list," he said, soapy chin thrust out.

"Heavens."

"Eight million followers, and I'm cut off from them, like the head amputated from the body." A pointing finger rose from the bubbly waters and shook angry suds at the air. "But if Huey was a surgeon, I am a dentist!"

"A dentist?"

"A social dentist. Pulling the decayed teeth of social ills. No intelligent person questions his dentist, does he?"

"Of course not."

"The patient must keep his mouth shut, and allow the tooth-puller to do his work!"

"If the patient has his mouth shut," I asked, "how does the dentist pull the tooth, exactly?"

"It's a figure of speech, man! Since Huey Long's death, Louisiana is riddled with social decay. The money demons of Wall Street and the predatory corporations have found willing accomplices in the likes of Seymour and his stooge, Governor Leche. Think of it—to cut a deal with Standard Oil, after Huey's blood had been shed in the capitol halls!"

I frowned. "What deal with Standard Oil?"

"It was in all the papers, man!"

"Not in Chicago. Catch me up."

"Why, Governor Leche cut a deal with those hounds of hell. Huey's five-cents-a-barrel tax was transmuted into a new, meager, one-cent-per-barrel tax. Of course, that's no surprise, is it?"

"It's a surprise to me," I said. "I would have thought Long's successors wouldn't dare dilute something that'd been such a public crusade of Huey's."

He snorted a laugh. "You know that lobbyist fellow of theirs—Louis LeSage?"

"Yes."

"Well, he and Seymour the Jew are old, dear friends."

"Seymour and LeSage? Friends?"

He thrust an arm from the tub and pointed. "When the

legislature isn't in session, LeSage lives in a palatial suite down at the Roosevelt Hotel. Which, of course, Weiss owns. LeSage stays there free of charge."

For a moment my mind reeled. One of the potential murder plotters Huey had sent me to see was a crony of Seymour's? Was there something sinister in it? Or was it just good sleazy politics, keeping a lobbyist happy?

"Now, if there's nothing else, Mr. Heller, I'm afraid this interview must come to a close," he said. "I have a rally to prepare for. . . ."

"Thank you, Reverend. Oh, there is one other thing."

"Yes? Anything to help your good efforts."

I stood and leaned over and pushed his head under the water. I held my hand on his skull like a yarmulke. He thrashed and burbled, and my suit got a little wet, though it was worth it.

After about thirty seconds, I let him up. He was coughing, and clouds of bubble bath were drifting like cotton candy in the shining bathroom.

"What . . . what . . . what was the idea. . . ."

"Just thought you should know," I said, drying myself off with a towel, before going out. "Heller *is* a Jewish name."

This bigoted madman had made several interesting points, on his way to Mars. Wild as the "FDR and the Jews" conspiracy theory he'd reeled off may have seemed, some of what the Reverend said had confirmed a conversation I'd had this morning with Elmer Irey.

From the phone in my hotel room, I had called Irey long-distance at his office at the Treasury Department in Washington, D.C.

"Is it true you guys took it on the lam out of Louisiana?" I asked.

"I don't know that I'd put it quite that way," Irey said dryly. "But we'd worked up ironclad tax cases against Seymour Weiss and many of the other Longsters, and last June the plug was pulled."

"At the President's direction?"

"Well, at the Attorney General's."

"You're sure you just didn't have enough hard evidence?"

His sigh hissed over the wires. "Heller—we made careful investigations and accumulated a mass of evidence that we felt, and still feel, would provide the basis for successful prosecutions. My office was not in favor of cancellation of the cases."

"And now the Long machine is in bed with FDR?"

"I can't really say." A pregnant pause was followed by: "But I can say that one of the journalists who covered the story referred to it as the 'second Louisiana Purchase.' "

Judge John Fournet made a similar point, when he met me for an early afternoon cocktail in the chrome-plated Roosevelt Hotel bar.

"I suppose it's not a surprise that Huey's insurance company would launch an investigation," the well-dressed, lanky judge drawled off-handedly.

Even seated in a back booth, Fournet, about forty, seemed tall. His dark hair was combed back and thinning, his dark blue eyes wide-set and piercing, his nose longish and bulb-tipped, his mouth a thin, measured line, his small chin jutting with self-confidence. His dark gray suit was silk, and his striped blue-and-gray tie bore a diamond-studded triangular pin that couldn't have cost any more than a new Packard. On his left hand was a silver ring with a diamond smaller than a golf ball. He might have been a prosperous bookmaker, but he was an associate justice of the Louisiana Supreme Court.

"I told Dick Leche," he continued in his cultured, molasses baritone, referring to the governor of the state, "it was a mistake not to have a full investigation of the assassination."

"Why didn't he?" I asked. "Leche campaigned on that, didn't he?"

"He certainly did. But he killed every bill the legislature passed, tryin' to initiate commissions to look into the matter. Trouble is, some lunatics in this state think the President of the United States himself was behind the killing. . . ."

"I met one this morning: Dr. Gerald L. K. Smith."

"I thought *he* blamed the Jews," Fournet said matter-of-factly.

"Oh he does. But they're in it with FDR."

He smiled and shook his head and sipped his drink, a Ramos Gin Fizz. We were having the house specialty in honor of Huey, who had helped popularize the drink, here and in the hotel's Blue Room.

"Problem is," Fournet said, "a full investigation would have brought such wild theories into the full view of a public forum. Silly as the charges are, draggin' the President's name into such an investigation would have been, on the one hand, embarrassin', and on the other . . . politically imprudent."

"Not exactly a wise way to woo federal funds."

"Precisely. Now, when you called my office, you said you were trying to establish that Carl Weiss was indeed the assassin."

I had told him this at Alice Jean's suggestion: had I said anything else, the judge would never have consented to meet with me.

"That's right," I said. "You see, Mrs. Long is rather financially strapped, so she's put in a double-indemnity claim. She gets a bigger death benefit if Huey died accidentally."

"Caught by a stray bullet from Messina or Murphy Roden, I suppose?" He shook his head sadly; he traced lines in the moisture on the cocktail glass—even in the dimly lighted hotel bar, the big diamond danced with reflected light. "It's truly sad. Can't blame the poor woman. Huey didn't put much cash away, for himself, y'know; it all went into his political life."

"You seem to be skeptical about that theory—that the death might have been accidental."

The dark blue eyes narrowed. "I was in the thick of it, young man." He looked into his cocktail, as if it were a crystal ball; but he was seeking the past, not the future.

He said somberly, "I was saying hello to Huey when this man of small stature, dressed in a white suit, flashed among us. He had a little black automatic in his right hand. He was right next to me—I put my hands on his arm and tried to deflect the bullet, as he was firing. Then another of the boys—I later learned it was Murphy Roden—grabbed at him, too, and I shoved the man, who I later learned was Dr. Carl Weiss, and Murphy went down with 'im, but not all the way."

"What do you mean?"

"Dr. Weiss was sort of . . . crouchin'. Tryin' to shoot again."

"You feel certain it was Weiss's bullet that hit Huey, and not one of the bodyguards'?"

"I should say. Huey cried out when he got shot, spun around, and ran down the hall like a scared deer. Then the gunfire escalated." He shook his head; the piercing gaze glazed for a moment. "I served in the World War—I was a machine gunner—but I never before heard anything like it. A machine gun fires, oh, three hundred to six hundred bullets a minute. Once the shooting started, it sounded like that and then some."

"You're lucky you weren't hit yourself."

"I just kind of stepped back and it went on before my eyes. Gunsmoke and marble dust made a fog." He sighed. "Then I went looking for Huey. You're the one that got him to the hospital, aren't you?"

"Yes."

"Otherwise, I don't know that I'd have talked to you. We both tried, didn't we?"

"Sir?"

"To save his life. He was a great man. Man of the people."

And he sipped his cocktail.

His diamond winked at me.

What visitor to New Orleans wasn't enraptured by the everyday drama and pageantry of the fourteen miles of docks along this half-mile-wide stretch of the Mississippi, where flags of all nations waved from mastheads, where ferries crossed and recrossed, where paddlewheels churned by invoking bygone days of ruffle-shirted gamblers, where seagulls from the nearby Gulf of Mexico cried mournfully as they trailed ships in search of food. Coffee docks, cotton docks, molasses sheds, bustled with activity; hundreds of sweat-stained workers carried green bunches of bananas from the holds of ships to waiting freight cars on riverside railroad tracks, while fat colored gals in snow white turbans wove their way through the laborers selling sandwiches and sweetcakes.

Administration of the Port of New Orleans was a formidable task, and a great responsibility, regulating commerce and traffic of the harbor, not to mention the wharves and public buildings, and construction of new wharves and sheds. After all, somebody had to collect fees from vessels using the facilities of the port's forty-three docks.

This grave responsibility fell to the Board of Commissioners of the Port of New Orleans, five public-spirited citizens appointed by the governor. I was about to call on one of these noble public servants, who served their six-year terms without pay.

His name was Joe Messina.

The dock board was at the end of, and facing, Canal Street, between the railroad tracks and the river; the *President* steamboat was docked nearby. The cheap concrete building—aggregate with shells stirred in, also used for the nearby wharves—was a two-story building with many windows; its blocky ugliness was offset by a vast, lovely, colorful flower garden that served as its front yard.

The downstairs was mostly a countered-off area with secretaries and clerks at desks; the board members had their offices upstairs. That's where I found Messina, beyond a wall of frosted glass and wood, through an unlocked door with his name on it—sleeping on his brown leather couch in a small wood-and-plaster office that had a desk but no file cabinets. The only paperwork on the desk was some crumpled napkins and a wadded-up paper coffee cup.

Windows looked out on the muddy river and its yellow banks and traffic that consisted of everything from driftwood to ocean-going vessels; at the right, a high viaduct cut off the view. The morning was cloudy, and shadows were sliding over the rippling surface of the river, as if great amorphous sea creatures were swimming just below the surface.

The great amorphous creature on the couch was snoring; he was wearing a white shirt unbuttoned at his thick hairy neck, buttons straining at his generous belly, and dark suit pants on his stumpy legs. His big flat feet were clad in socks with clocks; a pair of black, well-shined Florsheims were on the floor nearby. His suit coat and a tie were slung on a coat tree.

I pulled a chair around and sat; I nudged the couch, with

my foot, just a little. When it didn't stir him, I nudged harder.

He awoke with a start, his snoring turning into a snort that sounded like he was trying to swallow his nose.

"What's the deal?" he said, trying to right himself, like a turned-over alligator. "What's the deal?"

"Hi, Joe."

Finally he managed to sit up, and he rubbed his face with one catcher's-mitt hand and scratched his belly with the other; his slightly thinning dark hair was mussed. His dark little eyes focused on me.

"I know you! What's your name?"

"Nate Heller," I said.

"That's right!" The blank round face broke into an awful parody of a grin. "You're my pal!"

"I am?"

He stood and came over and patted me on the back; it about knocked the wind out of me. "You're the guy that rushed the Kingfish to the hospital! You're okay."

"Thanks, Joe."

"You want coffee? We got coffee."

I shrugged. "I wouldn't mind."

He padded out into the hall in his stocking feet and bellowed: "How about some coffee in here? *Two* coffees!"

He came back in, sat on the couch and got his shoes on. After he got them tied—which took all his concentration—he gestured around him, to his nearly empty office. The only art on the wall was a calendar of a little girl and her puppy and a framed photograph of Huey Long with his arm around a stiltedly smiling Messina.

"Some layout, huh?"

"Some layout. What do you do here, Joe?"

"I'm on the dock board!"

"Yeah, I gathered, but what . . ."

"We're in charge of the docks."

"Ah."

He got up and went behind his desk and sat. I turned my chair around to face him. Through the windows behind him, the Mississippi looked choppy; the wind was picking up.

"You're from Chicago," he said.

"Right."

"I remember you from '32."

"Right again."

His frown was puzzled, not hostile. "What are you doin' in town?"

"I'm looking into the Kingfish's death."

Now it turned hostile. "What do you mean, 'lookin' into' it?"

"I'm working for an insurance company, trying to establish that Dr. Carl Weiss was responsible."

He blinked. "What else could he be but responsible? He shot him!"

"There are other opinions."

The big round head shook, no, no, no. "I don't know anything about no other opinions. In a cowardly way, Senator Long was shot. That's the whole story."

A nervous bespectacled thirtyish male clerk, in a vest and suit pants, came in with two paper cups of coffee. He handed one to Joe, the other to me, and I thanked him. Joe, being a big shot on the dock board, didn't say a word to him. If anything, that seemed only to relieve the clerk, as he went out.

I sipped my coffee, which was strong and black but not very hot. Then I said, "It would help, Joe, if you told me your version of the shooting."

He took several gulps of his coffee, swilled it around in his mouth, possibly trying to eradicate the sleep taste of his nap.

"I don't know nothing till the time the shots were fired," he said. "When that doc fired the shot, I seen the Senator jump back and I knew he was killed."

"What did you do, Joe?"

"I immediately run up, pull my rod out and unload it in that bastard."

"Murphy Roden was scuffling with him, right?"

"I started firing when the guy broke loose from Murphy."

According to Murphy's story, Carl Weiss had been shot in the throat by this point; I doubted he'd broke away from anybody, after that.

But I asked, "He got loose from Murphy?"

"I guess. All I know is, I shot the man that shot Senator Long. I saw the pistol in his hand, too."

"Some people say he didn't have a gun."

He had the coffee cup in his hand when he slammed that hand on the desk; the desk *whumped* and the coffee splashed on Messina and the desktop. "They're goddamn liars! He had a pistol and woulda shot anybody there!"

Messina, glaring now, began licking the coffee off his hand.

Nonetheless, I ventured another comment: "Some people say the doctor slugged the Kingfish."

"He didn't slug him, he shot him." The Neanderthal brow furrowed. "I thought you were the Kingfish's friend!"

"I was." I smiled, shrugged. "You know how it is, Joe. *You* worked for the Bureau of Criminal Investigation. You know what it's like to have to investigate. . . ."

He slapped his chest with a thick hand; his eyes were tortured. "I was his favorite! Some people made fun of me, 'cause I slept at his feet, sometimes. But he had to be protected! They can see that now, now that it's too late!"

"Take it easy, Joe."

His fist quivered in the air. "I loved that man. He was

good to me. I was just sweepin' up hair in a barbershop when he found me."

"Joe, surely you've considered the possibility, that with all those slugs flying . . ."

He stood up, pushed his chair back with a fingers-on-blackboard scrape on the wood floor. "You accusin' me of somethin'?"

"No, I . . ."

He came around the desk and stood, facing me. His voice was trembling; his eyes had teared up. "You think I'd do that? Shoot the best friend I ever had?"

"I didn't say that. Some people think one of the bullets could have ricocheted—"

I didn't finish, because a huge fist was flying toward my face; I ducked back, to avoid it, which I did, but with his other hand, he shoved me, and I went backward, ass-over-tea-kettle, taking the chair with me, the rest of my coffee flying against the wall with a splash.

I landed on my back with a teeth-rattling jolt, and then I was looking up at him, and the grimacing little man seemed huge, towering over me, particularly his Florsheimed foot, which was poised to stomp me. I grabbed hold of it and yanked, and set him on his ass—hard. Everything in the room shook, and so did the frosted glass in the door and outer wall.

I got on my feet and so did he, and he crouched, like a wrestler about to make a play. So I picked up the chair and hit him with it.

In the movies, chairs bust in a million pieces when you do that; but this was a solid wood chair and it didn't break. It just whacked into him and hurt him. Tough as he was, it still made the stocky little bastard drop to one knee and hug himself.

He was crying. Whether over the pain or his dead boss, I wouldn't hazard a guess.

"Joe," I said. "Honestly, I meant no offense. I had to ask the questions. But Joe, a friendly warning—touch me again, and I'll fucking kill you."

And I kicked the chair into the wall, where it made a hell of a racket, and, I hoped, my point.

Messina didn't say anything. He was still on one knee, crying. Trying to scare him was probably about as useful as trying to put the fear of God into a potted plant.

The bespectacled clerk appeared in the doorway, looking like a startled rabbit.

"No more coffee, thanks," I said, and got the hell out.

Diamond Jim Moran wore a double-breasted money green suit and a pale yellow shirt with a light green tie with a diamond stickpin spelling out DJM; the tinted lenses of his gold wire-frames matched the suit.

"How many pair of tinted glasses do you own, Jim?" I asked him. It was just the two of us, in a booth in the Blue Room on the first floor of the Roosevelt Hotel.

"Nineteen," he said, as he studied the menu. He'd invited me for dinner and I'd accepted. "All different colors. Each one matchin' a different double-breasted."

Moran clashed with the blue-tinted glass of the glass-and-chrome cocktail lounge/restaurant with its circular bar and plush deco decor. Phil Harris would be performing later on the Blue Room's surprisingly small stage; it was early—a little after six. We'd already had a drink—I'd had the Planter's Punch (I was Ramos Gin-Fizzed out, house specialty or not) and Moran had something called a Roffignac.

"How's the slot-machine business?" I asked.

"Flourishin'," he said, reading the menu. "Flourishin'."

"You and Dandy Phil Kastel getting along okay?"

"Famously. Famously." He lowered the menu and looked over it at me; his battered pug's puss seemed mildly troubled.

"Though I am afraid, 'tween you, me and the lamppost, that we been a little overly ambitious."

"How so?"

He brushed his mustache with a thumbnail. "Well, gettin' the little devils put in places like restaurants, cafés, grocery stores, cigar stores—establishments that never seen a slot machine of any kind, before—that may be askin' for trouble. Some of the women's clubs and ministers are gettin' after Bob."

"Bob?"

"Mayor Maestri."

Alice Jean had mentioned His Honor the Mayor—a short, swarthy, inarticulate Sicilian whose business interests included whorehouses and gambling dens—who had been inserted, by Huey, into the office of mayor, unopposed, without an election.

I hadn't looked at my menu yet. "Will Kastel pull out, if the slots go?"

"Hell, no! We'll just move along onto the next thing."

"And what'll that be?"

"Pinball machines." He clicked in his cheek. "Wait'll you see the latest ones, with their electric lights and trick gadgets and bells and such. That'll be the next big thing, wait and see."

Those were made in Chicago, too.

I said, "Your invitation was a pleasant surprise."

"When I heard you were in town," he said, putting the menu down, "I wanted to get together."

"How did you know I was in town, Jim?"

His smile was teasing; I couldn't read his eyes—the green lenses blocked the view. "My office is here in the hotel, remember. Maybe the desk clerk told me."

"Why would he?"

"Maybe a little bird. Word's around you're askin' questions about Huey's killin'. Only, nobody seems to have a fix on just where you stand on it."

I shrugged. "I'm working for Mutual Insurance, following up on Mrs. Long's double-indemnity claim."

"Some people think you're pushin' fire."

"What does that mean?"

"Causin' trouble. Some people have the idea you want to clear Dr. Carl Weiss."

"What people?"

He picked the menu back up, opened it and began browsing. "You really should start with the bouillabaisse—the New Orleans variety is sure 'nuff second to none. And we'll have oysters Rockefeller, of course—even if this ain't Antoine's."

"Did Kastel ask you to warn me off?"

His expression was affable. "Nobody asked me to warn nobody off. I jus' invited an old fren' out to dinner."

"Jim—we're not old friends. We met, briefly, last year. I'm surprised you even remember me."

His expression turned somber. "I remember you. I remember 'cause it got back to me you tried to help the Kingfish. I loved that man."

Not again.

He said, "You were down at the dock board, earlier t'day, weren't you?"

"Yeah. So?"

"What kin'a fool thinks he can talk to Joe Messina and learn anything?"

"I learned Joe Messina is driving himself daffy thinking he might have killed his 'best friend.' "

He shrugged his furry eyebrows. "You're prob'ly right about that. Now, the jambalaya here is really quite respectable, for a fancy hotel . . . I mean, we'd have to go back down inta the Vieux Carré, to give you the true Creole experience."

"What do you want with me, Moran?"

"I like 'Jim' better. You're readin' a threat into this, Nate. No threat. I *am* your friend. And I admire ya for lookin' inta this killin'."

"You do?"

He sat back, viewed me appraisingly. "What are ya doin' goin' aroun' the dock board, anyway? Three of the five members are ex-Huey bodyguards, and Seymour Weiss hisself is head man. What a setup for dope and other smugglin' payoffs, and general waterfront shakedowns. . . . Those boys must be gettin' nice and rich—even a dumbbell like Messina."

"I hear *all* the bodyguards got cushy jobs."

"That's the truth. Big George McCracken? He's buildin' superintendent out at LSU, now—soakin' up this federal money that's flowin' again. Murphy Roden got appointed assistant superintendent of the state coppers."

"And none of 'em are going to like me poking around in this case. Not when maybe they accidentally shot their boss."

He looked at me over the tinted glasses. "*If* it was an accident."

"What are you saying?"

He shrugged. His voice was so soft it was barely audible. "I'm not saying anything. But somethin's been botherin' me a long, long time . . . and you're the first person who I can maybe risk sharin' it with."

"Sharing what?"

He sat forward, keeping his voice sotto. "Last year, 'round when you came callin', some of these guys bringin' them Chief slot machines down from Chicago was shootin' their mouths off to Dandy Phil about the Cermak rubout."

The back of my neck began to tingle.

"They said to Dandy Phil, 'If Huey Long's givin' ya money trouble, you oughta do what Frank Nitti done.' And Dandy Phil says, 'What?' And they tell Dandy Phil, 'Nitti bumped him.' And Dandy Phil says, 'You're kiddin'.' And they say, 'Kiddin' my ass! He bumped off the goddamn mayor of Chicago!' "

It was true. Most people thought a crazed assassin named Zangara had missed, when he shot Mayor Cermak, who'd been standing near FDR at a rally for the President-elect at Miami in 1932. Others—like me—knew that Roosevelt was not Zangara's target; knew that Zangara had been a one-man Sicilian suicide squad out to avenge the corrupt Cermak's own failed attempt to have Capone's successor, Frank Nitti, killed.

"Are you listenin', Nate?"

I nodded numbly.

"Anyway, they told Dandy Phil, 'Do it right, set it up from the inside, and the most important thing—find yourself a patsy. Do that, and it'll get written off as a political assassination.' "

"When . . . when was this?"

"When they was bringin' down one of the first loads of them Chiefs. Probably a few weeks before you come down, last year. Of course, they was prob'ly jus' shootin' off their big mouths. . . . You *are* familiar with the Cermak hit, Chicago boy like you?"

"I'm familiar with it," I said. "Too familiar."

"And why's that?"

I could barely get the words out. "I was there—in Miami. I was working as one of Cermak's bodyguards."

"Ouch! Remind me not to hire you for protection," Diamond Jim said, bugging his eyes. "Aw! Here's the waiter. Hope you're hungry, Nate. . . ."

22

State Police Headquarters was on the outskirts of Baton Rouge, out Florida Boulevard, in a flat, lushly wooded area. The building was new—a V-shaped white-washed brick two-story with its blunt bottom facing Foster Drive. I pulled my rental Ford into a driveway that divided to form a circle with a garden in the middle. Like the dock board building, this was a pedestrian structure whose appearance was gussied up: vivid flower beds were all around it, with moss-draped oaks here and there, providing a Louisianian touch.

Over the two front doors in the blunt bottom of the V were the bas-relief words: LOUISIANA STATE POLICE. A pair of troopers in spiffy green-and-black uniforms were coming out as I went in. At the reception counter inside the front door, a policewoman in gray sent me down the left wing of the V, where on either side was a row of offices with frosted glass and names.

One of them was MURPHY RODEN, ASSISTANT SUPERINTENDENT.

I knocked.

"Come on in," Murphy's voice said.

I stepped inside. Blond, rugged Roden, looking fit and trim as ever in white shirt and blue tie, was on the phone, swiveled to one side in his desk chair, looking out the window at the driveway flower garden.

His office was the opposite of Messina's: half a dozen file cabinets, a desk cluttered with paperwork and folders, and numerous framed photos of Murphy with the likes of the late Governor O.K. Allen, current Governor Leche and, of course, the Kingfish. There were also watercolor prints of aircraft from the World War on one wall, and a model Fokker atop one of the file cabinets.

"I'll be jinks swing!" Murphy said, as he swiveled around just enough to see me; his brown eyes lighted up. Into the phone, he said, "I'll get back to ya, Ted—ol' pal of mine just dropped by."

He hung up, stood behind the desk and stretched his hand across, grinning. "I wondered when you'd get around to me!"

I shook his hand, pulled up a chair. "You heard I was in town?"

"Who hasn't?" He sat. "You want some coffee?"

"No thanks. So what do you hear? Is somebody going to shoot me, for poking around?"

He rocked gently in his chair; his smile was wicked. "I don't think they decided, yet—'cept maybe for Joe Messina."

"I barely asked him a question," I said. "He just blew the hell up."

Murphy shrugged. "Sore point, with him. He's tore up with the possibility he mighta shot Huey. They had him in a private madhouse for a couple weeks, while back."

"No kidding?"

"If I'm lyin', I'm dyin'. They had him in a jacket that buckles up in back, if ya get my drift—he bawled his head off all day, all night, hollerin' about how he killed the best friend he ever had. Pitiful."

"Did he?"

"Did he what, Nate?"

"Kill the best friend he ever had?"

Murphy rocked; his mouth was smiling, but his eyes weren't. "What's your angle on this one, kid?"

"Well, that kinda depends on who I'm talking to, Murph."

He snorted a laugh. "I know that about you. But if you try the truth out on me, maybe I'll try it out on you."

"Sounds fair enough. I'm working as an impartial investigator, mutually acceptable to both the insurance company and Mrs. Long."

"The double-indemnity issue, huh?"

"Right."

His eyes narrowed. "Just how impartial are you?"

"I lean toward Mrs. Long, frankly. She got a raw deal on the financial end of the stick—seems to me all her late husband's cronies are a hell of a lot more flush than she is."

"Includin' me?"

"I didn't say that."

Now his smile turned sly. "This is awful noble of ya, Nate, takin' Mrs. Long's part in this. How much is she slippin' ya under the counter?"

I grinned. "Why, is that kind of thing just not done in Louisiana?"

He grinned back. "Why, hell, no. That's for them graft-happy Northerners, up in Chicago and such."

"Your turn."

"Pardon?"

"The truth."

He rocked in his chair. "First, answer me: you think this is goin' to go public?"

"If I can prove something that contradicts the public record? Hard to say. It shouldn't—it's a private matter, between Mrs. Long and her insurance company. But I suppose there's no guarantee the lid'll stay on. . . . That would ultimately be up to Mrs. Long."

"I don't think she'd do that," he said. "I don't think she'd trade her martyred husband for a damn fool shot down by his own overzealous men."

I said nothing; just waited for him to convince himself. He wanted to talk. I just had to sit and wait and let him.

Finally, he stopped rocking; sat forward. He folded his hands, prayerfully. "The truth is, Carl Weiss did shoot the Kingfish. I saw the gun in his hand. I saw him shoot the damn thing at him, point-blank."

"And it's that simple?"

He looked away from me. After a long time, he said, "I didn't say it was . . . simple."

"What is it, then?"

He gazed at me with eyes that were a hundred times more intelligent than Joe Messina's but every bit as tortured.

"The doc shot him, all right, but it's possible . . . just possible, mind you . . . that one of our bullets clipped Huey in the back, as he was runnin' off."

I sat forward. "But there was no talk of two wounds—just an entry and an exit. . . ."

He shrugged. "All I can say is . . . and I never told a soul on earth this, Nate, goddamnit . . . I heard Huey cry out a second time. Not as loud. But as he was runnin' away, he cried out, again."

"With all those bullets flying, it wouldn't be surprising if . . ."

"Nate, either way, it was that son of a bitch Carl Weiss's fault. No doubt about it." He slammed a fist on his desk and the paperwork shuddered. "But I have to wonder if one of our bullets didn't, goddamnit, finish the job."

"This is just a . . . feeling on your part. A hunch. A suspicion."

"A fear," he said. "And only one person would really know the answer."

I knew.

"Dr. Vidrine," I said.

"Vidrine," Murphy agreed. "The man who operated on Huey. Maybe you should talk to him. . . ."

I shook my head. "But *would* he talk to me? His public statements were that one bullet killed Huey—entry wound, exit wound, front, back. Not two *entry* wounds. Why the hell would he contradict himself, now?"

He blinked. "You mean, you don't know?"

"Know what?"

His laugh was humorless. "Vidrine's *already* disgraced. Governor Leche fired him from his job as superintendent at Charity Hospital, and he's been demoted from dean to assistant professor, out at LSU. Who knows? Maybe if you go talk to him, he'll come clean. Now, skeedaddle—I got criminals to catch."

I stood. "I appreciate the lead."

"No problem," he said. "Let me know when you're out from under, so we can go back to the French Quarter and find us a couple more college gals."

The stalls of the French Market in the Vieux Carré stretched along Decatur and North Peters streets, from Barracks to St. Ann. Though it was late evening—approaching nine o'clock—the stalls under the dark pitched roof of the tawny shed with its decorative ventilation towers and endless row of pillars were hopping with buying and selling. It was Thursday night—time to buy Friday's fish.

I wasn't buying or selling; I was looking for something for nothing. Guess at heart I was still a Chicago cop.

At one end of the market was the Café Du Monde. Designed to provide weary teamsters with a rest stop, the café

—and another, at the other end, the Morning Call—attracted all kinds. Farmers off wagons and trucks mingled in cheerful anonymity with posh couples in evening clothes, teenage lovers in sweaters and slacks and skirts, and the inevitable camera-carrying tourists.

Dr. Arthur Vidrine was seated in a corner, with his back to the world. But in the mirror that began halfway up the white wooden wall, I could see his dark hair, oval face, cleft chin—and morose expression. He wore a white linen suit, like Dr. Carl Weiss had, one Sunday night last year.

I pulled out a chair at the little black table and sat down. "Thank you for seeing me," I said.

"I appreciate the opportunity," he said quietly. He gestured to his small cup of dark steaming liquid. "You must try the café au lait, though if you like your coffee strong, I would suggest the café noir."

"You're the doctor," I said.

A young waiter in white shirt, black bow tie and black pants came for my order. I tried a serving of the powdered-sugar pastries everybody was eating. The waiter called them beignets, and said they were doughnuts, but he wasn't fooling me: they were square and puffy, with no hole.

"I'm pleased you caught me at the college this afternoon," Vidrine said between sips.

I'd phoned his office.

"I'm pleased you want to cooperate. I frankly had my doubts."

He sat forward, his dark eyes burning. "You know I've been demoted to a subordinate professorship."

"Yes . . ."

He glanced around furtively; the place was about half full. "You weren't followed?"

"I made sure."

"But you could be mistaken. . . ."

"No. I do this for a living. Nobody in this swamp has the detective skills of a Post Toasties Junior G-Man."

That actually made him smile, a little.

"Good," he said. "You know, I can blow the roof off this lousy state. . . ."

"You mind if I take notes? Or would that be indiscreet?"

"Go ahead. As long as you weren't followed." He leaned forward even further, as I got out my little notebook. "LSU is riddled with corruption. This laughable president, James Monroe Smith, is embezzling state funds."

I remembered President Smith: that ass-kissing yes-man I'd seen in Huey's twenty-fourth-floor suite at the capitol.

"Really?" I asked. "How do you know this?"

He sneered a tiny smile. "I still have *some* friends. Smith is speculating in whiskey-warehouse receipts. . . ."

"The president of LSU is investing in barrels of whiskey?"

"That's just the beginning. He's also playing the Stock Exchange. Trading in hundreds of thousands of dollars of wheat. . . ."

"This is fascinating, doctor, but—"

"And Smith's crony, this 'Big George' McCracken, a former Long bodyguard as you probably know, is up to his eyeballs in kickbacks from contractors and supply houses. McCracken's also been using WPA workers and materials on his own fancy estate, *and* those of his pals, including Governor Leche himself!"

I hoped my smile was sympathetic. "Dr. Vidrine—this is impressive, and these acts are undoubtedly criminal—and, coming from Chicago, I have no trouble grasping the concept of rampant graft. But it's *not* the information I'm after."

The waiter brought me my café noir and my "doughnuts." I tasted one; it was warm and sweet and delicious.

"Help yourself, doc," I said.

But he wasn't in the mood.

"You don't realize what you're asking," he said.

"You want to get even with Long's political heirs," I said, and shrugged. "Swell. But corruption in Louisiana ain't exactly a news flash. You want to do something to get back at 'em? Then you need to tell me what you know about the Long killing."

Vidrine stared into the little cup of creamy coffee. His face was white; his eyes haunted.

"I found a bullet," he said softly.

I leaned forward. "What?"

"Inside Senator Long." He sighed. Shook his head. "I found a bullet."

"Jesus."

I could barely hear him over the din of conversation and the clatter of dishes being cleared.

He didn't look at me as he spoke. "I . . . I don't have to tell you about the chaotic atmosphere at the hospital, that night—you were there. What you may not know is there were men standing around as we operated, Huey's men, bodyguards and political hacks, men who looked like gangsters, who refused to leave. The pressure, the conditions, were appalling."

He sighed again, closed his eyes, pressed thumb and forefinger to the bridge of his nose. Then he opened his eyes, sipped his coffee and continued.

"At any rate, two wounds had been noted—and we began the operation under the assumption that the frontal wound was an entry wound and the anterior an exit wound. . . ."

"But once you found that bullet," I said, "you didn't have an entry and exit wound anymore—you had *two* entry wounds. . . ."

"It could have meant that," Vidrine admitted, just the slightest defensive tone creeping in. "But the anterior wound might not have been a penetrating one. It looked more like a bruise, or a small trauma. . . ."

"And with Huey opened up, you couldn't exactly flip him over to have a closer look."

Vidrine nodded glumly. He sipped his café au lait; the cup looked like a thimble in a large hand that, frankly, did not look like a surgeon's.

"Even then," he said, "even during the operation, I knew I might have made a wrong diagnosis, a tragic decision. If I was dealing with two entry wounds, I'd . . ." He shook his head. ". . . I'd condemned the Senator to death."

"What did you do?"

His eyes pleaded for understanding. "What *could* I do? I . . . I palmed the bullet."

The doctor held out his other hand: in it were two spent slugs.

One of the slugs appeared to be a .38, the other a .45.

My mind was doing flip-flops. "Dr. Carl Weiss's gun was a .32 Browning," I said.

"And what did the bodyguards carry?" Vidrine asked, sarcasm faintly etching his words.

"They packed .38s and .45s," I said numbly. "You said you found *one* bullet. . . . I can count: that's two."

He dropped the gray slugs on the table, next to the little plate of square doughnuts.

"The second bullet came from the mortuary," Vidrine said.

"The mortuary?"

He nodded. "The body had been taken to Rabenhorst Funeral Home. Shortly before dawn, I got my nerve up and went there. Told the undertakers I needed a few moments with the Senator's body. I undid the sutures, put on rubber gloves and did a little . . . impromptu autopsy. Nothing major—just probed the retroperitoneal space, got lucky and came up with it."

"Why are you telling me this, showing me . . . ?"

He scooped the bullets up in a hand, turned the hand into a fist, shook it as he spoke.

"I'm resigning from LSU, Mr. Heller," he said. "I'm going to try to put my life back together, away from disloyal, dishonest men. But in the meantime, nothing would please me more than having someone like you making certain people's lives miserable." His smile was a study in irony. "Besides—what can they do to me?"

I shrugged. "Kill you?"

Now the smile turned enigmatic. He slipped the bullets in a pocket of his white linen suit coat. "Not with these trump cards tucked away."

"But you can't go public. . . ."

"No," he agreed and sighed. "The twin specters of malpractice and conspiracy would raise their heads. But it's something of a . . . what's the term?"

"Mexican standoff," I said.

"Yes," he said. "Yes."

"Not all of these men are smart," I reminded him. "But they're all brutal. There's little they'd stop at. . . ."

He shrugged one shoulder. "Should I turn up suspiciously dead, family members of mine will make sure these bullets wind up in the correct hands."

I tapped a finger on the table. "I could use those bullets, right now. . . ."

"Sorry," he said, and he stood. His mood had brightened. It was as if a heavy burden had been lifted. "But I've given you information, Mr. Heller. And that's a kind of ammunition in and of itself, isn't it?"

He plucked one of the doughnuts off the plate, took a bite and walked away, munching it. In a few moments, he was swallowed up into the French Quarter at night.

The gate to the private estate was a self-consciously rustic affair constructed of wagon wheels; it yawned open: I was expected. I tooled the Ford down the gravel drive through a corridor of towering pines, the afternoon sun shimmering through, casting flickering shadows; a day or so later, the grounds of the estate opened up, as rolling, and carefully coifed, as any golf course. A sprawling but modern brick and brown-shingle building—a hunting lodge with aspirations—looked out on the gently rippling, mirrorlike surface of the Tchefuncte River, where a boat landing extended, a motor launch with cabin docked there.

Near the main lodge were kennels, breeding stalls, pens, exercise areas, for the dogs, sheep, Hereford cattle and thoroughbred horses raised here; barns and stables spread behind the lodge, connected by gravel roads and paths. And all the while, towering pines looked on, unimpressed.

Well, I was impressed. Governor Dick Leche, moderately successful attorney, former secretary to O.K. Allen, was doing all right for himself. In the heart of St. Tammany Parish's Gold Coast, populated by retired financiers and company presidents and other affluent types, Leche had found not only an idyllic retreat, but another moneymaking enterprise.

I pulled the Ford up by several other vehicles parked in front of a triple-door brick garage; but my rental number was not in a league with the Lincoln and two Cadillacs I was joining. I'd barely got out of the car when Seymour Weiss was standing beside me, as if he'd materialized.

In his gray three-piece suit with black-and-white tie, he was as perfectly attired as a manikin in the men's department at Marshall Field's, only no department store had a dummy as homely as the iguanalike Seymour Weiss. On the other hand, Seymour was no dummy.

"The governor's inside," he said. "Make this brief."

"I'm disappointed," I said. "Aren't you glad to see me, Seymour?"

He said nothing, his pockmarked puss staying blank; but his dead dark eyes were scornful.

"Last time I saw you," I said, following him to a side door, "you were tossin' money at me."

He stopped, turned and said dryly, "That was so you would leave."

"And I left," I said. I smiled. "But I'm back."

Seymour's irritation hadn't been as apparent on the phone this morning, when I'd reached him in his office at the Roosevelt Hotel. At least, not at first. He knew I'd been investigating the Long case, but said he didn't know why. I told him I'd fill him in personally, if we could get together to talk, and he'd only said, "Certainly."

But he had bristled when I said I also wanted to meet with the governor.

"I can drive over to Baton Rouge this afternoon," I'd said, "to meet with Governor Leche, either at the capitol, or the governor's mansion. . . ."

"He's rarely there," Seymour had said. "He conducts

most of the affairs of state long-distance, from St. Tammany."

"Where's that?"

There'd been a long pause before he replied, with obvious reluctance: "Across the lake from New Orleans."

"Well, why don't you set up a meeting. I'd suggest, as soon as possible."

"Do I detect a threat in your voice, Mr. Heller?"

"I don't know. Do you?"

So, now—just a few hours later—I was in the governor's sprawling hunting lodge, following Seymour down a hallway with pelican-patterned wallpaper, decorated with framed photos of the governor and various dignitaries and celebrities. We moved into a cozy maple-paneled, open-beamed den with a large braided rug and an enormous, growling bearskin rug before a brick fireplace with a mantel crowded with stuffed ducks, beaver and geese. Though the back walls had built-in bookcases, looking on from every other angle were enough mounted deer heads to form a quorum of the Louisiana House of Representatives. A few long-dead fish swam the walls. The governor was apparently stuffing his taxidermist with cash.

Plump walnut-trimmed brown leather loungers with ottomans were angled toward, and at either side of, the fireplace; between them was a small matching sofa. Here and there, standing lamps wearing beige silk shades provided a woman's touch, slightly off-kilter in this man's man's room. There apparently was a Mrs. Leche.

Big George McCracken was sitting at a card table, playing solitaire. McCracken, with his lumpy, former boxer's face, still seemed to be buying his baggy suits from Hoodlum Haberdashery, Inc. His suit coat was over the back of the chair and he was in shirtsleeves and suspenders, blood red tie loosened; a stubby cigar smoldered in one corner of his mouth.

But at least he'd given up carrying a tommy gun in a paper bag. Unless it was under the table.

Huey Long's successor rose endlessly from the leather lounge chair at right and strode across the den like Paul Bunyan to meet us. An enormous man, both tall and heavyset, Leche wore a red-and-black plaid hunter's shirt and khaki pants and was in his stocking feet; black hair slicked back like George Raft's, Leche's facial features were pleasant, even boyishly handsome, though a little small for his bucket-sized head.

"I've wanted to meet you for a long time, Mr. Heller," Leche said, almost bubbling, extending his hand. Then, pointlessly, as if I didn't know who I was calling on, he added a self-introduction: "Dick Leche."

"And why's that, Your Excellency?" I said, shaking with him.

"Your efforts to get the Kingfish to Our Lady of the Lake are legend around here. Won't you sit down?"

He took me by the arm over to the sofa; big as he was, he could have flung me there. I sat on the sofa, and he settled back into his lounge chair, putting his white-stockinged feet up on the ottoman. Seymour took the lounge chair at my right; he sat with his legs crossed, hands folded, slowly twiddling his thumbs. Glowering.

"My efforts may be legendary, Your Excellency," I said, "but I obviously didn't do Huey any good."

"It was the effort, man! It was the effort. But please . . . call me Dick."

"Why, thank you, Dick. And call me Nate, if you would."

From an end table beside him, he took a pipe and relighted it with a kitchen match, as he said, "My pleasure. I understand you've been looking into the assassination."

"That's right."

Puffing at the pipe, getting it going, he said, "I'm a little . . . fuzzy on the exact nature of your investigation.

You know, we do have a Bureau of Criminal Investigation in this state."

"But, with all due respect, Dick—you never did investigate."

He shrugged, gestured offhandedly with the pipe. "It didn't seem . . . our place, somehow."

"I'm confused. You'll have to excuse me . . . I'm an out-of-towner, you know."

Leche's smile was a dazzler; he had teeth like well-scrubbed bathroom tiles. "Certainly."

"I'm told you ran on a 'Murder Ticket.' That you promised the voters you'd get to the bottom of the DeSoto Hotel conspiracy. . . ."

The smile withered around the pipe stem.

"Those were emotional times," Leche said somberly. "In the cool, reasoned light of day, it became apparent that the man who shot Senator Long was *already* dead. . . . So why waste the taxpayers' hard-earned money?"

Seymour said, "Besides, if the Long family wanted an investigation, Mrs. Long would have petitioned for one."

"In a way," I said, "that's why I'm here."

"It is?" Leche asked, surprised.

"I thought you were working for Mutual Insurance," Seymour said.

"Why, Seymour," I said, and give him a smile just as affable as Leche's if less toothy, "I thought both you and Dick, here, were 'fuzzy' about what I was up to."

"Are you trying to prove double indemnity," Seymour said crisply, "or trying to save your bosses some dough?"

"I'm sort of a cross between an investigator and an arbitrator," I said, settling back in the soft couch. "Both parties have agreed to abide by the findings of my inquiry."

"So, then," Seymour said, smiling for the first time, "there might be room for . . . negotiation."

"Sure," I said. "I'm from Chicago, remember? Of course,

to some people, having two clients who desire opposite outcomes might seem a conflict of interest. . . ."

"But to Nate Heller," Seymour said, with smooth, smiling contempt, "it's an opportunity."

Leche shifted in his comfortable chair, uncomfortable. Like most crooked politicians, he preferred staying behind the facade of respectability.

Seymour, his mood improved, called out to Big George. "Get us some drinks, would you, George? What would you like, Mr. Heller?"

"Got any Bacardi?"

Big George took our orders and lumbered morosely to a liquor cabinet where he got me my rum, some bourbon and branch water for Leche, and scotch straight up for Seymour.

As McCracken played waiter, Leche said, "George here is doing quite well out at LSU, these days."

"Yeah," I said, "I hear you're building superintendent out there."

"What else do you hear?" McCracken asked; there was something ominous in the tone.

That you're feathering your own fucking nest, courtesy of the WPA and the Louisiana taxpayers.

"Nothing," I said pleasantly.

Somehow I had a feeling McCracken's presence this afternoon had little if anything to do with his current university position: he was here representing the Bodyguard Contingent. After all, he'd been one of the brave lads who'd fired dozens of bullets into the fallen Dr. Carl Weiss.

Leche put his pipe in an ashtray on the endtable and sipped his drink. "Have you uncovered any . . . new evidence in your inquiry, Nate?"

"Possibly."

"What does that mean?" Seymour snapped. His good mood hadn't lasted long.

"Suppose," I said, studying the rum in the glass, "I was

in possession of a bullet or two, taken from Senator Long's body."

The room went deadly quiet: you could have heard a shell casing drop.

"Everyone knows the bullet passed through Senator Long," Leche said softly.

"Do they?" I sat forward. "What if I had two bullets taken from the Senator's body that were *not* bullets from Dr. Weiss's gun?"

A chair scraped back; I heard McCracken approaching.

"Bullets of a caliber," I said, "that instead matched those of the guns used by Huey's bodyguards."

McCracken, hovering behind me, said, "Let me handle this."

He wasn't talking to me.

Seymour said pointedly, "Sit down, and keep out of it."

McCracken said, "I can *handle* this sumbitch."

My nine-millimeter was under my left arm, incidentally. I wasn't licensed in Louisiana, but I was no fool, either.

"Sit down!" Seymour said. "Shut up! Keep out!"

McCracken's sigh could have put out a small fire. But he lumbered back and pulled the card-table chair out, scrapingly, and sat, heavily.

"Two lumps of lead," Leche said. He shrugged. "Who's to say where they came from?"

"Certainly Dr. Vidrine wouldn't testify," Seymour said. "He'd lose his medical license."

"Or something," I said cheerfully.

I was here to run a bluff. I had thought this through, and dangerous as it was, this was the best play I could think of, under these conditions, in this situation.

"Suppose I have witnesses," I said. "Witnesses from whom I've taken documented statements. Little loose ends running around hospital halls, and mortuaries, and capitol corridors and such. You've had a lot of inner turmoil in what used to be the Long machine. A lot of friends are now enemies. That kind of thing happens, when the spoils get fought over, and some get, and some don't."

"If you think any court in Louisiana—" Seymour began.

But I turned to Leche, whose face had fallen. "Governor —I realize I'm playing in your ballpark. The cops are yours. The courts. The legislature. But you forget—maybe you're no national figure, but the Kingfish sure as hell was. The assassination of Huey Long is of national interest and import . . . hell, *inter*national."

Leche tasted his tongue; he didn't seem to like the flavor.

I went on: "The press'll publicize this new evidence, and pretty soon you'll *have* to mount an inquiry . . . ballistics tests, testimony, you may even have to get the jackhammers out and chisel through that seven feet of concrete and steel you buried the Kingfish under, 'cause he's gonna have to be exhumed. He's evidence."

Leche looked hollowly at Seymour, who shook his head, as if to say, "Don't worry."

"Even if a wild bullet from a bodyguard did kill Huey, accidentally," Seymour said softly, "what good would exposing that do, at this point?"

"Well," I said, "there's a family in Baton Rouge who will have to carry with them the stigma of having an assassin for a son, brother, husband, father, for as long as anyone remembers the Kingfish . . . and that should only be as long as there's a Louisiana."

"But everyone agrees that Dr. Weiss *did* attack Huey," Seymour said.

Funny: here was a logical place for eyewitness McCracken to contradict me; but on this subject, he stayed silent.

"The doctor may only have slugged Huey," I said. "Neither of these bullets I'm talking about, remember, is a .32. . . ."

And now McCracken put in his two cents, only it wasn't a repudiation of what I'd just said. From across the room, he shouted, "Let *me* handle this!"

"Quiet!" Seymour said. He sat forward, his dark eyes locked on me, his hands gently patting the air diplomatically.

"If this is a matter of money," he said, "I can just make out a check for ten thousand dollars. Or would Mrs. Long prefer cash?"

Jackpot.

This sort of offer was exactly what I was fishing for. What better way to keep both my clients happy, and get myself that G-note bonus?

"I'll have to confer with Mrs. Long," I said. "But I think you might want to consider upping that amount."

"What for?" Seymour snapped. "That's all the double-indemnity clause would have paid her!"

"But that's not the only gauge we have to determine value here," I said, waggling a professorial finger. "Think of the next election. If Huey was killed accidentally, by a bunch of numbskull bodyguards . . ."

"Let me fucking handle it!"

"Shut up!" Seymour said.

". . . then you've lost a major talking point for future campaigns. After all, what price can you put on the political value of Huey's martyrdom?"

"What kind of money are we talking about?" Seymour asked, his eyes hooded.

"I'm not talking any kind of money," I said. "That's not my place. This is for you and Dick to decide. Now, if pressed, I might suggest you consider upping the amount, oh—ten times. Or maybe twenty."

Seymour reeled back as if I'd slapped him. "Are you *insane*, man?"

"Please don't change the subject," I said. "I just figured

if somebody happened to know what became of a certain 'dee-duct box,' they might want to treat Mrs. Long a little more . . . generously."

Leche was clutching the arms of the lounger like a man in the electric chair. "Seymour . . . ," he said. There was a lot in the one word: accusation, a plea for help, a demand that something be done. . . .

Seymour's dead eyes were fixed on me like the barrels of twin revolvers. Then he looked away, and said, coldly, quietly, "Suppose you talk to Mrs. Long. Talk to her, and get back to me with a figure."

I stood. "I'll do that. Governor, pleasure meeting you."

Leche had the expression of a pouting child; his affability was a memory. And sunk down in the chair like that, he suddenly seemed very small.

"I'll find my own way out," I said, and did, feeling pretty damn cocky but not relishing the savage expression on Big George McCracken's battered face as his eyes trailed after me.

Once again we sat in the solarium on dark-stained wicker furniture, drinking iced tea. It was late afternoon, and the tropical garden of Mrs. Long's backyard was cloaked in shadows that were gradually turning into dusk.

"Mr. Heller," she said, and it was as if every word she spoke pained her, "it's not that I don't appreciate your efforts . . ." The pale blue eyes in the attractive oval face were troubled. She sat on the wicker couch with her hands folded around a handkerchief; her navy suit was touched with a rose pattern, a pink cloth corsage sewn at one shoulder.

I winced. "I don't understand your reluctance, Mrs. Long. I'm certain we can get a considerable amount of money from Seymour and Leche and their cronies. . . ."

"It's blackmail money, Mr. Heller."

"Not really. Think of it as finally getting to withdraw a few bucks from the 'dee-duct box.' "

She shook her head, no. "It may be in name only, Mr. Heller, but I *am* a United States Senator. It wouldn't be proper."

I felt dizzy. "Aren't you the same Mrs. Long who offered

me a thousand bucks under the table, to favor her position in this investigation?"

Her smile was tiny and embarrassed as she looked at her lap. "Yes, I am. Perhaps it seems silly to you, having such a . . . flexible sense of ethics."

I sighed and sat back. "Not really. I do it all the time."

She looked at me with a painfully earnest expression. "What I want to know is, do you feel convinced that your investigation has shown my husband was killed accidentally?"

"I saw the bullets," I said. "I'm no ballistics expert, but I'd say they matched the caliber of the guns the bodyguards were packing. Even though Dr. Vidrine wouldn't hand the slugs over to me, I can say for a certainty that Senator Long was not shot by Carl Weiss."

"Will the insurance agency accept your opinion?"

I shrugged. "I see no reason why not. Both you and they agreed to accept my conclusions. This isn't a court of law—I don't have to attach evidentiary exhibits. All I have to do is write a reasoned, logical report, citing the various interviews I conducted that have led me to believe Carl Weiss approached your husband, an argument ensued, the doctor struck your husband a blow, and the gunfire began."

Her eyes were tight with thought. "And Mutual would pay the twenty-thousand-dollar double-indemnity claim?"

"I believe they would, yes."

Her expression relaxed; she raised her chin. "Then that's what I want you to do."

"Is *that* it?" I asked, still trying to make heads or tails of this. "You want the truth to come out?"

She sighed, sat back. "Actually . . . I haven't decided yet. The insurance company won't make your findings public, will they?"

"No. It's a confidential matter, between you and them." I leaned forward, shaking my head. "Excuse me, ma'am, I don't mean to be out of line . . . but I just don't get it. I mean, if you were planning to expose Seymour and those trigger-happy Cossacks, that would be one thing. But if you aren't, then this effort is strictly for the twenty-grand insurance payoff, and we can squeeze twenty *times* that out of those bastards! Excuse my French."

She smiled gently, leaned forward and touched my hand. "Mr. Heller . . . there are other factors at play here. I have to live in this state. My son Russell has become very interested in the world of politics. . . . He's fallen in love with Washington, and . . . well, I think Russell would like to finish what his father began, someday. But I believe . . . and I mean no disrespect to my late husband's memory, which I cherish . . . I believe my son is a different sort of man than my husband. Russell is honest, ethical . . . he views politics as a pathway to social change."

"He's young."

She nodded. "Yes he is. Huey was an idealist, once, before he learned to love power more than what he believed in. But Russell, Russell is different. Someday he'll run for office, and he will run as Huey Long's son. He will need friends, because as Huey Long's son, he's bound to have enemies, isn't he? And these men, Seymour Weiss and Richard Leche and the others, they're in political power, at least right now. For Russell's sake, I don't wish to alienate them."

Rose Long was a lovely woman. Huey had been lucky to have her at his side when he made his climb; but somehow I figured her son would appreciate her more. Anyway, he ought to.

"So—you *will* write that report?" she asked.

"Yes, I will."

Now she seemed embarrassed. "I'm afraid I don't have your thousand dollars in the house, right now. And I won't be able to get to the bank until Monday morning. . . ."

Tomorrow was Sunday.

"My phone call didn't give you much notice," I said. "I'll go back to my hotel room, write the report and drop by with it Monday afternoon, if that's convenient."

"As long as it's before Tuesday morning. We're heading back to Washington, Russell and Rose and I."

I stood, hat in hand. "A pleasure doing business with you, ma'am," I said. "And an education."

She walked me to the door, her hand on my arm. "You know, you're quite a remarkable young man."

That was a new one.

I said, "What makes you think that?"

"You took a great risk, going into the lion's den like that, this afternoon. Those men might have done anything."

"They're politicians. They pay people off, not bump people off."

"Perhaps. But it was ingenious, your plan to serve both my interests and those of Mutual Insurance. I'm sorry I wasn't able to accept it."

"Me too," I said. "I was figurin' on hitting you up for ten percent of whatever I squeezed outa Seymour."

We were at the front door. She shook her head and laughed; squeezed my arm. "Mr. Heller, you're terrible."

"That's more like it," I grinned, and went out.

She gave me a smile and a wave from the ornate entryway of the Mediterranean near-mansion, and I returned them as I walked out into a cool twilight, past broad-leafed banana trees, to the cement-block driveway. I climbed in the Ford, and I was just thinking there was an odd sort of medicinal smell in the car when something cold and hard and rectangular pressed against the back of my neck.

The nose of an automatic.

"How-do, you Yankee sumbitch," Big George McCracken whispered in my ear. "You 'bout to find out how the bug feels when he gits stepped on."

The nine-millimeter was in the glove compartment. I

hadn't thought I'd need it, calling on Mrs. Long, and hadn't wanted to alarm her with a glimpse of it.

"What do you want, George?"

"Those two bullets they dug outa Huey," he said.

"George . . . I don't have 'em. . . ."

"Sure you do," he said.

"I don't."

"We'll jus' hafta to talk about it, some."

And a hand slipped around and pressed a chloroformed cloth in my face. My last thought, before slipping into blackness, was *so* that's *what the medicinal smell was. . . .*

When I woke up I was in a pitch-dark place, on my side, a fetus in what I soon realized was the cramped metal womb of an automobile trunk. The car was jostling along a gravel road—I could hear the rocks kicking up under the car and against the fenders.

I had barely figured this out when the car rolled to a stop. I felt around for something, for anything, maybe a tire iron, but the lid of the trunk lifted and the moonlight was so bright I squinted as Big George McCracken looked in at me with a sneer of a smile. Next to him was a dark-haired, hook-nosed, bull-necked tough in a dark suit and a tie. He looked familiar, but in my dazed condition, I couldn't place him.

"Git 'im outa there, wouldja, Carlos?"

Carlos.

Last year at Dandy Phil Kastel's warehouse, this short, muscular hood had been uncrating slot machines, and doing Kastel's bidding.

Carlos's big hands grabbed on to my suit coat and he hauled me out of the trunk like a sack of grain. My feet tried to keep my body upright, but my knees wobbled. Carlos held on to me by the waist and dragged me along.

The car, I noted for no good reason, was a black Studebaker two-door coupe. It had pulled up on the grass incline with perhaps a dozen other vehicles, ranging from new sedans to beat-up pickup trucks, in front of a rambling ramshackle oversize shed of a building alive with lights and laughter and honky-tonk piano; a crude wood-burned sign sat on two legs in the unmowed yard: WILLSWOOD TAVERN. Silhouetted behind the gray, unpainted wooden frame structure, with its split-log shingles, loomed the ghostly, foreboding shapes of a swamp.

They dragged me behind the building; through open windows, I glimpsed a burly bartender with no apron dispensing sweaty bottles of beer, drunken men dancing with loose women, long picnic-type tables where spaghetti and oysters and crawfish were being chowed down by a rowdy clientele, smaller tables where men were playing cards with piles of cash on the table.

Behind the building, across a short yard with tall unmowed grass, the darkness of the swamp beckoned me to make a break for it. Whatever dangers lurked there, they were surely preferable to the certainty of what faced me with Big George and Carlos.

But my muscles weren't working yet; my brain barely was.

McCracken opened a door, and Carlos pushed me through. I stumbled into a dark room and rolled on a hard dirt floor, bumping up against a wooden chair. A door slammed, and a cone of light clicked on from a hanging lamp, and I was a huddled shape in the spotlight.

"Put 'im in the chair, Carlos."

The big hands were on me again, and I was hoisted off the floor and slammed into the wooden chair. Carlos got around behind me and yanked my arms behind me and rope looped around my wrists and around through the rungs of the chair. I could feel him knotting them, tying me into the chair; at least the hemp wasn't so tight as to cut off the circulation. Thank God for small favors.

It was a small supply room—shelves of canned goods, stacked cartons of bottled beer; a big gray metal washer tub was shoved against the slats of one wall.

"I can handle this by myself," McCracken said to Carlos.

"Thanks," Carlos said. "No good de boss not bein' 'round on Sat'dy night."

The bullnecked hood—and apparent proprietor of the Willswood Tavern—opened a door that must have led into the kitchen, because the pungent aroma of tomato sauce filled the room. Dishes and kettles clattered.

"You get tired, George my fren'," Carlos said, "jus' let me know. I send Bucky Boy back."

Then it was just me and McCracken.

He took off his suitcoat and rested it on the stacked beer cartons. A .38 revolver was shoulder-holstered under his left arm. He unbuttoned his cuffs and rolled up his sleeves. Then he plucked something off a shelf—he was outside the cone of light, and I couldn't make out what it was—and stepped into the light, right in front of me, the hand with the object, whatever it was, behind his back.

His battered fighter's mug worked up a smile. "We already tossed your hotel room, didn't find 'em. Didn't find 'em in your car, neither. . . ."

The noise of drunken merriment, from out in the saloon, leached through the wooden walls.

"I don't have the goddamn bullets," I said.

"Sure you do. You said you did. I heard ya tell Seymour and Dickie."

"I was bluffing."

He frowned; thinking was an effort. "Bluffin'?"

"There *are* no bullets. I was just tryin' to extort some dough out of Seymour for Mrs. Long."

"Bullshit."

"It's the truth, goddamnit! George, listen to me—I knew those sons of bitches rooked Mrs. Long outa the dee-duct box money. Asking around, I figured out Carl Weiss just punched Huey, and set you guys off!"

"I'll ask ya again," he said, and his hand came out from behind his back.

A rubber hose.

"Please don't," I said. In Chicago, it was called getting fed the goldfish; and it was a meal I'd been served before.

It hadn't agreed with me.

"George, goddamnit, I'm telling you truth. . . ."

The hose swished through the air and whacked into my left forearm; the sting was followed by a deep ache.

"I want those bullets, Heller. Where *are* they?"

It swished again, and again, and each time I cried out, but nobody out there having fun could hear me, and the sting would be followed by the ache, and he kept questioning me and I kept telling him I didn't have the goddamn bullets and he moved on to my right arm and then my thighs and my calves and shins and by that time I had stopped yelling and started whimpering and then I stopped whimpering and started crying my fucking eyes out, and then, thank God, I passed out.

Somebody threw water in my face and I came out of it, coughing, choking, sputtering, spitting, not knowing whether I'd been out a minute or an hour or a week; but the pain was living agony and I began to scream and McCracken slipped a hand over my mouth and I screamed into it.

The sound of drunken revelry continued from the next room.

McCracken took his hand away from my face. "Keep your voice down, Heller, or you get the next one in the jewels."

And he whapped me on the thigh, alongside my balls, and the pain shot through me like an arrow, but I clenched my teeth. Didn't scream. Just moaned.

A hillbilly scarecrow in coveralls and no shirt on his hairless sunken chest stepped into the shaft of light. He had an awful, crooked, bucktooth smile that was black and yellow and green—everything but white; his eyes were large and yellow and his nose was straight and pointed, like a bee stinger. His sunken cheeks were stubbly, but his chin was nowhere in sight; his Adam's apple was prominent and bobbed as he laughed, which he was doing right now, watching me suffering in my chair.

"This is Bucky Boy," McCracken said. "Bucky Boy's gonna he'p me out."

"I'm the fella 'round here what makes the Yankee gumbo!" Bucky Boy chortled. He kicked the big gray washer tub. "Mix 'er up in there, I do."

McCracken folded his arms; the rubber hose hung limply, but threateningly, from his right hand. "Why don't ya ask Bucky Boy what Yankee gumbo is?"

But I didn't have to.

"I dump me a Yankee in this here tub," he said, and kicked it again, and laughed idiotically, deep in his throat, making his Adam's apple bob some more, "and then I pours in *lotsa* lye! Then I let 'im *soak* a spell!"

Leaving a partly decomposed, liquefied corpse. . . .

McCracken picked up the recipe from there: "Before long, all we got to do is pour that fool Yankee into the swamp."

Ingenious way to dispose of a corpse; send it flowing into a waterway.

"I . . . I don't have the damn bullets. I told you. I was bluffing."

McCracken beat on me a while. Every blow sent pain shooting through my system until I was drunk with it; I started to laugh, to join in with the good time that was leaking in from the saloon out front.

"He's gettin' slaphappy," Bucky Boy said, a frown indicating some degree of thinking ability.

McCracken was rubbing his right arm with his left hand. "I'm gettin' wore out. You wanna pound on him some, Bucky Boy?"

"Shore!"

"Don't kill him, now."

"Try not!"

Bucky Boy had pipe-cleaner arms, but he found power somewhere; the wiry hillbilly had the sense to get behind me, and find new territory, slamming the rubber hose into my shoulders, even whapping it through the rungs of the chair. I wasn't laughing anymore, but he was, filling the little storeroom with raucous, down-home glee.

When my body was one enormous sea of anguish, I did myself a favor and passed out again.

When I came to, I was alone. I was throbbing with pain, like my body was covered with boils about to burst; though they hadn't touched my face or hit me on the head, my head was splitting.

I tried to stand. Maybe I could make it over to that door, if I could get my feet and legs to work. It took all the effort I had, but I stood. My legs were flimsy things under me, like a card table that wasn't put up right, but I dragged myself over to that door, hunching over, carrying the chair on my back like a slave with a cotton bale, and turned my back to the door, and, with no more effort than it takes to thread a needle with your toes, tried the knob, turned the knob.

But it was locked.

Now what?

I could try to smash the chair against the wall—it was spindly enough that it might come apart—but would the racket attract somebody out there? The sounds of drunken laughter and honky-tonk piano continued; it had covered my screams—would it cover this?

The walls that weren't lined with shelves were either blocked by beer cartons or that Yankee-gumbo tub, so the door itself, which was a solid-looking slab of wood, was the best bet. I rammed myself into it, and the chair didn't give, though every bone and muscle in my body seemed to; but I did it again, and again, and tears were rolling down my face, mingling with sweat, when McCracken came bolting through that kitchen door and dragged me back over toward the middle of the little room and slapped me, twice, hard. My mouth was bleeding, but I was starting to go generally numb.

When he began waling on me with the rubber hose again, I hardly felt it; I was just a big dead slab of meat, barely holding onto consciousness.

"I want those fuckin' bullets! I want those fuckin' bullets!"

I could have told him about Vidrine, and if the pain hadn't turned to numbness, maybe I would have; but I knew, punchy as I was by this point, that telling him about Vidrine would only get the doc killed. It wouldn't help me. Oh, maybe McCracken would stop beating on me. But he was going to kill me, anyway. I knew that.

So did he.

Because you have to kill a man you give a beating like this to.

Or he'll kill you.

My chin was on my chest. McCracken was standing talking with Carlos; beanpole Bucky Boy was looking on.

The washer tub had been moved out from the wall; it was filled within a few inches of its rim with a cloudy liquid. An acrid aroma flared my nostrils.

"I don't care whether you do this thing or not," Carlos said, "but dawn's comin' . . . and Sunday's my *big* mornin', you know. The cops and the crooks and the boodlers be comin' by, to pay Carlos his cut'a de week's take. So eider way, I want 'im outa here. 'Live or dead, sho' 'nuff."

McCracken sighed, shook his head and said, "Hell—he ain't gonna talk."

"Do whatever y'think best. I ain't no part of it, dough."

And Carlos went back through the kitchen. No sounds or smells came out. The saloon was quiet out there. After hours.

The lye smell was starting to crowd out the air in the little space; McCracken started to cough. Then he dug in his pants pocket and came back with a key and unlocked the door that led out back, let that door stand open to air out the room a little.

Bucky Boy stood in front of me and said, "You bet' let me kill 'im, boss, 'fore we dump 'im in the tub. He might thrash aroun' some, and get that mean ol' stuff on you and me."

That's when I stood, chair and all, and, heaving all my weight into it, butted Bucky Boy in the pit of his stomach, and he went careening backward, head knocking against the conical lamp, sending it swinging, throwing its light wildly around the storeroom, while he went awkwardly back, windmilling his arms like Huey giving a rabble-rousing speech, instinct making him look over his shoulder to see where he was going, and splashing right into the tub of lye, getting it on his bare arms, chest, the side of his face, and more; he had lost balance, he was in the tub, splashing and kicking and screaming like he was being skinned alive, which in a sense he was.

But he didn't get much if any of it on me, splashing around, because I was busy ramming backward into McCracken, who was clawing for the gun in his shoulder holster, only he didn't get to it before my chair splintered against him, sending him into a wall of canned goods. The shelves collapsed and the cans rained on him, and he was on his ass down there, under the wood and the scattering of cans, dazed.

I moved through the open door and outside, shaking the remnants of the chair from behind me, free, or as free as a man with his hands bound behind him can be, and ran into the early daylight, moving toward the swamp. McCracken would soon be after me, with his gun, and hazardous as the unknown of that marshy wilderness might be, it was a place where I might find cover, where I might have an even chance.

As soon as I crossed the waist-high grass of the yard and stumbled into the trees, the ground got soft, spongy. Would it go out from under me, and put my chin at ground level? Words like *snake* and *quicksand* flashed through my city-boy brain. What was I doing in this grotesque world of sharp, spiky palmettos and canes? This macabre jungle of ferns and vines, some green, others gray, a gloom brightened (I suddenly noticed) by the morning chirping of a thousand birds.

I knew I shouldn't go too far, or I'd never come out. My only goal, for the moment, was to hide; stay away from the man with the gun who wanted to kill me. If I could find something sharp, to work the ropes around my wrist against, I could quit thinking defensively, and fight back . . . but right now: hiding. Survival. . . .

The land gave way to water suddenly, a forest of cypress trees standing like impossibly tall men, but they were dead men, as gray as the Spanish moss they were so lavishly draped with; the trees of this ghost forest were no less formidable dead than alive: their out-flaring, swollen trunks separating into twin arms reaching into a sky they blotted out, their root systems above the water, gnarled, skeletal, horrible, beautiful.

One step at a time, I tested the water, to find the land

beneath. I saw something sliding along the water's surface, about ten feet away; I froze. Waited. Then, whether harmless or poisonous, the serpent had passed, and I had this hellish Eden to myself again. Another step, and another, over one ankle, one more, another, to my knees, and then I was up on the roots of the biggest cypress in Louisiana.

I knew the direction I'd come, so I got behind the tree, figuring I could peek around and watch for McCracken, and in the meantime try to work the rope on the bark of the cypress. I had already twisted my fingers around to check the knot; it was hopelessly tight. It might take a while, but eventually the rope would wear through.

As I worked the ropes against the rough bark, I heard the rustle of fronds as he moved through. I had hoped that spongy ground would swallow up my footprints, but even so, maybe he could track me by broken branches and tramped-down foliage. I hadn't been too careful; I'd just been moving.

I peered around. He was standing at the edge where the marshy land gave way to water and the ghost cypress forest began. He wasn't twenty feet away.

"Heller!" he called, voice echoing across the water. "Give it up. You gon' *die* out here!"

A bird called a mocking cry by way of response.

"Look—I believe ya . . . you *were* bluffin'. There ain't no bullets. Me, I made an honest mistake. I'll put my gun away, if you call out to me. I swear it on my mama's grave!"

Not even a bird answered him this time.

"Heller! They done rushed Bucky Boy to the hospital! No harm done. He's gon' be jus' fine. No hard feelin's. We all took a beatin' on this one. Come on, boy!"

He wouldn't step out into that water. He wasn't sure I was out here. All I had to do was wait him out. I already had a sense, from what Carlos said, and from McCracken himself, that McCracken was acting on his own accord.

There'd be no reinforcements. *All I had to do was wait him out.* Something nudged me, and I turned quickly and the snout of a dull gray alligator, a creature easily eight feet long, was right beside me.

I lost my balance and fell back splatteringly into the water, arms waving. I was on my ass, knees up, and the view through them was the gator looking at me with its beady eyes, considering whether I was worth the trouble.

"Heller!" McCracken called, almost cackling. "Got ya now!"

He came running, and hit a deep spot, which made him lose his footing, sending him *splat*, face first into the water, and his gun went flying and splashed into the swamp, only a few feet away, gone forever. The fuss was too much for the gator, who slithered away, but I had to make the best of it.

Maybe my hands were bound behind me, but McCracken was unarmed now, and I kicked up water as I ran toward him and as he was just getting back on his feet, I played bull and rammed my head into his belly, sending him back down, throwing water everywhere. But when I went to kick him in the head, he reached up and grabbed my foot and threw me backward, with considerable force, and I slammed into a cypress and got the wind knocked out of me.

I slumped there, gasping for breath, beyond pain, as the dripping McCracken, his battered fighter's face twisted into a smile as grotesque as the most gnarled, twisted branch in this gruesome landscape, staggered toward me, each footstep splashing. He was reaching into his pocket for something.

His hand came back and he flipped the razor open and its blade caught the sun streaking through the hanging moss.

"Maybe them bullets are inside'a you," he said. "We gon' have a look-see. . . ."

I tried to stand, but I couldn't get my footing on the knobby cypress roots, my hands still roped behind me.

His throat exploded in a blossom of blood as something *thunk*ed into the tree trunk, above me. He dropped the razor and it *plink*ed into the water, as he clawed with both hands toward his throat, but blood was billowing out and he staggered a few more steps and fell face down at my feet, turning the swamp water around him a spreading red.

At the edge of the swamp, where the water began, Murphy Roden was standing, expressionless, a heavy revolver in his fist, trailing smoke.

"Nate! You alive, kid?"

"And kicking," I said, or maybe I just thought it.

Either way, I passed out.

The shades were drawn, but morning sun peeked around the edges and threw streaks of sunlight on my face, prying my eyes open.

I was in my underwear, in bed, a comfortable bed, or as comfortable as any bed can be when your body is covered with welts and bruises. At least my head wasn't aching. My watch was on the nightstand: 8:10. Nice to know. Now, what *day* was it?

The bedroom I recognized: Alice Jean's, in the Beauregard Town bungalow. Pink stucco walls and a five-piece art moderne waterfall bedroom set with contrasting grains of walnut veneer creating angular designs, like the shooting pains in my arms and legs whenever I tried to move.

I couldn't get back to sleep. The sun was in my face and turning over would have been agony; so I just lay there, moving only enough so that the strip of sunlight at least fell between my eyes. Lay there and felt sorry for myself.

And thought.

And fitted pieces together, like those contrasting wood veneers that formed the pattern of Alice Jean's bedroom set.

I had breakfast in bed about an hour later. Alice Jean looked in on me, noticed I was awake, informed me it was Monday morning, and asked me if I thought I could eat. I said yes, and scrambled eggs and toast and orange juice went down surprisingly well. Of course, she was spoon-feeding me off a tray, a buxom angel of a nurse in an appropriately white frock with blue trimming.

After the meal, she took the dishes down and came back with another tray bearing a cup of coffee with cream and sugar on the side. I took it black. It went better with my bruises that way.

I said, "How'd I get here?"

She was sitting on the edge of the bed. "Murphy Roden brought you. He thought you needed looking after, and figured I'd be willing to do it."

"Wouldn't do for me to show up in a hospital."

She frowned. "Why? What the hell happened to you, anyway?" Then she seemed embarrassed, blurting out what she'd been dying to ask. "You don't have to talk about it. You don't have to talk at all. Just get feeling better."

"I feel fine. I feel like goddamn Fred Astaire. All I lack is the top hat and tails."

"Settle down, now. . . ."

I tried to sit up a little. "I need to make a phone call. Not right away, but before tomorrow."

"I can make it for you."

"No you can't. It's to Mrs. Long."

She lowered her gaze. "You should try to sleep some more."

"Okay. Can you get that sun out of my face?"

"Sure," she said, and got up and adjusted the shade.

I closed my eyes.

I opened my eyes.

She was leaning over me, to see if I was sleeping, which I had been, but I'd sensed her, and woken; and now her lovely, heart-shaped face, framed by those dark flapper curls, was before me, a vision of concern.

"You have a visitor," she said.

"Murphy?"

"Yes."

Figured.

I said, "Prop an extra pillow behind me, would you?"

"Are you sure . . . ?"

"Yeah."

I allowed her to push me forward enough to slide another pillow under me; it didn't hurt any worse than falling down a couple flights of stairs. But I wanted to be in a sitting-up position.

"Now send him up."

She nodded and went off, and a few moments later, Murphy, in a white linen suit, peeked in. He took off his Panama fedora and smiled, a little.

"Need somebody to hold your hand, kid?"

"I prefer Alice Jean. But come on in. Pull up a chair, Murph."

He did—the dainty one from the vanity; he sat forward on the tiny chair, turning the fedora in his hands like a wheel. "At least they didn't mark your face up. Mouth's a little puffy, but otherwise, you're still the same ol' ravin' beauty."

I gave him half a smile, using the side of my face that wasn't puffy. "How did you happen to be there, Murph? Or do you usually stroll through the swamp around dawn, Sunday mornings?"

A grin flickered. "Just like a dick. No gratitude, just questions."

"Thanks for saving my life. What the hell were you doing there?"

"Carlos called me."

"*Carlos* called you?"

"Yeah. He's no flunky, you know—he's a modern-day Laffite over there in Jefferson Parish, on the West Bank. It's wide-open over there. They make money hand over fist."

"And he called *you*."

He shrugged. "He and Dandy Phil Kastel and Mayor Maestri got a good thing goin'. Got a lot of good things goin', in fact. Carlos is no fool—he figured Big George had gone off on a personal tangent, and wanted to make sure helpin' bump you off was kosher with the boys in the backroom."

"And you weren't about to let Big George 'bump off' your good pal, were you?"

"Course not."

"Killing an insurance investigator from up North, who was working on the Long case—think of the trouble it could stir up."

"Well, that's true—but friendship . . ."

"Fuck friendship. You used me."

He frowned, more confused than irritated. "Used you? Now, how the hell did I *use* you?"

"You wanted to find out what Dr. Vidrine knew. What he *had*." I gave him a full, lovely smile. "What better way to do that than send somebody working to take the Longsters down? Somebody like me."

"You're talkin' fool nonsense, Nate."

"Well, he has the bullets, Murph. Two of 'em. One's a .38, the other's a .45."

His face whitened; his expression was long and lifeless.

"But," I said, "he isn't gonna use 'em."

Relief showed through. "Not gonna use 'em?"

"If I'm lyin', you're dyin'," I said cheerfully. "He just wants to be left alone, to live his life, and do his work. An admirable point of view. If you boys stay away from him, everything will be just fine. But he's got those slugs spread out with relatives or lawyers or something, and if he dies under circumstances that even seem the least little bit mysterious, the bullets will surface. And somehow I don't think it'll be the assistant superintendent of police whose desk that evidence gets delivered to."

"Nobody's gonna bother Vidrine," he said somberly. "You got my word."

"I don't need your word. Vidrine's got you good ol' boys by the short and curlies. And you know it."

He shook his head, laughed humorlessly. "You don't seem very grateful. . . ."

"What about Big George, Murph? You're a cop. How did you handle it? How's it gonna play in the papers? It was justifiable homicide, sure, but one of the state's top cops, shootin' down the building superintendent of LSU? That won't look good."

Murphy said nothing.

"Or did Big George take a permanent vacation? Let me guess—don't tell me. Do Carlos and his boys also make *Southern*-style gumbo, from time to time? Right now, McCracken wouldn't happen to be in that big gray washer tub, marinating in lye, would he?"

Murphy stood. "You don't seem to be in the mood for a visitor. . . ."

"By the way," I said, "d'you think you could have your coppers take a look for that rental Ford of mine?"

"Already did," he said softly. "It's out front."

"Good. My gun's in the glove compartment. It's got sentimental value."

"We at the state police are always anxious to serve the

public," he said dryly. He waved a sour good-bye with his Panama, and was halfway out the bedroom door when I called to him.

"Hey, Murph—stick around. I want to fill you in on my investigation. I want to tell you what *really* happened in that capitol hallway, on a certain Sunday evening last year."

"Is that right?" His attention was piqued. "If mem'ry serves, I took that 'un in, firsthand. . . ."

"Forget it, then."

He strolled back in. "Run it by me, why don't ya?"

"All right," I said. "Sit back down. Like we say around these parts—set a spell."

Murphy sighed heavily and sat back down on the little vanity chair; he began twisting his hat in his hands again.

"It starts with Seymour Weiss," I said. "Seymour, and probably a number of others in the Long organization, were getting unhappy with Huey. Specifically, with Huey's unquenchable—and unrealistic—thirst for power. Let's face it, state political machines all over the country were getting fat on New Deal dollars . . . but *not* the Long machine. The Kingfish was too busy battling FDR, alienating the cash source and *blocking* funds from getting to Louisiana. Now, sacrificing short-term profits for long-term goals is fine—but Huey's presidential ambitions were a pipe dream."

"The Kingfish had followers all over the country," Murphy said. "His Share the Wealth Clubs . . ."

"Eight million strong. Impressive number. But not enough votes to put a man in the White House, not by a long shot. And just recently Huey'd come a cropper trying to put his man in power in neighboring Mississippi—and if the Kingfish couldn't sway his own next-door neighbor, if he couldn't even guarantee carrying the South, what in the hell was the point of a presidential push?"

"Some say he was setting the stage for 1940," Murphy said.

"And maybe he was. Trouble is, it was 1935 and the federal tax boys were breathing down the Longsters' collective necks. Now, Seymour knew that without the Kingfish around, he could deliver enough votes to FDR to end both the federal tax probe *and* the pending congressional inquiry into the constitutionality of Long's dictatorship."

"All of a sudden you're an expert on Louisiana politics."

"I'm from Chicago, Murph. I've been an expert on corrupt politics since grade school. Anyway, it's just a little over a year after the assassination, and where are we? The Long machine is backing the man Huey used to affectionately call 'that crippled fucker.' Federal money's flowing like water into the Pelican State, and all the tax investigations and congressional inquiries have mysteriously shut down."

A smile twitched. "You know what they say about politics making strange bedfellows."

"I sure do. And Seymour has a long history of strange bedfellows—like Louis LeSage, for instance, lobbyist and vice president of Standard Oil. Standard, Huey's arch enemy, who on the eve of Huey's murder were just champing at the bit to make a backroom deal. A deal Governor Leche, of course, has since cut. You see, Seymour is one savvy character—he could read the handwriting on the wall: the Long machine could run much more smoothly, and profitably, *without* the Kingfish around. After all, the Long machine was designed to work on the state level, not national. Huey's megalomaniac ambitions were derailing that smooth-running machine."

Murphy smirked dismissively. "But without Huey, where did that leave his 'machine'?"

"Well, it's running on all cylinders right now; I saw Leche's little hunting lodge. It's as simple as this, Murph: at some point last year, it became clear to Seymour that Huey Long would make a better martyr than a leader."

He was shaking his head, no. "Seymour and Huey were like brothers."

"Cain and Abel *were* brothers. Seymour was also Huey's treasurer, and he alone knew how much unrecorded cash money was in Huey's 'dee-duct box' . . . it was at least a million. Probably much more . . . and all that money disappeared when Huey was murdered."

"Murdered," Murphy said, "by Dr. Carl Weiss."

"No. Somebody else, Murph."

"*Who* then? Overzealous bodyguards? Even if that were true, it wouldn't be 'murder'. . . ."

"Oh, it's murder, all right."

He smirked. "Yeah? Then who 'done' it?"

"You done it, Murph."

He blinked. Laughed. "Me?"

"Not you alone, of course."

He shook his head, laughed again, harshly. "Of course not! It was a *conspiracy*, right, Nate? And *everybody* in that crowded corridor was a conspirator!"

"Not everybody. Just you and Big George McCracken . . . who I've helped you conveniently remove . . . and maybe Judge Fournet."

"Judge Fournet? Now you've completely lost your mind."

"Well, maybe you can find me a padded cell next to Joe Messina—who wasn't in on it, by the way. He truly loved the Kingfish. Seymour, of course, the master puppeteer, made sure he wasn't in that hallway at all; he didn't even come to town. As for Fournet, I'm honestly not sure about him. At any rate, there were enough people involved for a lawyer pal of Huey's to warn him about a 'murder plot.' " I managed a shrug. "Anyway, this is a case with many a loose end. But I've tied one hell of a lot of 'em up. . . ."

"Really? Then, tell me—how'd we pull all this off?"

"It began with a phone call or two from a 'friend' from within the Kingfish's inner circle to Dr. Carl Weiss. Getting that idealistic young doctor all riled up about the 'nigger blood' issue was the first step. Then Dr. Carl was contacted by this same 'friend'—you, possibly McCracken, maybe even Fournet, or another party—and told to come to the capitol, and wait at a specific place, the corridor outside the governor's office. Dr. Carl was told the Kingfish was willing to listen to him plead his case; this embarrassing subject was not one the young doctor would likely discuss with his family. This was something he had to do on his own. Now, Dr. Carl had to know he couldn't stop the gerrymander of Judge Pavy . . . but he could appeal to Huey's sense of decency not to defame his family with this racial slur."

Murphy said nothing; he had stopped turning his hat.

"Somebody—probably Big George—held a parking place right out front for Dr. Carl . . . if the doctor had stopped on impulse, as he's supposed to have, it's highly unlikely he would've lucked into such a prime parking place right out front. The lot was packed, and the show inside was in full sway, with a full house."

"Supposition," Murphy muttered.

"Perhaps," I said. "But Big George wasn't in the House with the rest of us in the bodyguard contingent that night—he slipped away . . . though he did turn up *later*, in the hallway. Only he wasn't carrying his usual toy: that submachine gun in the paper sack."

"So what?"

"So, maybe he already knew there was going to be gunfire in that narrow passageway, and didn't want to take his tommy gun into such close quarters."

Murphy swallowed. Said nothing.

"As Huey stepped out of the governor's office," I said, "Judge Fournet attracted his attention, stopping him . . . and that's when Dr. Carl Weiss stepped forward, thinking he had, essentially, an appointment with Huey. Huey, knowing nothing about it, probably brushed him off, rudely . . . and the doctor hauled off and slugged him—the perfect cue for you to go into your act."

The brown eyes widened. "*My* act?"

"You dove forward, coming up alongside the doctor, shooting Huey point blank with your own .38, and tackling Dr. Carl, as if he were the assailant."

The brown eyes narrowed. He was slumped in the chair.

"Then as you wrestled him down, you shot Dr. Carl in the throat, killing the poor 'sumbitch,' making him an instant dead patsy. . . ."

He was looking at the floor. Turning the hat slowly in his hands.

"But you took a hell of a risk, didn't you? Maybe you hadn't figured on your trigger-happy brothers turning that hallway into a living hell. They almost blinded you, didn't they, with their muzzle flashes, so anxious were they to help you drill that poor little doctor. In fact, one of 'em . . . probably Messina . . . accidentally nailed the Kingfish in the back, as he was fleeing."

"Bullets *were* ricocheting," Murphy said hollowly.

I tried to get more comfortable; it didn't work, but I could see him better. "You obviously had a throw-down gun, the doctor *had* to be armed, but later . . . when Big George moved the doctor's car around back, to a less suspicious position, he found the doc's own weapon in the glove box. Since the word from the hospital mistakenly confirmed the notion that the bullet had gone through the Kingfish, this was perfect: after somebody fired a round or two out of it, you substituted Dr. Carl's real gun for the throw-down piece."

Silence hung in the room like a storm cloud threatening thunder.

Finally he said: "Finished?"

"Yeah."

"Quite a yarn." He stood slowly. His eyes gazed at me unblinkingly. "But can you prove it?"

"No."

He laughed, once. "I didn't think so."

"Particularly not in this state. Besides, my sympathy's with Mrs. Long. If I tell the insurance company this really *was* a murder, it'd just cost her ten grand."

He squinted at me, trying to read me. "Can you *live* with that?"

"Sure. After all . . . you saved my life—you're my pal."

The sarcasm made him wince; at least he had that much humanity left.

"What I wonder," I said, "is, can *you* live with it?"

His eyes tightened.

"With what you did to Dr. Carl Weiss," I continued, "and his pretty widow and his baby son, and their whole goddamn family, and the Pavys. . . ."

His frown had both irritation and frustration in it. "What else can I do? What's done is done. Jesus, Nate. What do you *expect* me to do?"

"Go to hell," I said.

He just stood there looking at me, for several long moments.

Then I pointed toward the door; the effort hurt, but it was worth it. "Get a head start, why don't you?"

Murphy started to say something, thought better of it, put on the Panama and went quickly out.

The rest of that Monday, I slept, mostly. The only thing I accomplished was getting out of bed to use the bathroom; I also used the upstairs phone, in the hall, to call Mrs. Long. Not wanting to concern her, or muddy the waters, I didn't let her know about the beating I'd taken. Or about my thoughts regarding Seymour Weiss and Murphy Roden and the murder plot. That's what Huey had hired me to uncover, wasn't it? And I finally had, hadn't I?

"I'm down with influenza," I told her on the phone.

"Oh dear," she said. "I'm sorry. I hope it's not too serious."

"Just some sore muscles and stiff bones is all. But I won't be able to show you my report before you leave for Washington tomorrow. Could I send you a carbon?"

"That would be fine. I'll give you my address in Washington. Oh, and I have your thousand-dollar bonus here, in cash. Shall I have it messengered to your hotel?"

"Please," I said, and called the hotel to ask them to put the envelope from Mrs. Long, when it arrived, in their safe.

And that was that.

By Tuesday I was up and around, and spent the morning sitting at Alice Jean's dining-room table, using a typewriter she'd sneaked home from her office back in her capitol days. Referring to my little notebook from time to time, I plowed through the report to Hugh Gallagher at Mutual Life Insurance—policy number 3473640.

Alice Jean kept me plied with coffee and doughnuts, and fixed tuna salad sandwiches and iced tea for lunch; I was getting used to drinking it sweet. Both today and yesterday, she'd made an attentive, sympathetic nurse, as thoughtful as she was attractive. But she'd been uncharacteristically quiet; almost brooding.

Something was troubling her, and I didn't think it was just my injuries.

The report was finished by two o'clock; it ran eight pages, and concluded thusly: "There is no doubt that Huey P. Long's death was accidental."

I was lyin', but at least I wouldn't be dyin'. This was best for all concerned, except possibly for Mutual Insurance, and somehow I thought I'd get over that.

Later that afternoon, I again sat in an easy chair in the living room of Yvonne Weiss's bungalow on Lakeland Drive, in the shadow of the capitol tower. Again she sat on the mohair sofa. Her plump, dark-haired year-and-a-half-old son, in a pale blue playsuit, was amusing himself at her feet, playing with his ball, which was also one of a handful of words he was gleefully trying out.

The swelling around my mouth was down, and the rest of my bruises didn't show, but Yvonne Weiss was a doctor's wife and she could tell by the way I moved something was wrong.

"You've been injured," she'd said, when she met me at the door. Her look of concern touched me; I almost got teary for a moment, for some goddamn reason. Maybe it was my two hundred and thirty-six bruises and welts.

"I fell down a flight of stairs," I said.

"Oh, my! Clumsy you."

Now she was sitting quietly, reading my report.

As she got toward the end, she read aloud, in a somewhat halting, dignified tone: "There is no doubt that Dr. Carl Weiss attacked Long physically, but there is considerable doubt that he ever fired a gun. Witnesses stated that the bodyguards were firing blindly, repeatedly and wildly. The consensus of informed opinion is that Long was killed by his own men and not by Weiss."

As she read, her son looked up from his ball and studied her, cocking his head from side to side, transfixed by his mother's words; it was as if she were reading it to him, and he had understood everything.

Her smile wasn't very big, but it was a heartbreaker. "Thank you, Mr. Heller, for letting me see this."

"Ma!" the boy said. He was smiling his own heartbreaking smile, even if he didn't have much in the way of teeth yet.

"You understand," I said, "that this is a confidential report. The insurance company won't make it public, and, talking to Mrs. Long, I doubt she ever will. She has political aspirations for her son, and in the long run, it's better for her to get along with her husband's political heirs. . . ."

"Better to leave her husband a martyr," she said, with only a hint of bitterness.

"Ma!" the boy said.

"But even if the public will never know," I said, "I thought you . . . and your family . . . had a right to know the truth."

She looked down at her son, who was playing with his Fresh Air Taxi. "You're most considerate, Mr. Heller. . . ."

"Cah!" the boy said. I think he meant "car."

"Thank you, Mrs. Weiss."

Her gaze moved from her son back to me; she locked onto me with dark steady eyes, her lovely face a cameo of serenity. Her smile was faint, like the Mona Lisa's.

"But, meaning in no way to belittle your efforts, or your kindness," she said quietly, "we already did know that Carl was not a murderer."

Clumsy me.

"Ball!" the boy shouted merrily.

And she showed me out.

That evening, Alice Jean fed me a delicious rice dish called congri; there wasn't much to it, except rice and peas and onion and a little ham, a few spices. But it hit the spot.

We ate in the small white-tile kitchen. The dining room table was still spread out with the typewriter and my notes and several drafts of my report. Alice Jean wore an apron over her white blouse and pleated tan slacks.

I touched a napkin to my mouth. "I can't make up my mind whether you look like a movie star or a housewife."

Her bee-stung lips pursed into a little smile. "Funny you should say that."

"Oh? Why?"

"I've been thinking about going to California, for a while."

"Alice Jean Crosley, leave Louisiana? Seems unthinkable."

"Well, I'm going to," she said, but didn't explain any further.

She wouldn't let me help with the dishes—I was still an "invalid"—so I waited in the living room, on the sofa. Only one lamp was on, and its soft light filtering through the silk shade softened the sleek modern lines of the furnishings. I was feeling better. I could almost get comfortable.

The apron was gone when she drifted into the living

room—the mannish slacks and blouse were made feminine by her generous curves. She settled next to me and put her hand on my leg.

"Does that hurt?" she asked.

"If it did," I said, "it'd take somebody bigger than you to make me admit it."

"You're leaving soon, aren't you?"

"Yeah. I called and got train reservations, this afternoon."

"When do you leave?"

"Tomorrow morning."

She looked away from me, looked at nothing for maybe a minute. Barely audible, from the kitchen, on the radio she'd turned on doing the dishes, Bing Crosby softly sang "Pennies from Heaven."

"Before you go," she said, "there's two things I want to give you."

"You've given me plenty, Alice Jean. Starting with throwing up in my lap."

She laughed a little, and nestled her head against my shoulder. "Does that hurt?"

"No. Alice Jean?

"Yes?"

"Are you . . . crying?"

"Yes."

"Why? Usually when I catch a train, the girl's relieved."

She laughed again, but it choked in a sob. "I . . . I heard it."

"Heard what?"

"I was outside the door. Yesterday. Eavesdropping. When you and Murphy were talking . . ."

"Oh. Oh, Jesus."

She looked up at me and the hazel eyes were streaming tears. "They killed my Huey. They murdered him. . . ."

I slipped my arm around her, patted her, soothed her. "Nothing we can do," I told her. "Nothing we can do. . . ."

She wept a long time, and I patted her a long time, and the radio shifted to an instrumental version of "There's a Small Hotel." Then, suddenly, she shot to her feet and scurried off, like she just remembered she had something on the stove.

She was gone so long, I started to get worried; must have been half an hour.

When she came back in, she was self-composed, her eyes red but no tears, and had redone her makeup, her pretty Clara Bow features looking as perfect as a movie queen's eight-by-ten glossy. She was carrying with her a briefcase—it was old, battered and brown, and rather large, and looked like a suitcase in her dainty fist.

She slammed it onto the sofa.

Through her tiny white teeth, she said, "Can't do anything, huh?"

I frowned. "What's this?"

She snapped it open. The briefcase was piled with official-looking papers and folders; I began thumbing through—there were reams of the stuff, government documents, both photostats and originals.

"What . . . ?"

"Under Huey's tenure," she said, with arch formality, "a lot of public and not-so-public documents passed through my hands."

"No kidding," I said.

Ledger books, too! After all, she'd been Secretary of State, Revenue Collector, Supervisor of Accounts. . . .

"*I* don't *have* a life insurance policy with Mutual," she said. She patted the papers in the briefcase. "*This* is my life insurance policy."

Flipping through page after page, I could barely focus my

eyes; my head was reeling. "It's one hell of a policy, Alice Jean."

"I want you to have it, Nate. I want you to take it."

It was like I'd been slapped. "What?"

She closed the lid of the briefcase with a *thud*.

"I want you to use these," she said coldly. "Use them to bring those bastards down."

I gave her an astounded grin. "Alice Jean, I'm just a private operator. I'm in no position . . ."

Her jaw was tilted and firm. "Anybody with these documents I pilfered is in a position to do *a lot* of damage. They're yours, Nate, to do with as you please—but not for blackmail purposes. I'm not giving you this material so you can make a buck. Promise me."

And a buck could be made. Many bucks.

But I said, "I promise," and I meant it.

Then I laughed, and shook my head. "You know, baby—Huey made a big mistake, putting a pretty young thing like you in such a position of responsibility."

She actually smiled. "Think so?"

"Yeah. He should have stuck with dumb clucks like O.K. Allen and Dick Leche."

She clicked shut the latches of the briefcase; put it on the coffee table on top of her movie and romance magazines.

I looked at her carefully as she settled back next to me on the sofa. I said, "Two things."

"What?"

"You said there were *two* things you wanted to give me, before I left. That's only one."

"It's pretty substantial, though, don't you think?"

"Oh, yes. Pretty substantial indeed. But what's the other thing?"

The cupie smile turned wicked. She began to unbutton the blouse and reveal the creamy slopes of her bosom overflowing the white lacy brassiere.

"Pretty," I said, "substantial . . ."

Indeed.

We stayed there on the couch, and she kissed every bruise on me, and—for a while anyway—made all the pain go away.

27

A week later, back in Chicago, I was sitting at my desk in the big single room that was my office on the fourth floor of the four-story building at Van Buren and Plymouth. I was batting out another insurance report for Mutual, an investigation that had been far less troublesome than the Long case. But also less profitable.

Business was pretty good; I'd brought back two grand and expenses from my Louisiana excursion. I was thinking about taking an apartment at the Morrison Hotel; for too long a time I'd been sleeping on the Murphy bed in this office, playing night watchman for the building in exchange for my rent. After all, I was beginning to move up in the world. . . .

When the phone rang, I figured it was that North Side bank wondering about the credit checks I was supposed to be running. I'd started thinking about putting on an op or two. What good was being president of a firm if you didn't have somebody to boss around?

"A-1 Detective Agency," I picked up the phone and said. "Nathan Heller speaking."

"Is this some kind of joke?" The voice was male and tightly wound.

"Is that you, Elmer?"

"Yes," Elmer Irey said, softly. "This package that came in the mail—are these documents legitimate?"

"Well, I don't know if I'd call anything about those documents 'legitimate,' but if you mean, are they for real, they're for real, all right. Genuine pilfered files, records, what-have-you, largely pertaining to finance during the administration of Huey P. Long, and shortly thereafter."

"Where in hell did you get them?"

"Where do you think? From an insider who got screwed over, and wants to get even."

"I . . . I don't see how I can use these in any court of law. They're . . . stolen. Illegally obtained . . ."

"I don't know anything about that. Anyway, you didn't illegally obtain 'em. They're a . . ." I laughed to myself. ". . . hell, Elmer, they're a lagniappe."

"A *what*?"

"A gift. A little something extra."

There was a long staticky pause.

"You know, Elmer, as a taxpayer, I kinda resent this cavalier use of long-distance."

"Heller, I don't know what to say . . . I had figured this investigation was over, but from what I see here, there's no way even the Attorney General could stop it, now. But, damnit, I still don't think these are admissible as evidence. . . ."

"Maybe not, but they sure as hell tell you what's been going on, who's been stealing what, and point you in all sorts of interesting right directions."

"That's true. That's certainly true. . . ."

I leaned back in my swivel chair. "I didn't go all the way through those. I'm no accountant. But I did hear some other rumors, only I don't think they're rumors."

"Such as?"

I told him what Dr. Vidrine had told me about President James Monroe Smith at LSU, and about the building scams and misappropriation of WPA funds and materials by one George McCracken, whose current whereabouts were unknown.

"This will take some time," Irey said cautiously. And then something unusual began creeping into the dour T-man's voice: happiness. "I'll have to be discreet. We'll have to go through these records with a fine-tooth comb . . . but I do believe we'll see some results."

"Have fun."

"Something I don't understand, Heller."

"Yeah?"

"What's in it for you?"

"Jesus, I told you it was a lagniappe, Elmer!"

"It's not like you, Heller."

"Just don't audit me, okay?"

He chuckled. "Not this year," he said, and clicked off.

Irey was right: it did take a while; but in 1939, Seymour Weiss got a four-year sentence for mail fraud relating to a 1936 "commission" he received for the sale of a hotel to be used at LSU as a nurses dormitory. One of the codefendants in the scheme, also found guilty, was Louis LeSage.

Irey's man John Rogge got Seymour on another four years of income-tax evasion, as well, but the mail-fraud and tax-evasion terms ran concurrently. Sent to the federal pen in Atlanta, Seymour was paroled in 1942, after cutting a deal to pay his back taxes.

Seymour deserved much worse, of course, but I felt Alice Jean's thirst for revenge had been fairly well served: by 1940, the Long machine had crumbled—scandal, jail terms, millions in back taxes and court fines, a number of suicides.

Most of the Longsters landed in jail, fulfilling Huey's prediction that without him, that's where all his people would wind up. Dr. James Monroe Smith of LSU beamed cheerfully in prison stripes for the news photographers, before trying to kill himself in his cell. Governor Dick Leche resigned, in the wake of the LSU building scams and rumors of his own hunting-lodge estate being built with WPA materials; and Rogge destroyed Leche on the witness stand, getting him to admit to having made one million dollars in kickbacks while governor. Leche drew a ten-year sentence on income-tax evasion. He died in 1965.

Not everyone in the Long camp fared badly. Judge Fournet, despite being on the LSU board when corruption was running rampant, remained untouched by scandal. By 1949 he had risen to chief justice of the State Supreme Court. In later years, the once tall judge, now stooped with age, walked with a cane, because (he said) of the disc he ruptured scuffling with Dr. Carl Weiss in that capitol corridor. He died in 1988.

Murphy Roden had a long, successful career in Louisiana law enforcement, taking time out to serve in the Navy during the Second World War; he held high police positions throughout his life, eventually becoming State Police Chief under Huey's brother Earl, and Commissioner of Public Safety under Governor Jimmie Davis. He resigned in 1962, citing poor health, including a bursitis-plagued shoulder.

Earl Long, despite being Leche's lieutenant governor, remained standing, unscathed, when the old Long machine fell. Perhaps, in retrospect, he was grateful to Huey for not allowing him in the inner circle. His own three terms as governor were both colorful and checkered, but unlike Huey, whose shadow he never escaped, nor stopped resenting, he was content with Louisiana for his kingdom.

Alice Jean Crosley returned from California to make closed-session appearances before several federal grand juries during the various inquiries into the Longsters. She was active in campaign work for Earl, and married a man who had a high-paying job with the state. Childless, the couple remain happily married to this day, and live in a quiet, exclusive neighborhood in Baton Rouge.

Dr. Arthur Vidrine returned to his native Ville Platte where he lived quietly and well, founding a private hospital in 1937, which he ran until he retired in ill health. He died in 1955.

Yvonne Weiss left Louisiana. She went to New York with her young son, returning to school for a master's degree in French. She remarried, became a librarian, and always spoke of her late husband fondly. When the rare journalist would track her down, Yvonne—who died in 1963—would gladly speak of Carl—but not of the shooting.

On the other hand, Dr. C. A. Weiss, Carl's father, was vocal on the subject: whenever a national publication referred to his son as an "assassin," he bitterly—and eloquently—demanded a retraction. He died in 1947, never losing faith in his son's innocence.

Carl Weiss, Jr., only three months old when his father died, is a successful orthopedic surgeon in Long Island, New York, where his uncle, Dr. Tom Ed Weiss, also practiced.

After finishing out her husband's Senate term, Rose Long never again entered public life; her later years were quiet and, due to the accomplishments of her son Russell, proud. Russell was elected to the United States Senate in 1948 and retired thirty-eight years later, a respected and powerful Senator. He seemed to devote himself on the one hand to praising and protecting the good things his father did; and on the other, to make up for the bad with good works and ethical practices. Along the way, he became exactly the kind of career politician his father abhorred.

The Reverend Gerald L. K. Smith never regained his national prominence, although he built a small empire in Eureka Springs, Arkansas, with a Bible college and a yearly

Passion Play that attracted big crowds. He died, in 1976, a minor-league Oral Roberts.

I don't know what became of Diamond Jim Moran, other than he was a high-profile presence in New Orleans throughout Mayor Maestri's election-free six years in office. But Dandy Phil Kastel went on to build the Tropicana in Las Vegas in partnership with Frank Costello; in the late 1950s, Kastel was found with six bullets in him—it was ruled a suicide.

Kastel's assistant, Carlos, went on from the rustic roots of his Willswood Tavern to be undisputed ruler of the mob in New Orleans. He was implicated in a later political assassination. His last name, incidentally, was Marcello.

Most of these people I kept track of casually, through the papers, chats with Eliot Ness, Wilson and Irey, and via sporadic correspondence and phone calls with Alice Jean. The only other one I ever had direct contact with again was, ironically enough, Seymour Weiss.

In 1955 I was in New York with a lady friend of mine for a long weekend of Broadway plays, shopping and fancy dining. On nostalgic impulse, I stayed at the Hotel New Yorker, and in the lounge, Seymour Weiss—looking like a fat, urbane lizard in his green-silk suit and narrow green-and-white tie—appeared at our table just after my female friend had gone to the powder room.

"Nate Heller?" he said, and that homely puss of his smiled; at age sixty or so, he didn't look a hell of a lot older, but a little pudgier. Prosperous.

"Hiya, Seymour. Sit down."

He did. "What brings you to New York?"

"Pleasure trip. Still hangin' out in Huey's hotel, after all these years?"

His smile was small and self-satisfied. "I own the hotel, Nate. I own a lot of hotels."

"You must have invested wisely."

"I did. I'll buy you a drink. . . ." He waved for a waiter.

"Swell. Just as long as it's not a Ramos Gin Fizz."

I had a rum-and-Coke, and he had some Dewar's. Too casually, he asked, "You didn't really believe that nonsense you told Murphy Roden, way back when?"

"How *is* Murphy?"

"Ailing. Did you, Nate? Do you?"

"What?"

"Believe that nonsense."

I sipped my drink; smiled nastily. "Seymour, I'm at an age where I'm not believing in much of anything. You tell *me* something."

"All right."

"Way back when, why did you bring me here from Chicago, to deliver your damn birthday present to Huey?"

He shrugged; the dead eyes avoided me. "Because I was worried about him. I thought he'd listen to reason, coming from you."

"I think it's because Huey'd had a tip that somebody on the inside, somebody close to him, was gonna betray him. Maybe you just wanted him to *think* you were worried about him."

The pockmarked face was immobile. "Is that any way to repay my hospitality?"

"I was just curious. Certain things, certain loose ends from cases long ago, can keep a detective up at night."

He saluted me with his scotch glass. "I sleep fine."

"I bet you do."

He was looking past me now. "Is this your lady friend moving across the room? Very lovely."

"Beautiful women are a habit I just can't seem to break."

"Tell you what, Nate," he said genially. "For old times' sake. To prove there's no hard feelings. . . . Why don't you and your young lady join me for dinner tonight in our restaurant. It'll be my treat."

"No thanks, Seymour," I said. "I couldn't properly dress for the occasion."

He blinked. "It's not formal. Just a tie and jacket."

"Maybe. But I forgot my bullet-proof vest."

I introduced him to Linda, and he was very suave, very charming, before leaving our table to stop by and chat with other guests.

"He seemed nice," Linda said.

"Seymour's a gracious host, all right."

"Kind of ugly, though, don't you think?"

I sipped my free rum-and-Coke—another Weiss lagniappe. "You don't know the half of it."

Seymour—who in his later years got involved with extreme right-wing political organizations and became close pals with J. Edgar Hoover—died in 1969 at age seventy-three.

Many of the others are gone, too: Murphy Roden, Joe Messina, Louis LeSage, Edward Hamilton, even Frank Wilson and Elmer Irey. Carlos Marcello died (as I write this) just a little over a year ago. On the other hand, the questions surrounding the shooting of the Kingfish are alive and well.

In 1985, the fiftieth anniversary of the assassination prompted the usual journalistic rehashes. But one of the articles inspired the public relations director of Mutual Life to look up his company's policies on Huey Long.

My long-forgotten report was dredged up and its contents made available to the press; considerations of privacy were cast aside in the public interest. A flurry of publicity followed, when it was discovered that, in 1936, Mutual had paid double-indemnity on the accidental-death policy of a political figure that history had declared the victim of an assassin's bullet.

By this time, I was retired, living in a condo in Coral Springs, Florida, with my second wife. I did a number of interviews for both print and electronic media, and reiterated the "accidental death" conclusion of my report, implicating the bodyguards, all of whom were dead and buried by now. It took about five minutes for my fifteen minutes of fame to lapse.

Then Coleman Vidrine, Jr., a retired captain of the Louisiana State Police, came forward and announced that his late father, Dr. Arthur Vidrine's first cousin, had passed down to him a bullet—a spent .38 slug—and a story that went with it. Seemed Dr. Vidrine had given the bullet to his cousin for safekeeping. Coleman Vidrine, Sr. had told his son that Arthur was concerned for his safety, and considered the bullet part of his "life insurance policy."

The .45 slug never showed up, but in the midst of this renewed interest in the case, Merle Welsh—the funeral director who embalmed both Huey Long and Dr. Carl Weiss—confirmed the story of a predawn impromptu autopsy by Dr. Vidrine, during which a .45 slug was recovered from the body of the Kingfish.

The funeral director, who was familiar with gunshot cases, also identified both wounds in Huey Long's body as wounds of entry.

None of this was enough for the Louisiana State Police to reopen the case.

Then in 1991, a flamboyant but renowned forensics expert, Dr. James E. Starrs of George Washington University in Washington, D.C., took an interest in Huey Long and Carl Weiss. He convinced the Weiss family—Carl Jr. and Tom Ed—to allow him to exhume Dr. Carl Austin Weiss's body. Although many argued that this was the wrong body to exhume (the right one being under tons of concrete and steel), Starrs was able to establish a number of facts that tended to show Dr. Carl's innocence.

A hollow-point .38—undoubtedly from Murphy Roden's gun, though no one said so—was found in the doctor's brain case. Fibers from Dr. Carl's white shirt were found embedded in the hollow point of the slug, which—along with bullets smashing into left wrist and right arm (apparent via skeletal damage)—indicated the doctor's arms were up in a defensive posture when that fatal shot into his head was fired.

The skeleton, which was about all that was left of Carl Austin Weiss, also disclosed—through a study of trajectory of the twenty-four bullets that caused bone damage (those that passed through or into flesh without striking bone are lost in the mists of history)—that at least a dozen bullets were fired into the fallen doctor's back.

Roselawn Cemetery, where Dr. Carl Weiss had been buried, wasn't the only place the forensics expert made an important discovery. Starrs also tracked down long-missing, key evidence in the estate of the late Louis Guerre, head of the B.C.I. at the time of Huey's death: the state police files on the investigation; and the "murder weapon," Dr. Carl Weiss's .32 Browning.

Also found among Guerre's effects was a spent .32 slug, initially thought to be the "fatal bullet," but ballistics experts soon established it had not come from Dr. Carl's gun. Both proponents of Dr. Carl's innocence and of his guilt found ways to use that bullet as ammunition in their arguments. In reality, it was just a spent slug among a deceased copper's odds and ends, with no chain of custody to connect it with that Browning.

On February 21, 1992, Dr. Starrs presented his arguments, tending to favor Carl Austin Weiss's innocence, at the forty-fourth annual meeting of the Academy of Forensics Sciences, which by coincidence was held that year in New Orleans. Four months later, the state police held a press conference declaring Dr. Carl Weiss the one-man, one-bullet assassin. Their conclusions were largely based on photographs (which had a poor chain of custody themselves) of the clothing Huey was supposedly wearing when he was shot.

There were indications, in the photos, of powder burns from a point-blank entry wound to the right abdomen. And of course, the police stated in support of their brother officers of bygone days, this meant Dr. Carl Weiss had to be the assassin. After all, he was the only one close enough to Huey Long to shoot him point-blank, leaving a powder burn. . . .

Murphy Roden's name wasn't mentioned.

All of this latter-day attention to the case hasn't served to do anything but raise the same old questions. If anything, things are more clouded now than ever.

When I saw Carl Weiss, Jr., a distinguished-looking man in his late fifties, speak on TV of his belief in his father's innocence, I remembered a little boy playing with a Fresh Air Taxi and figured now was the time to come forward with what I know.

It doesn't put anyone at risk, at this late date, not even me. But don't you think it's time people know that history *almost* got it right?

That a man named Weiss did kill Huey Long?

I OWE THEM ONE

Despite its extensive basis in history, this is a work of fiction, and a few liberties have been taken with the facts, though as few as possible—and any blame for historical inaccuracies is my own, reflecting, I hope, the limitations of conflicting source material.

Most of the characters in this novel are real and appear with their true names. Any readers intimately familiar with the story of Huey Long's life and death will be aware that I have focused on the key players, while omitting other, more minor ones, in an effort to streamline the narrative, and not overburden the reader with superfluous characters. For example, Long's secretary Earle Christenberry is absent; as he served many of the same advisory (and glorified "gofer") functions as Seymour Weiss, I considered his presence as a character redundant (several male secretaries and advisors are referred to here, in passing). Accordingly, some of Christenberry's majordomo–type actions have been given to Seymour Weiss.

A similar liberty was taken in depicting Dr. Arthur Vidrine as performing the impromptu autopsy on Long at Rabenhorst Funeral Home; Dr. Clarence Lorio, who assisted Vidrine in the operation, was the man identified by undertaker Welsh. Similarly, while both Elmer Irey and Frank Wilson were indeed in New Orleans investigating Huey Long, it was another agent—Mike Malone (sometimes identified as Pat O'Rourke)—who went undercover at the Roosevelt Hotel. The agent *was* identified in the lobby by a Chicagoan with mob ties, who was hustled out of there by the agent, just as Heller is by Wilson in this novel.

The theory that Seymour Weiss orchestrated the assassination, using Murphy Roden as his triggerman, is my own, and, to my knowledge, new to this work. I do not mean to present it as the definitive solution to the mystery of Long's death, but—despite its presence in a fictional work—it is rooted firmly in fact and fits the specifics of the case at least as well as any other theory.

Edward Hamilton is a composite character, but a fair representation of the "Square Dealers" leadership. Big George McCracken is also a composite, based primarily on Long's bodyguard George McQuiston and "Big" George Caldwell, building superintendent at LSU. McQuiston did carry a tommy gun in a grocery sack (although some sources say the weapon was a sawed-off shotgun) and Caldwell indeed was mired in building scams and WPA malfeasance at the university.

Alice Jean Crosley is a fictional character, although she has a real-life counterpart; however, Long's former mistress—disappointed by Long replacing her in Washington, D.C., with Earle Christenberry—married shortly before the Senator's assassination, making the love affair between Alice Jean and Nate Heller purely fanciful. The notion that Huey's former mistress (and the former Secretary of State, revenue collector, etc.) was bitter after her ouster by Long's heirs, and that she was in possession of damaging pilfered documents, is based on material in *Louisiana Hayride: The American*

Rehearsal for Dictatorship (1941), Harnett T. Kane's classic, darkly amusing examination of Huey and his political heirs.

The story of Huey rejecting a bullet-proof vest from Chicago has a factual basis, as does the assigning of police liaisons to escort the Kingfish and his pistol-packing, deputized "Cossacks" to the 1932 Democratic Convention in Chicago.

Mutual Life Insurance Company did send an investigator to Louisiana in the last week of October 1936 to look into Mrs. Long's double-indemnity claim. The investigator—the sublimely named K. B. Ponder—undertook an inquiry similar to the one Heller conducts in this book (the quotes from Heller's report are near-quotes from Ponder's seven-page document). Mutual did pay the double-indemnity claim.

Some authors contend that in 1936 Mutual considered death by assassination included under the umbrella of accidental death (which is apparently the case today), but this does not jibe with either logic or the facts: if such payment was automatic, why would Mutual have gone to the expense and trouble of sending Ponder to Louisiana to undertake a full investigation in dangerous, enemy territory?

My longtime research associate George Hagenauer did his usual stellar job of rooting out magazine and newspaper material (including Huey's own, wildly outlandish *American Progress*). George also spent many hours with me, discussing this convoluted, fascinating, frustrating case; his feel for the more eccentric aspects of the American political scene was most helpful, and an overview of the case he prepared, exploring its political ramifications, was crucial to the development of this narrative. George is a valued collaborator on the Heller "memoirs"; I continue to appreciate his contribution, enthusiasm and friendship.

The relentless Lynn Myers dug out key material, including two vital early biographies: *The Story of Huey P. Long* (1935), Carlton Beals; and *The Kingfish: Huey P. Long, Dic-*

tator (1938), Thomas O. Harris (journalist Harris is a minor character in this book). These contemporary accounts were crucial in this attempt to re-create a sense of the times, as was *Huey Long: A Candid Biography* (1935), Forrest Davis.

I was particularly fortunate to have the aid of one of the foremost collectors of Huey Long material, Michael Wynne of Pineville, Louisiana. Mike's expertise was matched only by his friendliness: my constant, intrusive, impromptu phone calls, with lists of questions, got immediate detailed answers; and when Mike didn't know an answer, he came up with it in a few days. He provided me with photocopies of rare, in some cases confidential, documents, about which I can say no more. My thanks, also, to bookseller Jim Taylor, of Baton Rouge, for putting Mike in contact with me . . . and for introducing me to the concept of lagniappe.

Another person was instrumental in the writing of this book: my talented wife, writer Barbara Collins, who accompanied me on a research trip to Baton Rouge and New Orleans in May of 1993. My son, Nate, was helpful, too, in our exploration of Huey's fabulous art deco skyscraper capitol—even if he did break the rules and snap a photo in the House of Representatives (Huey broke his share of rules there as well).

A special thanks to Georgene Jones of Baton Rouge, who sent me articles on the reopening of the case, in the early stages of my research for this novel. Mystery writer Bob Randisi provided information on New York City, and my father, Max Collins, Sr., shared his reminiscences of the Hotel New Yorker.

Three nonfiction works focus on the assassination, and all are of considerable merit: *The Huey Long Murder Case* (1963), Hermann B. Deutsch; *Requiem for a Kingfish* (1986), Ed Reed; and *The Day Huey Long Was Shot* (1963), David Zinman. Deutsch's work benefits from the author being an eyewitness to many of the events, and is flawed only by a too-ready acceptance of Dr. Carl Weiss as the assassin. Reed's privately printed work broke extensive new ground, and his research and analysis were crucial in the development of this book. Zinman's lengthy postscript, in the 1993 expanded edition of his work, provides a detailed look at the James E. Starrs investigation and the subsequent controversy; also, Zinman alone of the three authors spends as much time on the story of Dr. Carl Austin Weiss as he does on that of the Kingfish.

Huey Long: A Biography (1970), T. Harry Williams, is a Pulitzer Prize–winning work with a grand reputation; certainly its wealth of detail was helpful to me, though its pro-Long bias (and Williams's tendency to accept at face value the word of such dubious sources as Seymour Weiss and Long's bodyguards) limited its usefulness. My purposes were better served by the much more balanced (and, to my thinking, readable) account, *The Kingfish and His Realm: The Life and Times of Huey Long* (1991), William Ivy Hair.

Long's sketchy autobiography *Every Man a King* (1933) and his fanciful, posthumous *My First Days in the White House* (1935) were also beneficial. Dozens of books and pamphlets about Long were consulted, but the following were of the most use: *Hattie and Huey* (1989), David Malone; *Dynasty: The Longs of Louisiana* (1960), Thomas Martin; *Favorite Huey Long Stories* (1937), Hugh Mercer; *The Longs of Louisiana* (1960), Stan Opotowsky; and *Huey Long's Louisiana: State Politics, 1920–1952* (1956), Allan P. Sindler. Two books on would-be American dictators were of help: *Huey Long, Father Coughlin and the Great Depression* (1982), Alan Brinkley; and *Forerunners of American Fascism* (1935), Raymond Graham Swing. First-rate chapters on Huey Long were found in *Mainstream* (1943), Hamilton Basso, and *The Bosses* (1972), Alfred Steinberg.

The following books provided background on Earl Long:

Peapatch Politics: The Earl Long Era in Louisiana Politics (1991), William J. "Bill" Dodd; and *Socks on a Rooster: Louisiana's Earl K. Long* (1967), Richard McCaughan.

The specter of Robert Penn Warren's classic, Pulitzer Prize–winning novel *All the King's Men* (1946) hovers over any book about Huey Long, particularly any work of fiction; I read the novel in high school and, because of it, developed an interest in Huey Long. But I made the conscious decision not to reread it before the writing of *Blood and Thunder*, not wanting to be either influenced or intimidated.

I did screen Robert Rossen's award-winning 1949 film adaptation of the book, as well as Raoul Walsh's 1953 film based on Adria Locke Langley's Huey Long–inspired novel, *A Lion Is in the Streets* (1945). Surprisingly, in what I am aware is a minority opinion, I found the former film flat and artificial, particularly Broderick Crawford's one-note performance, and the latter more lively and on target, with James Cagney capturing the huckster charm of a Kingfish.

Other films were more useful: Ken Burns's excellent 1985 documentary, *Huey Long*; and the well-researched docudrama *The Life and Assassination of the Kingfish* (1977), from writer-director Robert Collins, who used many of the real locations. Also helpful were a 1992 segment of NBC's "Unsolved Mysteries" that dramatized the viewpoints of both Ed Reed and Professor Starrs; and the 1965 David L. Wolper documentary, *The Longs: A Louisiana Dynasty*, written by Bud Wiser and directed by Alan Landsburg.

Huey Long's connections to organized crime are documented in numerous sources, but I turned primarily to the following: *Mafia Kingfish* (1989), John H. Davis; *Uncle Frank: The Biography of Frank Costello* (1973), Leonard Katz; *Lansky* (1971), Hank Messick; *Double Cross* (1992), Sam and Chuck Giancana; *All American Mafioso* (1991), Charles Rappleye and Ed Becker; *The Grim Reapers*

(1969), Ed Reid; and *Frank Costello: Prime Minister of the Underworld* (1974), George Wolf with Joseph DiMona.

Elmer Irey and Frank Wilson's efforts to nail Long and his Longsters are detailed in Irey's own *The Tax Dodgers* (1948), with William J. Slocum, and Wilson's autobiography, *Special Agent: A Quarter Century with the Treasury Department* (1956) with Beth Day. Also helpful was *Secret File* (1969), Hank Messick. Thanks to Jim Doherty for providing further material on Frank Wilson.

The WPA Guides of the late '30s and early '40s are the backbone of my recreations of the era, never more so than with the *Louisiana State Guide* (1941), *New Orleans City Guide* (1938) and *Gumbo Ya-Ya* (1945). *The WPA Guide to New York City* and *New York Panorama: A Companion to the WPA Guide to New York City* were also helpful, as was *Oklahoma: A Guide to the Sooner State* (1941).

My attempt to re-create a sense of Louisiana in the thirties was dependent on the following sources: *Louisiana's Message 1930–1931*, no date, no author, a guide issued by the state of Louisiana Department of Agriculture and Immigration; *Do You Know Louisiana* (1938), issued by the Louisiana State Department of Commerce and Industry; *John Law Wasn't So Wrong* (1952), Hodding Carter; *The Louisiana Capitol* (1980), Ellen Roy Jolly and James Calhoun; *The Bayous of Louisiana* (1963), Harnett T. Kane; *All This Is Louisiana* (1950), Frances Parkinson Keyes; *A Self-Guided Tour of Baton Rouge* (1974), John P. and Lillian C. King; *The Louisiana Capitol: Its Art and Architecture* (1977); and *New Orleans in the Thirties* (1989), Mary Lou Widmer. Mary Jane Smith, at the Old Governor's Mansion, gave me a gracious guided tour as well as a worthwhile illustrated pamphlet.

Information about the Stork Club came from *No Cover Charge: A Backward Look at Night Clubs* (1956), Robert

Sylvester; information about radio star Phil Baker was found in *Tune In Yesterday* (1976), John Dunning. As is the case with previous Heller novels, pickpocket information came from the definitive *Whiz Mob* (1955), David W. Maurer.

Finally, I would like to thank my editor, Michaela Hamilton, and her associate, Joe Pittman, for their support and belief in Nate Heller and me; and my agent, Dominick Abel, for his continued support, both professionally and personally.

ABOUT THE AUTHOR

MAX ALLAN COLLINS has earned an unprecedented six Private Eye Writers of America Shamus nominations for his Nathan Heller historical thrillers, winning twice (*True Detective*, 1983, and *Stolen Away*, 1991).

In addition, Collins has three contemporary suspense series—Nolan, Quarry and Mallory (a thief, hitman and mystery writer, respectively)—and has also written several widely praised historical thrillers about real-life "Untouchable" Eliot Ness.

A Mystery Writers of America Edgar nominee in both fiction and nonfiction categories, Collins is also film reviewer for *Mystery Scene Magazine*; his recent work includes short fiction, trading-card sets, graphic novels, and occasional movie novelizations, including the best-selling *In the Line of Fire*. Two of his screenplays—*The Expert* and *Mommy*—were produced in 1994 for release this year; he executive-produced and directed the latter.

He scripted the internationally syndicated comic strip "Dick Tracy" from 1977 to 1993, is cocreator (with artist Terry Beatty) of the comic-book feature *Ms. Tree*, and has written both the Batman comic book and newspaper strip. He is currently developing a comics project, *Mike Danger*, with Mickey Spillane.

A longtime rock musician, he records and performs with two bands. Collins lives in Muscatine, Iowa, with his wife, writer Barbara Collins, and their son, Nathan.

· A NOTE ON THE TYPE ·

The typeface used in this book is a version of Sabon, originally designed in the 1960s by Jan Tschichold (1902–1974) at the behest of a consortium of manufacturers of metal type. As one who began as an outspoken design revolutionary—calling for the elimination of serifs, scorning revivals of historic typefaces—Tschichold seemed an odd choice, but he met the challenge brilliantly: The typeface was to be based on the fonts of the sixteenth-century French typefounder Claude Garamond but five percent narrower; it had to be identical for three different processes, working around the quirks of each, such as linotype's inability to "kern" (allow one character into the space of another, the way the top of a lowercase *f* overhangs other letters). Aside from Sabon, named for a sixteenth-century French punchcutter to avoid problems of attribution to Garamond, Tschichold is best remembered as the designer of the Penguin paperbacks of the late 1940s.